FLETCHER KNEBEL

Night of Camp David

VINTAGE

1 3 5 7 9 10 8 6 4 2

Vintage
20 Vauxhall Bridge Road,
London SW1V 2SA

Vintage is part of the Penguin Random House group of companies
whose addresses can be found at global.penguinrandomhouse.com

First published in Vintage in 2018

Published in the United States by Vintage Books, a division of
Penguin Random House LLC, in 2018
First published in the United States by Harper & Row in 1965

penguin.co.uk/vintage

A CIP catalogue record for this book is available from the
British Library

ISBN 9781529111576

Printed and bound in Great Britain by Clays Ltd, Elcograf S.p.A.

Penguin Random House is committed to a sustainable future for our
business, our readers and our planet. This book is made from Forest
Stewardship Council® certified paper.

To Mary and Jack

Night of Camp David

1.

After Midnight

Jim MacVeagh's burst of laughter came so unexpectedly, his hand jiggled the stem of the wineglass, and a splash of champagne spotted the linen tablecloth. Sidney Karper, the Secretary of Defense, sitting on his right, grinned in shared appreciation and shook his head.

"Unbeatable, isn't he, Senator? He just won't be topped."

"Nobody can touch him when he's determined," agreed MacVeagh. He wiped at his eye with a corner of his napkin and turned back toward the center of the long head table, cluttered with late debris of ashes and crumpled menus amid the sparkle of glassware.

The speaker, President Mark Hollenbach, was mock-solemn again after flashing a responsive smile for the spray of laughter which greeted his first sally. His was the honor chore of the night—the brief reply to the toast to the President of the United States which signaled the closing of another annual Gridiron dinner. The newspaper correspondents had lampooned the Hollenbach administration and its foes in a series of musical skits, some sharp as stilettos but one belabored in its buffoonery, while the Marine Band orchestra in shining scarlet coats played for the 550 diners.

Behind the President hung the emblem of the club which had satirized every White House occupant since Benjamin Harrison. It was a huge, illuminated, rose-festooned gridiron, patterned on the type used by nineteenth-century housewives for roasting over a wood fire. Before Hollenbach sat the elite of America's delicately interwoven political-industrial society, the men who ran the political parties and the big corporations. These were men whom, for the most part, the President called by their first names. They were mellowed now by the whisky and wines, the terrapin and the filet mignon chateaubriand, yet they sat watching him attentively in the manner of that always vigilant breed, the President-watchers. Yes, he was on trial, as ever, and the long rows of roses and daffodils, the shimmering silver and wineglasses, the amiable droop of white ties and once stiff shirt bosoms, did not deceive him. It was 11 P.M., and the faces turned toward him beamed like pumpkins on a vine. The men of wealth thought the fare deserved well of them, and even those who had rented their white-tie-and-tails for $15 shared a sense of well-being. It was at just such an hour of camaraderie that an average man would lower his guard. But not President Hollenbach. He could never afford to be bested.

"As you know," he resumed, "one of my closest advisers is renowned for his abstinence." He paused. Timing was of the essence in a speech of witticisms. "The worst part about being a teetotaler like Joe is that when he gets up in the morning he knows he already feels as good as he's going to feel all day."

Another roll of mirth. Mark Hollenbach smiled, and Jim MacVeagh thought he detected a touch of vindication in the smile. The gag was an old one—used years before by Governor George Romney of Michigan—and MacVeagh knew that Hollenbach's speech man had tried to dissuade him from using it. But Hollenbach ruled that it would sound fresh on the lips of a President. It did. MacVeagh glanced again at Sidney Karper beside him, but the Secretary of Defense was not smiling. Instead, he seemed absorbed in a study of the President. Karper's huge head, with the prominent beak and the bronze tint of the skin, reminded MacVeagh of a profile of an American Indian. He had to crane his neck to get an unobstructed view of the President past Karper.

"I am delighted to be here this evening," said President Hollenbach, "and hear the nation's leading newspapermen tell the truth about me—for a change." More laughter. Hollenbach kept his face blank this time. "I was especially heartened to see my friends, the Republicans, laughing. . . . They don't often succumb to attacks of good humor, you know. Of course, tonight, they never quite got around to laughing at themselves. For a Republican to laugh at himself requires a severe psychological upheaval. Still, tonight, they laughed at me—and that's a start. After all, they have to begin somewhere. I have great faith in this country, and I'm confident that someday, somewhere, somehow, a Republican is going to break out in a big, hearty guffaw, just for the fun of the thing."

The President paused and took a sip of water. "The Republican capacity for solemnity constantly mystifies me. Perhaps the clue lies in what they say to one another. I've often wondered what Republicans talk about in the cloisters of their own minority clan. I've given the matter a great deal of thought, and I think I've hit on a way to find out. May I advance a suggestion for your consideration? . . .

"I propose," he said after a brief hesitation, "that the FBI be empowered to maintain an automatic tap on all telephones in the country. The tremendous advantages for crime detection are, of course, obvious. On the other hand, no decent, law-abiding citizen would have anything to fear, since nothing he said could be of interest to a federal investigative body. But—and here's the point—with a standing wiretap, we Democrats could learn what mysterious substance provides the glue for Republicanism, what indeed it is they say to one another that makes them so gloomy."

There was a ripple of tittering among the diners and a few laughs. Jim MacVeagh, grinning, turned to Sidney Karper.

"He's really soaring, isn't he?"

The Defense Secretary did not smile. "Even in fun," he replied, "that's a chilling suggestion."

MacVeagh eyed his seatmate in surprise, and was about to protest, but another presidential thrust brought a wave of laughter that carried MacVeagh back into the current of Hollenbach's talk.

". . . and so," the President was saying, "let's agree that life is short enough without waiting around for the day Republicans begin to enjoy themselves. For real humor, for that earthy gusto of the people, we must turn to my own party and to the White House where, I concede, some strange things have been happening."

On a tide of chuckles, Mark Hollenbach was off on five minutes of pungent commentary on his own administration. His stories were barbed, yet salved in an after-dinner lubricant of self-derogation, and when President Hollenbach sat down, 550 men rose to their feet and applauded him. The rows of white-vested stags locked arms and sang "Auld Lang Syne" in mottled harmony. The 91st annual Gridiron dinner was over.

The Marine Band struck ruffles and flourishes and swung into "Hail to the Chief." Hollenbach walked down the long head table, bracketed by two Secret Service men. When the President saw Senator MacVeagh, he leaned over and whispered to him.

"Come on over to the house in a few minutes, Jim. I want to talk to you. I'll buy you a nightcap."

"Be honored, Mr. President," said MacVeagh.

Hollenbach quickened his pace and at the door of the broad Statler Hilton mezzanine lobby, he was swallowed by a new brood of Secret Service agents. The buzz of conversation in the banquet hall rose in volume, then fractured into clattering fragments as the diners bunched at the exits on their way to the after-dinner drinking rooms. MacVeagh found his host, columnist Craig Spence, and thanked him for the evening. Spence's fringe of red hair sat on his otherwise bald head like a tiara of poinciana. He wobbled slightly as he shook hands.

"Come on up to 1240," said Spence. "It's open house all night."

MacVeagh shook his head. "Thanks, Craig, but I need air. You wined and dined me too well."

The junior senator from Iowa threaded his way through the knots of flushed faces and pearl-studded shirt fronts, lingering here, chatting there, then joining a long line at the hat check counter. At last, he looped his white silk scarf about his neck, got helped into his black topcoat by Grady Cavanaugh, a good-humored Supreme Court justice, and left the hotel by the main 16th Street entrance. A jostling crowd gathered under the bright lights to watch the dignitaries leave. MacVeagh waved and shook his head at the Secretary of Defense, who offered him a ride in a Pentagon limousine. Instead he walked bareheaded into the frosty March night.

As he turned left on 16th Street, heading toward Lafayette Park and the White House, James F. MacVeagh felt on good terms with himself and even relatively at peace with the world. In his chosen profession, politics, he had risen as swiftly and as effortlessly as a kite in a gust, and the glitter of the Gridiron dinner seemed a minor summit for Senator MacVeagh. At age thirty-eight, a first-term senator, he had been placed at the head table and now he was summoned to the White House for a private midnight drink. In Washington terms, he was in, very much in, and while his status did not surprise him, he was buoyed by it. The whisky and wine mingled smoothly in his big frame and the chill wind on his cheeks contrasted with the warmth within. He ran a hand through his tangle of black hair as he passed the imposing headquarters of the AFL-CIO, with its illuminated lobby mural of gilded toilers, and he began to whistle a song from the Gridiron show, "I've Got a Feeling I'm Falling." The lyric had aptly characterized the rapidly descending political fortunes of Vice-President Patrick O'Malley in the wake of revelations about his part in the federal sports arena scandals.

MacVeagh cut through Lafayette Park, where mounds of snow from last week's storm still had failed to thaw. He noted a tiny sign in a flower bed and bent over to read it in the light of the shrouded moon. "Tulips sleeping here," it read. MacVeagh made a mental note to use the phrase in a Senate speech. Such souvenirs of imagination in the vast, gray federal bureaucracy merited recognition. He looked up at the central statue of Andrew Jackson and found a chunk of dirty snow oddly clinging to the rump of Jackson's rearing charger. The statue's metal was tarnished, so that both Jackson and his mount had turned a bilious green, as though suffering companionably through eternity with the same affliction. Old Andy, how different a president from the urbane and complex man who now lived in the same White House across the street, a house which seemed to embrace the glow from the big portico lantern with friendly arms. Why Jim MacVeagh for a Saturday night visit? He knew the President well, had advised him on midwestern strategy in the campaign, but he was no confidant. Come to think of it, was anybody?

But MacVeagh felt too carefree for fretful speculation. He jaywalked across Pennsylvania Avenue, and nodded to the White House policeman guarding the high iron gates of the west entrance.

"Jim MacVeagh," he said.

"I know, Senator," said the guard, standing close and inspecting his face. "We got a call from the house."

MacVeagh walked up the curving driveway past snow-topped Japanese yews bordering the drive like ermine balloons. The west wing was dark, but the center of the mansion threw a circle of light in which the great elms, preserved from blight by constant spraying, cast shadows of embroidered linen over the snow. A gardener had shaken the snow off the ancient boxwoods in front of the portico and they shone bright green, as with new leaves, in the light of the hanging lantern.

Inside, in the museum-like foyer, MacVeagh was undoing his scarf when a young man with a swarthy face walked toward him. He was grinning, his teeth white as limestone in a rainstorm. MacVeagh recognized him as a member of the White House Secret Service detail.

"Luther Smith, Senator," he said. "Don't bother taking your things off. The man went to Camp David and I've got orders to bring you along."

"Camp David!" MacVeagh looked at his wrist watch. 11:50. Camp David, the presidential mountain retreat built by Franklin D. Roosevelt under the original name Shangri-la, was 80 miles away in the Catoctin range of Maryland. That meant two hours over icy roads. "Good Lord, did he say why?"

"No. We don't ask," said Smith. "All I know is that he just left and I've got orders to take you by your home for a change of clothes and then drive you on up to the lodge."

"Orders, huh?"

"Orders, sir." Smith grinned again with his flash of white teeth. MacVeagh liked the man.

"All right. Let's go."

A long, purring limousine waited on the curved driveway on the south lawn of the grounds. MacVeagh got in the front seat with Smith and they drove over the Memorial Bridge and out

George Washington Parkway to MacVeagh's home in McLean, Virginia.

The old stone house squatted darkly under its television antenna, like a slumping sentinel with upraised rifle on a wintry border outpost. Only the footprints of the paper boy marred the sheet of snow still refusing to melt a week after the storm.

"Come on in and make some coffee while I change," said MacVeagh. "My wife and daughter are out in Iowa for a week and I'm batching it."

"No, thanks, Senator. I'll stay here and keep this heater going."

MacVeagh fumbled for his key just beyond the rays of the car's headlights. If Martha had been with him, the carriage lamps would be on, casting warm amber circles, but with Martha away, he'd forgotten. In the bedroom, MacVeagh unhitched his formal harness, swore twice over the studs and collar button, and put on a fresh pair of socks. Then he wondered about his attire and went back to the front door in his shorts and undershirt.

"Hey, Luther," he yelled. The agent pressed a button to lower a front car window.

"What am I supposed to wear?" he called. "I've never been to Camp David before, let alone in the middle of the night."

"Old clothes," Smith called back. "The man always wears khaki pants and a sweater up there."

MacVeagh settled for gray slacks, a flannel shirt, and a fleece-lined windbreaker he used for fishing on cold mornings. He thought fleetingly of phoning Martha in Des Moines, decided it was too late, and trotted back to the limousine. Smith motioned him into the back seat.

"You might as well get some shut-eye," he said. "It'll be after two when we get there."

But the whisky and wines swam in MacVeagh. His head felt fluffy, and so they talked for half an hour, chiefly about Smith's trade of protecting presidents. It was tough with this one, said the agent, because he insisted on changing the drill at the last minute. Tonight, for instance, they had to call three agents out of bed and get them to scout the highways ahead of the President. Oh, well, the pay wasn't much, but the pension wasn't bad and you met a lot of interesting people, including the zombies who threatened to set fire to the White House with a blowtorch. Protecting the President became your sole cause, and you'd turn in your own brother if you suspected him of compromising the man's safety. They were almost to Frederick before MacVeagh fell asleep.

He awoke with a flashlight shining in his face. When it had been lowered and he had rubbed his eyes, he saw a Marine sergeant saluting briskly from the steps of a log guardhouse. The snow lay deep here and the towering firs were silhouetted in the fragile moonlight. A snowplow had cleared the road, leaving ridges almost two feet high on either side. The forest was thick, no wind stirred, and only the crunch of the car's tires could be heard in the hush of the night hours. Smith stopped the limousine before the largest of a cluster of wooden buildings. A dull green paint, the drab uniform of service bases, attested to the retreat's maintenance by military crews.

Mark Hollenbach, wearing an open-necked shirt and cardigan, stepped to the side of the car and opened a door for MacVeagh.

"Welcome to Aspen, Jim," he said. "Come on in. It's colder than the hinges out here."

MacVeagh entered, uncertainly, and found himself in a low, rough-beamed room in which firelight flickered at one end and a single floor lamp burned at the other. The room was illuminated largely by shifting patches from the veiled moon which came through a huge picture window. Outside, on a stone patio, stood a pedestal with mounted binoculars similar to those placed in public parks for scenic viewing. Inside the room, sofas, wooden tables, and a big easy chair made moundlike shadows. President Hollenbach walked to the fireplace, rubbing his hands. Jim followed and they stood there warming themselves, backs to the fire.

"Want a drink?" asked Hollenbach.

"A drink I don't need, Mr. President, not after Scotch and five wines tonight. But I could use a glass of tomato juice, if you've got one."

"Good idea," said Hollenbach. He walked into an adjoining pantry and came back with two tall glasses. "I put a little A-1 sauce and some pepper in this. Is that all right?"

"Fine." MacVeagh raised his glass to Hollenbach's. "Here's to a great speech tonight, Mr. President. It was right on the nose."

"They did seem to like it."

What was this all about? MacVeagh wondered. Here he stood at two o'clock in the morning, drinking tomato juice with the President of the United States and looking out a window which framed an expanse of lonely white. The lodge, Aspen, stood on a shelf of the mountain. A one-hole golf course, MacVeagh knew, ran to the brow. He could see the flagless pin, marking the green which had been sodded years ago for President Eisenhower. Just beyond was a stand of hardwood trees, and through their bare branches could be seen the next mountain range, merging into the gray blur of the horizon like a distant fleet at sea.

A mantel clock ticked behind them. Firelight fingered the side of Hollenbach's face and Jim found himself thinking of this unusual man in khaki pants and the ragged gray sweater. Hollenbach's crew cut, stiff as an old wire brush with its mixture of sandy and gray hair, made him seem younger than his fifty-seven years. The neck above the open collar of his green sport shirt showed wrinkles, but no sagging flesh. His long face, with its thin bone structure, was not handsome, yet it etched a sensitivity that lured women voters. Not a delicate face, but possibly a professorial one. Jim could imagine Hollenbach expounding the style of Hawthorne and Poe to freshman classes in American literature. Actually, he recalled, it was history that young Mark Hollenbach taught at the University of Colorado in the days before he got into politics.

The President was trim. No stomach bulge, no flabby muscles. Physical fitness was part of his creed; ten minutes of vigorous setting-up exercises before breakfast, a swim in the White House pool at noon and always two late afternoons of golf a week at the Burning Tree Club when weather permitted. A call to excellence had been his campaign appeal to America, and in the White House, President Hollenbach tried to live an example for the people. Excellence in all things, including the care of the human body, he said time and again.

"What did you think of the dinner, Jim?" he asked.

"I liked it. That Republican skit dragged, but those on us were great, really funny. They sure picked on us where we're vulnerable."

"O'Malley was duck soup for them, of course," said Hollenbach. "And it's always easy to kid the President. He's everybody's fall guy."

"Your little speech at the end was terrific. And you know why—because you spent half the time ribbing yourself after you kidded the opposition."

"What did you think of my wiretap suggestion?"

"I got a kick out of it," said MacVeagh with a grin. Then he recalled Sidney Karper's strange reaction. "But apparently it misfired with some people. I guess the idea of a wiretap on every phone jolted them and they couldn't take it as a joke."

"I didn't mean it as a joke," said Hollenbach.

"You what?" MacVeagh stared at him.

"Oh, of course I was jesting in that context—of listening in on the Republicans," said the President. "But I've thought a lot about the rising crime rate and, Jim, we've got to do something drastic. Access to every phone conversation would give the FBI and other federal agencies a terrific weapon against criminals. And it's quite feasible, you know, if worked through the Bell System."

"You can't be serious, Mr. President." Fragments of a dozen of his own indiscreet telephone remarks whipped through Mac-Veagh's mind and he thought briefly and guiltily of Rita. "Good Lord, that's police state stuff. There isn't enough privacy left as it is."

"I am very serious, Jim," said Hollenbach. "It would have to be done carefully, with great legal restraints and protection, naturally. But no respectable citizen would have a thing to fear. It's the hoodlums, the punks, the syndicate killers, and the dope peddlers we're after. Automatic wiretapping, aided by computers to store the telephone calls, would drive them all out of business."

MacVeagh was dumfounded, unable to find words for an immediate reply. He thought he knew this President fairly well, could sense the trend of his political philosophy without asking, yet here was a proposal suddenly dropped from the skies, like a giant boulder in a cyclone, to block a familiar and well-traveled roadway.

"Mr. President," he said slowly, "I'm no civil liberties fanatic, but I do understand our basic freedoms. This thing of yours could be an awful weapon for evil in the wrong hands. Who knows what type of man may succeed you? And then, there are the political repercussions. A proposal like that could murder you this fall."

Hollenbach's jaw line tensed and he waved a hand as though to dismiss the subject. "All novel ideas involve a political risk," he said. "That doesn't frighten me. But enough of that tonight. I've other things I want to talk to you about."

Hollenbach set his glass on the mantel and pressed the tips of his fingers forcefully together. Isometric exercises were part of his formula for the fit body. Often, when sitting at a conference table, he would curl his toes and try to push them through the soles of his shoes. At other times he jammed his elbows against the back of a chair, hardening his biceps and chest muscles. In a crowd the movements were invisible, but with friends he made no effort to mask the practice—even after two o'clock in the morning. Now he motioned to a long, white monk's-cloth sofa which faced the wide window and the stretch of white beyond. He sat at one end and half turned toward MacVeagh, sitting at the other.

"Jim," he said, "let's talk business. Those Gridiron fellows didn't tromp on O'Malley as hard as they could have. A matter of not kicking a man when he's down, I suppose. But you and I know the Republicans won't be that easy in the fall. I just won't have O'Malley on the ticket with me again."

Hollenbach's flat statement of intent on the vice-presidency came as no surprise to MacVeagh, even though this was the President's first mention of it, as far as he knew. Leading Democrats assumed it was only a matter of time until the President announced that Vice-President Patrick O'Malley would not be his running mate in the fall campaign for re-election. O'Malley had been muddied beyond scouring in Senator Bryce Robinson's one-man investigation of the John F. Kennedy Memorial Sports Arena. The Republican senator, tracking as always like a wolf who scorns the pack, had found favoritism in the building contract. It was not fraud. No bribery had been uncovered, no venality, no mysteriously fattened bank accounts.

Instead, the case evolved as a classic Washington example of influence buying through campaign contributions. The contractor for the sports arena had contributed heavily to O'Malley's primary campaign fund when O'Malley was challenging Hollenbach for the Democratic presidential nomination four years earlier. The contractor was Art (Jingles) Jilinsky, a Pittsburgh Democrat long a fringe figure in party councils. O'Malley's role had not been particularly impure. He merely introduced Jilinsky to the chairman of the Fine Arts Commission and followed up with telephone calls asking the status of the contract awards. If O'Malley had admitted the whole affair at the outset, if it had not been a presidential campaign year, and if the building had not been dedicated to a martyred president, the incident might have withered after brief partisan combat. But it was a Kennedy memorial, it was a campaign year, and O'Malley had not come forward at once with the full truth.

Senator Robinson, a master at trapping the unwary, first revealed that Jilinsky contributed $3,000 (the limit before the start of gift taxes) to O'Malley's futile presidential bid and that three years later—last year—O'Malley had introduced Jilinsky to the Fine Arts chairman who had a major role in awarding such memorial building contracts. When reporters questioned Vice-President O'Malley, he conceded that he had received the contribution and made the introduction. But, he protested, he had received hundreds of similar contributions and made scores of introductions of American citizens to officeholders. It was a political smear of the lowest sort, he contended, to link the contribution with the introduction. He would, he said, have done the same for any voter.

The episode flared briefly, then sputtered out. But two weeks later, Senator Robinson took the Senate floor to reveal a $3,000 campaign gift to O'Malley from Mrs. Jilinsky. O'Malley brushed this aside as a matter beyond his recollection. Two days later Robinson released a chart showing a total of $36,000 in gifts from Jilinsky, members of his family, and six of his subcontractors. Questioned by newsmen, the subcontractors confessed that they actually had given Jilinsky's money in their own names, since each received three $1,000 bills from Jilinsky several days after making the contributions. "Six Give and Get Three Grand," headlined the Washington *Daily News*.

Vice-President O'Malley, badly jolted this time, said that he had never inspected the list of campaign contributions, that all finances had been handled without his knowledge by his campaign treasurer. This appeared to conflict with his first ready acknowledgment of Jilinsky's own gift. Senator Robinson let this controversy rage for a week before tripping his last political land mine. O'Malley, he charged with supporting affidavits from the personal secretary to the Fine Arts chairman, had made three telephone calls asking the progress of contract negotiations on the Kennedy arena. This contract, Robinson showed, was awarded to Jilinsky & Sons, Inc., on a cost-plus basis with potential profits to the Jilinsky family running as high as $600,000.

The episode had its irony, for O'Malley could not have leased the arena for a week without borrowing. He produced his income tax returns for the past five years, showing only a trickle of income outside his salary as vice-president and earlier as a congressman. Clearly, O'Malley had not enriched himself. What he had done was in the hoary political pattern—permitting a friend to "buy access" to a federal official via campaign contributions. Politicians in both parties sympathized with O'Malley, realizing that his conduct differed only in timing and degree from that of thousands of elected officials from county courthouses to Congress. But, they shrugged, that was the ill luck of the Irish. O'Malley had been caught in the old game in the wrong year, on the wrong contract, and the penalty, they assumed, would be the loss of the vice-presidency.

None of this recent history had to be recounted by the President and the senator as they sat together in early morning. Both had writhed through the slow unfolding of Senator Robinson's tale of money and Democratic politics. Both assumed that President Hollenbach's personal popularity remained uncharred despite the scandal, yet they knew the country expected the President to act promptly.

"I'm going to announce at my Wednesday press conference that O'Malley has decided not to be a candidate for re-election," said Hollenbach. "That's just between us, of course."

"Has he told you that?"

"No." Hollenbach stretched out his legs and MacVeagh noted that he wore battered moccasins. "But I'm going to phone him tomorrow and ask for such a statement in writing. He can't refuse."

"No, of course he can't." Jim knew it had to come, but hearing O'Malley's fate stated so irrevocably, he felt a twinge of sorrow. Pat was not a venal man. Jim doubted he had ever taken an illegal dollar in his life. He had merely played the game as he had learned it in Pennsylvania. Pat's real weakness was his readiness to help a friend—and Jilinsky had been a friend. It was a frailty endemic among those who plied the trade of politics. Or any trade, for that matter.

"I can't help feeling sorry for Pat, Mr. President," said MacVeagh. "He's a big, likable Irishman who goes by a code he never thought much about, I guess. But if I were in trouble myself, he's probably the first man I'd go to."

"I wouldn't," said Hollenbach. The words exploded, as though fired from a gun. "O'Malley did it for the express purpose of embarrassing me in an election year."

The President's eyes locked on MacVeagh's, but the younger man grinned. "Oh, come now, Mr. President. Pat made the introduction and those calls last year. I doubt if he thought about the election, one way or the other."

"No, no." Hollenbach shook his head impatiently. "I mean the way he handled it. Instead of making a clean breast of things right at the start, he let Robinson paint him—gradually, one coat at a time—until he looked like a crook. That was intentional, Jim. O'Malley did it to defeat me in November. I know."

MacVeagh was startled by the velocity of the President's speech. Words tumbled out in a rush and Jim noted that color speared upward in Hollenbach's cheeks.

"But that's not logical, Mr. President." Jim thought his own voice unduly subdued after the President's eruption. "After all, in trying to beat you, O'Malley would be ruining himself. He has no future except on a ticket with you."

Hollenbach rose from the sofa and began pacing the floor. On one turn he clicked off the floor lamp, leaving the room with only thin moonlight, reflected from the snow outside, and the lazy orange tongues curling from the fireplace. The President's features were shadowed, but MacVeagh felt eyes searching his own in the half-light.

"You don't understand a man like that," said Hollenbach. The words hurried from him as though fleeing an unseen enemy. "His own future is nothing compared to his objective. . . . He's out to grind me down. . . . All right. I'll say it . . . to destroy me. . . . What does Patrick O'Malley risk? He's fortunate to be vice-president. Even that office stretches his limited talents. . . . He had nowhere else to go. . . . So let's face facts. His entire aim was to soil me, to rub some of his mud off on me, to make people think that I'm the kind of man who winks at sordid political pay-offs in his official household. . . ."

Hollenbach came close and MacVeagh felt uncomfortable, as though he had unwittingly intruded on another's privacy. A disquieting emotion nettled him. Outside the snow lay blank and cold. MacVeagh saw a dead tree, its branches missing. Then he noted that the trunk moved and he realized, with relief, that it was a guard, probably a Marine, on duty. The man blew on his hands and moved away, out of eye range.

Hollenbach walked in small, nervous steps to the big window. He stood there, mute, looking at the gray mass on the horizon. For a minute the ticking of the mantel clock and the pop of burning logs were the only sounds. Then MacVeagh heard a familiar, booming laugh, so deep in tone from such a thin, wiry body that it always seemed to come from some hidden spring of resources. Hollenbach returned to the sofa and slouched in the corner.

"Forgive me, Jim, for getting so worked up," he said easily, "but the man has always irritated me. The country paid attention when I spoke of excellence, but not O'Malley. As far as he was concerned, I might as well have been gabbling in Bantu. He never heard me."

Hollenbach smiled and fingered the frayed border of his sweater. "O'Malley will soon be ancient history," he said quietly. "What we have to do now is pick the best man available for vice-president. Time's passing. It's only five months until the Detroit convention."

"Five months and eight days," corrected MacVeagh. They both laughed. Jim felt at ease again.

"All right, five months and eight days. What do you think I ought to do, Jim? Who's the right man for us?"

"That's strictly your business, Mr. President. I may be a new boy, but not so new that I start advising presidents on their running mates."

"Put it another way, Jim." The tension was all gone now. Hollenbach stretched out his legs again and his moccasins found the end of an unfinished cherry coffee table to rest on. "Suppose you were in my place. Whom would you pick? I'm not going to hold you to anything. Just think out loud for me."

MacVeagh recognized Hollenbach's most persuasive mood. When the President slid into this informal but persistent quest for advice, it was useless to deny him, for he would wheedle, coax and implore until the wall was breached and the besieged came forth, laden with the gifts of tribute—a name, a place, a policy.

"You've got me," MacVeagh sighed. "Well, I see only two men and there isn't much to choose between them—Karper and Nicholson."

William Nicholson was the able, if too ponderous, Speaker of the House of Representatives. Sidney Karper, beside whom Mac-Veagh had sat that evening, was the keen, blunt Secretary of Defense whose sometimes acid comments on the nation's dilemma abroad gave a kind of curious comfort to Americans in a world obviously devoid of solace.

"Nicholson is too heavy." Hollenbach held up a palm as if warding off a falling object. "He smothers me with that elephantine way of his."

"I know," said Jim, "but he's steady and the people like that feeling of reliability."

Hollenbach ignored the observation. "As for Karper, I agree he's the smartest man in Washington and one of the most admired. But the country isn't ready for a Jewish vice-president."

"Of course I think you're wrong on that, Mr. President. Look at the polls. He runs right after you in most of those 'most admired Americans' things."

"As a Cabinet officer, yes. As a man next in line to be president, no. Besides, he took the liberty of going through with a project I didn't approve of. He showed his arrogance."

MacVeagh waited, questioning, but the President did not elaborate.

"Even if you're right on the country's attitude, which I doubt," protested MacVeagh, "your popularity would carry him through without a scratch. And you've got to concede Karper's tremendous ability."

Jim heard the echo of his own words, like a man talking into a steel barrel. What the devil was Mark driving at? And what was he doing on this mountaintop, 80 miles from home, in the middle of the night? Middle? It wasn't far from dawn. And why wasn't Evelyn Hollenbach up here with her husband? Jim felt disembodied, unreal, no more substantial than the pale light which hardly cast a shadow any longer in the darkened room. Why, for one thing, had Mark turned out the only light? He decided to ask.

"It's one of my whims," Hollenbach replied. "I think better in the dark. Besides, I love this view, night or day, and any lamp in the room reflects on the glass and spoils the effect." A small smile moved the President's lips. "Back to the subject, Jim. You've only given me two names. No governors?"

He's relentless, thought MacVeagh. He wants me to trot out every possibility in the Democratic party. MacVeagh mused silently, his eyes on the fire with its growing bed of pink-white coals. There seemed to be no pressure for an immediate reply and his mind ran idly down the list of governors as he could picture them, alphabetically in tiny print, in a page of the Congressional Directory. At last he named three men whose records were known favorably to the country.

Hollenbach discussed each man at length, a dispassionate analysis of assets and liabilities. MacVeagh was amused by the President's unerring talent for singling out vulnerable characteristics, and he was relieved that James F. MacVeagh was not being similarly dissected. The process reminded him of a surgeon, deftly pushing aside arteries and nerves and probing with his knife to the core of suspicious tissue. In the end, the three men suggested by MacVeagh had an excess of liabilities, as did another governor added by Hollenbach.

"Perhaps, Mr. President, the day of the governor has passed." The warmth of the fire lulled MacVeagh and he was growing sleepy again. He generalized more to make conversation than from a conviction in his words. "Governors aren't identified any more with the big national issues that trouble people. They build the roads, the colleges, and the state hospitals, but even there they have to depend on federal money. Everything centers on Washington, our old friend Barry Goldwater notwithstanding."

"Right." Hollenbach's agreement had a hearty, explosive ring. Didn't the man ever tire? MacVeagh rubbed at his eyes and suppressed a desire to yawn.

"That brings us to the Senate," said the President. He leaned toward MacVeagh, his arms resting on his khaki pants, but his fingers flexing as though squeezing sponges. "Suppose I narrowed it to the Senate. Whom should I pick?"

"Now, Mr. President, please don't prod me into discussing my colleagues." MacVeagh was bored with a game that appeared to have no part for him. He yearned for bed. "You know, the world's most exclusive club, and all that. One member doesn't talk about another—much. We're all capable, all distinguished, all Rhodes Scholar types."

Hollenbach would not be deflected. "How about Hempstead?"

"The name's against him," said MacVeagh. "Hollenbach and Hempstead? It sounds like some old law firm that's gone to seed."

Hollenbach grinned briefly, but MacVeagh could see he was really not amused. Mark cared little for bantering, and he seldom made light remarks in conversation. While the President performed superbly with witticisms in a public speech, as at the Gridiron dinner earlier, MacVeagh knew that Hollenbach felt that humor was a waste of time. And now the President was deep in one of his quests. He's a single-minded Dutchman, thought MacVeagh wearily. God, but he could be inflexible in these moods. Hollenbach seemed to sense MacVeagh's resistance, so he named five Democratic senators himself and again he aligned their good and bad points. Jim was amazed how much the President knew about the personal lives of the senators. His character vignettes were shrewd, his instinct for the vulnerable as keen as it had been with the governors. But the rhythm of the President's monologue and the glow of the fire relaxed MacVeagh like a warm mist. He caught himself beginning to nod once and shook his shoulders to stay awake.

"So that's the lot," said Hollenbach at last. He smiled. "Except for one man."

"Who's that?" MacVeagh's response was automatic. After all, it was the President's problem, not his, and who could think clearly at—what time? Three-thirty? Four? Some ungodly hour.

"You."

"Me!" MacVeagh straightened suddenly from the little nest his back had burrowed into the corner of the white sofa.

"Yes, why not? As long as we're discussing bloodlines, why not look at the pedigree of the junior senator from Iowa?"

Well, why not? thought Jim. His mind, its torpor shed, promptly set to work unbidden. After all, his name had figured in some newspaper speculation inspired by O'Malley's difficulties. One columnist had even pointed out MacVeagh's assets. True, the writer was his good friend, Craig Spence, but assets were assets: youth, intelligence (a matter of opinion perhaps, that one); from a solid midwestern state where Hollenbach was weakest right now; handsome (his daughter Chinky used the word "manful" to describe his looks); sincerity on television (well, damn it, he tried to be sincere off camera as well). He'd made a good impression as chairman of the Armed Services Subcommittee investigating defense costs. He was a Congregationalist, communicant in a homey faith which contrasted with Hollenbach's somewhat aloof brand of Episcopalianism. He had a lively wife and a wholesome kid (Chinky was everybody's breathless teen-ager). Of course, Spence hadn't stressed his shortcomings: too easygoing, inclined to skirt the rocky way, too much of an optimist. And then there was the affair with Rita. (But no one knew about that, and it was over anyway, wasn't it?)

"I know you're lazy, Jim." The President's voice cut into MacVeagh's reverie on his personal balance sheet. "And you've come up too fast for your own good. Still, slave driver Hollenbach would work the fat off of you. All in all, I'd say you'd have to be considered."

"Are you serious, Mr. President?"

Hollenbach rose again from the sofa and went to the fireplace mantel, leaning an elbow near the clock. Jim thought the hands registered 3:55, but he could not be certain in the strange half-light. The President gazed down on him, fixedly as though appraising a piece of furniture.

"I'm not sure," he said. "Jim, you've got the flare for politics, but you are lazy, aren't you?"

"Maybe you'd call it that. I take my time about things. I guess I kind of go in spurts."

Hollenbach grinned. "Not a headful of steam all the time, like me, eh?"

MacVeagh made an effort to keep it light. "You're a man apart, Mr. President. Nobody could be expected to duplicate your energy."

"No, I suppose not. Jim, joking aside, I want to make the right choice on this one. It's not just the winning in November, although of course I don't want a man who'll hurt the ticket. But this is important for the country. A hundred things can happen to a president—any time—and the vice-president should have the capacity to take over quietly and confidently, so there's no loss of leadership and no crisis for the country. As Johnson did from Kennedy, if you will."

Through the window MacVeagh could see the curve of the snow as it blanketed Ike's old pitch-and-putt golf fairway and then fell away to the unseen valley below. The distant range was a gray blot. Clouds masked all but a sliver of moon. No stars shone, and the denuded hardwood trees seemed to appeal to the sky with bony hands. Was the President really considering him for vice-president or merely toying with him? Probably neither. He was just thinking aloud on a problem which absorbed him at the moment. Still, a word from the President on a cold March night and he'd come suddenly awake. He wasn't sure what it portended, but Jim wanted to tell someone. He thought of

Martha and Chinky, visiting in Des Moines. He thought of his young, brash assistant, Flip Carlson. And then, almost against his will, he thought of Rita. Her number in Georgetown was Briarwood 9-8877.

"I'm definite on one thing." Hollenbach's voice again thrust into MacVeagh's thoughts. "The man I want nominated isn't going to be another O'Malley. He isn't going to be a man whose moral values are so lax, he doesn't know right from wrong. I've had a bellyful of that for one administration."

Well, that would eliminate me, thought Jim, if it ever got down to the wire. Not that he regarded himself as immoral, but he was sure Hollenbach wanted no man with a Rita in his recent past. Past?

Hollenbach stood wrapped in the glow from the crackling logs. A pink flush had spread over his cheeks. He was talking swiftly again, occasionally glancing at MacVeagh.

"Jim, I want my second term to be a great one. A concept is forming that could reshape the world. But to carry it out I need an intelligent man at my side, a man who can think long-range. And when I think of O'Malley—trying to disfigure me from his sordid little dung heap—I'd like to throttle him. Because he sank in his own muck, he tried to pull me in too. Thank God, the American people are too smart for that."

"Mr. President," protested MacVeagh, "you've got Pat all wrong there. He wasn't trying to embarrass you. He was just trying to save his own skin."

Hollenbach dismissed the objection with a wave of his arm. He hurried on as though MacVeagh had not spoken. "O'Malley tried and he failed. Never, never again is there going to be an O'Malley in this administration if I can help it. And, by God, I can help it."

The President's fervor shot ruddy streaks up his cheeks and MacVeagh's mind jumped back, in one of those inexplicable shifts of time and scene, to his early soldiering days in Viet Nam. He saw a medic's shack and a corporal gesticulating, but the image quickly vanished and Jim wondered why he'd been reminded of it.

The President's mood softened. He smiled at MacVeagh. "Well, that's enough for tonight. It's after four o'clock, and time to turn in. O'Malley can wait until Wednesday. Jim, I've got a bed waiting for you in one of the guest cabins. You can take your time getting up in the morning."

But MacVeagh felt an urge to leave. To be an obedient sounding board for a president was one thing, but to remain on this bleak plateau, with its darkened Aspen Lodge and its occupant obsessed with the imagined spite of a subordinate, was another. He preferred the stone house in McLean with its familiar furniture, and the walls, shutters and windows he knew. He could even hear the rattle of the metal heating ducts which he'd promised Martha twenty times to get fixed, but which he always forgot until nightime.

"If you don't mind, Mr. President," he said. "I'd better get home. I've got some documents to read before our committee session Monday . . . and there are some things to do around the house . . . Martha and my daughter are in Des Moines for a few days. . . . So, if you can spare Luther Smith for the drive . . ."

Hollenbach placed a hand on his elbow. "I understand, Jim. I think it's senseless to drive back to Washington this time of morning, but good senators are hard to come by. You have to humor them."

MacVeagh smiled. "After a big night like this, I guess I need my own bed."

Hollenbach nodded and walked through the dark to a telephone in the pantry. "Wake up Smitty," Jim heard him say. "We've got a madman here who insists on being driven back to Washington."

The President chatted for a minute about MacVeagh's family and about his own son, Mark Jr., a senior at Yale. The boy was smart, he said, but college boys were inclined to taper off the last semester. He wanted to see young Mark keep the pressure on.

They heard the squeak of tires on hard-packed snow. Hollenbach held the door open.

"I'm glad you could come up, Jim. I think we ought to have another talk before too long."

"Good night, Mr. President. I don't need to say thanks."

As the door remained open, MacVeagh caught a last glimpse of the dark room with its great, shadowy beams. A single shaft of moonlight, pale and delicate, pierced the big window. Mark Hollenbach, silhouetted, was pressing the knuckles of both hands hard against the doorjamb. It was cold outside. Jim zipped up his windbreaker and got into the limousine.

2.

Georgetown

Jim MacVeagh was in that billowy zone between sleep and wakefulness where fragments of dreams slide into conscious thought, slip away, burst into formless greens, reds and yellows, then fade again. The drawn Venetian blinds admitted only thin bars of light. He was flat on his belly and his arms were wrapped around a pillow. Groggy, he got out of bed and opened the blinds. The sun was low in the west. God, he'd been sleeping all day. It must be four in the afternoon. His gray slacks and flannel shirt were slung over Martha's gilt dresser chair and the debris from his pockets was strewn over the glass top of her dresser. Then he remembered. He threw himself back on the bed and lay staring at the ceiling.

A chance for vice-president! Was Mark serious? He seemed so, but of course he'd made it plain that MacVeagh was only one of many. Still, with the others Hollenbach had hammered at the reasons why they wouldn't do, whereas with him, Jim MacVeagh, the President mentioned only one thing—that he was lazy. Was he? No, not really. It was just that there were other things in life besides work, besides the politics that engrossed Hollenbach like a man in a cell with only one book to read. There was all manner of life to be savored, and at thirty-eight the taste buds weren't jaded. There was a tang still. He could see the lake in northern Minnesota, a day's drive from Des Moines. He pictured it black and glassy smooth with the first pale hint of dawn through the tall pines to the east, the air chill to the cheeks and the stillness of an empty cathedral. And then the quick whine of the reel, a hooked trout thrashing, and the pulsing tug against his wrists. In a quick shift of scene, he could see Chinky, her legs wide apart, proud of the first little bulges at her breast, grinning her affection at him. He could see the white arc of a golf ball, high into a cloudless sky from a No. 9 iron, plopping on a green and lying, egg-bright, eight feet from the pin. He could feel the sun baking his back as he lay beside a pool on Green Turtle Cay in the Bahamas, while he squinted drowsily at the blinding brilliance of coral and green water. He could see Martha, with her snubbed nose and tight-clipped brown hair, chattering at the telephone, flicking him a hurried smile as she dipped, restless as a bee, from one budding enterprise to another. Her gay, skittering life sometimes appalled him and occasionally irritated him, but her vivacity and bounce were antidotes for his own languid temperament and her presence gave him a curious, amused contentment. He saw Rita, an arm thrown languorously over his chest and her face lax and half-hidden by tangled strands of black hair. Then he saw Mark Hollenbach again, intent, flexing his fingers, his crew cut as aggressive as tiny spikes . . . the strange pallor of Aspen Lodge at 4 A.M., a reach of unmarred snow outside and little curls of flame licking from the fireplace.

Just how had Mark said it? "So that's the whole list, except for one man." He had seemed in earnest. But then Mark always was. Probably it was just Hollenbach's way of complimenting a guest he'd yanked up to the mountain in the middle of the night, just a needed auditor for his monologue. And yet . . . what was the purpose of summoning Jim MacVeagh, a first-term senator and no confidant, to Camp David on a wintry night? He could find no answer. His brain still felt woolly. Too much high living and late hours. He yawned and stretched.

A hot shower opened his drugged pores, and after he let final needles of cold water drill into him, he felt so good he began to whistle. He put on the gray slacks again, a clean blue jersey polo shirt and loafers, and went downstairs. He pulled in the Sunday papers, *Post, Star, New York Times*, with the thought that he'd beaten the morning paper boy only by minutes. It must have been 6:30 A.M. when Luther Smith delivered him in the White House limousine. The papers were still soggy at the edges from the melting snow on the stoop. MacVeagh glanced at the head-lines as he fried bacon and eggs and plugged in the electric percolator. But the food tasted flat and dry, and he pushed it away with the thought that 4:30 P.M. was a witless hour for breakfast. He switched instead to a bloody Mary and sat sipping it at the glass-and-driftwood coffee table in the living room. He read the news idly, focusing only on the political stories and skimming the rest. A disorderly heap of papers grew at his feet.

He felt puffy in the face, always a sign that the good life was becoming too good for him, and he rubbed the heel of his hand over the bristles of his jaw. His weight, he knew, was nudging 190, too much for a man who wasn't quite six feet tall. But his stomach was flat, no middle-age pot yet. The blue eyes under the heavy black brows were still appealing to women, at least some of them still told him so. The thatch of black hair showed no signs of thinning. For a man with the blood of the Scots in him, he'd been told he had a Gallic appearance, and he wondered whose genes had gotten mixed up where and under what circum-stances. He hoped they had fun. He grinned at the thought. It wasn't a bad life, if you had a little luck—and got outdoors enough. That's really all you need, MacVeagh, he told himself, just a little more exercise and a little less liquor on the social circuit.

Although he tried, he could not for long suppress the thought of becoming Hollenbach's vice-president. He was "manful" enough, to use Chinky's phrase, for a vice-president, but was he too boyish in appearance? People didn't trust boys any longer around the nuclear war codes, the rockets, and the computers. Was Hollenbach serious? If he was, then Joe Donovan ought to know something. Donovan, the Democratic national chairman, might act out his role as the cynical politician to the point of exasperation, but he knew what was developing sooner than most. A little gossip with Joe might produce a clue of some sort.

MacVeagh went to the hallway phone and looked up Donovan's unlisted home number in his memorandum book of private Washington telephones. Donovan's voice was heavy, sardonic, purposely slovenly in syntax. Joe had gone to Penn, but he detested Ivy League mannerisms. Save for his refusal to drink anything alcoholic, he played the role of the tough Irish politician, one of the boys, as though he were Patrick O'Malley—who didn't act that way at all.

"Hi, pal," Donovan opened. MacVeagh could see the pale eyelashes almost meeting, alert, suspicious, and the studied curl in the corner of Donovan's lips. "You got patronage problems? Call tomorrow. No, on second thought, don't call us. We'll call you."

"You can have the jobs, Joe," said MacVeagh. "That last hassle over the Cedar Rapids postmaster cost me a thousand votes."

"We took your man, didn't we?"

"That's just it," bantered MacVeagh. "It turns out the guy has more enemies than stamps. Anyway, I just wanted to yak, nothing special."

"About what?" Donovan slurred the words intentionally, indicating suspicion.

"Just gossip. What do you hear, Joe?"

"Now, come off it, Jimmy." Donovan was the only man in Washington who called him Jimmy, but he was not the only man who knew that MacVeagh didn't particularly relish it. "You got something definite in mind, say it. I don't blush easy."

"Well, some of us were talking about the convention," said MacVeagh. "It's only five months off, you know."

"Five months and seven days," corrected Donovan. Mac-Veagh laughed at the echo of his exchange—minus one day—with President Hollenbach last night.

"Right. So what do you hear about vice-president?"

"We got a vice-president," snapped Donovan, "or ain't you heard the name Patrick O'Malley?"

"But the word's going around that O'Malley isn't long for this world."

"You said it, Jimmy. I didn't."

"Act your age, Joe," chided MacVeagh. "You really think Hollenbach is going to keep O'Malley on the ticket after the Jilinsky thing?"

"As national chairman, I'm sayin' nothin'. As Joe Donovan, I think O'Malley's had it. Does that answer your question?"

"Partially. But if O'Malley's out, who's in?"

"Why all the sudden interest on a Sunday afternoon?" Donovan's tone was one of admonition, but then speculation, as it usually does with politicians, got the better of him. "Who's in if O'Malley's out? Mind you, I said *if* O'Malley's out. Well, I hear a lot of names. There's Karper and Nicholson, couple of governors, some fellows on the Hill. You know, the usual run."

MacVeagh probed casually. "Who do you think would run best with him, Joe?"

"Me? Who do I think? Hell, I think we can run an Ay-rab with a goiter for second place, so long as we got Hollenbach at the head of the ticket."

"No favorites?"

"No favorites. And if I did, what would it matter? Hollenbach picks his own men, always, and pays no attention to me. You know that. I don't say he wouldn't be better off sometimes if he'd listen to me. He just don't. And the way he looks in the polls right now, maybe his judgment is best."

"Is the President mentioning anyone yet, Joe?" asked Mac-Veagh.

"Never even brought up the subject, not directly anyway. Oh, I know he's thinking about some fellows, because he drops names in connection with other things and asks me what I think of them." Donovan paused, then fell into his man-to-man confidential tone, as though the walls were eavesdropping. "Matter of fact, Jimmy, he talked about you the other day. He asked me what I thought of your character. Character! That's a hell of a thing to ask me."

"Well, what did you tell him?" MacVeagh tried to say it casually, but he felt a quickening of his heartbeat.

"None of your business. I don't repeat conversations with the President." Donovan paused again. MacVeagh knew he was relishing the suspense. "But I don't mind telling you what I think in general, Jimmy. They've all been speculating Karper. I don't buy it. Karper is smart and he's a Jew. The voters will take a Jew maybe, but they don't want no smart Jew, believe me. Nicholson would be all right, but he's not the President's type. Frankly, I think Nick bores the stuffing out of him. So that leaves lots of guys. Like I said, we could run an Ay-rab with Hollenbach this time. If it happens to come up you, well, that's all right with me. You got the looks, youth, messy black hair, and a nice way with the dames."

"Thanks," said MacVeagh. "Thanks a lot."

"Oh, you got more than that," continued Donovan. "Sincerity, integrity—all that jazz."

"You sound overwhelmed," said MacVeagh. He was brusque. Sometimes Donovan carried his cynic's role to juvenile lengths.

"I'm trying to give it to you straight, Jimmy. If I had to guess now, I'd say Hollenbach is considering maybe a dozen men. Maybe you're on his serious list and maybe you're not. Either way, it wouldn't surprise me."

MacVeagh knew that Donovan was trying to be objective, trying to tell him as much as he knew—or sensed. MacVeagh softened. After all, he was the one who was trying to pump the national chairman.

"Thanks, Joe. And I mean it. I just got to wondering about the whole situation."

"You haven't heard anything, have you?" Now it was Donovan's turn to probe.

"Not really," replied MacVeagh, fencing. "I just got word from a source that maybe Hollenbach had thought about me, and naturally I was interested."

"Natch." Donovan was sympathetic. "If I hear anything more, I'll call you. I've got a hunch Hollenbach is going to break it off in O'Malley any day now. I can't blame him, of course, but, jeez, I hope he doesn't make me do the dirty work. I like Pat, arenas or no arenas. But I guess Hollenbach will do the job himself all right, and if you ask me, I think he kinda has a hankering for it."

"What do you mean?"

"Aw, Mark is sore at O'Malley. Thinks he let the party down, loused up his own defense, and left some fingerprints on the White House wallpaper. Like I say, I can't blame him. Pat didn't help us none."

MacVeagh thought of the President's outburst against O'Malley the night before. "Did you get the idea," he asked, "that the President thinks O'Malley intentionally botched his own defense in order to hurt the administration?"

"On purpose? Oh, no, I don't think so. He's just mad as a bastard at O'Malley. Well, I'd hate to bet on Pat's summer replacement. On that one, I've got no solid dope."

"Thanks for talking to me, Joe," said MacVeagh. "And, by the way, I liked that commercial you got last night from the President."

"You mean about me not touching the stuff?"

"Yes. And listen, I'd like to get a good, sober man on my side. I'd be different, I'd pay attention to what he recommended."

Donovan laughed. "Maybe we can work out a deal someday. So long, Jimmy."

MacVeagh walked back to the living room, his hands in his pockets, his eyes on his scuffed loafers. And so he was in the running and he had a chance, however small, to be nominated in August at Cobo Hall in Detroit by the Democratic party as its candidate for vice-president. What a zany game, politics.

Six years ago he was just a lighthearted state representative in Iowa who had inherited an insurance agency from his father. The agency yielded a good living without undue work—the clients trusted the son as they had old Jamie MacVeagh—and his political chores were not onerous. Then came the revision of the state tax laws with young Jim MacVeagh chairing the subcommittee on reform. He worked for five months—hard as a hired hand for a change—and, wonder of wonders, the new tax law pleased almost everybody: farmers, businessmen, teachers, the little guys. So when the wheels of the Democratic party in Iowa asked him to run for the Senate, he accepted without too much thought. The campaign would be a novel experience, and even if he flopped, it would probably help his insurance agency. He started the campaign as a lark, worried only the last week—chiefly because a newcomer appeared ill-matched against a two-term incumbent—and then swamped Elmer Jencks, the Republican candidate. Elmer was solid and dull, two qualities admired in many country precincts, but he looked dour and he'd picked up a shoulder twitch in Washington which apparently the voters mistrusted. And so now, a flicker of a chance to be vice-president. He had to tell Martha.

But the phone rang, calling him from the faded rose sofa. He kicked away the newspapers and went to the hallway again.

"I lost a bet with myself, Jims." The voice was low, cotton-soft. "I thought you'd call right after the Gridiron dinner."

"Rita," he said with a trace of annoyance. She should have better sense than to call him at home. It had never happened before and he felt a twinge of disloyalty hearing her voice in this house with Martha's possessions all about him.

"Don't worry your Puritan heart, Jims," she comforted intuitively. "I read the papers too. Mrs. MacVeagh and her daughter are in Iowa for a week."

"I know but . . ."

"Are you coming over?" The voice continued low, but the tone taunted.

"For God's sake, quit using that boudoir throat like the weather girl on the radio."

"Are you, Jims?"

"Are I what?" He sounded flustered and this time his irritation was directed at himself.

"Coming over. It's only twenty minutes from McLean to Georgetown, even in Sunday traffic."

"Listen, Rita. I'm beat. I stayed up until all hours this morning and my stomach's fluttering."

"Have a drink, darling."

"I had one."

"Have another. You're always better when you've been drinking." It was her factual voice now, as dry and as uninspired as a bookkeeper's. It always excited him, for reasons he had yet to fathom.

He hesitated. The day of reckoning, the day when he should close the books on the Rita affair could be tomorrow. It didn't have to be tonight, did it? It could be done later, tomorrow or Tuesday or . . .

"All right," he said. "I'll see you after a bit."

He puttered for a few minutes, brushing his teeth again, running an electric shaver over his beard, and making two trips to the kitchen for short drinks of Scotch, straight. Then he stood by the phone and thought of calling Des Moines, but the idea of talking to Martha or Chinky just then repelled him. Instead, he wondered what would be his excuse if Martha called while he was out. Oh, he'd figure out something later, a meeting, a formal conference. Somebody was always conferring about something in Washington, even on Sunday.

In the Ford convertible, he turned the heater up high and drove without thinking. He was over Chain Bridge and speeding past the leafless maples and oaks lining Canal Road before he realized that it wasn't just the junior senator from Iowa who was going to an evening tryst, but a man who might be under consideration for vice-president. Good Lord, driving to see Rita when his name was in the hat! He ought to have his head examined. But there was the old tingle in his muscles and the course of desire deep within him.

The room was dark, the musk of perfume lay in the air like overripe fruit, and Rita's body, slack and smooth, lay against his. Her head rested on his bare shoulder, her hair faintly tickling his skin.

"You fell asleep for a few minutes," she whispered. "Gurgles with the snores, yet. Such noises."

"Uh-huh." He closed his eyes again and felt the luxurious fatigue of consummation. How long had this thing with Rita been going on now? Three years since he met her in the campaign, wasn't it? There had been no seven-year itch with him. Instead, it was an eleven-year itch. Rita had been Joe Donovan's secretary then and when Donovan, Mark Hollenbach's campaign manager, became national chairman, Rita Krasicki moved into K Street headquarters with him. For a long time Rita and

Jim flirted casually, on the phone or when MacVeagh called at Donovan's office. Then came occasional dinners at Paul Young's or Le Bistro, and finally, last fall, Jim spent his first night at this apartment. Suddenly the affair gained force like a mounting fever.

She was a big girl, built like a peasant, with a broad bottom and cushion breasts that always made men look a second time. Her skin had a light olive tint and her eyes matched her hair as exactly as a pair of ebony earrings. Rita's mother was Italian, her father Polish, and she grew up in the dreary, wood-frame Polish section of Buffalo, a city she never revisited if she could help it. Rita excited men. Even bent over her typewriter, in Donovan's outer office, her body evoked visions of the urgency and the solace of sex. Visiting politicians never minded being kept waiting by Donovan. "Joe's sex annex," they called the outer office, but Rita's appraisal of her body and the yearnings it inspired was too candid for jokes. Rita Krasicki assumed that men and women were born to mate and that passion was a fact of nature. Since she was a Catholic of reasonably faithful habits, Jim MacVeagh often wondered what she confessed to the priests at St. Matthew's Cathedral where she missed Mass only occasionally. Once, in a moment of intimacy, he asked her. "I don't confess things outside the church," was her only reply. Jim never mentioned the subject again.

Why Rita hadn't remarried after the death of the young husband to whom she never referred, MacVeagh couldn't imagine. He assumed she would someday, but she was thirty-one now and seemingly in no hurry to find another legally certified partner. Was she in love with him? MacVeagh really didn't know. Weren't all women in love with somebody? All he knew was that her willing passion, the ever-renewing lure of her great, smooth body fascinated and consumed him in a way that Martha never had. With Martha there was none of the slow, swelling surge of lust he knew with Rita, an emotion so complete that it left them spent and speechless. Why? Was that really fair to Martha? Jim wondered vaguely whether subconsciously he didn't approach Martha with restraint, inhibiting her by his own standards of what a wife and mother should and should not do. Whereas with Rita, his lust, boastful and challenging, compounded hers. But Jim pushed the comparison away, as he always did when he felt his thoughts verging on anything deeper than surface self-analysis. Introspection was a distasteful trait. He was what he was and he felt what he felt, and that was that.

He shifted under the bed-sheet, moved her head gently, and placed his hands behind his own head, swinging the elbows lazily. How many times had he been in this bed in the narrow Georgetown apartment with its copper-colored wallpaper, its tiny shaded lamps on the dresser, and its heavy scent of perfume? Ten? Twelve? And would he be here again, or was this the last time? As a man who had a chance to be a vice-presidential candidate. . . . Vice-President . . . Good Lord! . . .

MacVeagh sat upright so quickly that he yanked the sheet off both of them. She pulled it back, swathed her full breasts in it, and turned to him.

"Who shot you?" she asked. "Or is your usual moral hangover coming in instant packages these days?" She was pleasantly derisive, for after their lovemaking, he usually fretted until he was dressed, as though the whole MacVeagh family—and its Swensson in-laws—were suddenly to march through the door and find him naked, shorn of the decorous garments of fatherhood.

"No, it's not that," he said. "I just thought of something I keep forgetting, something that happened last night."

She waited quietly, cupping a hand at the black curls which hung in disarray about her head. MacVeagh slid out of bed, pulled on his shorts and began fussing with his socks and pants.

"Politics?" she asked.

He nodded.

"In that case, let's be formal. I'll put on something too."

They dressed and then MacVeagh sat at a pink, plastic-topped table in the little kitchen while Rita made coffee. Her coral shirt-waist made a vivid contrast with a full, gray skirt, faintly figured. Her olive legs were bare. Thong sandals exposed the crimson tint on her toenails which blended with the blouse. The painted toe-nails reminded Jim of their first night. He had fondled her toes and remarked idly that red against flesh was an exciting combi-nation. Now it was a ritual with them.

He knew he would tell her. With another woman in Washing-ton, relaying a conversation with the President would be the act of an innocent. A man might as well make an announcement at a press conference, for the word would be all over town in twenty-four hours anyway. But Rita was a political pro. She knew every-thing Joe Donovan knew and sometimes more. She was full of political gossip, much of which she shared with Jim, and her discussion of past events helped him to store away the small miscellany of people, dates and places that enable a politician, like a squirrel in autumn, to prepare for an uncertain future. But Rita held her tongue, never repeating what Jim told her in the intimacy of her O Street apartment. In return MacVeagh hon-ored her confidence. The compact was unspoken. Even to men-tion the necessity for secrecy would have been a rebuke to their code. In a word, they were politicians.

"Mark asked me up to Camp David last night after the din-ner," he said. "The surroundings were kind of spooky, but not the subject."

She laughed, low in her throat. "You mean the lights-out bit and the ghostly view of the mountains in the wee hours?"

He looked at her sharply. "Don't tell me you've been up there too in the middle of the night?"

"No, Jims. President Hollenbach and I only talk to each other over the phone—when he calls for Joe."

"Well, then . . ." Jim was surprised. Presidential idiosyncrasies were the bloodstream of Washington gossip, yet he'd never heard of Hollenbach's apparent penchant for sitting on a mountain perch in the dark.

"I've got my sources." Her black lashes fluttered, teasing him.

"I'm sure there are none better, Rita, but mine aren't bad, and I've never heard anything about Camp David. Honestly."

"Maybe you don't know the right Secret Service men," she said. "As I get it, it's different than it was with Lyndon Johnson. Lyndon turned off the lights to save money. Mark does it because he loves to think in the dark—or some such. But let's hear it from the horse's mouth. Was it really spooky?"

"No, not exactly," he said, knitting his brows as he thought. "He turned off the only light, and there wasn't much of a moon. Lots of snow outside. What I thought was a dead tree trunk turned out to be a Marine guard. But the fireplace was cheerful enough. Oh, what the dickens, if it hadn't been the President there, I wouldn't have given it a second thought. Still, it was kind of strange."

"I think it's priceless," she said. "Mark Hollenbach, our Mr. Perfection. It's nice to know he's a little strange at times, like the rest of us. But what happened up there that made you jump like a Jack-in-the-box a few minutes ago?"

Yes, thought Jim, what actually did happen up there? Not much, really. A mere mention of his name along with a dozen others, and yet that mention was sticking to his mind like adhesive tape.

"I don't want to make a federal case out of the thing," he said, "but it was kind of intriguing." He told her of the vice-presidential conversation, trying to remember it as precisely as he could.

She smiled affectionately and shook her head.

"So Jim MacVeagh's on the list!" She said it with a touch of incredulity.

"Is that so surprising?"

"Surprising?" She studied him a moment.

Damn it, he thought, there's that statistical look again, as different from her mood of a few minutes ago as sandpaper from honey.

"No, not surprising, knowing how Hollenbach's mind works." She smiled, quickly laving him with tenderness again. "But it's an idea that takes a lot of getting used to. James F. MacVeagh being considered for vice-president. Jims, honey, you don't have any more business being thought of for vice-president than I do. You're a lovable bum. You've got a tantalizing Scotch cleft in your handsome chin. You're sweet, you're kind, and you're usually on the side of the angels—when the angels aren't against what the corn farmers in Iowa want—but you use only half the brains God gave you. Also, sweetheart, you're lazy."

"Thanks, baby." He lowered his brows in simulated displeasure. "I'll make you head of the MacVeagh Forever fan club."

"Well, aren't you lazy?"

"I guess so." He fingered the bridge of his nose, musing. "At least, Mark told me I was last night."

"Are you taking this thing seriously?"

"No, I guess not. Still, the party has gone further and done worse, as the man said."

Rita reached across the table and took his face in her hands, framing it as a mother would a child's.

"Jims, if you won't be serious, let me. I've watched you for a lot of months now and, God knows, I've thought about you plenty. I think you're a pretty good senator, but please, honey, don't get bitten by this vice-presidential bug. Oh, I know you'd make a fascinating and glamorous candidate, but a vice-president could be a president if something happened to Hollenbach. . . . And do you really think you've the stature for it? Do you think much about foreign policy—what we should do in Europe, in Asia and Africa? Have you got what it takes to steer the economy, to quiet racial turmoil, to be sensible and steady about the bomb? Have you got the wisdom to do all these things and more?"

She'd withdrawn her hands and was searching his face, not unkindly, but intently, with her black eyes. He was too taken aback to answer. Their knowing political talk had always been about the mechanics of the business—the method of getting elected—never the ability to govern. Rita's questions reminded him of those he heard from troubled housewives at women's club meetings or from high school students on TV panel shows. He'd always fabricated his answers hurriedly, relying on platitudes and textbook generalities, and he'd realized they often sounded vapid and dissatisfying. Such questions were outside the trade, almost immaterial, as though you were to ask a real estate agent whether he loved the land.

"I'm asking as a citizen, Jims," she continued, "not as a woman who's been around politics for ten years. But have you ever studied yourself to discover whether you've got what it takes?"

"Oh, for God's sake, Rita." He was testy. "You sound like the emoting little mothers who gush around at the civic associations. If a man knows the ropes in this business, he can handle any job. It's as simple as that."

"Is it?" Her large eyes were fastened on his and she was not smiling now. "One thing I do know about you, Senator Mac-Veagh. You loathe self-analysis. You're afraid to mar the trim little picture you have of yourself—loving father, family man, good provider, happy politician—and a very discreet and very satisfying lover."

He bridled. If he was as shallow as that, why did she bother to coax him to Georgetown with a voice of cashmere? "My, aren't we scratchy tonight." He held out his arm. "Here, dig in your nails and draw some real blood."

She ignored the move. "Oh, I have no illusions that we can turn you into a statesman. The MacVeagh career will go onward and upward regardless, as gorgeous as a fireworks display on the Fourth of July. Jims, you're one of the lucky ones. You've got a hex on destiny."

"To be blunt about it, you don't think I'm the caliber for vice-president, do you?"

"To be blunt, no. I don't."

"And who, in your unlimited sagacity, would you pick?" His voice grated now and he was glad of it. There was the bitch in every woman.

"Karper. And be honest, darling, so would you, now, wouldn't you?"

He thought a moment while his irritation ebbed. He grinned. "Yes, I guess I would. For ability anyway. Maybe Nicholson on straight politics."

She leaned forward, her chin in pinched fingers, and searched his face again, seemingly striking a balance of his features. "Give up the hope, Jims. In the first place, Mark won't pick you, believe me. Second, even if he did, you're not the cut for it. You're gentle, you're wonderful in bed, and you're nice to have around the house—but not the White House. Let's face it. You play at life, Jims. You don't work at it."

Her voice was soft, but it stung like needles hidden in fur. Her mood offended him. Personality dissection was a rare trait with Rita.

"You make me sound foolish," he said.

She came around the little table, framed his face again in her hands, and kissed him on the lips, so hard he could feel the sharp edge of her teeth. She released him quickly.

"Jims, Jims, you don't understand a thing about women, do you? It's part of your low-life charm. The minute you mentioned what Mark said last night, I thought of us. Don't you realize? If you ever ran for vice-president, we'd be through."

"Through?" He tried to put unfelt surprise in the question, but failed.

"Of course. If Mark picked you, you'd be trailed by news-papermen everywhere you went—and it wouldn't do any good to put your convertible in a parking garage three blocks from here. Jims, it would be all over."

"Rita." There was a plea in the sounding of her name. He rose from the table and put his arms around her, but she gripped his wrists and held him away.

"It's only a matter of time anyway, darling," she said. "You were going to end it sometime soon. I could feel it. Tomorrow, next week, next month."

"How about you, baby? Weren't you ever going to end it?"

Her black eyes, wide and staring, were moist.

"Don't ask things like that, Jims, please," she pleaded in a whisper.

"Rita, you know it doesn't figure . . ."

"No, Jim MacVeagh, it never figured. And now, with this new ambition eating at you, I know for sure it's over."

She dropped his wrists and walked from the room, her sandals slapping the floor, a barren sound. From behind the door, Jim could hear muffled noises and he knew that she was crying.

He felt suddenly alone, immersed in nostalgia and misty re-grets, as he had when, as a boy, he left summer camp to return to school. He was alone, in a ridiculously small kitchen in a house where he didn't belong, and he wouldn't feel right until he left. His eyes caught a pair of tall wooden salt and pepper shakers in a wall recess. They were exactly like Martha's. You're a louse, MacVeagh, he told himself. And he almost meant it.

When she returned, her face orderly with cosmetic repairs, he was sitting at the pink kitchen table and rubbing the bridge of his nose. His thoughts were on a darkened lodge at Camp David, with the fingers of firelight, the moon's pencil tracings, and the President whose torrent of anger spilled over the hapless form of Patrick O'Malley.

"Trouble?" asked Rita.

"Not concerning me, no. . . . It's the way the President talked and acted. I didn't tell you, but he made a joking reference at the Gridiron dinner about the need for a national wiretapping law— so the FBI could automatically listen in on everybody's phone. Naturally, I thought he was kidding. But later at Camp David he said he was in earnest, and he convinced me he was. Good God, imagine monitoring every phone conversation!"

"Especially ours," she said lightly. He could see she wasn't taking the proposal seriously.

"And then," continued Jim, "he really blew his top over O'Malley last night. He even accused Pat of deliberately trying to smear him and the administration. It didn't make any sense. Jesus, Pat was only trying to save his own skin, maybe not too intelligently. But Mark has the screwball idea that Pat was trying to sabotage him—Hollenbach—personally."

She laughed and shook her head. Black wavelets fell across a cheek. "As I said, dear, everyone's a little strange at times, even Mr. Perfection. I'll never forget the time his temper shot up like a rocket—over not much, it seemed to me. Yes, everyone has his hidden peculiarities. Except you, of course. You don't change, darling. You're as transparent as a glass bowl."

"And not much inside, to hear you tell it," he replied. His mind was elsewhere, fastened on the picture of Hollenbach, rest-less, agitated, fired with indignation over O'Malley's supposed malice. What had Rita said?

"You say Mark lost his temper once with you?"

"Not with me," she said. "All he ever says to me are flirty little things, very flattering from a president."

"But he blew his top about somebody else?" MacVeagh was intrigued.

Rita scooped up the coffee cups and saucers, and kissed the cleft on his chin as she stepped past him to the kitchen sink.

"Hand me those spoons," she ordered. "I never give information over a messy table."

She tidied silently for several minutes, then sat down across from him again with a swirl of her wide-flaring skirt. She tapped a cigarette on the table and leaned forward while he lit it for her. "Unlike you, darling," she said, "I have all the vices. But I'm doing better. This is my first today."

"And so the President got mad once?" he asked.

She pursed her lips in reproof for his insistence. "Yes, Mr. Chairman," she said. "Yes, he did. Usually the only things I hear from the President are pretty nothings, all about how nice I look over the phone and when is Joe going to let me get married—that kind of thing. It's supposed to flatter me and it does. After all, how many girls can say the President sweet-talks them?"

"Four hundred eighty-three. I know. I'm taking a poll."

She thrust the tip of her tongue at him. "Anyway, I thank him and I put Joe on and that's that. but one day the gentlemanly Mr. Hollenbach, with all his talk of excellence, wasn't excellent at all. Actually, he sounded off and he came through just a little mean and shabby. Or maybe human is the right word."

"When was that?"

"Couple of months ago—January, I guess. I know it was a Friday morning because I get my hair done on Fridays at noon, and I remember it was a mess that morning." She inhaled deeply and blew out a spike of smoke. Jim noted that she invested even so routine an act with a sensuousness that stirred him.

"Your hair is never a mess, baby," he said, skipping its appearance when her head rested on his bare shoulder earlier.

"You're a liar, Jims, among other charming traits. Anyway,

the President called that Friday morning and asked for Joe. There was none of the usual sweet talk. I told him he must have forgotten, that Joe was on his western tour. Oh, yes, he said, well, did I know about the Davidge appointment. Davidge was being considered for assistant secretary of the treasury."

"The Chicago banker?"

"That's the one."

Jim frowned. "I never knew his name was up. Hollenbach appointed Lavallier and we confirmed him."

"I know, dear." She drew a final draught on the cigarette and mashed it out. A faint smudge of lipstick adorned the stub. "But here's the story. Davidge is an old friend of Joe's, and Joe asked the President to give him the post as a personal favor. Mark indicated he liked the idea and would think it over. But then that morning, without any of the usual kidding, he told me that Davidge was out, that he had learned that Davidge was trying to ruin him, and that the fellow was only trying to infiltrate the subcabinet in order to spy on him."

"Davidge spy on anybody? My God, he's the least devious man in America."

"I know." She nodded. "I tried to say something of the sort to the President, but he ranted on about Davidge, his words all running together. He was like a regular volcano erupting. Then, all at once, his voice got so chilly, it scared me. He cautioned me not to say a word about this to Joe, that he would call Joe himself in Salt Lake City and tell him Davidge wouldn't do."

"What did he say Davidge had done to him?"

"I couldn't make out at first," she said. "Everything came out so fast. It was a jumble, really. The only thing I caught was his charge that Davidge had made a traitorous speech about the administration and that was 'the self-revelation of a wicked man' —those were about the words he used—who was determined to hound him out of office.

"Well, when Joe got back the next week, he said the President had called him to say Davidge wouldn't do. The President apparently was very polite and apologetic with Joe, saying he hated to turn down a good friend of his, but that he'd found a better man for the job. So they sent Lavallier's name up to the Senate, and that was that. But the thing about Davidge's speech bugged me, so I called Davidge's secretary in Chicago and got her to send me all of his speeches for the last year or so. I went through them line by line and found only one sentence that was even faintly critical of the administration. And it was the tiniest little thing, you'd hardly notice it. All he said was that the Hollenbach administration ought to review its policy on some technical aspect of interest rates. That was all, so help me, about fifteen words."

"Did you tell Donovan any of this?" asked MacVeagh.

"No, I didn't. I don't repeat what I've heard—unless some guy with rumpled black hair and a sweet chin keeps pestering me. But that's what I mean by strange. It was a funny outburst, so different from anything the President has done before or since. I guess he was working too hard. Or maybe Davidge did him dirt once and we don't know about it. Anyway, it proves that with all his talk about the life of excellence, our Mr. President is human too. And I think I like him better, knowing he can fly off the handle once in a while. Don't you?"

MacVeagh, thinking of Hollenbach's similar outburst over O'Malley, only half heard. "Yes, I guess so," he said.

"You don't sound like it. . . . Well, that's enough politics for the night. This is supposed to be our day off."

She parted the curtains over the sink and looked out. The windows revealed a square of dirty snow in the handkerchief back yard. The night was overcast, a gray swab, and in the light from the window Jim could see water dripping from branches of the bare sycamore tree against the high board fence. The fence, similar to those which most Georgetown residents used to snare a few square feet of privacy, enclosed the tiny plot like a prison wall. Jim felt it pressing in upon him. Rita dropped the curtains.

"A miserable, stinking night," she said. "I don't know about you, but I'm glad I don't have to stir out of here until tomorrow."

MacVeagh stretched awkwardly. He wanted to leave at once, to get back to the familiar furniture in the McLean house, to get about the business of being the junior senator from Iowa again. He thought of Martha and Chinky, and felt the sourness of remorse in his mouth.

"Rita, I've got to go." He glanced at his wrist watch as he rose. Ten minutes after nine. "We have a committee meeting at ten tomorrow and I've got a batch of reports still to read."

Her smile was a sharing one that made him feel even more uncomfortable. "Okay, Jims," she said. "I understand."

And of course she does, he thought. She knows the tug of guilt, the tremor of impatience within him, the way his mind was trying to shut her out even as he watched the rise and fall of her bosom each time she breathed. He took a step and embraced her, kissing her lips and folding her close. Her body slackened and her breasts pressed his chest like warm pillows. But his arm muscles remained taut and there was no dissolving. When he released her, she reached behind him into his back trousers pocket for his handkerchief. She rubbed the lipstick from his mouth.

"Now our ambitious senator is spotless and pure," she said.

At the door, she took his hands in hers, lightly.

"Jims, I know the little bug is biting you, and that you're telling yourself that it has to be all over now. But if Mark passes you by, the number is Briarwood 9-8877. You just start at the top and slide downhill. Remember?"

He looked into her eyes, darkly wet, and he felt a surge of compassion for this undissembling woman who gave without demanding a down payment on the future.

"I'm not sure anything is over, baby."

"You know it is." Her voice had dropped to a whisper. "But without regrets. No regrets, Jims?"

"No, Rita. No regrets."

He stepped through the doorway onto the side stoop which served her first-floor apartment. By habit, he looked both ways on O Street. Seeing no one nearby, he trotted down the four brick steps and walked rapidly toward the Wisconsin Avenue garage where his car was parked.

The overcast was a brooding gray, slush covered the sidewalk like old sponges, and drippings from the ginkgo trees spattered his white raincoat. The air was soggily chill on his hatless head, but he felt unfettered, almost buoyant, as though he had ridden through a long tunnel and burst into open countryside again. His mind saw Rita standing by the door, her broad shoulders sheathed in the coral shirt, her olive face lax with memories. She was right, of course, more honest than he, as always. It had to be over. With even a glimmer of a chance for vice-president, he couldn't afford to take the risk. Another president might wink at extramarital affairs, but not President Hollenbach. No, sir, not Mark Hollenbach.

MacVeagh drove to McLean just inside the speed limit, the tires squishing through the slush and spraying muddy water from little pools at the edge of the pavement. He thought of President Hollenbach and his outburst against O'Malley, and of Rita's story of a similar explosion over Davidge, hardly a man to arouse anyone's ire. Neither one made much sense. And that incredible wiretap idea. Was something eating Mark? He'd never heard of Hollenbach's letting his temper get away from him like that. And the scene at Camp David had been eerie. Apparently, at least according to Rita, this wasn't the first time the President had sat around in the dark on his lonely mountain. Who really knew the tensions the man must be under? Jim found himself thinking again of a medic's shack in Viet Nam and a corporal leaping from his bunk and shouting. Pressure had a way of squirting free of a man somehow. Oh, well, as Rita said, we're all a little strange . . . except, of course, Jim MacVeagh, the glass bowl man.

Maybe he was transparent but, damn it, he wasn't as shallow as Rita tried to make out. To hear her tell it, he was all play and games, and no thinker. His resentment rose as he drove. Just name over the men in the Senate, he found himself retorting to her, and how many savants do you find? Or look at the Cabinet. How many Walter Lippmanns there? Or Winston Churchills? Men of stature? Sidney Karper maybe, but after him, period. He simmered as he drove across Chain Bridge. Then he remembered her remark about his lack of understanding of women, and he smiled. Of course, that was it. Rita downgraded him because she feared she had lost him . . . to the tiniest hint of an offer of the vice-presidency. Well, she was right. As long as there was a chance, he would keep to the straight and narrow. And, by God, if it came his way, old Jamie MacVeagh's boy could do as well at the job as the next man. But face it, he told himself, the chances are almost nil. Still, maybe he ought to apply himself more than he had, broaden out, give the brain some fodder now and then. He thought of the handsomely bound edition of the *Federalist Papers* which Martha had given him for his thirty-fifth birthday. The books rested on the corner of his desk in the den, unopened for almost three years. Oh, the devil with Rita and her psycho-analyzing. He was a tradesman—not a statesman—and a darn good tradesman too. How many could say as much?

At home, the chairs, carpet and draperies—the new turquoise draperies over which Martha had pondered and pouted for days —looked snugly in place. The scattered Sunday papers awaited him like old comrades and the faded rose sofa appeared inviting.

He knew he should telephone Martha. The thought occurred that only two hours before he had been in Rita's bed, an interlude of indecently short duration. But, he rationalized, he hadn't called Rita. She'd called him. The fact consoled him, and he placed a call to the Swensson home in Des Moines through the operator. No, he didn't care to dial direct, thank you.

His wife answered and he could hear her little gasp of delight when the operator said, "Washington calling." Martha treasured the telephone as a debutante loves dances. A.T. & T. stockholders had no better friend.

She would be standing by her mother's teakwood table, with the frieze carvings of fat squatting Buddhas, and she would be looking across the parlor at the weathered grandfather clock to mark the time of the call in case it brought news of the Senate wives, the P.T.A., the foreign students exchange, a reception at the Italian embassy, the United Fund drive, her Wednesday afternoon bowling league, the Committee for More Effective Urban Renewal, the Congressional women's fashion show, or any of the medley of good works and social routs which spangled her life like an overtrimmed Christmas tree. She would be patting at her precisely waved hair, waiting tensely. Jim felt vaguely annoyed.

"Relax, Marty. It's only me—with a little gossip."

"Oh, Jim." Martha was the only woman he knew who could verbally heave a sigh of relief. "What kind of gossip?"

"Can I swear you to secrecy? Nothing to Chinky? Not a word to your mother? This has to be kept deep in the well, maybe for a long time."

"Of course." Her tone was eager now, and Jim could imagine her pale eyebrows arching in anticipation. Curiosity livened her face like a child's. He could see her little Swede's nose and the soft wisps of hair that trailed behind her ears from the closely set coiffure.

"Cross your heart . . ." It was their old game since courtship days.

"And hope to die . . . yes, yes. . . . Please, Jim!"

"Hold on to the phone," he ordered jovially. "Last night Mark Hollenbach summoned me up to Camp David after the Gridiron dinner—and said he was considering me for vice-president."

"For what?" It was almost a shriek.

"Vice-president," he said proudly. "Or, I should say the Democratic nomination for the job. Of course, he's considering umpteen others too."

"But you're honestly one of them?" Every landmark in life, Jim thought, excites Martha as though it were Fort Knox on a platter. But this time he thought her bubbly response justified. "But what about O'—" She caught herself. "What about Mr. You-know-who?"

"O'Malley? He's out. It had to come. Mark is demanding a statement in writing, saying he's not a candidate for re-election."

"Honey, how many others is he thinking about? Do you know?"

"Oh, a dozen maybe. Really, Marty, there isn't much chance, but I wanted you to know."

"Jim, I'm so proud of you. I know you're at the top of the list."

He compared her quick assessment of his chances with Rita's cynical rating—the opinion of a professional—and he felt the least bit depressed. Martha spoke from the ignorance of wifely loyalty.

He sighed. "Not much chance of that. Nice thought, though, Marty."

"I've got a feeling about it, Jim. Intuition. Honey, you'd make a grand vice-president. You've got the heart for it."

MacVeagh chuckled. Martha says he has the heart for it. Rita says he doesn't have the brain for it. Maybe they're both right.

"And young and handsome too," said Martha.

He laughed. The two women agreed on that. The thought cheered him.

"But, Jim." Her voice fell. "If you're picked, think of the work. All that traveling, and speeches, those horrible jet planes, and those awful veal cutlets they always serve at the banquets."

He understood. Did any politician's wife ever really enjoy campaigning? Election night maybe, but the crowds, the interminable rallies, the late hours, the clutter of pols and stale whisky glasses in the hotel suites, the corsages from the Girl Scouts and the Eastern Star chapters, the eternal smiles that made a woman's cheeks, they said, feel like cracked leather. No, he guessed none of them did. And for Martha it would mean severing a frenetic chain of civic, social and personal uplift meetings, the sparkling links in the life of a lady doer.

"Don't worry, Marty," he soothed. "There's not much chance Mark will pick me. He was probably just flattering me, a little sweetening to keep me in line on administration programs."

She didn't believe him, obviously, for she said: "I'm so proud of you I could cry. In fact, I think I am. Oh, dear." He laughed again. Her sniffles were real, and he was grateful she felt strongly about him.

"Oh, I almost forgot," she said after a moment. "Do me a favor, will you Jim?"

"Sure."

"Call Bertha Hempstead," she ordered, briskly, "and tell her she'll have to get the speaker for next Thursday. And, honey, one other thing. In my dresser drawer you'll find a program for the Smith alumnae dinner. . . ."

"Now just a minute." He bridled. Martha was in her madam chairman's role which swept all other concerns aside like an imperious broom. "I said a favor. Now you want two."

"Don't be grouchy," she said. "The Smith program just has to get to the printer's by tomorrow night."

"Anything else?" His voice was spiked with irritation, and he didn't mind.

"No, Mr. Vice-President." She said it fondly, ignoring his tone.

"Get Chinky to the phone, will you? But no telling her, now."

"Ja-ane!" She called it in two syllables. "Your dad's on the phone."

There was the clap of oversize loafers on the floor and then his daughter answered, more breathless than her mother. "Hi, Number One! You two-timing me while I'm away?"

He could see her brown eyes and the flush of exuberance in her cheeks. He remembered how he'd nicknamed her Chinky when she was a fat little lump, with wide, pleading eyes and a chin that trembled. For some reason, she pronounced "dr" as a hard "ch," and when she wanted a drink of water, she'd hold out a tiny fist and say, "Chink, daddy. Chink." Now he knew her feet were planted wide apart, like those of the models in *Vogue,* and that her pony tail reached to the small of her back. The hair was tied with rubber bands. This year, her thirteenth, rubber bands were in.

"I'm true-blue for you, Chinky," he said. "If only I had an orchid, I'd place it in front of your picture tonight."

"Always the cornball, Pops." She snorted. "Ugh. Why do I go for you? I must be weak-minded."

"You still coming home Wednesday?" he asked. "One week is long enough to be out of school, even for an IQ of one-twenty."

"One-twenty-four, you dragger-downer," she yelped. "Oh, Pops, have you heard Porky Jones yet . . . on l-p?"

"Haven't had the pleasure—or punishment. Who's he?"

"Who's Porky Jones? Say, man, what outpost of civilization have you been hiding out in? Like off with some Indian squaw, huh?" Jim cringed, as though he'd been slapped. "Porky's on the drums, stupid. He's divine. Mom let me buy the album. I mean neat. Wait'll you hear."

"Okay, Chinky. Wednesday night. Okay?"

"Right, pops. We'll have a blast. 'Bye, now."

Jim felt good, and he replaced the receiver slowly, as though to prolong Chinky's image. He thought of the one subcommittee draft report in the den upstairs, then shrugged. Tomorrow would be time enough. He had fibbed to Rita about a "batch of reports" to be read. He saw Rita briefly, fuzzily, then put her from his mind. It was not hard, for the Georgetown apartment and its languid aroma of perfume seemed a thousand miles away.

The pleasant mood lasted while he undressed and got into his pajamas. He opened the window and found that a new snow, light and fluffy, was falling lazily. The scattered flakes shone for a moment as they passed the window's beam of light, then vanished below him.

Senator Jim MacVeagh fell asleep almost as soon as he crawled into the unmade bed, and his last conscious thought that Sunday night was that President Hollenbach had a list—and his name was on it.

3.

The List

A half hour before President Hollenbach's Wednesday press conference, newspapermen began arriving at the sloping State Department auditorium. They chatted in little knots in the glass-fronted lobby, flipped open wallets to show their color photographs on White House press cards to entrance guards, and sauntered down the aisles to their seats.

In the unwritten but slavishly honored protocol of the correspondent corps, those who covered the White House as a regular beat had reserved seat status. Metal nameplates on the first rows spelled prestige—AP, UPI, CBS, NBC, ABC, New York Times, Washington Post, Washington Star, Baltimore Sun, Chicago and Los Angeles papers, and a score of others, including the big multiple-ownership names of American journalism, Scripps-Howard, Newhouse, Cowles, Hearst, Knight, Gannett, Copley. The foreign correspondents collected in self-segregated pockets, pierced only occasionally by an American reporter who covered the diplomatic run and wished to polish his French or Italian. A dozen Japanese businessmen, bespectacled and blandly courteous, filed into a rear row to watch the show as trade mission guests of President Hollenbach. In front of them five African newspapermen chortled over some private joke. They were one-year fellows of the State Department and they were twitting the mulatto foreign service officer serving as their escort.

Five minutes before the press conference, scheduled to be televised live beginning at 10:30 A.M., all correspondents and visitors were in their seats. A Congressional press gallery functionary walked up and down the aisle, holding aloft a white card with the numerals 412—the total attendance as the doors closed. It was an unusually large turnout. It had been three weeks since the President's last conference. In the interval the case of Vice-President Patrick O'Malley and the Kennedy sports arena had boiled to a froth. An air of knowing anticipation tingled in the room. Next to a declaration of war, nothing titillated the nerve ends of Washington journalism like a full-bodied, old-fashioned scandal. The habitual rustle of newspapers was missing. Reporters talked behind cupped hands or wrote out questions in notebooks. In the front row Craig Spence, his fringe of red hair framing his shiny dome, chewed on a pencil and studied his own question: "Mr. President, did Vice-President O'Malley violate your administration's code of ethics when he made three phone calls to the chairman of the Fine Arts Commission?"

A cameraman took a last-minute stance behind the podium, marked with the presidential seal, so his colleagues could focus lenses and adjust light meters. In the glassed television booths above the crowd, commentators talked into microphones and ad-libbed as they cast anxious glances at the second hands of clocks. Two Secret Service agents appeared at the corner of the auditorium's stage. The crowd hushed.

Promptly on the stroke of 10:30 President Hollenbach entered from stage left and walked briskly to the centered podium. His steps were short, fast, forcing his two press aides, one white and one Negro, to hurry to stay in his wake. The President wore a two-button brown suit, immaculately creased, and a matching figured brown tie with a small knot at his button-down shirt collar. His crew cut, the color of gravel, was trimmed neatly and recently. The correspondents rose as one, with a creaking of seats and a bustle of bodies. Hollenbach's long, thin face wrinkled in a smile of appreciation for this traditional salute to the office of President of the United States. He held a typed sheet and spoke into the cluster of microphones.

"Thank you, ladies and gentlemen. Please be seated. I have a statement to read. You won't have to take notes, as copies will be available in the rear as you leave. While I do not wish to thwart your zealous pursuit of the news, I must tell you in advance that no questions will be entertained on the subject of the prepared statement after I have read it. The statement follows:

"Quote. Vice-President Patrick J. O'Malley hand-delivered to me last night a letter, stating that he could not, under any circumstances, allow his name to be presented to the Democratic national convention in Detroit as a candidate for renomination as vice-president. Since the letter is personal in nature, I am not at liberty to divulge its contents, except to say that Mr. O'Malley is fully cognizant of the fact that his actions with respect to the Kennedy memorial sports arena did not conform to the standard of ethical conduct as announced by this administration shortly after the inauguration. That ethical code was widely published and reprinted, and every American knows, in general, what it provides.

"Vice-President O'Malley amplified his position in a talk with me last night. While I regret the circumstances and the unavoidable embarrassment to the Vice-President, I agree that Mr. O'Malley took the only honorable course open to him. I applaud his decision to place country and party before his career. At the same time, needless to say, I most emphatically do not condone his conduct in the sports arena case.

"As President and as a candidate to succeed myself in this

office, I accept the Vice-President's decision in the spirit in which it was made. While a Democratic convention is the master of its own house, I shall, in due course, make my own recommendation to the delegates as to the man I think best fitted to occupy the office of vice-president. Unquote."

A dozen reporters sprang to their feet. Hollenbach, honoring custom, nodded to the Associated Press correspondent, senior man on the White House beat, who stood in the favored front row aisle position.

"Mr. President," he asked, "could you say whether the Vice-President's action was prompted by any prior discussion with you."

Hollenbach gripped the podium and those in the front rows could see that his knuckles went white. "With due respect to your diligence," he said, "I refer you to the formal statement. As I said, I cannot entertain any questions on that subject." Hollenbach nodded to Craig Spence, who thrust up his lanky body on the closing syllable of the President's reply.

"Respecting your limitation, sir, could you tell us when you expect to announce your own preference for your running mate?"

Hollenbach nodded affably. "Oh, I would expect to notify the delegates in plenty of time—say two months before the convention, perhaps late June at the latest. Mind you, Craig, the delegates will have the last word." He smiled. "My views amount to a recommendation only."

Laughter engulfed the room. Hollenbach's answering smile was only a wisp, but his flecked green eyes showed a sparkle. With an arching finger, he indicated a newsman in the rear.

"Mr. President, can you give us some idea of the type of man you're considering?"

Hollenbach nodded again. "Clearly, the basic quality we're looking for is the same the American people want—an all-around ability to assume the office of President of the United

States at a moment's notice. While I feel fit enough, and I assume the Republican candidate will be equally healthy, we all live by a fragile thread. The Vice-President must be qualified in every respect to lead this country. None of us will forget the dignified and considerate, yet resolute, manner in which Lyndon Johnson took over the reins in those first awful moments in Dallas. It's that definite, but indefinable, mark of leadership that we want in our vice-president."

"Do you have a list of men who meet that test, Mr. President?"

"Yes, I do."

"Could you say, sir, how many are on it?"

"Seven."

"Exactly seven, Mr. President?"

"Well, seven at the moment, but that, of course, is subject to change. Fortunately, our party—and I wish I could say the same for the Republicans—is blessed with an abundance of talent."

A bureau chief on Craig Spence's right whispered: "He left himself wide open with that one. By tomorrow the Republican committee will be billing this lash-up as 'Snow White and the Seven Dwarfs.'"

Spence beamed at him. "Not if I can get it into print first," he said. "I'm swiping that one from you."

The newsmen sought to burrow into the political future for the next fifteen minutes, but Hollenbach blocked all attempts at further enlightenment. No, he would not name names. He refused to say whether any Cabinet members were on the list. He would not limit it by sex, or race either, for that matter. He declined to say whether or not he had conferred with anyone on his list. Finally, frustrated reporters turned the inquiries to other channels: the state of the economy, the status of his legislative program, the world's trouble spots. A German correspondent, speaking in a heavy accent, asked his views on the new outbreak of skirmishing on the Israeli-Egyptian frontier, and the conference closed with a fervent presidential plea for peace and his hopes for success of the United Nations truce mission.

In his office in the old Senate Office Building, Jim MacVeagh leaned across his littered desk, switched off his portable television set and sat watching the picture of the emptying State Department auditorium fade to a pencil point of light in the center of the screen. So the plot was thickening—and narrowing. Instead of the dozen possibilities that Joe Donovan estimated, the number was down to seven. And he was one of the seven. Or was he? Yes, he was sure he was, so that made the odds no more than six to one against him. And Karper and Nicholson were both out, judging by what Mark had said Saturday night, so that removed the most formidable competition. Who could the others be? He took the Congressional Directory from its position next to the donkey-shaped bookend and began leafing through the alphabetical list of senators, then the Cabinet and the state-by-state list of governors. Six other men? He could find but three who seemed to mesh smoothly with Hollenbach's own complex personality. He sensed a rising warmth within, as though with the onset of a fever. God, it was tantalizing not knowing. He paced to the window and looked down at the traffic on Constitution Avenue. Rita was right. The bug had bitten him and there was no throwing off the virus.

Rita. He wanted to see her tonight. Inwardly he reproached Martha for calling him that morning to say she and Chinky could not return until Saturday. Her mother had picked up a cold, and at her mother's age, Martha said, she wouldn't feel right leaving her. Old ladies got pneumonia so easily, she'd said, and he agreed. But, damn it, her mother had no business getting a cold right now. It exposed him, left him vulnerable. By her physical presence, Martha could protect him—and this gnawing ambition—from temptation. He grew petulant. Didn't Martha realize that he had a chance to be vice-president, and that her duty was to be beside her husband? . . . The Congressional Directory lay open before him, but his mind went back to Rita and the curve of her wide, bare shoulders. He could smell the scent of rich perfume on her olive skin, and feel the warmth of her breasts on his chest and the soft nuzzling of her lips on his throat.

MacVeagh reached for his personal telephone, the one that did not connect through the Capitol Hill switchboard, and dialed the number of the Democratic national committee.

"Mrs. Krasicki, please."

She answered in her low voice that made his skin feel as though it were being brushed by satin. "Mr. Donovan's office."

"Rita, it's Jim. What are you doing tonight?"

Silence, except for a muffled clink of her thin, gold bracelets.

"I'd like to come over after work," he said. "I'll bring the groceries and do the steak."

She whispered into the mouthpiece, and he could imagine that she had turned her back on someone in the room.

"We said it was over." He could hear her breathing. "There isn't even a scar on the wound yet."

"It's only a scratch, baby," he bantered. "I can heal it. I know just the right medicine."

"Jims, please. I don't want to be hurt again."

"Rita, I need you."

"Need or want?"

"Does it matter?"

"It matters a great deal." She was still whispering. "Don't be cruel, Jims."

"I'm not. I'm gentle—by your own admission."

"Oh, sweetheart. I do want to see you."

"Six-thirty?"

"Make it seven. This is one of those days around here."

"Okay, martinis at seven. Until then."

"Good-by."

When he hung up, he found he felt none of the anticipatory elation which usually accompanied their telephoned arrangements. Instead, he felt vaguely depressed. She was hurt, she said, and he realized with a wince that he hadn't thought of her feelings at all on Sunday. He had walked down the four brick steps, with only a stray backward thought, and he had driven to McLean with his mind on the vice-presidency, on himself and on the relief he felt that it was over. And now he persisted in going back to Georgetown and twisting the knife in a woman who had given without complaint. It had to end, and yet he was prolonging it, like the final kiss held too long at the end of a movie. No regrets, she'd said, and now there would be everything to regret. Had he really ever considered her feelings? No, he'd played a role: casual lover to a girl who desired, supposedly, without involvement, as though any woman ever did. Rita said he played at life. She was right. Why the devil couldn't he have let it die, peacefully and forever, on Sunday night? Now when it ended there would be a wrenching and an acrid taste in the mouth because he had come back into her life unbidden, guilty of a spiritual charge of breaking and entering. If he had the courage, he thought, he'd telephone back right now and cancel everything. But he didn't do it. For a man who disliked self-analysis, he realized wryly, he had been indulging in a great deal of it lately. And then his eyes went back to the Congressional Directory and he wondered again who the other six men were.

The wall bell rang once, rudely clattering like an old alarm clock, signaling the opening of the Senate session. MacVeagh checked his desk calendar to find the pending business. It was the Independent Offices appropriations bill and he had to be at his desk on the Senate floor, for the measure carried a number of Iowa projects, including the important one of erecting a new federal building at Davenport. He buzzed for his administrative assistant, Roger Carlson.

Carlson, a huge, corn-haired young man who had played basketball at the University of Iowa, came into the room carrying a manila folder stuffed with papers.

"Most of that poop is about that Davenport project," he said, "but you'll find some stuff on the others too."

Carlson gave the folder to MacVeagh and leaned on his big palms against the edge of the desk. He was coatless and his shirt was open at the neck, tie pulled to one side. Carlson was getting beefy after three years in Washington.

"Jim, I've got a bet you're on the list. Right?" His eyes searched MacVeagh's for confirmation. Carlson loved the inwardness of politics, regarded any development of which he was not apprised in advance as a personal affront.

"What makes you think so, Flip?" Carlson's zest for the game amused MacVeagh. Jim sometimes thought the office of the junior senator from Iowa would operate more efficiently if their roles were reversed. And he suspected the thought was not alien to Carlson.

"Just a process of elimination, Jim," said Carlson. "If Mark, the pure in heart, says there are only seven on the list, I believe him. Right? And you'd have to be one of the seven."

"I appreciate your confidence in me, Flip, but what's your reasoning?"

"You don't reason in this business." Carlson grinned and held a finger aloft. "You get it by divine inspiration. Right? Wanna bet against yourself?"

"No, thanks. There'd be no way of proving it anyway. When he announces his choice, nobody will ever know who the other six were."

"Well, how about a one-to-three bet that he picks you? Your thirty bucks to my ten?"

MacVeagh laughed. "I should bet thirty dollars against myself? Flip, I've got enough troubles. Now get your big hams off the desk. I'm going over to the floor."

Carlson held the corridor door open for him. "It's bugging you just a little, isn't it, Jim?"

MacVeagh nodded. "A little," he admitted, "but not as much as it does you."

He rode the open subway tram to the Capitol, took the "Senators Only" elevator to the Senate floor level and settled himself at his antique mahogany desk on the rear row of the Democratic side. The majority leader was wrangling, in his high-pitched drone, with the minority leader over some obscure procedural point. The two leaders faced each other, politely combative, yet already dejected of voice, as though they had contested the point all night and would continue all day until reason outpointed opacity. Jim put a hand to his mouth to mask a yawn. Parliamentary pettifogging bored him, and he doubted he would ever have the patience to master it. He had lost several floor skirmishes because of his distaste for the Senate manual and its rules, and thereafter he'd brought Flip Carlson to sit beside him whenever a parliamentary snarl threatened one of his rare legislative ventures. Carlson knew the Senate manual as small boys knew the major league batting averages.

A Senate page, in white shirt and black trousers, whispered in MacVeagh's ear. The head of United Press International's Senate staff wanted to see him in the lobby. Glad of an opportunity to escape the majority leader's nasal delineation of the rule book and righteousness, MacVeagh sauntered out to the President's room, with its immense gold chandelier and its faded rococo walls. The UPI reporter, a thin little man with a cheek tic that bespoke a thousand old wire service deadlines, wanted to know if MacVeagh had a candidate for vice-president, what he thought of Hollenbach's "dumping" of O'Malley, whether he had reason to believe his name was on "the list," his own guess as to Hollenbach's eventual choice. MacVeagh answered cheerfully, parrying obliquely, managing to sound sincere while saying nothing. Being interviewed was an art and Jim was happy that he was intuitively adept at it. The UPI man scrawled his answers in a looping half-shorthand, seldom looked up, then hurried off to the press elevator as though pursued by demons.

It was the first of a dozen such interviews for MacVeagh. Every senator in sight was quizzed as the newsmen gathered reaction to President Hollenbach's announcement, biggest political story of the year. Senators shuttled on and off the floor like ponderous beetles, and the fate of the nation's public works was forgotten while all hands played the joyful game of politics. The newsmen's traffic in senators was especially heavy since they could not find Vice-President O'Malley, who had gone into seclusion, no one knew where. MacVeagh found himself answering the same questions so often that he could brighten his phrases and even get off a few bon mots.

It was midafternoon when Craig Spence called him from the floor and met him in the little vestibule off the Senate's center aisle. Alcoves on each side, originally built for statuary, now contained red leather pads where senators could sit while conversing with callers. Few newsmen used this location. Spence liked his sessions with his friend MacVeagh to be as private as possible. The angular columnist stood with his hands in his coat pockets. The companionable freckles on his bony face matched his carrot fringe of hair. MacVeagh always felt at ease with Spence. It was understood that they spoke off-the-record always, unless the columnist asked permission to quote him.

"Jim," he said, "I've got a tip that the President really cussed the bejesus out of O'Malley at their meeting last night. You heard anything?"

"Nothing. But I wouldn't be surprised. I know that Hollenbach is mad at Pat, to a degree, I'd say, that isn't justified by Pat's behavior. Pat was dead wrong, of course, but it's not as if he'd looted the Treasury or mugged somebody on the Mall."

"You mean the President is angrier than the facts justify?" Spence was lounging against the wall, but his eyes watched Mac-Veagh's face alertly.

MacVeagh thought of the flickering fire at Aspen lodge and the ruddy streaks in Hollenbach's face as he exploded about O'Malley. "Yes, I'd say so. But why, I don't know."

"Funny," said Spence. "I got a hint of that from another source today. Wonder what's bugging him?"

"I wonder too," mused MacVeagh. "It's out of character for Mark. He's usually beautifully controlled."

Spence switched topics. "Speaking of Snow White and the Seven Dwarfs . . ." MacVeagh grinned. "Tell me, Jim, have you any reason to believe you're on this list of seven?"

MacVeagh answered carefully. He could never mislead his friend, but neither could he divulge his meeting with the President. "I don't know whether I am or not, Craig. Flip Carlson thinks I am, but he's speculating. A process of elimination, he says. Let's put it this way. I've heard nothing definite, one way or the other."

"Logic says you ought to be on it."

"Are you speaking as a friend or a political expert?"

Spence's grin bunched the freckles on his cheeks. "In politics, you know as well as I do, there are no experts. We write a lot about the pros, but then every four years a bunch of young, sharp-eyed amateurs comes along and steals the party machinery for some candidate and gets him the nomination for president. It's happening all over again with the Republicans this year."

"Let me ask you something, man to man, Craig. Be honest with me. Do you think I've got the stuff to be vice-president?"

Spence was surprised. "Oh," he said, "so you're taking the thing seriously, huh? Well, you want an honest answer and I'll give you one. Jim, I think you've got the potential. You're intelligent, honest, and you want to do the right thing. But, damn it, man, I don't think you do your homework. There's still a lot of the playboy in you."

"Playboy?"

Spence hunched his shoulders. "Oh, I don't mean with women. You may or you may not be in that league." He winked. "I don't know about that. But I mean your whole attitude. You take things pretty easy."

MacVeagh smiled, somewhat sadly. "That makes it unanimous. Two other friends have told me the same thing recently."

"But the potential's there, fellow." Spence poked a fist lightly into MacVeagh's shoulder. "Personally, I'd like to see you go to work."

They stood a moment in silence, both embarrassed at rummaging into MacVeagh's character. Old friends take one another for granted, and MacVeagh was sorry he had forced Spence to cross the line.

"As long as we're on personalities, and I've got you in the mood," said MacVeagh, "let me ask you about somebody else. Assuming that Hollenbach has lost his temper over O'Malley, which I suspect is the truth, have you ever heard of his doing it before?"

Spence appeared puzzled. "No, I haven't, I don't think. No, never. Why do you ask?"

MacVeagh tilted his head in a gesture of unconcern. "No special reason, except that it's not like Mark to lose control of himself. And from what we've both heard, he apparently did this time."

"Of course, you can't blame him. A spotless record for more than three years for the Hollenbach administration, and then in a couple of weeks O'Malley louses it up. I guess the President takes it as a personal insult."

"Yes," said MacVeagh. "I guess he does."

A page boy had appeared through the swinging doors and was standing respectfully a few paces away, waiting for MacVeagh to finish speaking. Spence indicated the boy with his head, shook hands with MacVeagh, and departed.

"You're wanted on five in the cloakroom, Senator," the page said. "The White House is calling."

It was Rose Ellen, the President's personal secretary, speaking in a soft Alabama drawl that had no "r's" and had never known the harshness of a stone fence.

"Senatah MacVeagh, the President would be pleased if you could come by his office at fo'-thirty. Would that inconvenience yo' schedule, suh?"

"If it did," replied MacVeagh, "I'd be there anyway, Rose Ellen. Did you say four-thirty?"

"Yes, ah did. An' the President said to bring your cah in the back gate and come through the rose gahden." She trilled a laugh. "We'ah off-the-record today, Senatah."

Now what? Two sessions with the President in five days, more than he'd had in the whole previous year. He ran over the pending legislative business in which both he and Hollenbach were involved, but could think of nothing significant. Something on vice-president? No, certainly not this soon. That was weeks away. Still speculating, he went back to his office, dictated for half an hour, then hailed a cab on Constitution Avenue for the ride to the White House.

A White House policeman admitted him at the back gate on East Executive Avenue, and he walked up the curving asphalt driveway toward the rear balcony of the big house. The snow had melted now, and the late-afternoon sun bathed the lawn in a golden haze. There was still no hint of spring in the air, but water bubbled in the fountain and the broad leaves of the magnolia trees shone moistly. The scene had a pastoral peace, and the singsong of traffic on the wet streets behind the iron fence was a muted hum.

The Secret Service agent standing at the rose garden was Luther Smith. He grinned, his teeth like ivory in his swarthy face.

"Nice to see you in daylight, Senator," he said.

"Just looking at you reminds me of all the sleep I lost last Saturday," said MacVeagh.

"He's waiting for you." Smith motioned to the President's office under the portico.

Mark Hollenbach was stepping through the French doors to greet him. They shook hands, the President's grip as strong as iron. Then they were inside the oval office and MacVeagh was seated in the short-backed chair facing the President's desk. Hollenbach's green eyes were alight and his thin features radiated enthusiasm. Aglow with another project, thought MacVeagh. Just where did he get this unflagging energy? It was 4:30 P.M., and a man of fifty-seven should be tapering off, feeling an ebb of the spirit.

"Jim, I've decided what I want to do on the vice-presidency." The President made a triangle of his fingers, pressing the tips firmly together.

"Oh." MacVeagh waited.

"I told my press conference this morning that there were seven under consideration," said Hollenbach. "That's true enough, but the more I ponder this thing, the more I keep coming back to you."

MacVeagh experienced a pervasive tingling sensation, as though he were wired and the electricity had shot through his whole body. In the moment of exhilaration he said nothing. Hollenbach smiled shortly, watching his reaction, then got up and stood with his arms on the back of the black leather swivel chair.

"You make sense politically, Jim, but there's more to it than that. I've got some major plans for my second term, and I need a partner with youth and vigor—intelligence too. You've got all three, Jim, and you've got another great asset. You're not wedded to any particular ideology, not opinionated or locked in the clutch of semantics. In short, you've got an open mind and that's exactly what I need next time."

An open mind? Jim was bewildered by the speed of the President's words. Rita would say it was an unused mind, and he guessed Craig Spence would agree with her. So it was open, was it? The thought pleased him.

"I can't announce anything this early." The President was hurrying on, elated by his plans. "As I said this morning, June is soon enough for that. The climate might change, of course, but right now I see you as the man. Now, here's what I think we should do."

Jim could feel the throb of excitement, a heady sensation. The President was silhouetted against the French windows, the twilight behind him softening the shrubs and seeming to lie on the lawn like orange gauze. Vice-president! MacVeagh's eyes held to the form of the President as though hypnotized.

"I'm going to pass the word quietly to Donovan this evening that you're the man, and let the idea seep around the committee. We'll try you out in a couple of those new Vice-Presidential primaries. New Hampshire is gone, of course, but we could work up a quick write-in for you in Wisconsin and Indiana, maybe Oregon. The national committee can put the muscle on for you and the word will get around that I'm for you. When I'm asked at a press conference, I won't commit myself, just say it's a free country and an open party. That way, you'll make it on your own and you'll come into office when we win in November—with much more prestige."

The shock had passed now, and MacVeagh was following closely. You fox, he thought. If I fail in the primaries, it's my fault and I'm out. But if I win, it's with your power and help, and I'm under complete obligation to you for the duration. What a torturous trade, politics. Candid as two men might be with each other, when the magnet of the White House began its powerful, circular attraction they all played the game to the limit, each according to his aptitude. And Hollenbach's skill was matchless.

"It will set you up." Hollenbach sat down at his desk again and surveyed MacVeagh. "When I announce my choice in late June, everybody will say that I couldn't do anything else. They'll say you earned it."

"What are the ground rules?" Jim was cautious now. "I assume I can't tell anyone that you've given me the nod?"

"No, no. Nothing official until June. Let gossip do its own work. We want this to be your show, an exhibition of your strength in the party."

My strength? Jim laughed, inwardly and wryly. This show was about as much his as Ringling Brothers belonged to the man on the high wire. Hollenbach's reversal of the facts rankled. He decided to play his own hand.

"One question, Mr. President. What makes you think I want to be vice-president?"

Hollenbach did not smile. "I measure my man," he said.

"That I won't dispute, sir. But there are some other factors. What about my state? Iowa has only nine electoral votes. Even assuming I'm in good odor there, that isn't much to add to the ticket. And what about my ability? Several good friends have put me down as a fair senator, but they don't think I have—well, uh, the stature, to be next in line to run the country. I was inclined to differ with them, but I've about come to the conclusion they're right."

"Modesty, Jim, like poverty, is an overrated virtue. Take the first point. You've got the stamp of the Midwest on you, and frankly if I'm weak anywhere it's with the farmers. You'd help some. Now as to your ability. Your aversion to hard work I concede, but I know you've got the makings and you're not hampered by a lot of antique preconceptions of how to operate the Republic."

MacVeagh grinned. "Kind of like clay, ready to be molded. Is that it, sir?"

"If you will." Hollenbach leaned forward over his desk, his face alive. "Look, Jim, I'm full to the brim with a new idea. I want you to hear it."

First, thought Jim, I wonder if he shouldn't hear something else? Shouldn't he be told that there is—or was—the complication of another woman? How should he say it? Jim looked at the President and saw the green eyes boring into him, the face glowing with his idea. No, this was not the time. It would sound ridiculous. Later, perhaps, when the chance occurred.

"This new idea," continued the President, "has immense possibilities. I want to outline it to you and get your counsel on it. Could you come up to Camp David again Saturday night—say about nine?"

"Of course, Mr. President," said MacVeagh, but he wondered what he would tell Martha and Chinky, due back Saturday.

"Good. I'll have Luther Smith pick you up at your place a little after seven. We can think better up there, away from all this." Hollenbach swept his hand around the oval room, as though indicating a myriad vexations of the presidency leering at him from under the tables and chairs.

The President walked around the desk and gripped MacVeagh's elbow, gently propelling him in the direction of the door to the rose garden.

"I'm glad to get this thing under way," he said. "I'll call Donovan right away and see if we can't get something stirring for you in Wisconsin."

MacVeagh walked across the lawn like a groom on his way to the wedding, dazed yet vibrant with dreams. He was halfway down the driveway before he realized that he hadn't been asked whether he'd accept the nomination. He had been ordered into it

—or rather toward it—and his own disclaimer as to his talents had been brushed aside as a parent disregards the whim of a child. He bristled momentarily, but the mood quickly gave way to euphoria again. He crossed East Executive Avenue toward the shadow of the Treasury Building as though he were treading on foam. It was dusk now, the street lamps had come on, orange circles in the lowering darkness, and the homegoing traffic drummed impatiently. He thought of walking up Pennsylvania Avenue to Capitol Hill, then changed his mind and stepped into the Round Robin bar of the Willard Hotel.

With the first sharp taste of the martini-on-the-rocks, he thought of Rita. Martinis at her place at seven, they had agreed. But God, he couldn't now, not with the vice-presidency within his reach. The risk was too great. He hadn't been able to bring himself to mention the problem to the President. How could he have said it? "Mr. President, before you commit yourself, I must tell you there is another woman in my life." Christ, it sounded like showboat melodrama. Besides, the affair was over, a thing of the past. Rita knew it and he knew it. He had slipped this morning and she'd called him "cruel," but it wasn't really that. It was the insistent pull she exerted, like a twitching rope which slackened only occasionally. That was her fault, not his. Besides, it took two to make an affair. Women always managed to arrange these emotional denouements so that the man came out the insensitive villain while the woman, bruised and crushed, appeared to weep for unrequited love. That was the cunning of the sex, and even Rita, with her factual, bookkeeper's mind, was not above playing the woman who nurses her wound.

He took a large swallow of the drink and ordered another. He downed the second one, then searched in his trousers pocket for a dime. By the time he got to the pay telephone booth he had become the champion of all the world's duped males. Blast the feminine mystique.

Rita sounded harried when she answered.

"This is Jim again," he said. "The heel calleth. Rita, I've got to cancel out tonight after all. I hate to do it, but something important has come up."

"I know," she said. The tone was frigid. "Mr. Donovan got a call from the White House just now."

"I knew you'd understand, Rita. I guess, well, there isn't much more to be said."

"Oh, yes, there is." The ice had turned to fury and each word came down distinctly like the rhythmic blows of a hammer. "You're not a heel. You're a selfish, adolescent bastard with about as many moral inhibitions as a rabbit. If I were your wife I'd take you out of the house and tie you to the apron strings of my worst enemy." She paused for breath. "And one thing more, lover boy. If you ever call me again—on any pretext—I'll call the police and the Associated Press, simultaneously."

She slammed down the receiver and Jim stood in the booth looking foolishly at the telephone and feeling the ringing in his ear echo through his skull.

Then he taxied home to McLean and that night, for the first time in two years, he got drunk. His last thought, before he fell into a sodden sleep, was that he would deliver a brilliant acceptance speech in Cobo Hall in August, and Rita Krasicki, Mark Hollenbach, and the six unknown dwarfs could all go to hell.

4.

Aspen

Jim was ready in corduroy pants, flannel shirt, and his fleece-lined windbreaker when agent Luther Smith drove a White House limousine into the McLean driveway a few minutes after seven Saturday night.

The week had sped by, for Donovan worked fast. On Thursday the Democratic city chairman in Appleton announced he was opening a vice-presidential write-in campaign for Senator James F. MacVeagh in Wisconsin's April primary. The next day two Milwaukee businessmen revealed creation of a citizens' committee to urge Democrats to write in MacVeagh's name for vice-president. Jim had been kept busy on the phone Saturday, denying to newsmen that he was a candidate. "I'm flattered by the friendly advertising in Wisconsin," he said, "but there has been absolutely no encouragement from me, nor can there be. This is President Hollenbach's choice, and his alone." Would he "demand" that the work in his behalf cease? No, that would be presumptuous. Wisconsin was a sovereign state. All he could do was say that he was not a candidate.

Martha and Chinky, who arrived home that morning from Des Moines, first protested his evening trip to Camp David, but when Jim told Martha of President Hollenbach's decision, she'd kissed him, cried just a little, and then washed and ironed his flannel shirt and pressed his old pants, complaining the while that this was no way to dress for an appointment with the President. But both mother and daughter were excited. The flurry of phone calls kindled the household.

On the drive to the Catoctin Mountains, Jim sat in the front seat with Smith, and they talked while the agent drove. MacVeagh joked about Hollenbach's custom of sitting in the dark at the mountain lodge, but Smith said the agents rather liked it. Despite their security precautions, some nut could always wriggle up the far side of the mountain with a rifle and take aim through a telescopic sight. If the lights were on, the President would make a fine target through the picture window. No, if a president had to have a quirk, that was a good one to have. Hearing Rita's story of frequent light dimming at Camp David thus confirmed, MacVeagh wondered whether her source was this handsome, dark-featured agent with the shining teeth. He asked Smith if he was a bachelor. "Yeah, still lucky after thirty-two years," he replied. Well, Smith could do worse than Rita, thought MacVeagh, even if she had shown that she could blaze like a wildcat. He cringed at the memory.

MacVeagh had to knock at the door of the President's lodge this time. A muffled voice bid him enter. The room was darkened again, and Jim had some trouble finding the President in the gloom. Hollenbach stood in a far corner, his back to MacVeagh, and he was looking through the big window down the stretch of parkland which served as the one-hole golf course. The snow had melted now, save for ragged clumps near the lodge and under the pines and hardwoods which framed the fairway. A half-moon rode high behind a puff of cloud, and the hilltop shadows were sharply etched as though in an engraving. In the fireplace one huge log smoked above a bright bed of coals. The room held the tang of hickory smoke.

Hollenbach turned and walked toward MacVeagh. There was

no greeting and his long face was set without a smile. He wore khaki pants, moccasins, and a black turtleneck sweater that made him look as though he had stepped from a vintage photograph of a college football team in the days before the forward pass. Hollenbach reached into his pants pocket and handed Mac-Veagh a crumpled newspaper clipping.

"Just what kind of man is this Craig Spence?" he demanded. His voice rasped.

MacVeagh tried to read the clipping, but the print was too small for the dim light. He looked questioningly at the President.

"Because I happened to say that seven people were under consideration for vice-president," said Hollenbach, "Spence has the gall to liken the situation to 'Snow White and the Seven Dwarfs.' Just for the purposes of a cheap quip, he's willing to hold the office of President of the United States up to ridicule. I thought he was a friend of yours."

"He is, Mr. President." MacVeagh chuckled. The President was joshing him. "Actually, it does describe the thing pretty deftly, doesn't it?"

"You think that's funny?" Hollenbach glared at him.

"Well, sure . . ." MacVeagh stopped. If Hollenbach was fooling, he was the world's best actor.

"I definitely do not." The President's voice grated like rock rubbed against rock. "It's a snide little crack designed to demean the President. Snow White! As though I were some juvenile innocent wandering around in a wicked world, ready to be fleeced."

"Oh, now, Mr. President," said MacVeagh, "you're reading too much into it. I imagine Craig was merely indicating that you're a good president faced with a choice of men who are all a considerable cut below your ability."

"Nonsense!" Hollenbach shouted the word. He clenched his

fingers into fists. "It was the phrase of a crafty columnist who knows exactly what he's doing. He's trying to belittle the presidency and drag it down to his own smart-aleck level."

MacVeagh was too flabbergasted to reply. He could feel the anger flowing from the President in the shadowy room, but it seemed to have an unreal quality, like a river without a source. They stood silent for a moment. Then the President sat down heavily on the couch facing the window and motioned Mac-Veagh to a seat beside him.

"Something has to be done about these irresponsible newspapermen," said Hollenbach. He bit out the words. "Freedom of the press is one thing, but unbridled license to degrade and ridicule officials who devote their lives to this country is something else again. I know we can't legislate responsibility, but one thing I can do. I can cut off Craig Spence's sources at the White House."

MacVeagh frowned in the dark and looked at Hollenbach as though seeing him for the first time. What the devil . . .

"Spence is an ingrate," continued Hollenbach. "He's had the run of the White House, four or five exclusive stories. I've given him at least an hour of my valuable time in two separate interviews. And then to repay the favor with a crack like that. Talk about biting the hand that feeds you . . ."

Hollenbach halted and watched the firelight for a moment. When he spoke again, his voice was still edged. "I'm beginning to wonder, Jim, if there isn't some kind of conspiracy afoot to discredit me in the eyes of the country. First O'Malley's outrageous action and now this. And these aren't isolated cases, believe me. I could tell you of other instances . . ." His voice trailed off, and when he resumed it was just above a whisper. "Other men have tried . . . I know . . . I've had to take steps to protect myself. It's almost as if there were a net closing . . ."

Hollenbach's voice slid away. He sat brooding, his legs outstretched toward the fire, his thin face, tautly furrowed, held in dim profile to MacVeagh. There was a canyon of stillness between them.

"Damn it!" The President's curse exploded in the quiet room, and MacVeagh realized that this was the first time he had ever heard Hollenbach swear. "O'Malley is the worst. He was more than a vice-president. He was part of the family, privy to every decision and secret of the administration. No president ever treated his vice-president with the courtesy and solicitude I gave to Pat O'Malley. And then, like a murdering brother, he turned on me and tried to crucify me with his filthy little deals. And then he had the audacity to stand in my White House office Tuesday night and say that he was sorry. Sorry! When he plotted the whole sordid business, from start to finish, in an effort to defeat me in November. Well, it didn't work. Thank God, the American people have a conscience, which is something that can't be said for a man who was never anything but a Pittsburgh ward boss."

The President paused for breath, then he plunged on. "It proves the need for a law that would let law-enforcement agencies, such as the FBI, monitor telephone calls. With that law on the books, O'Malley never could have got away with that arena deal. When he made those calls to the chairman—and talked to Jilinsky—we'd have known something was up and could have moved in to stop it."

Tap the telephone of the Vice-President? Jim felt glazed and numb, as though he were midway in a dream where the scenes kept repeating themselves endlessly. The man beside him, speaking with measured fury, seemed an utter stranger, and he wondered what had become of the self-assured, radiant Mark Hollenbach. Whatever the object of this Saturday night session, thought MacVeagh, it was lost now. Mark needed sleep and rest.

"I think perhaps I'd better go," said Jim. "We can have our talk another time."

Hollenbach looked startled. He swung around to face Mac-Veagh, stared at him a moment, then burst into laughter. It was the deep, hearty, familiar laugh that MacVeagh had heard a dozen times.

"Oh, excuse me, Jim," he said. "I had no right to foist one of my moods on you. You're up here to learn about our plans. Thank goodness, you're a new breed. With Hollenbach and Mac-Veagh, a team of the old and the new, it will be a brand-new administration next January. The O'Malleys, the Spences, and the rest will be forgotten. We've got things to do, boy."

Hollenbach rose, took several long strides and swung around, his back to the fireplace. He stood framed in the gossamer light cast by the rosy mound of coals, and an easy, relaxed smile spread over his face. He thumped the heels of his palms together. MacVeagh felt a quick easing of tension, as though someone had slapped his back in a moment of fright. The President he knew and admired was back again.

"Jim," Hollenbach said slowly, "I want my second term to be a great one. I want intelligent men around me, men who can think long-range, as I said, and I want a vice-president who can grasp new concepts without being shackled by prejudice. Look, let me explain it—and this is the reason I wanted you up here tonight.

"Despite our prosperity, this country is in deep trouble— abroad. We all recognize that. The changes in the world are violent ones, and they're hurtling along with a speed unknown before in history. We've got to find an anchor to help ride out the storm. We've been searching since the end of World War II— foreign aid, alliances, containment, massive retaliation—but we've never found one. But, Jim, I think I've found the anchor. I can't mention it before the election. The people will have to be educated up to it. But after the second inauguration, I'll reveal it."

The President was exuberant now. The familiar flush came to his cheeks and his eyes shone like the dropping coals in the fireplace behind him. He was talking swiftly, occasionally glancing at MacVeagh, but for the most part speaking toward the great window as though addressing a multitude beyond. Jim knew the signs. The President was in the vise of one of his ideas, and the intellectual seizure became a physical emotion, a force in the room.

"I call it the grand concept, Jim," said Hollenbach, "or the concept of Aspen, if you will, since I first thought of it here one night."

The President paused. There was no sound in the room save for a sputter amid the fireplace coals. Hollenbach's eyes seemed fastened on a distant point beyond the picture window. Jim felt a tremor of anticipation. He leaned forward on the sofa.

"The idea," continued Hollenbach, "is to forge the mightiest core of power the world has ever known. Not just an alliance, but a union—a real union, political, economic, social—of the great free nations of the globe."

Hollenbach glanced at him, and Jim knew a comment was called for.

"If you can name the great nations, Mr. President, you're a genius." He kept his tone light, but he found himself caught up in Hollenbach's enthusiasm. "After the United States, I add Russia and Red China and then I run out. And I assume you're not talking about the Communists."

"No. No." Hollenbach flung an arm toward one end of the room. "Look to the north, Jim. . . . Canada! Canada!"

"A union with Canada?" MacVeagh squinted at his wrist watch in the gloom. 10:15. A little late for bizarre jokes, he thought.

"Right. A union with Canada." Hollenbach stared at Mac-Veagh, and Jim could sense, if he could not see, an intensity in the gaze.

"Canada is the wealthiest nation on earth." Hollenbach's words raced after one another. His eyes were fixed on Mac-Veagh's and he tensed again as he had when speaking of Spence and O'Malley. "The mineral riches under her soil are incredible in their immensity. Even with modern demands, they are well-nigh inexhaustible. Believe me, Jim, Canada will be the seat of power in the next century and, properly exploited and conserved, her riches can go on for a thousand years."

The fervor seemed to radiate from Hollenbach now, almost as real as the circle of firelight. MacVeagh wondered why he himself never heaved with such profound emotion. Perhaps that was the difference between the leader and the led. He tried to shake the spell by breaking into the President's hurrying monologue.

"The new imperialism, huh?" he asked.

Hollenbach eyed him suspiciously for an instant, but suspicion melted quickly and the President's features were gripped anew in trembling excitement.

"An enlightened imperialism, yes, in a way," he said, "but really a union of survival for both countries. But Canada is only part of it, Jim. Canada is latent power. What this country needs almost as badly as more power is character and stability. For a perfect union, we also need Scandinavia."

"We need what?" MacVeagh experienced an odd floating sensation as he often did when witnesses before his Senate sub-committee drifted into the abstruse jargon of the space age.

"Scandinavia." The President's voice quivered, and with spread fingers he pressed hard against his hips. "Sweden, Denmark, Norway and Finland, to be specific. They will bring us the character and the discipline we so sadly lack. I know these people, Jim. I'm of German extraction, but many generations ago my people were Swedes who emigrated to Germany. . . . Your wife's of Swedish stock, isn't she?"

MacVeagh nodded a hypnotic assent.

"You know what I mean then. You see, Canada will bring us the power for the future, Scandinavia the character, the steadiness. . . . It's the grand concept for survival . . . a union of know-how, that's us, with power and character. . . ."

Hollenbach sped on like a runaway train, barely pausing for breath, leaving no gaps into which MacVeagh could move with a question. He appeared to anticipate all inquiries. Why not England? Great Britain was finished as a major power, attenuated, effete, jaded. All that the English had to contribute—and it had been tremendous in its day—America already had absorbed. England was weak, introspective, plagued by memories of faded glory. France was too flighty and defensive, inclined to bicker any decision to death unless it emanated from Paris. Italy had culture, but no power or root stability. Germany, proud of her industrial growth, was arrogant and domineering again. . . . But with the merger of know-how, power and character, the United States, Canada and Scandinavia, the new nation under one parliament and one president could keep the peace for centuries. The president of the union should be a man who dreamed the dreams of giants. This was the grand concept. To it, Mark Hollenbach would dedicate his entire second term, his life if necessary. It was the only sensible bulwark against creeping Communism in Africa, Asia and Latin America. In union, America would survive and prosper. Alone, shielded only by the paper ramparts of NATO, SEATO and the rest, America would perish.

It was after eleven o'clock when Hollenbach concluded on a swelling evangelical note. His face flamed like the firelight, his fists were clenched and sweat studded his forehead. Though the effort had been the President's, MacVeagh felt exhausted. The silence in the long, low room had a clamor of its own. A gust of wind raised a flurry of old snow beside the lodge and the snow swept high on the window like frozen lightning. Bewildered, Mac-Veagh felt as though his head were stuffed with wool. He searched for words.

"That's an awful lot to take in one night, Mr. President," he said lamely.

"Of course it is." The President spoke softly, sympathetically, some of the heat seeming to drain from him.

"But I can't understand why you exclude England, France and Germany from such a union," said MacVeagh. That wasn't all he didn't understand, but he felt like an ant before a confusingly mammoth cake. He had to nibble somewhere.

"I only exclude Europe at the start," said Hollenbach, and his face quickly lighted again. "Right now, Europe has nothing to give us. But once we build the fortress of Aspen—the United States, Canada and Scandinavia—I predict that the nations of Europe will pound at the door to get in. And if they don't, we'll have the power to force them into the new nation."

"Force?" MacVeagh's voice sounded distant to his own ears.

"Yes, force." Hollenbach smashed a fist into the palm of his other hand.

"You mean military force, Mr. President?"

"Only if necessary, and I doubt it ever would be. There are other kinds of pressure, trade duties and barriers, financial measures, economic sanctions if you will. But, never fear, Jim. England, France and Germany, and the Low Countries too, can be brought to heel. The union of Aspen will have the force to exert its will. We'll be the lighthouse of the world, a beacon of peace for centuries."

"Have you thought about the type of man who would lead such a union, the prime minister or the president, I think you said?"

"Yes, I have." Hollenbach turned his face upward and his eyes seemed to measure the beams above him. "He should, of course, be a man above national boundaries, a dedicated man, an idealist perhaps, yet a practical politician. The Scandinavians have produced many of that type, some of whom have served devotedly at the United Nations. I'm not sure, Jim, but if I could see the union come to life in my second term, I would, of course, do everything humanly possible to help it through the formative years. If the call came to lead, I would not shirk my responsibility."

"I see." MacVeagh saw that Hollenbach's sensitive features were rapt, as though infused by a holy vision. "As I said, Mr. President, that's an awful lot to absorb in one session."

"Sleep on it, Jim," advised Hollenbach quietly. "You're the first man I've confided in, and I've done it because I want us to be true partners of government. Naturally, the grand concept is difficult to assimilate, all in one dose. You'll need to think about it, but when you have you'll come to the same conclusion I have. Together, Jim, we can save this country and change the course of history for centuries to come."

"I certainly will think about it, Mr. President." He knew his words sounded remote and trifling, but he could think of nothing else to say. His thoughts failed to navigate properly in his head of wool.

Hollenbach waggled a warning finger at him. "That's all between us, Jim. Keep it to yourself. There are people who are out to get me, and the grand concept—if it leaks out too early without proper explanation—could be used against me. If little men, mean little men of no vision like the O'Malleys, the Spences and the others, if they got hold of it, I could be made to look the fool." He shook himself, as though to ward off the mere mention of O'Malley and Spence.

"I realize that, Mr. President," said MacVeagh.

Hollenbach put an arm around MacVeagh's shoulders and guided him toward the door. "I suppose you'll want to get home to your waiting wife," he said. "Besides, Evelyn is coming up early tomorrow. We're going to try to relax for a day. I owe her the day. She deserves it. She doesn't get many any more."

Hollenbach called for the car, and while they waited, he steered MacVeagh to a wall bookcase, and drew out an object from a small case on a shelf. He held it out, and in the flickers of firelight Jim saw that it was a silver fountain pen.

"I used that to sign the last nuclear treaty," said Hollenbach, "but someday I want to use it to sign the new union into life. I would dearly wish that the union could come into existence right in this room—the union and the creation of Aspen."

The President swept his arm toward the big window, and Jim could see the gaunt, leafless trees casting their intricate shadows in the moonlight. In the distance the next mountain range shouldered the gray sky under a headdress of tiny stars. Hollenbach sighed.

"I love it here," he said. "It's the only place to breathe the first life into the union. Until then, Jim, I want you to keep the fountain pen. Let it be our talisman, and let's hope it brings good luck to a president and a vice-president who've got mountains of work to do."

"Thank you, sir." Jim fondled the pen, then slid it into a pocket of his windbreaker.

The President opened the door. The car was there with Luther Smith at the wheel again. Hollenbach shook MacVeagh's hand in parting.

"Remember, Jim, together you and I can do great things for our country."

"Good night, sir."

MacVeagh climbed into the back seat of the limousine. As they passed the guardhouse and the saluting Marine, Smith attempted to open a conversation, but Jim turned it aside and sat staring out the window. He cupped his chin in one hand and sat immobile, almost transfixed, and only half saw the trunks of trees march by as the car twisted and turned down the mountain road and sped into the high valley and through the darkened town of Thurmont.

His thoughts became weird flashes which changed abruptly like a kaleidoscope. Sweden, maroon on a map, Norway in green. A vice-president with a wife of Swedish stock. . . . My God, he hadn't caught the significance. Could that be his link with the grand concept? . . . Mark Hollenbach, his crew cut bristling like a mop of spikes, striding toward Hudson Bay in a black turtleneck sweater. Walking, walking, with earphones strapped to his head and the murmurs of a thousand exotic conversations pouring in from telephone lines across the continent. O'Malley, Spence and the Chicago banker, Davidge, standing mute and stunned in the background. . . . Hollenbach on a dais in Stockholm, wearing robes of royal purple, and studying a military map of Europe with a cluster of generals in strange uniforms. . . .

Then Jim saw a medic's hut in Viet Nam, and now, for the first time, he did not resist the full memory. The picture formed. A corporal, in the early grip of fever, leaped from his cot and, arms waving crazily, cried that he was being pursued by snakes. Then he began to babble of a shapeless scheme for victory. A doctor and two nurses seized him and the man soon collapsed on his cot again in a spasm of chills, but the grotesque scene remained etched in a recess of MacVeagh's memory.

Through the night, speeding on the superhighway below Frederick, another thought formed, ugly, menacing. He could not banish it, even though it brought a knotting of his stomach muscles, the way fear always affected him. He felt shattered, undone, and he knew he needed the advice of someone he could trust. Pat O'Malley? No, not Pat, although it was ironic that he should think first of the man he was tapped to succeed. Grady Cavanaugh, the Supreme Court justice with whom he'd fished and philosophized? No, not on this problem.

Maybe Paul Griscom? Yes. Griscom, the discreet old political lawyer who wore his clothes like an unmade bed. He'd been consulted by every administration since Harry Truman's and his clients stretched from Seattle to New Delhi. R. Paul Griscom. He would call him first thing in the morning. Then he realized why he had selected Griscom. The old lawyer was not only a friend of his but a close family friend of President Mark Hollenbach.

In his jacket pocket Jim felt the fountain pen—talisman of Aspen. Warm waves of air blew over him from the car's rear heater, but he found himself shivering, and he knew it was the clutch of fear. Jim MacVeagh had reached the conclusion that the President of the United States was insane.

5.

Cactus

Lieutenant General John M. Trumbull flipped the folder to the center of the conference table. The folder was red-bordered and bore a stamped legend, TOP SECRET, in black letters. It slid on the polished wax and came to rest in front of the pudgy man from the Rand Corporation who wore his pipe straight down like a sagging goatee.

"I've read the damn thing ten times," boomed the general, "and it won't march, as the French say."

The psychologist from Harvard, whose hairless scalp met his brow like the edge of a cliff, put his hands to his ears. "Not so loud, General," he said. "It's too early in the morning."

It was 10 A.M., Monday, in the Pentagon. General Trumbull spoke again, reminding his auditors of approaching thunder. "It's spinach and to hell with it, as the kids say."

The man from the State Department fiddled with his lapel and looked vaguely bored. A Navy captain, the communications expert, squinted down his yellow pencil as though it were a gun barrel. Butch Andrate, Secretary of Defense Sidney Karper's nonvoting "observer" on the committee, continued his doodling. He had just drawn General Trumbull with a head shaped like a genial megaphone.

The secret five-man committee for Project CACTUS—in

Pentagonese, "Command And Control, The Ultimate System" —was meeting again this Monday morning as it had every Monday for five months. Its mission was to refine and improve the method by which the United States government decided to fire a nuclear warhead at an enemy, reducing to absolute zero, if possible, the chances of firing one by mistake or miscalculation. Or, in the words of Secretary Karper's directive, the committee was ordered to "study the command and control system and recommend improvements, with particular attention to insulation of human aberrations."

Ever since the first atomic bomb exploded over Hiroshima, incinerating the city with a fireball that generated 100 million degrees of heat at its core, command and control of the weapon and its monster progeny had occupied countless officers, committees and commissions.

Over the years, the system had been perfected gradually. An elaborate but instantaneous communications network, complete with foolproof codes and authenticators, permitted swift response to a surprise enemy attack. It also reduced the chances of individual error to almost nothing, so that not once in a million times could a nuclear warhead be fired by mistake. But "almost" was not good enough for Sidney Karper. He wanted the chances squeezed down to zero.

Under the law in existence since the late forties, only the President of the United States could authorize the use of a nuclear weapon, but under the system as it actually operated in recent years, responsibility was spread among three men—the President, the Secretary of Defense and the Chairman of the Joint Chiefs of Staff. These three had been designated the National Command Authorities in 1962 when Defense Secretary Robert S. McNamara established the National Military Command Center. This hub of instant communications and intelligence was located behind heavy oak doors in the restricted JCS area of the

Pentagon along the ninth corridor of the second floor. Here four watch crews maintained a 24-hour vigil and here, in times of crisis, the five members of the Joint Chiefs of Staff gathered about an egg-shaped table. Each officer had direct links to bases around the globe. Four loudspeakers brought instant word of critical developments from the Strategic Air Command in Omaha and the North American Air Defense Command in Colorado Springs.

While the President alone had the final authority to release atomic and hydrogen weapons, in practice the other two National Command Authorities had to advise him that a nuclear strike was justified. In the event of a surprise enemy attack, a communications labyrinth of incredible complexity—computers, codes, long lines, authenticators, buttons and gold telephones—permitted a command decision within minutes. If the President's two subordinates, one military and one civilian, did not agree that nuclear warheads should be launched, the system called for another swift consultation with the two men and a presidential decision—within six minutes. In theory, the President could overrule anybody, but again in practice it was held highly unlikely that the President would reverse both men. In sum, academicians of the grisly subject foresaw that unless at least two of the three men involved gave the "Go" signal, no warheads would leave their berths.

In all the years since Hiroshima, this overture to holocaust had remained, blessedly, a matter of theory among the nuclear powers. Yet it preyed on men's minds through a dozen crises on all continents, and there had been many days, cloaked from the public, when the men involved in the final American atomic judgment rehearsed their parts in the split-second pageant of life and death, fearful that the next moment might transform the stage to reality. In these long, somber hours, the men of decision could see shattered, wasted cities, imagine the drifting pall of lethal radiation, and hear the whimper of a legless child in the rubble of a playground. In those hours the great became humble, and when the crisis passed, the mark remained on every man, seared on his heart as though with a branding iron until the day of his death.

Sidney Karper, who veiled his compassion with rough humor and crisp talk of megatons, had lived through such a crisis as a minor Pentagon official in a prior administration. Although he had no role in the swift cycle of decision then, he had known what took place, and so the scar was upon his heart too. Thus his assistants were not surprised when Karper, soon after he took the oath as secretary of defense, began to worry about perfecting "C and C." With his keen, roving mind, he pried into hundreds of crevices in the huge military establishment—in a manner unknown since McNamara—but always he came back to the harrying question, the nuclear decision.

Karper created the committee in the utmost secrecy, picked the five members with care, financed the project with $250,000 from the Secretary's contingency fund and imposed rigid security precautions on the committee and its inevitable task forces. President Hollenbach approved the project casually one afternoon and asked for a progress report every three months.

Only to Butch Andrate, his confidential special assistant, did Karper reveal the fears that inspired Project CACTUS. The plump Andrate, tie loosened and horn-rim glasses pushed up on his pompadour like a freakish owl, came into Karper's office near the Pentagon's River Entrance for final instructions before the first meeting of the CACTUS committee. Karper sat at his clean desk, flanked by the Secretary's flag and that of the United States. Through the window, Andrate could see white bristles on the Potomac and the spin of traffic on the approaches to the Pentagon.

Andrate tapped the CACTUS directive. "I get everything except this thing about 'insulation of human aberrations,' " he said. "Whatcha got in mind, boss?"

"Forrestal," replied Karper.

He was a huge man, hard muscles under blue pin-stripe suit, and with the bronze tint of his skin and the imposing hooked beak, he looked more American Indian than Jewish. Karper lived as a man of style, in dress, in speech, in posture, and only one habit gave a hint of his tough boyhood days on Chicago's near South Side. At work, he frequently had a quill toothpick dangling from the corner of his mouth and occasionally he blew through it, as he did now, making a noise not unlike a peanut whistle.

"Forrestal?" asked Andrate.

Karper nodded his great head. "Jim Forrestal was off his rocker long before that night in 1949 when he started to copy Sophocles's 'Chorus from Ajax,' and then jumped out of a sixteenth-story window at Bethesda Naval Hospital."

"I didn't know he was copying a poem," said Andrate.

"Our first secretary of defense," said Karper, "looked solid as a rock, with that bulldog chin and the boxer's broken nose. Gentiles can deceive you. Now me, if I cracked up, it would show in every pore. But Forrestal was breaking up for weeks before anybody guessed."

"And we don't want that to happen to anybody involved in C and C today?" Andrate jiggled his glasses on the top of his head.

"We can't prevent a man from going nuts," said Karper, "but if he does, we've got to find a way to isolate him from the big decision. It's that simple. That's what I want the CACTUS committee to come up with."

"Boss, you don't look goofy to me." Andrate liked to keep it light.

Karper blew through his toothpick, a whining whistle. He

rolled his big body in the swivel chair. "Anybody can smash up," he said. "There are three of us involved in the 'Go' decision now, and who knows what goes on inside any of us? If any one of the three blows his top, we've got a right and a duty to know it as soon as possible. Then we've got to insulate him from the decision. That man has no business being in a spot where he can . . . how did Lyndon Johnson say it? Oh, yes, mash the button. . . . The last time a madman mashed the button, we got the Second World War and six million Jews were cremated. The next time the button is mashed, we could cremate the human race."

Andrate said nothing and for minutes the only sound in the room was the muffled click of a typewriter from the other office.

"Okay, I got the message, boss," said Andrate at last. "But it's a large order. It won't fly by itself."

"No, it won't be easy." Karper grinned and got up, his six-foot-four body looming over his chubby aide. "As far as the President alone is concerned, Congress did its best on the disability question, although there's no real machinery to spot mental instability. Here, on this side of the river, we've got a special responsibility. We've got to make sure, somehow, that when the three National Command Authorities confer on the decision of life and death, all of them are thinking as normal men. So just tell the CACTUS bunch that I want that button kept away from the loony bin. How they do it is their job."

Under Karper's directive, the CACTUS "bunch" worked harder than any Pentagon group before it. Lieutenant General John Trumbull, called back from Air Force retirement, might bray at his colleagues, but he was astute, a canny leader, and he had long personal experience with the command and control system. At the first session in the pale-green conference room on the executive E ring of the Pentagon—big John Trumbull complained the room made him so seasick he should have joined the Navy—Butch Andrate made it plain that it was the last clause of the directive, "insulation of human aberrations," which concerned the Secretary. The committee got down to work. First it considered and discarded a Rand proposal, outgrowth of a continuing study under Air Force contract. Then the Harvard professor put a joint Harvard-M.I.T. task force to work for two months, but the committee rejected that plan also, as it did a proposal by a group of communications officers headed by the Navy captain.

After five months of labor, the CACTUS group had not been able to do the job. They had tried—and discarded—almost every conceivable idea: a panel of psychiatrists making quarterly examinations of the Big Three—JCS Chairman, SECDEF, and the President; regular examinations by a psychiatrist of the official's choice; granting authority to the surgeon general to give the National Command Authorities a clean bill of mental health after investigation; entrusting the job to a computer with periodic questionnaires to be filled out by the principals; a special committee of Congress authorized to conduct mental tests under its own rules; a law, or perhaps a constitutional amendment, creating the office of psychiatrist general who would have broad powers to delve into the mental status of all top government officials.

And now, this Monday morning, the committee was down to what all knew was the last proposal, a formula concocted by the Harvard psychologist and the Rand man. It was complicated and cumbersome, but in essence it provided that if one of the Big Three had reason to doubt the "mental normality" of either of the others, he could notify the surgeon general who would then convoke a panel of psychiatrists. The psychiatrists would examine the supposedly faulty mind under prescribed methods and then make a recommendation to the surgeon general. If the examinee, in the surgeon general's opinion, was mentally unbalanced, the surgeon general would report to a joint committee of the Congress. This committee, in turn, could either refuse to act or it could demand the resignation of the official. Should the official refuse to resign, the committee would institute impeachment proceedings through regular channels in the House of Representatives.

The Harvard-Rand paper had been submitted to the full committee the previous Monday—and now big John Trumbull had given his answer by flipping the document down the table. The little Rand man, sucking his pipe like a straw in a soda, slowly patted the spilled papers back into the folder.

"It's no criticism of you fellows to say your plan won't go," said Trumbull. He cleared his throat like a dredge at work. "But it's still the old fourth man theme."

The "fourth man theme" had become the group's nickname for any proposal which would stipulate another person or group to inquire into the mental stability of the Big Three involved in the nuclear decision.

"The old fourth man theme," repeated Trumbull, his voice rolling through the room like a boulder. "Only this time we've got about thirty people as the fourth man. This hydra-headed fourth man is supposed to winnow the sane from the insane. We have to assume that he's omniscient—or they are—with the wisdom of Solomon and the righteous wrath of Jehovah. Gentlemen, you don't hardly find that kind no more . . ."

"As the comedians say," finished the Harvard professor tartly. The psychologist privately tagged big John a "negativist." He'd had a hunch from the start that the general believed they were wasting time. The Harvard man felt deeply that they should make a beginning—anything reasonable. Frustration chipped at his nerves.

"With all due respect to our friends from Harvard and Rand," said the State Department man, politely aloof, "their plan is web-

footed. It might take a year to work through that maze of procedure."

"Meanwhile," added the Navy captain, "the troubled mind,
if such be the case, would be getting no more normal."

"Or the world might be gone." The State Department man
said it without emphasis, as though the globe could encounter
worse fates.

"But we've tried every other approach," complained the Rand
man. He was deflated and his pipe hung down over his chin. "At
least our plan is politically feasible. It ties in Congress with the
executive branch."

General Trumbull thumped the heel of his hand on the table.
"I've had five tours in this rabbit warren, and I think I know
something about how the town works, inside the Pentagon, on
the Hill, and over on Pennsylvania Avenue. Christ on a raft,
gentlemen, this place leaks like a sieve. How could you keep the
whole thing secret, with thirty people cut into the show? Why, it
would be all over the front pages within a week that the Chairman of the Joint Chiefs or the Secretary of Defense was suspected of not having all his marbles. And if that wouldn't make
Peiping trigger-happy, I don't know what would."

"And suppose the man is really as sane as we are, after all?"
asked the Navy captain. "Even if he got cleared eventually by a
committee of Congress, his career would be wrecked. I agree
with John. In any plan involving this fourth man theme, you've
got to have God as the fourth man. Unfortunately, you don't ask
God to fill a billet. He asks you."

"I'll admit our proposal isn't simple," pleaded the Harvard
man, "but it will work. If it's time that's bothering you, we could
recommend a time limit on each step. For instance, the panel of
psychiatrists could be required to report back to the surgeon
general within two weeks."

"Great God," exclaimed Trumbull, "it takes one of those head shrinkers two weeks just to find out whether his man was trained to the potty as a kid."

"The major flaw, it seems to me," said the State Department man, "is that this procedure would require an act of Congress to set it up. That means endless debate in the country before the system could go into operation. Even assuming you could get an enabling bill through both houses, it wouldn't bear the faintest resemblance to this Harvard-Rand proposal."

"Of course," said Trumbull. "Any fourth man idea requires Congressional sanction before it could be put into operation. By the time the debate ended, the country would think that everybody and his brother in Washington were crazy."

"But," protested the Rand man, "we agreed long ago that any plan in which the National Command Authorities were the judges of their own—uh—well, relative sanity would be impossible."

"So we did," agreed Trumbull. "And now, it appears to me, we've also exhausted the fourth man theme."

"I refuse to believe that the five brains around this table can't come up with a single recommendation for the Secretary," said the Harvard psychologist.

"Thanks for conceding I've got a brain, professor." Trumbull grinned and shook his hands aloft like a boxer in the ring.

"Vote!" said the Navy captain.

General Trumbull shot a look of gratitude at his military colleague, as though his suggestion was the best of the morning. He banged the heel of his hand on the table again.

"All in favor of recommending the Harvard-Rand plan to the Secretary will raise their right hands."

Harvard and the little Rand man crooked their right elbows. The two hands waved weakly, like men overboard who see the lifeboat pulling away from them.

"All opposed, raise their hands."

Trumbull, the Navy captain, and the State Department officer shot their right hands high.

"By vote of three to two," said Trumbull, "the committee declines to recommend the plan to the Secretary."

Butch Andrate, still doodling with his head lowered, wrote on his yellow pad: "Long-hairs 2, short-hairs 3."

"I move," said the Navy captain, "that this committee do now adjourn and that the chairman report to Secretary Karper that we have been unable to agree on a feasible plan."

"Do I hear a second?" asked Trumbull, forgetting that he had not bothered with such parliamentary procedure on the first vote.

"Second the motion," said the State Department man.

The vote was the same, three to two. Project CACTUS was dead.

"With your permission, gentlemen," said Trumbull, "I'll amend that last vote to provide for a report to Secretary Karper by the full committee in person. On a matter of this importance, I think he'd understand our dilemma better if we all go in and talk informally with him. How about tomorrow morning at ten, if his schedule is free?"

They all nodded agreement and Andrate, speaking for the first time that morning, said he was sure the Secretary could devote several hours to the subject the next morning.

"We brought in a dry well, gentlemen," said Trumbull, rising from his chair, "but I, for one, think I learned something."

"What?" asked the Harvard psychologist. Except for his shiny head, he looked sunken, worn, and a bit useless.

"I think," said Trumbull, "that I learned what we really all know, intuitively, but never quite admit to ourselves—that in any human endeavor there are some points that can't be covered by law, and that, in the last analysis, you've just got to trust the men involved."

"Even if insane?" asked the Rand man.

"The other way round," replied Trumbull. "You trust a man to remain as normal as he was the day he got the job."

Papers were pushed into briefcases. Wearily, the Harvard man held out the red-bordered folder to the Rand man, but he shook his head with a wag of his pipe. The folder went into the Harvard dispatch case instead. Locks snapped, and the CACTUS thinkers filed out the door to the E corridor with its oil paintings of men storming atoll beaches in a war that never knew the horrors of the towering mushroom cloud until its final days.

Big John Trumbull detained Butch Andrate at the doorway. He closed the door and stood with his hand on the knob.

"No one will tell the Secretary tomorrow," he said, "but there was just one sticky point in this whole thing. If it weren't for that, we could have come up with something concrete weeks ago. You've heard all our discussions and I think you know what I mean. You're the man to lay it on the line to Karper."

Andrate frowned and rubbed his perched glasses across the top of his head. "I'm not sure I get you, General. What sticky point?"

"Andrate," said Trumbull, "nobody—but nobody—in this country can tell a president of the United States that his mind is sick."

Andrate said nothing, merely stared at the general like an owl with four eyes.

"The SAC commander, yes," said Trumbull. "The Chairman of the Joint Chiefs, yes. Your boss, yes. The head of the Ford Foundation, yes. The Speaker of the House, yes. The chairman of the Red Cross, yes. The President of the United States, no."

Andrate blinked. "That's one man we have to trust?"

"That's one man we have to trust," said Trumbull.

The general opened the door and marched, shoulders thrown back, down the corridor and back toward Air Force retirement. Andrate watched until the general turned a corner and the dull echo of his footfall was swallowed by the Pentagon's sound-proofed halls.

6.

World Center

As Project CACTUS dissolved in bootless disagreement that Monday morning at the Pentagon, Senator Jim MacVeagh walked toward the World Center Building in downtown Washington. A chill rain began to fall and it ran off his white raincoat in rivulets. He wore no hat, as usual, but he was oblivious to the moist mat the rain was making of his hair. Jim felt frayed and itchy-skinned. He had slept but little since returning from Camp David, and such snatches of sleep as he had managed had been torn by weird, crooked dreams which made him toss. Once Martha punched him in the ribs to wake him. He was growling and he had cried out, she said.

He had called Paul Griscom after breakfast Sunday, and the lawyer agreed to see him at eleven today. MacVeagh skipped the Armed Services Subcommittee meeting he was supposed to chair, and now he was trying to put his tangled thoughts into some orderly sequence before facing Griscom.

The law offices of Griscom, Fotheringill & Hadley bore the hushed accent of opulence. This was not the largest law firm in Washington, but it was regarded as the most influential—especially when the Democrats were in power. In the reception room, wall-to-wall carpeting of a cinnamon hue, its pile an inch thick into which the shoes of callers sank luxuriously, merged with dark-walnut paneling which showed tiny nicks of a cabinet-maker's tools. This was no plywood veneer, but rich, thick wood. Currier & Ives prints, framed in tasteful green, graced the walls at spacious intervals. A blonde receptionist, comely but not too young, typed on a muted, electrically operated keyboard. Her smile was gracious, as though she were about to pour from a silver urn at a garden party. Her accent was British.

"Senator MacVeagh? To see Mr. Griscom, isn't it?" The syllables ran together in the muddily dentured style of the Empire's lower-upper classes. MacVeagh nodded. The receptionist dialed a number and spoke to someone in chapel-like tones.

"Would you please be seated?" she asked, as though he might not. "Mr. Griscom will be with you in a moment."

Paul Griscom loped toward him down the long corridor. He was a tall, spare man of about sixty. His tanned face had deep grooves as though time had clawed him and the wounds only recently had healed. His rimless spectacles reflected the light in darting rays, and deep, veined pouches under his eyes indicated an adult life of hard work, a poor liver or a riotous youth, perhaps all three. He wore an old gray suit, baggy at the knees. His long legs were bowed slightly. Paul Griscom had arrived in Washington as a law student forty years before, but he still referred to himself as a "country boy" from Wyoming.

"Jim! It's nice to see you. Come on back to the office, and I'll give you a towel to dry off that hair of yours."

He conducted MacVeagh down the hall past a number of open doors. Young lawyers worked in smaller rooms, but amid the same quiet paneling and rich carpeting as those surrounding the receptionist.

Griscom's office, wide-windowed on the corner of 16th & K streets, had bare walls, painted a stark white, and rickety furniture that had the stamp of a secondhand sale. It was as though, having tiptoed through the cathedral, Griscom was saying to his clients: "Here's where we get down to business." The only wall decorations were autographed pictures, chiefly presidents of the United States. The one of Mark Hollenbach, Jim noted, was signed, "To my old friend, Paul." Beside it hung a photograph of Mark Hollenbach, Jr., in a Yale varsity sweater, autographed "To Uncle Paul, a great guy and better pal." MacVeagh was glad he had not come here as a client. The mixture of restrained elegance, country lawyer, and autographed influence was a heady one, and Jim was sure the fee would galvanize the effect. Griscom seemed to read his mind.

"It always impresses them," he said as one insider to another. "I don't care whether they're fresh from Peoria or whether they run the biggest corporations in New York."

MacVeagh used the towel Griscom handed him while the lawyer laboriously stuffed an old, silver-trimmed pipe. Griscom seated himself behind his desk, yanked out a tail of his shirt, blew on his spectacles and polished the lenses with the shirttail. They traded the amenities as Jim remembered the first time he'd met Griscom—when the lawyer came to Des Moines to testify on a model state tax law he recommended for MacVeagh's legislative tax revision committee. Since then he had been Griscom's guest for golf at the Chevy Chase and Burning Tree clubs. Griscom belonged to all the best clubs, including the 1900 F Street, the Metropolitan, the Sulgrave, and even the Waltz Group. Griscom was, among other things, a tax expert, and Jim assumed his membership dues were all deductible business items. It was income tax return time now. A pile of manila folders rested on the corner of Griscom's desk, and Jim saw that the top one was tagged, "Hollenbach, M. & E."

"Well, Jim, what's your problem?" Griscom eyed him through a screen of pipe smoke. The lawyer's tone was soothing, as though any human affliction, from sore feet to a federal antitrust indictment, could be cured in the offices of Griscom, Fotheringill & Hadley, the last of whom had been dead ten years.

"This isn't a legal problem, Paul," said MacVeagh. Although he had rehearsed his opening, he felt like an actor who'd forgotten his entrance cue. "I came to you because . . . well, because you've got a wise head. Call it trust if you want, Paul. I'm deeply troubled, more than at any time in my life. And still I'm not sure you can actually help much either."

"Suppose you let me be the judge of that," said Griscom. He puffed slowly at his silver-ringed pipe.

"Paul . . ." Jim felt his pulse quicken as he took the first step. "Paul, I've become reasonably convinced that an influential man in this government is having severe mental problems, maybe a breakdown, maybe worse."

Griscom grunted. "He wouldn't be the first." He said nothing more, merely fingered the bowl of his pipe, studying the grain as though inspecting it for flaws.

"I'm at a loss as to what I should do about it, if anything," said MacVeagh. "As I say, this isn't a legal problem, and I'm not here as a client. All I want is advice from a friend."

The dark pouches under Griscom's eyes widened slightly as he smiled. "Don't worry, Jim, we scale down the fees to meet any pocketbook. And the way you're buttering up my ego, that will be payment enough. Come on now, let's dispense with the preliminaries and have the whole story. I've got plenty of time."

MacVeagh shifted in his chair and rubbed the bridge of his nose as he thought again of just how to say it. "Paul," he began, "if this man were just an ordinary citizen, I wouldn't waste your time. But he's a prominent figure in Washington, and he's in a position to influence both domestic and foreign policy. I've had occasion to observe him closely in recent days, and frankly, Paul, I think perhaps his mind is going to pieces. I'm deeply disturbed, even frightened by what I've seen and heard. Let me tell you in some detail."

Using no names and masking the scenes, MacVeagh told of Hollenbach's savage outbursts against O'Malley, Spence and Davidge. When he recounted the Davidge incident, he faltered occasionally as he tried to recollect Rita's exact words. He described Hollenbach's physical appearance as he strode about and ranted, but he deleted Hollenbach's habit of sitting on a lonely hill in the dark, for he felt sure Griscom would know of this idiosyncrasy and correctly identify his friend. Nor did Jim mention the wiretapping proposal. He knew Griscom had attended the Gridiron dinner and would promptly recognize the source of the idea. Otherwise MacVeagh pictured the Camp David scenes in detail. His recital took almost twenty minutes.

Griscom yanked out his shirttail again to polish his glasses. "Tell me," asked the lawyer, squinting at the results of his handiwork, "did your friend give any indication that he thought his . . . uh . . . tormenters were allied in any way?"

"No . . ." Then Jim remembered, and he nodded quickly. "I mean yes. Yes, he did. His voice rather faded away once, and he mumbled something about a conspiracy, a 'net closing' around him, I think he said. I remember he said he was forced to take measures to protect himself."

"Anything more?"

"Plenty," said MacVeagh. "This man has been smitten with an outlandish idea of saving the world through a new union of nations—and what a strange conglomeration they are!"

MacVeagh described the "grand concept" of the United States-Canada-Scandinavia merger and tried to make Griscom understand the passion which had seized Hollenbach while he talked. As he explained the project, MacVeagh watched Griscom closely. If Hollenbach had told others, Griscom would be a logical man in whom to confide. But the lawyer's face showed no recognition. He was leaning back in his ragged swivel chair, the springs squeaking now and then, and he was smoking his pipe in a passive face.

"And that's not all," said MacVeagh. "He actually proposed to use force—economic first, but military if necessary—to make the nations of Europe join this new super-union. Then I got the distinct impression, from several things he said, that he fancies himself as the head of this huge Western government. Paul, he talked like some kind of fanatic Messiah, and I don't mind saying that he sent chills up and down my backbone. I've been frightened in my life, but not often. This fellow scared me as I haven't been scared since I was in the service in Viet Nam."

"Jim," said Griscom. "I think you said earlier that this man is in a position to influence government policy. Am I right?"

MacVeagh nodded. He could sense that Griscom was waiting for him to divulge the name. For a moment, he was on the verge of doing so, but the moment crumbled. He did not dare. He just could not bring himself to accuse the President of the United States of having a sick mind. For one thing, he wasn't sure. No man could make a charge like that without a mass of corroborative evidence—not even in private. For another thing, there was the awe of the office and the fear of what might happen to Senator MacVeagh if his suspicions proved groundless. He had half hoped that Griscom might put two and two together and sense the identity, but obviously the lawyer had not.

Griscom stood up, shucked his coat and placed it on the back of his chair. "Come on into this next office, Jim, and let's see what we can find."

The adjoining room was furnished in the rich, sleek brown colors common to the entire suite save for Griscom's own office. Floor-to-ceiling bookcases lined the four walls and a long walnut table, equipped with several reading lamps, occupied the center of the room.

"The firm has its own law library," said Griscom, "but this is my private reference room. Here's where I burn the midnight oil now and then, sometimes with one or two of the young lawyers to help. But I don't think there's a lawbook in the place."

He made a brief tour with MacVeagh at his side. "It's amazing what a man has to know when he gets on a tough case," he said. "Now this whole section here is construction stuff—how-to books on electricity, wiring, foundations, air-conditioning systems, God knows what all. We get a lot of building contract cases. This tier is all our old criminal stuff. We don't do much of that any more, but in the early days I had to know everything about firearms. Just about every gun made in the world is described somewhere in one of these books."

He stopped before the bookcase adjoining a window which overlooked 16th Street. The rain had slackened, but umbrellas still bobbed along the sidewalks like enormous black bugs. Tires whined on the wet pavement.

"This is my psychology section," said Griscom. "To practice law today, a man has to be goddam near a couch man. Thanks to the Supreme Court, you've got to know motivation, psyche, neurology, and God knows what, everything from exaggerated trauma to the dynamics of the menopause. You get through one of these cases with a psychiatrist testifying about ego defense mechanisms, and you begin to think the whole world is screwy."

Griscom ran his fingers across the books on one shelf as he talked. "But I'd say your man isn't too complicated a case. . . . Ah, here we are." He took down a thick, tan book. Griscom grinned, his face a network of wrinkles. "If you were an expert as I am, Jim, we'd go into something more exotic, but for the layman this is a fine book."

Griscom opened the fly-leaf and MacVeagh read: *"Abnormal Psychology and Modern Life*. Scott, Foresman and Company, by James C. Coleman, University of California at Los Angeles."

"This is an excellent, basic introduction to the whole kit and kaboodle of mental ailments," said Griscom. "If your symptom isn't in here, you're a human cipher. You bite your nails? Take cocaine? How about satyriasis? . . . That's where you need a woman three or four times a day. Nice thought, eh? Maybe you stammer? You name it, and the professor's got it all catalogued, filed and explained for you. But kidding aside, this is a great textbook and a tremendous amount of research has gone into it. Now, let's see if we can't find your man."

Griscom perched his glasses on his thin, desiccated nose and peered through the lower part of the lenses. He riffled the pages of the book. "Yep, here we are. Page 289. It's headed 'Paranoid Reactions.' Now let's see if we recognize anyone here."

The lawyer stepped to the window and began to read aloud:

" 'The individual feels that he is being singled out and taken advantage of, mistreated, plotted against, stolen from, spied upon, ignored, or otherwise mistreated by his "enemies." . . .' "

Griscom glanced up at MacVeagh. "Now let's skip a little here," he said as he turned a page. "Quote. 'Although the evidence which the paranoiac advances to justify his claims may be extremely tenuous and inconclusive, he is unwilling to accept any other possible explanation and is impervious to reason.' Unquote. You said you argued with your man about the motives of these so-called persecutors, but he ignored you? Does this sound like your man?"

Jim nodded. Griscom skipped over a few paragraphs. "Now let's go into the other phases. Listen:

" 'Although ideas of persecution predominate in paranoid reactions, many paranoids develop delusions of grandeur in which they endow themselves with superior or unique ability. Such "exalted" ideas usually center around Messianic missions, social reforms, and remarkable inventions. . . . Such individuals usually become attached to some social reform movement such as prohibition, and are tireless and fanatical crusaders, although they often do their cause more harm than good by their self-righteousness and their condemnation of others.' "

Griscom paused and peered over his glasses at MacVeagh. "Now you say, however, that usually your man appears quite normal, and that he's a fellow of quick intelligence with a lot of sound ideas?"

"Yes," said Jim. "That about describes him and the situation, I'd say."

"Well, then," said Griscom, "listen to this under a section entitled 'Paranoid States.' Quote. 'In paranoid states the delusions are less systematized and bridge the gap between the paranoid proper and the paranoid schizophrenic. There is often some evidence of disordered thought processes, as well as hallucinations and other psychopathological symptoms, but without the severe personality disorganization, thought fragmentation and loss of contact with reality which are found to be typical of paranoid schizophrenics. In many cases these delusional systems develop rather suddenly, often following some particularly traumatic life experience. They are usually transient and of short duration, clearing up spontaneously without psychotherapy.' "

Griscom closed and replaced the book, and led MacVeagh back to the bare corner office. He settled into his swivel chair again and banged his pipe on a thick glass ashtray, scattering ashes over the tax file.

"It seems fairly reasonable to assume that your man is evidencing some paranoid symptoms," said Griscom, "but we don't know whether this is just a transient case or whether the man is in a bad way and needs psychiatric help. Of course, Jim, as a starter, I don't understand why you haven't got your man into the hands of a good psychiatrist."

"He won't go," Jim lied swiftly. He could think of no other adequate explanation for failure to pursue this obvious course. "I tried to persuade him, but he insists there's nothing wrong with him."

"I see. Well, perhaps some big emotional upset has occurred, something in his personal life that rips at him and produces this reaction. A woman perhaps? That's always the first assumption, you know."

"No," said Jim quickly. "I'm sure there's no woman trouble of any kind. He's happily married, quite content in that department, I'd say."

"But," mused Griscom, "you never know what goes on beneath the surface of these supposedly placid marriages." The lawyer tapped his pipe on the ashtray. "Well, let's try to narrow our problem. As I get it, you're concerned because this man has an influential hand in government policy. Then I'd say the simplest thing on earth is just to take the story to President Hollenbach and let him ask for the fellow's resignation. Even if he's not a permanent mental case, he probably needs rest and relief from tension, so the President would be doing him a favor."

"It's not that easy." Jim was guarded now. "You see, Paul, this man is an elected official. He can't be removed like that."

"Oh," said Griscom, "a member of Congress?"

"I'd rather not say."

"Now, Jim, you're not too alert this morning." Griscom smiled at him. "If he's elected, he has to be a member of Congress, unless, of course, you're talking about Pat O'Malley."

"Don't worry. It isn't O'Malley, although he'd have ample cause right now." He noted that Griscom mentioned only O'Malley and not Hollenbach, the No. 1 elected official in Washington. Not even Griscom's mind would link a president to such a story. MacVeagh grinned, a bit limply. "You boxed me in there, Paul. I wasn't thinking too fast."

Griscom leaned back and folded his shirt-sleeved arms. His eyes dwelled on MacVeagh and there was sympathy in his look.

"For some mysterious reason," he said, "you decline to name names. That's no way to treat a lawyer and ordinarily, under the circumstances, I'd refuse to take the case." He smiled warmly again. "But as you said at the outset, you're deeply troubled, and I appreciate your feeling. Look, Jim, are you sure you're not exaggerating?"

"I certainly don't think so."

"All of us are lacerated from time to time," said Griscom, "over an endless number of things. It's a rare man who hasn't felt himself slipping, who hasn't wondered whether perhaps he has loosed his mental moorings. And the pressures of this thing we call civilization don't help us any." Griscom was eying Mac-Veagh closely as he talked. "I see these people troop through this law office. Something has cracked their shell and then they stumble in here, shattered people, looking for a legal out. But many of them pull themselves together and manage to work back to a normal life—whatever that is, precisely."

Griscom dropped his eyes and seemed to be inspecting his pipe as though it were a slide rule and he needed a measurable answer. "For instance, as you know, Jim, I live on O Street in Georgetown."

Jim started. "I'd forgotten that," he said.

"I thought perhaps you had," said Griscom softly. "At any rate, several times I've seen a man who very closely resembles a well-known senator leave a house on O Street. He looks around, somewhat furtively, and walks rapidly away. In this particular house, Jim, lives a very attractive and sensuous woman who works for a politician whom we both know. Now the man, if he is the senator I believe he is, has a lovely wife and a fine daughter. It's pretty obvious that he's carrying on an affair of some sort with this woman on O Street. Now, how do you explain behavior like that? It happens every day, sure, but in the context of mental adjustments and problems, just how do you explain it?"

MacVeagh went rigid and stared Griscom in the eye without blinking. What kind of game is this? he thought. He made an effort to keep his voice cool. It came out quite cold.

"I don't know about the explanation," he said, "but it sounds to me like you're in a position to blackmail somebody if you want to."

Griscom smiled kindly, the seams in his weathered face relaxed. "Oh, no, nothing like that, Jim. I'm not the kind. Besides, I couldn't positively identify the man. I just use him as an example. What goes on in a man of intelligence, position and stature to make him lead two lives like that? A simple appetite for sex isn't quite sufficient answer. But we don't know, do we? Is he normal? Who's to say? Of course, admittedly this isn't on a par with persecution complexes, delusions of grandeur and all that, but couldn't the tension of such a double life produce, in some individuals, a sharp psychological wrench that might lead a man into a temporary paranoid state?"

MacVeagh was too stunned to answer. My God, he thought, Paul actually thinks I've been describing myself, and now he's trying to tell me, not very subtly either, that he knows I'm the one with the mental ailment. Jim was prompted to deny the implication at once, but, no, he reasoned, what good would that do? Paul would merely think he was lying out of self-protection. Besides, to make the point, he'd have to confess about Rita to distinguish between the two persons, himself and Hollenbach. The idea of mentioning Rita's name to a third person was repugnant. He couldn't do that, even if she had screamed at him over the phone like a mother tern.

Griscom was still talking in a quiet, leisurely vein: "So in the case of your man, Jim, I wouldn't do anything right now. Don't be in any hurry. The government's in no crisis that I know of, and I doubt if your man could unduly influence the course of events a great deal anyway, at least not over the short haul. Look at it this way. If it's a paranoid state, maybe it'll all be over in a few days. If not, there's always time to consult a psychiatrist if the condition becomes worse. Why don't you give the case a little time?" Griscom grinned. "I've never heard of a piece of litigation yet that didn't mellow under a little judicious delay."

"I guess you're right," Jim muttered. Balls of fire, how could he extricate himself from this zany web Griscom was weaving?

"Here's one concrete suggestion, Jim. Why not do some prodding and probing into the man's early life? The psychologists tell us that the seeds of breakdowns in adult life are often sown back in the formative years." He looked fixedly at MacVeagh. "And in this particular case, Jim, I don't think you'd have much trouble looking back into the man's early days."

An anger of frustration welled up in MacVeagh and he felt his skin growing warm. By God, he does think I came here to describe myself. He thinks I'm either indulging in some damned self-purgative or I've come to him for psychiatric advice about myself. Me, the most normal guy in town. Jim felt like lashing out at Griscom, upbraiding him for his pose of being a "country boy" attorney from Wyoming when actually he was a canny lobbyist-lawyer who traded on highly placed friends and wasn't above hinting that he knew the trade of blackmail. MacVeagh raged inwardly. Yes, an adroit, posing manipulator, who joined all the exclusive clubs and went around with unpressed pants. And as for the sly reference to Rita, MacVeagh decided he detested Paul Griscom for it. Jim found it an effort to get himself in hand for a decorous exit. He rose slowly and put out his hand.

"I appreciate the advice, Paul." He knew it sounded stiff. "It was more than considerate of you to take the time."

Griscom came around the desk. He grasped MacVeagh's hand and held it in a warm, firm grip. "Jim, I've seen some items in the press about you and the vice-presidency. Apparently some leaders in Wisconsin are getting up a write-in campaign for you."

MacVeagh was in no mood to discuss politics, but he nodded curtly. "I do have some friends out there," he said. "Of course, it doesn't mean a thing. The decision is exclusively the President's."

"I know," said Griscom. He continued to hold MacVeagh's hand. "But it means you're definitely in the running. I congratulate you. It's a high compliment to your ability."

"Thanks."

"Jim," said Griscom, "I understand how you feel about your —uh—friend. I've gone through some gritty periods myself and I know what it's like. Let time be the healer. At least, it's worth a try. And if it fails, and our man doesn't recover, then come back and see me. I think a lot of you, Jim, and I'm anxious to help all I can."

His voice was sincere, the friendly voice of a man who would soon know old age and needed nothing more from life now but good marks from those he liked or respected. But Jim was still seething. He broke off the handshake.

"Thanks, Paul. You've been a big help."

The British secretary's smile was one of approval, complimenting him for having the sound judgment to bring his difficulties to Griscom, Fotheringill & Hadley. MacVeagh lunged out of the office without a good day, yanking the door behind him. But it did not slam. A pneumatic device slowed the door's motion, and Jim heard it click sedately behind him.

He was still in vile humor when he arrived at his Senate office. The idea that Senator MacVeagh might suffer a mental lapse because of an affair with Rita Krasicki was so ludicrous that Jim couldn't understand how a man of Griscom's discernment could possibly reach such a conclusion. Either Griscom was a lightweight whose reputation overshadowed his talents or he, MacVeagh, had botched the mission horribly. He had gone to the law office as a frightened man seeking counsel, and he had come out in a frustrated rage. He had accomplished absolutely nothing—except to learn that Griscom knew of Rita. He could imagine Griscom standing in his living room, peeping at him from behind a curtain. Griscom's knowledge rattled him, and Jim wasn't sure who angered him more at the moment, Griscom or himself.

Flip Carlson called on the intercom with news—another Wisconsin mayor had come out for MacVeagh for vice-president—but Jim cut him off. Later, he said brusquely. Right now he had other things to do.

Then, as he sat at his desk, digging at the big blotter with a letter opener, his ire began to drain away. Griscom had made a logical deduction, especially in view of Jim's refusal to name names. And what did Griscom's conjecture matter, really, when weighed against Jim's own growing belief about Mark Hollenbach? He saw Hollenbach again, striding about shadowy Aspen lodge, poisonously assailing his fancied persecutors and, alternately, immersing himself in the rapt vision of a preposterous union of nations that would prove the world's salvation.

Jim had to do something, but just what? Well, the first thing was to do his homework—which Craig Spence had accused him of neglecting. To start with, he ought to know precisely what the law and the custom was in cases where a president's physical or mental condition was called into question. What was that fellow's name at the legislative reference service of the Library of Congress? Oh, yes. A Mr. Brunton, one of those hundreds of faceless civil servants who knew everything a senator didn't.

He telephoned the Library of Congress, got the proper extension, and heard the pale, courteous voice of Mr. Brunton.

"This is Jim MacVeagh of Iowa, Mr. Brunton," he said. "Say, I need whatever you've got on the subject of presidential inability. What? A speech? No, no, just a request from a constituent."

He listened for a moment. "Yes, that's it. The early agreements, Eisenhower-Nixon and Kennedy-Johnson, and now the one between President Hollenbach and Mr. O'Malley. And those Senate hearings run by Senator Birch Bayh of Indiana. Also, the American Bar Association recommendations. In short, everything you've got."

"I'll send over what I've got this afternoon, Senator." Mr. Brunton was apologetic. "But right now a great deal of that material is out to somebody else. There's always a lot of interest in that subject, you know, and our folder keeps making the rounds. But as soon as the other material comes back, I'll shoot it right over."

Jim tilted back in his chair. That was a starter, but he ought to be doing something else. The fear he'd felt when riding back from Camp David came seeping back. Was Mark really . . . ? He hesitated to think the word again. But time might count, and he ought to act somehow. Then he thought of something Paul Griscom had said. Yes, that certainly should be done.

He ruminated for almost half an hour, planning his course. Then he dialed his assistant on the intercom.

"Flip," he said. "Come on in here. You're going on a trip for me."

7.

La Belle

Six days later, on a Sunday afternoon, Jim MacVeagh was sitting in the upstairs den of his McLean home with the window wide open. The calendar marked the first day of spring, and an unseasonable blaze of heat sucked at the winter's moisture deep in the earth of suburban Virginia. The MacVeagh back lawn perspired under the sun. The vacant field beyond the back fence steamed and glistened in the sudden thaw. The last of the snow had vanished overnight. Branches of a dogwood tree outside Jim's window gleamed moistly, and he could see the first green fuzz of new buds. The smell of the opening land was full and pungent, and under his sport shirt Jim could feel a trickle of sweat.

The sunlight, bursting through the window as though newly freed of confinement, sparkled on a tray of knives in a corner of the room. The velvet case of old surgical instruments, some dating back two hundred years, reminded Jim of his father and of old Jamie MacVeagh's disappointment. He had wanted to be a surgeon, but the family lacked the tuition for medical school, and Jamie had wound up selling insurance. A frustrated physician all his life, he'd used much of his spare funds to accumulate one of the country's finest collections of ancient medical weaponry. On his father's death, Jim had sold most of the collection, given some of it to a medical museum, and retained only the case of knives. Life has its odd twists, thought Jim. His father, balked in his ambition for a medical career, spent most of his life collecting symbols of the profession. And now here was the son, supposedly the leading candidate for vice-president, collecting all the information he could find about the man who had offered him the post. The situations weren't analogous, thought Jim, but somehow he better appreciated his father's frustration today.

Jim MacVeagh was curved in a red leather easy chair on the base of his spine, his sneakered feet propped on a hassock, while he read a typewritten report from his brash young assistant, Flip Carlson.

In his despair the Monday before, Jim recalled something Paul Griscom had said—that he ought to look into the early life of the man whose mental stability he suspected. Seeds of breakdowns often are sown in the formative years, he'd said. Griscom, of course, was urging Jim to look back on his own childhood, thinking as he did that MacVeagh was his own patient. But the more Jim thought of the advice the better he liked it. What, indeed, had Mark Hollenbach's early life been like? Nobody really knew much about it, only cursory mentions in highly favorable campaign biographies and a few broad sketches in the magazines. Everyone knew the highlights. Hollenbach's father had been superintendent of schools in rural Hendry County, Florida, and the boy was reared in the little county seat of La Belle. Then Mark had gone north to college at Denison University, Granville, Ohio, and later joined the faculty of the University of Colorado at Boulder as a history professor. From there he'd gone into politics, rising to governor of Colorado and finally president.

MacVeagh had wanted to swing around the country himself, interviewing those who knew Mark Hollenbach as a boy and young man, but realized he'd be recognized as a U.S. senator and that he would have no excuse for prowling about on such a bizarre mission. So he had enlisted his administrative assistant, Flip Carlson, whose zest for politics was matched only by his craving for travel. Jim told Carlson that he had decided to do a biography of Hollenbach, a quick job hopefully to be printed in a hurry and placed on sale during the fall campaign. The author's credentials—a Democrat, a senator and a friend—would ensure at least a modest reception, he told Carlson, but suppose he were selected as vice-president? Then the novelty of a book about the candidate, written by his running mate, might produce a best seller. Carlson agreed the idea had "schmaltz," as he put it, and he was eager to do what he could.

Despite the need for speed, MacVeagh cautioned, he wanted to picture the young Hollenbach in depth ("How about width and breadth for a change?" asked Carlson), so he needed to know everything Carlson could dig up. How did the boy's mind work? What were his emotional responses as he went through school and college? Who were his friends and what were his dreams? In short, it ought to be a real personality study and not the traditional banal tale of an aspiring youth who was sure to become president. Carlson, intrigued by the venture, left Washington the next day with a portable typewriter and a carton of notebooks.

Carlson's research had produced a sheaf of documents, all the usual material. There were grade reports from elementary school, transcripts of high school and college scholastic records, a battered college annual, photostats of newspaper clippings, several photographs of Hollenbach and his boyhood home and a bibliography of books and magazine articles which mentioned the President's early life.

MacVeagh had skimmed through it all. Now, as the hot sun flooded the room, Jim turned to Carlson's typewritten account of his interviews and began to read carefully from the first page:

Memo to JFM from RC.

Interviews on the Rising Mark.

Tuesday. Arrived Tampa in late morning, rented car and drove down to La Belle. Right? This town is on the Caloosahatchee River, halfway between Lake Okeechobee and the Gulf of Mexico and about the same distance between the 19th and 20th centuries. Sign on highway coming into town reads, "La Belle, Birthplace of Mark Hollenbach," but that's one of the few new public improvements since the war. Went to Glades Motel, noisy air conditioner, ice machine, but no pool. Got room for $5 single. (It's only $6 double, but I worked so hard in La Belle, I didn't have time to meet any broads.) Town is flat, dusty, scrub palmetto, live oaks with Spanish moss, natch, yellow brick courthouse. Some hot nights, the sheriff takes prisoners out of the county jail and lets them sit outside. La Belle actually is the intersection of Routes 80 and 29, with about 1,300 people gathered around to watch the traffic. Hasn't changed much since Mark was a kid. No big developments like the coastal cities. Everything sleepy. Guys clomp around in levis and cowboy boots—snakeproof on account of rattlers out in the brush. Went right to work, starting with the names I had. Right?

AMOS PALMER. Auto repairs. Playmate and grammar school friend of Hollenbach. Find Palmer at shop. Wizened old face like a conch shell. Cracker. Real smart. Cagey too. Wipes hands on overalls. Drinks Coke. Doesn't offer me one. Oh, one of them, he says. Says been pestered by three, four writin' fellows. Okay, though, he says, fire away. So, what kind of a kid was Hollenbach? Skinny as a bamboo fishing pole, he says. Had good times. Fished, played ball, sneaked swims in the Caloosahatchee. But Mark didn't break no rules much. Maybe because his daddy was head of the county schools and pretty strict. When they got older, maybe seventh, eighth grades, Mark takes to swallowing books like a heron snatches pinfish. He keeps way ahead of the other kids in learnin'. Broody sometimes. Remembers him once by river swimming hole, skeeters thick as mangrove roots around him, readin' some damfool book. Rest of kids was swimmin'. Mark tries hard at everything, but not much at sports. Always wants to be first in everything, but only manages to be tops in studies. Says got to quit talkin' now and finish the clutch on this car. What did he think of Mark in those days? Same thing as now, he says. Kind of have to admire him, but never felt none too close to him. Mark was more of a loner. From what he hears, still is, ain't he?

PHOEBE HENDRIX. 77. Nice old dame. Spry. Never married. Lives in little white frame house with Key West tin roof. Musty old-maid smell inside. As young girl out of teachers' college, she had Mark in first grade. You never get over the first class you teach, she says. Remembers all the kids in it. Hollenbach the smartest. Had to quit calling on him because he always knows the answers and it makes the other kids afraid to speak up. Once he cries because she won't call on him when his hand is up. (Not sure, but maybe the poor kid wanted to go to the john, but I don't mention this to Phoebe.) He could read like a third-grader at end of that first year. Nice, quiet boy, but sulky and irritable if he isn't first in everything, spelling, arithmetic, music, the works.

WINSTON E. GROVER, ins., real estate broker. Big, heavy, slow guy. Full of bull. High school graduate with Hollenbach. Praises him like he was always name-brand genius. Knew he'd be president, etc., etc. Grand fellow, Mark, gracious, gentleman, solid. Grover talks like he's making a recording for the National Archives. Not much help. I learn more about Grover than about Hollenbach. Says he tried to give 25 acres of prime road property on the main road to Fort Myers—road to river—to Hollenbach. Good publicity for town, especially if Mark retired there. But President wouldn't take it. Sends Grover a letter with a little lecture about conflict of interest and accepting gifts, as I get story. Grover keeping letter. Says it will be worth lots of money someday. No, he won't show it. He laughs and slaps his leg and says ol' Mark still knows how to tell a fellow off. Reminds him of one night at high school dance when Hollenbach blows his top at another guy over a girl. Nope, won't tell. Just as well these things aren't said about presidents. But would be great story, if he could tell it. But why rake up that kind of stuff? Phooie.

MRS. FREDERICK (MAE PAULINE) RICHARDSON. Married to banker, but used to have some dates with Hollenbach in high school.

Plump—no, fat—gentle and hospitable, but inclined to chirp and twitter. Oh, yes, Mark was a perfect gentleman. Took her to dance once. Got in fight with Ed Broyle over her, but don't print that in book, please. Her husband Fred would be embarrassed. Ed's dead now, but he gave Hollenbach a cut lip. All a mistake. Ed cuts in on dance floor and Mark won't yield, and accuses Ed of trying to flirt with his girl. (All this same dance Grover talking about? I dunno.) Boys rag Mark because he enunciates so well, almost like an actor on stage or something, and he never drawls like everybody else in Hendry County. Some thought he was stuck up. Had a right to be. Oh, Mark never changed. She knew that when she saw him on television, during campaign, pleading for excellence. He was just about perfect in everything he tried. But would it be fun to live with a perfect man? She giggles. Never saw him after he went off to Denison because he worked in the North summers and came home only a few times. Hollenbach's dad was strict, but the boy more so, and that's funny, isn't it, to be stricter than the parent? Made his own high standards and rules. Now, don't put my name in that book. I've talked too much already. What's the First Lady like? (Come to think of it, she's not unlike Mae Pauline Richardson. Right?)

No more people in La Belle who knew him well. Adults at that time mostly dead now. Most of his classmates all moved or died (two steady occupations in La Belle) except three who couldn't even remember what he looked like. No use writing down their names. Waste of time interviewing them.

Wednesday. Working on Denison University annual, with first preference for his fraternity brothers in Beta Theta Pi. Most in Ohio still. Drove to Miami and turned in rental car. Flew to Cincinnati, tourist. Saved you money.

HOMER RIDENAUER. Saw him Wednesday night at home in Cincy. Lawyer. Lots of dough. Although Republican, he thinks Hollenbach a great president and will vote for him this fall. Wants to talk current policy. Hard time getting him back on campus. Says Hollenbach different, very different. No smoke, no drink, no cusswords, no frittering away time in front of console radio-phonograph in fraternity house or in all-night bull sessions. Only sees him take drink once, when sophomore, and Mark spits that out. Mark doesn't mind others drinking, but Ridenauer says Mark can't waste his own time. Always calm, cool, good judgment. Gets mad only once, when chapter falls below fraternity average in grades. Raises Cain at chapter meeting. Gets very excited, but doesn't do much good. Mark is no good at team sports, but pretty fair golfer, tennis player, and an average miler at track. Plugs away at the mile, wins a few dual meets. Solid citizen even then. Ridenauer says he's anxious to read book when finished. Thinks nobody's really pegged what makes this great man tick.

Thursday. Columbus, O. PETER McCREARY. Star auto salesman. Big, husky, breezy guy. Captain of football team and treasurer of fraternity chapter when Hollenbach was president of Betas. Says Mark excellent student, fine man, very mature for years. Knew he'd go far. Praises him highly. Can't explain why, but get clear impression McCreary never likes Hollenbach. Nothing he says. His inflection, maybe.

Still Columbus. TOM (SPIDER) CRAWFORD. Hotel manager. Small, dapper guy. Doesn't look like spider, but says he used to. Says Mark was drivingest boy he ever knows. Lots of self-discipline. Hits the books late at night. Felt sometimes Mark was all stretched out tight as a drum and would have done him good to relax, get drunk or something. But only time he takes a drink he knows of, he spits it out. (Same scene as with Ridenauer. Right?) Spider no pal of Mark's. Says he likes the free-and-easy kind better. Maybe that's why he's in hotel business. You see plenty in a hotel. Winks. Still, he guesses he's glad Hollenbach's running the country. Sounds like grudging concession to me.

Saw two other fraternity brothers in Columbus area, but they contributed nothing. Not worth mentioning.

Friday. HOWARD RENTZSCH. Celina, Ohio. Jolly guy, hard worker. Runs small department store. First man I ever meet who has seven consonants and only one vowel in his name. Celina nice town. Big, wide main drag. Houses with pillars set way back. Turn of the century atmosphere in this part of town. Rentzsch says he was good friend of Hollenbach, he thought. Brought him home couple of times. Admired his ability, but thought Mark ought to loosen up and have some fun. Hard to get close to the guy. They're no longer friends. Rentzsch says he doesn't know what happened, but after Hollenbach got into politics, didn't seem to have time for old acquaintances. Written him couple of times, but only gets one formal White House Christmas card two years ago. No note, no nothing. Rentzsch says he never really figured Mark out in school, although he tried, but if I really want to know what Mark was like as college boy, try and contact Tina Faraday, the former TV actress. Says she used to go with Mark and, from what he hears, give her a couple of drinks, and she'll talk your ear off. Used phone in Rentzsch's store to call Miss Faraday in L.A. Got her after long delay and made date for Saturday. Rentzsch pleasant fellow. Bought blouse from him for a girl—when I find one.

Saturday. (Pardon the typing. This written Sunday morning, coming back on plane to D.C. from L.A. Portable hard to use on knees in a jet.) TINA FARADAY. Former TV actress, 58. Real maiden name, Ida Jones. Married names in rotation: Lomax, Jacobs, Pinckert, Stacey. Divorced all four. Lives alone, with maid and cook, in Santa Monica. Big house, somewhat deteriorated, on cliff overlooking Pacific. This interview worth whole price of tour. Wait'll you read it.

Spend six hours with Tina, until 3 a.m. Sunday. She gets plastered. I get swacked too, but keep old brain cells alert, I hope. Wildest dame I ever meet. Cusses worse than Joe Donovan. More exotic in choice and range of profanity. Chin sags despite face-lifting, but still attractive in kind of beat-up, vulpine way. Good word, vulpine. Right? She wears black, slinky thing which wraps her hips tight and leaves one shoulder bare. Open-toed shoes. Shoes gold. Toenails painted green. Honest. Or maybe emerald. Bright as hell, anyway.

(Pause while I call stewardess for aspirin. Take two. Feel better. Back to report.)

Tina drinks beaucoup gin-on-rocks. First two had some vermouth, but after that straight gin. Lose count at eight. She spends couple hours quizzing me. How many books have I written? Where do I live? I say Omaha. (Well, Council Bluffs is close enough.

Right?) Do I know the God-love-'em screwball somethings in Omaha? Get out of that one, just barely, but she remains suspicious until fourth drink. Then can't make her stop talking if I'd wanted to. Talks like Niagara Falls, gushing and cussing and slogging the stuff down. She was transfer to Denison from University of Toledo, so she only knew Mark in junior and senior years. Decides he is smartest man in school and she is going to have him for hers, maybe marry him.

She is hot article then. Proves it by old picture. Jesus, yes. A knockout—all willowy curves, wide, sexy mouth, and a white chest with two honeydew melons. Makes your mouth water. She is in Spanish class with Mark. Starts by asking him to help her with the Spanish. He does. Plenty of nights. But he only kisses her once and then not with much bejazz. Takes her to some fraternity dances. She presses against him. (Tina illustrates all this by the indoor fountain with bullfrogs. I mean she has bullfrogs in the fountain.) But Mark pulls away, always dances proper. So after couple of months, she gets mad. (She illustrates this too. Wonderful display of rage. Great actress.) Denison campus built around the football field, which is sunken like a real bowl into the earth. One night Tina and Mark are lying on the rim of the bowl. The stars are out and it's soft, murmuring spring with the divine scent of God-love-it clover in the air. (That's what the woman says.) She nestles close to Mark and this time they kiss very feelingly, she says. (No illustration here, though. Too bad. She's terrific with a bullfrog chorus in the background.) They kiss some more, and get real pash like college kids should. All of a sudden, he rears back and says, "No more," or words to that effect. (Tina acts out this scummy double-cross by our lover.) He starts to preach her a lecture on purity, morals and conduct, etc., and gets going like a goddam (censored) (censored) circus tent revivalist. He's all hopped up and waxing eloquent while she's doing a slow burn. Finally, she hauls off and cracks him in the God-love-it mush with both fists, one, two, plop, plop. His nose starts to bleed. (Worse than the cut lip in La Belle, I gather.) He's trying to stop it with his handkerchief while she stalks off, haughty and proud. (Another little off-Broadway drama by the fountain.)

Next day he apologizes in Spanish class for being such a prude, but says he can't help himself. She scorns him. Now it's the reverse and he's after her. She holds him off awhile, but then they begin to have dates again, very quiet, sweet, soulful affairs, all full of the longing of youth and stuff. You remember? Right?

The next fall, their senior year, she invites him to her home in Columbus for the weekend. Ohio State is playing a home game and the town is football crazy again as usual. They go to game, which she thinks Ohio State wins. After game, they go to her home, but it turns out her folks are away. Actually, they are in Europe for a couple of months, which she knows all the time. She plays slow music. They dance. She sneaks a couple of shots of straight gin in the kitchen (this broad has noncorroding copper piping), then chews gum furiously because he's death on alcohol for fair sex. Gradually she works things so they're in the bedroom upstairs. (Why don't these things ever happen to me?) She tells him he can undress in the bathroom and he goes in there. She sheds her dress and whatever she has underneath, which probably isn't much, judging by her body profile last night by the bullfrog pond. Anyway, she climbs into bed after a slosh of cologne. She waits and waits and then she waits some more. Wonders if he's sick or something. Finally, the door opens and Mark comes out—with all his clothes on. His eyes are damp. "I can't," he moans, very agitated. "We're not married." With that he hurries out of the room, clatters down the stairs and out of the house. She wants to throw the dresser out the window at him, but instead she has herself a nice, long cry—and then a few belts of gin.

They're not in any classes together this last year, so she sees him only occasionally and then avoids him. He never asks for another date, and if he had, she'd have whopped him again, she thinks. The last time she sees him, they are lining up for graduation in caps and gowns and he comes close to her while trying to find his place in line. "Married yet?" she asks in sarcastic, viperish whisper. He looks at her, throws her a saintly, pitying smile, according to her, and shakes his head. She hasn't seen him since and what's more, she doesn't vote for him. Thinks he's a (censored) (censored) ass. Later, she hears he gets married to a Colorado girl named Evelyn Willett (the current

First Lady) and she hears this is a homey, sweet type girl who doesn't need much in the love department, which, she says, serves Mark right. Thinks from glitter-eyed pictures of him she sees in the papers, he gets about as much loving as Tibetan monk.

From 2 to 3 a.m., I hear about her God-love-'em four husbands, none of whom, it seems, majored in fidelity, but guess you don't want any of that. We're now over good old Iowa and the stewardess is bringing me one more aspirin with coffee. I may live, but my head won't. After reading over this last part, I'm not sure whether you should keep it for the book, seal it for 75 years at the Library of Congress or burn it. Right?

Your private private eye,
Flip.

MacVeagh chuckled, then laughed aloud. Carlson, red-eyed and jittery, had delivered the typewritten sheaf to him an hour earlier, then implored Jim not to phone him until evening after he'd had some sleep. Jim could imagine Tina Faraday, in gold shoes and green-lacquered toenails, swaying on the edge of a fountain while she portrayed love scorned. The image reminded him of Rita, wrathfully exploding over the telephone, and he wondered whether any woman ever accepted rejection gracefully.

Then he thought of the youthful Mark Hollenbach and tried to piece together a picture of the boy: proud, lonely, tormented by rigid, self-imposed standards, determined to excel, a natural student who nevertheless drove himself, obsessed with self-improvement, aloof, unable to form close, relaxed friendships, stirred by sexual guilt, yet a leader who earned the admiration and respect, if not the affection, of his fellows. Add almost forty years to the picture of the college boy, thought MacVeagh, and had the tone and shading changed much? Isometrics was unknown when Mark was at Denison, but had it been practiced, Jim could imagine young Hollenbach flexing his fingers and tightening his biceps, even as he did now.

Jim's mind went back once more to the sessions at Camp

David, to the eerie half-light, the volcanoes of anger over O'Malley and Spence, the talk of a conspiracy to ruin the President, and the gaudy, spangled vision of a super-union with Mark Hollenbach as the prime minister of everything from Bering Strait to the Baltic. The sun poured through the open window, warm as fire, but Jim felt the chill of fear as he had when riding back from the Catoctin Mountains the week before. He sensed that something was radically wrong with the man who sat in the White House, but he was at a loss as to what to do. Was he the only person in Washington who felt this? Rita had heard Mark erupt purposelessly over Davidge, the banker, but she dismissed it as an ordinary temper tantrum. Was MacVeagh alone in his surmises? And were they valid hunches, or was he beginning to fabricate and imagine a pattern that did not exist?

And this complex, driven man whose mental balance he doubted, had picked him as his vice-president. Mark had confided in him, trusted him with the vision, proposed that they shoulder the future together. What right had he to soil this trust by secretly investigating the man's youth as though he were a shoddy public welfare case? And was the picture he'd formed of the young Hollenbach an honest one or was he chinking in the gaps with suppositions drawn from the memory of Aspen lodge? Jim wondered whether he had the right to weigh the President's mental stability. After all, he was but one of a hundred senators, a single cog in the intricate machinery of government, unauthorized by law to investigate anything or anybody, unless empowered by vote of a Senate committee.

Still, didn't he have a duty to—well—to the country to pursue his misgivings and somehow settle this question which baffled him? If Mark Hollenbach was unbalanced, action had to be initiated. . . .

His circuitous ruminations were interrupted by a shout from downstairs.

"Hey, Pops," yelled Chinky in her fluttering soprano. "There's a good-looking man down here who says he has to see you right away."

"All right. Send him up."

As his visitor came up the steps, MacVeagh could see a broad smile and the flash of white teeth in a swarthy face. It was the Secret Service agent Luther Smith. He entered the den, closing the door behind him.

"Senator," said Smith, "I don't like to barge in on you like this on a Sunday afternoon, but I'm ordered to ask you some questions."

"Questions?"

"Yes." Smith stood uneasily, holding his felt hat in his hands and fingering the narrow brim. "Senator, I've just come back from a little town in Florida named La Belle."

8.

Sweet Water

Slim Carmichael hung his blue suit carefully in the closet, smoothing the crease in one sleeve and arranging the trousers on the hanger so that they would remain neatly pressed until he donned them again for church next Sunday. He was glad to be out of his once-a-week town clothes with the collar and tie which always made a prisoner of his neck and the coat that seemed to put a bind on his shoulders.

He pulled on blue dungarees, work boots, and a short-sleeved khaki shirt with a feeling of relief. He was a good Baptist by his own accounting, but he felt the Lord could be worshiped more earnestly if custom didn't dictate that he must listen to the preacher in clothes that gripped like a vise. He preferred his own nightly prayers. The idea was to nourish the spirit, not strangle it.

Slim strode to the wooden porch of his loose-jointed frame house, jammed his big hands into the front pockets of his dungarees, and stood looking proudly at his land. It stretched flat and powdery gray to the west, like a bed of ashes pressed smooth by a giant hand iron. Slim owned 2,000 acres of this shimmering, treeless ground and he loved every foot of it, for there was twenty years of himself lying there. A generation of sweat had oozed from his body, leaving him bony and parched, as dry as old leather that will no longer absorb oil. His joints ached occasionally now, as though the very juices of his marrow had seeped into the soil.

The ever-blowing wind was coming from the west this Sunday noon. The window frames rattled and the sign near the gate, which read CARMICHAEL, creaked as it swayed. Slim tilted his straw sombrero, flared sharply at the sides like the banks of a gully, and gazed across the land to the south. The sun drilled fiercely, making an oven of the porch and turning the soil almost white in the glare. Squinting toward the horizon, and the hazy bulk of the Davis Mountains, Slim could see two brown funnels rising to the sky. With the end of the thaws, the great dust storms would soon begin, sweeping across the west Texas plains like airborne armies. The dirt would drift through the cracks of the house, lay a powderlike film over the furniture and burrow into the fence posts, filling them as though they were sponges. Out in the fields in a sudden dust blow, a man could only squat like a frog and bury his head in his arms, waiting for the suffocating fury to pass. For a cotton farmer like Slim, the soil was always with him: in his hair, thick in his nostrils, embedded in his pores. No amount of scrubbing could entirely free him from the brand of his own land.

But Slim loved this bare, dusty expanse, perhaps more than his wife Betsy, certainly more than any man-made article he owned. The land lay there, flaky and gray, burnished by the sun, annually churned by the tractor-drawn harrows, fortified by costly fertilizers, and laved by some of the purest water in America.

The water was the miracle. It sprang from a deep, underground river and turned a narrow band of near desert in West Texas into a bursting garden. Years ago, before World War II, this had been cattle country. Then the rains ceased, the grasses withered, and the cattle died of famine. Hard times throttled the country along the Pecos River. The towns, which had rung with the shouts of the cowhands who knew no "law west of the Pecos," began to shrivel in the dust clouds swirling across the grassless plains. Then a blessing, the miracle of the underground river, was discovered. Soon great irrigation pumps were hoisting the clear, cold, sparkling water to quench the thirst of the topsoil. A single pump would fetch up hundreds of gallons every minute of this colorless, liquid gold, and within a few years more than 100,000 acres whitened with high-priced cotton.

Slim Carmichael came after the pumps, a migrant from East Texas with a bent for farming and $10,000 in savings. First he leased 500 acres in the watered band south of Pecos and north of Saragosa, and borrowed heavily to make his first cotton crop. Weather and luck were with him. He made enough to put a down payment on acres of his own. In the years that followed, he and Betsy, childless, gave everything to the land, stinting themselves, never buying a fancy town house as so many of the cotton men did, spurning the new model cars, and seldom taking a trip outside Reeves County. Slim Carmichael became a good credit risk and the bankers trusted him with bigger loans each year. Now he owned 2,000 acres, mortgage free, and of the $100,000 it would cost him this year to make his crop, he had to borrow only $40,000. The rest was his own money.

Slim Carmichael was in sounder financial condition than most of his neighbors, but recently he also had differed in another respect. His name now was known beyond Reeves County, for last summer Slim had the son of the President of the United States, Mark Hollenbach, Jr., working as a hand on his cotton farm. The boy had roomed at Yale with the son of Doc Peyster, and Peyster had come to Slim when young Hollenbach wrote, saying that he'd like to work a summer in the West Texas cotton fields. The kid had done well, Slim thought, working easily with the dozen Mexicans whom Slim employed. Young Mark was a big boy, powerful in the shoulders, a rugged towhead who didn't mind hard work. He was serious enough about the labor that blistered his palms, but he joked around the house and delighted Betsy by calling her his "second girl"—anybody under twenty-five he could find would be his first. Slim was pleased because some of the timidity and anxiety seemed to leave Betsy when Mark Jr. was around the house. Betsy lived in fear of a crop failure because of the big loans Slim had to negotiate each year. She always envisioned them impoverished by one bad year, and the strain sapped her spirit and nagged at her worn body like a chronic sore. But with Mark Jr. around, blithe and carefree, her eyes brightened and her worries faded. It was like having a son of their own in the house for the first time.

The early part of Mark's stay had been annoying for Slim, for they were plagued by newspapermen from Pecos, Odessa, San Angelo and Dallas, and even a writer-photographer team from *Look* magazine. But after three weeks Mark Jr. and Slim agreed that they'd had it. No more reporters, they vowed, and they shook hands on it. After that, the kid worked with the Mexicans, getting his shirt wringing wet, driving the tractors, operating the pumps, turning the big valves and repairing the machinery in which the dust fought a constant battle with lubrication for the life of the small parts.

The boy fitted easily into the routine of farm life, and Slim even became accustomed to the chubby Secret Service agent who stayed in the guest room and paid his bill as a boarder. While the agent never allowed more than a few hundred feet to come be-tween himself and the President's son, he was remarkably unob-trusive. Dressed as a hired hand, the agent frequently worked in the fields and smilingly shook his head when Slim tried to pay him the going hourly rate. He was doing all right on government per diem, he said. At first, after a day in the sun, young Mark was too tired to stir after supper, except for Saturday nights when Slim took the boy and the agent to a highway beer hall for a few drinks and a game of darts. By the end of the summer, though, Mark Jr. had built up his stamina, and many week nights, he would play his guitar while the Mexicans sang old folk melodies in Spanish and the agent beat out an accompaniment on an oil drum.

Slim was thinking of young Mark this Sunday as he left the farmhouse and walked across the fields, scuffing at the dirt and adjusting his straw sombrero to deflect the rays of the sun. Slim was thinking of Mark Jr. because the boy would be back in a few months for another summer of work before he went to law school. But Slim also was thinking of his young friend because of this thing about the water—the sweet, icy water which sprang wondrously from far beneath these arid plains.

Slim and Mark Jr. had exchanged a number of letters last fall, and then at Christmas time, Slim had received a White House card and an accompanying handwritten letter from the President, on official stationery with the President's seal. The President thanked him warmly for helping young Mark and for keeping an eye on him. The President also said that he would like to repay the favor, and if he could be of any assistance, Slim should be sure to write him.

So, in January, after considerable thought, Slim did write the President about his chief worry—the sweet water. The water under the land in this part of West Texas, he wrote, was a priceless natural resource that should be preserved. But, wrote Slim, he was afraid that too many pumps were going to bring up too much water to produce too much cotton that wasn't needed. Slim cited geologists and their reports. He urged that the federal government could help by sponsoring a conference of the cotton farmers and trying to find some formula to put a limit on the pumping. Slim wrote that he, for one, would be glad to cut back voluntarily, but others refused, so the prestige of the federal government was needed. Perhaps the government could produce an agreement which all farmers would sign. Or, if voluntary methods wouldn't work, perhaps there ought to be a federal law limiting the take of water. But something ought to be done, concluded Slim, so that the flow could be preserved for years to come. He labored over the letter for several nights, for words were not Slim's trade.

By return air mail, Slim received a polite letter from the President, this one typewritten, saying that the President thought Slim's idea had merit and that he was referring it to the Interior and Agriculture departments for recommendations. But now, Slim had heard nothing in six weeks, and his interest was piqued as to just what Hollenbach's federal men would come up with as a solution.

He was standing near one of his pumps and gazing down a long, boarded irrigation channel, which stretched to the horizon like a ribbon of silver, when he heard Betsy call him. Her thin, piping voice was almost lost in a freshet of wind, but he turned to see her on the porch. She was waving something and motioning to him. When he reached the house, she held out a letter to him.

"It just came special delivery," she said. "It says White House on the envelope, so I guess it's the one you've been expecting."

Slim took the letter and went to the kitchen, first swallowing a glassful of the cool water which, he assumed, was the subject of the letter. The stationery was a pale-green color, bearing the presidential crest, and the handwriting was the President's, the same, clear, neat loops that Slim remembered from the Christmas note. He read it carefully:

Dear Mr. Carmichael:

As you know, and as I wrote you, I was very appreciative of the help and counsel you gave my son last summer, and I was anxious to do anything of a personal nature that I could to return the favor.

But I am irritated and distressed that you presumed on this relationship to try to foist onto the federal government a problem which is essentially an individual one. Frankly, my dear Carmichael, you are completely out of bounds when you solicit the aid of the federal government in general, and the President in particular, in solving a problem that is one of your own making. Time, effort and money in considerable quantities would be required here in Washington to fulfill your request.

At this particular time, the administration has its hands and its heart full with enormous responsibilities on the national and international scenes. Our very survival as a nation rests on the manner in which we confront these difficulties and surmount them. I am, at this very moment, seeking to formulate a concept by which our nation and our world can live in security and peace for the unknown centuries ahead.

You could not, of course, know this, but it does seem to me that the broad outlines of America's dilemma would have penetrated even your area of West Texas and that you would have been aware of the burden we are carrying.

In short, Carmichael, these are hours when every citizen should do his utmost to find his own way over the personal obstacles which face us all.

It was President Kennedy who said, "Ask not what your country can do for you, but what you can do for your country." It is not too late for all of us to heed those words.

Sincerely,
Mark Hollenbach

Bewildered, Slim, ran his finger over the presidential seal, as though assuring himself it was genuine. He snapped the letter and read several sentences again. Then he shoved it across the kitchen table to Betsy.

"Read that," he ordered, and the harshness in his voice made her look up in surprise.

When she finished reading, her brows creased in a frown. "I

don't understand," she said. "There must be some . . ."

"Some mistake?" he asked. "Oh, no. That's the President's handwritin' all right. I know it from the Christmas note. Now just where in the hell does he get off telling me that this water is a personal problem of ours?"

He thought a minute, and as he thought, Betsy could see the skin tightening on his bony features. His jaw set. Slim was getting angry.

"I was trying to help," he said, "and he reads me a snotty lecture on citizenship. Why, that high-horse professor! Who does he think he is anyway?"

"Now, Slim," Betsy protested. "There has to be some explanation. It sounds to me like he never read your letter."

"Sure he did." Slim's reedy voice was rising. "He said he liked the idea and he was askin' two departments about it. Now he gives me the back of his hand."

Betsy fingered her cheek nervously. She hated these outside troubles. They had enough of their own. "Probably the letter was written for him by somebody else and he never even saw it," she suggested.

"Oh, no. I tell you that's his own handwriting, all cute and careful like an old-maid schoolteacher. Damn these eastern smart-alecks. They think the rest of us are a bunch of slobs."

"Slim," she admonished. "President Hollenbach's from Colorado. He's no Easterner."

Slim slapped the table. "Oh, it's all the same. A fellow goes back there to Washington, and he gets all slick and know-it-all like that New York crowd. Just because he's in the White House he thinks he can insult ordinary people. And I wasn't askin' for help. I was trying to help him. That's what gets my goat. By God, I've got a good mind to stump Reeves County this fall and whip the tar out of that guy."

"Slim, please," she pleaded.

He snatched the letter and read it once more. When he spoke again, he had calmed somewhat.

"On second thought, Betsy," he said, "I think maybe somebody got to that ol' boy. He's a politician, and no politician would write a letter like that, especially in a year when he's runnin' again, unless somethin' was up. Maybe Bill Spicer and his gang got in the act. Spicer and 'em don't want no meters on the pumps. They want to take that water until it dries up and to hell with the future. Maybe I ought to show the letter to the county agent and see what he knows."

She shook her head. "Please don't do that, Slim. Why should we get involved? It's none of our business. I don't like messing in something like that. The government has too many ways to get back at you."

Her pinched little face, as fleshless as his own, showed the years of sun and toil. The worry lines bunched about her eyes and her fingers plucked at a place mat. Everything seemed to unnerve Betsy these last few years.

"Well, all right," he said, "but how about sending the letter to Mark, Jr.? He's a sensible young fellow, and he might have an idea. Maybe, just maybe, this is the President's idea of a joke."

"Please don't, Slim," she implored. "It would only upset young Mark. What could he do about it anyway? Why not wait until he comes out here this summer? Then you can show him the letter someday without making anything special out of it."

Slim looked at his wife and sighed. "All right, Betsy." He replaced the letter in the green envelope and carried it into the dining room. He put it in a small drawer of the old roll-top desk which both he and Betsy used for their accounts. "We'll just leave it there for the time being and forget about it," he said.

But he couldn't forget. After Sunday dinner and a cigarette, Slim sat in a rocker on his porch and looked out at the baking land. Fragile clouds, as small and as delicate as bits of lace, hung motionless in the pale-blue sky, and the earth seemed to flinch under the hammer of the sun. Far to the south loomed the peaks of the Davis Mountains, wrapped in a wavering haze. These Sunday afternoons were hours of contentment for Slim. Even the steady heat, which settled in the shade of the porch like the bed of a furnace, did not bother him.

But today he could not put the letter out of his mind. Those bastard politicians, he thought, they're all the same, Republican or Democrat. A man worked until his back ached, paid his taxes through the nose, obeyed the law, and hoped those rattlebrains in Washington would someday learn the value of a dollar. A man tried to act responsibly, even suggesting that he cut his own profits for the sake of conserving a resource for the whole country. And what did he get for his pains? A thumb at the nose by the President of the United States, a man who even had the gall to suggest that a farmer in West Texas was too ignorant to know any better. It was a lousy, stinking deal.

Slim batted angrily at a fly which streaked to safety on the crown of his straw sombrero. One thing was sure. This year they ought to clean out that insolent gang in Washington—from top to bottom.

9.

Secret Service

Chief Arnold Brothers, slumped in a chair in his office in the old Treasury Building, didn't like the taste and the smell of the whole business. It was one thing to track down the nuts who wrote anonymous letters, jumbled and obscene for the most part, which threatened the President of the United States. They were harmless usually, and it was no great problem for the U.S. Secret Service to persuade local mental health officers to take over the surveillance or to aid in quiet commitments to mental institutions. But something else again were these not infrequent incidents involving apparently normal, even influential, persons. People grew emotional about politics and the issues, particularly in a campaign year, and they made alarming remarks about the President that they didn't really mean. Still, the Service had to investigate. It couldn't afford to take a chance on anyone.

Chief Brothers was a chunky, methodical man with curly brown hair and a bland face which masked his own nest of anxieties. Foremost among them was retirement. He could quit the Service on full pension next year, and that he intended to do. The life of an agent was all right, despite the irregular hours and the endless, tense waiting for the unexpected when one was a member of the White House detail. But this administrative job, crammed with budget disputes and laced by the intricate cross-webbing of politics, was for the birds, in Brothers' opinion. The required obeisance to minor politicians grated on his pride. The errand boy role in which the White House frequently cast his men was galling. Despite the public glamour attached to his job, in the inner world of Washington everyone knew the Secret Service chief just did not have the stature, the prestige or the funds of the FBI director. And yet, if anything went wrong, it was his neck nevertheless.

And now had arisen this curious, prickly situation involving the junior senator from Iowa, just when the chief's head felt like a stuffed cabbage from a bad spring cold. Brothers sneezed, yanked at his pocket handkerchief, and dabbed mournfully at his red-rimmed nostrils. He frowned as he thought of how the MacVeagh business had started. An auto repairman in the little town of La Belle, Florida, a man named Amos Palmer, had called Washington headquarters to report that a suspicious young man was nosing around town asking personal questions about President Hollenbach. Palmer said he hadn't liked the fellow's attitude. The agent on duty gave the matter little thought, assuming the questioner was merely a newspaperman or magazine writer, but he dispatched a teletype to the Miami office, requesting a routine check.

Miami ran the check, tracing a rental car through a license number which appeared on the motel registration card in La Belle. The Miami office found that the car had been rented in Tampa to a Roger Carlson of Washington, D.C., although that was not the name which appeared in the La Belle motel's registration file. Carlson had a rental car credit card, and another routine check with the national office of the company revealed the card had been issued to a Roger Carlson, administrative assistant to Senator James F. MacVeagh of Iowa.

That's when Chief Brothers decided to send Luther Smith down to La Belle to case the situation. Not that Brothers thought there was anything suspicious. He'd assumed that Carlson was simply on some private political mission—one of these wheels-within-wheels affairs he encountered all the time in Washington. Still, he'd taken the precaution of sending Smith into the field because President Hollenbach was not the sort who'd appreciate someone padding about, making secret inquiries into his early life. Brothers knew intuitively that if Hollenbach ever learned of the La Belle case he'd demand an immediate report. So Brothers wanted to be in the clear, ready with the full and undiluted word. This presidential flunky aspect of his job especially annoyed Chief Brothers. He and his agents were supposed to safeguard and protect the person of the President, and ever since the assassination of President Kennedy—Brothers had been an agent in Dallas that day—the task weighed on them all like a shroud. But the SS men were distracted from their job by these auxiliary chores every president thrust upon them. They were required to run errands, carry speeches, function as a valet at times, act as a president's private detective and, sometimes, even as baby-sitter or wife-comforter.

Brothers sighed wearily and patted at his oozing nose with his handkerchief. He resented Smith's detailed report on his trip to La Belle and his interview with Senator MacVeagh because it spelled unneeded grief. Suddenly the chief found himself pitched into one of those swampy messes from which he instinctively recoiled. MacVeagh, apparently, had lied to Smith. His explanation of Carlson's poking about La Belle, asking strange questions about the President, had been a limp one. It was one of those flimsy cover stories that any agent would suspect. So Brothers felt compelled to order an investigation of MacVeagh, and he didn't like it one bit. A senator, if harassed or offended, could make life miserable for a bureau chief. And that, Brothers well knew, was all he was. The public might invest his job with mys-

tery and thrills, but Brothers knew he was just another government employee with his neck out—for anybody to take a swipe
at.

He only hoped that Smith had proceeded with discretion, so
that Senator MacVeagh wouldn't get word of the checkout.
Chief Brothers looked at his wrist watch and flipped a switch on
his squawk box.

"Is Smith there yet?"

"He's just coming in now, chief," was the metallic response.
"I'll send him right in."

Agent Luther Smith swarmed into the room, alive with
energy, flashing his pearly smile. Brothers eyed him apprehen-
sively and then sneezed, a small explosion that rocked his padded
frame. Smith took an armchair near Brothers' desk and opened a
loose-leaf notebook.

"This thing is getting gutsy, chief," he said. His voice had the
buoyancy of the investigator who has just discovered a corpse on
the patio.

"What have you got?" Brothers asked it like a man who'd
rather not hear.

"I've questioned five . . . no six . . . pretty good friends of
MacVeagh, all on a security basis."

"You sure they won't talk?" asked Brothers moodily. "I don't
trust anybody in this town."

"Positive," said Smith cheerfully. "I told them all this was a
routine check, and we didn't want to embarrass anybody. They
all promised to keep mum. Anyway, I'll make out a full report
for you, but there isn't a great deal in it except for Paul Griscom,
the lawyer."

"What did he have to say?"

"Plenty, but he didn't want to at first. He said because of his
special relationship to the President and MacVeagh, he'd rather
not mention any discussions with the senator. But I kept pressing

and he finally agreed to talk. He says MacVeagh came to see him last week, with an odd story about a man high in government who, MacVeagh claimed, was having some kind of severe mental trouble. MacVeagh described the symptoms which Griscom says added up to paranoia—a persecution complex, all sorts of people out to get him, coupled with some screwy scheme to save the world, a delusion of grandeur. MacVeagh, says Griscom, was highly agitated and refused to name the person. Said he wanted advice from Griscom on what to do. Griscom says it was so obvious what should be done—either get Hollenbach to give the guy the bounce or take the fellow to a psychiatrist—that he began to wonder about MacVeagh. The more the senator talked, says Griscom, the more he became convinced that MacVeagh was describing his own condition. In a word, that MacVeagh was the guy who was off his rocker."

"Oh, no." Brothers groaned. "We need that like a hole in the head. Did Griscom give you any idea what he thought MacVeagh's trouble was?"

"Yeah," said Smith, with more relish than Brothers thought seemly at the moment. "Griscom lives on O Street, and he says he has seen a guy who he swears is MacVeagh coming out of an apartment that belongs to a real sex cart. Her name is Rita Krasicki and she works for Joe Donovan at Democratic headquarters."

"You know her?"

"Yes, I've talked to her some. She's an eyeful, chief." Smith's dark face reddened slightly. "In fact . . . well, I don't blame MacVeagh."

"But what's the girl got to do with the price of oats?" asked Brothers. "I couldn't keep count of all the wheels in this city who have a little piece tucked away somewhere."

"I know, but Griscom thinks it may be different in MacVeagh's case. MacVeagh has a swell wife and daughter, and

Griscom thinks he's the kind of man who can't two-time his wife without brooding about it and rebuking himself and getting all messed up generally."

"You buy that?" Brothers' blue eyes questioned sharply from his smooth, bland face.

"No, I don't, chief. I think MacVeagh is a pretty uncomplicated guy who wouldn't think much about it. He's not one of those worried introverts. At least that's my hunch, and I've talked to him quite a bit."

"But he lied to you about this La Belle business."

"Yeah, I can't understand that. He says he's writing a biography of Hollenbach and he needs this early background stuff. But it seems funny that he'd be writing a book, with everything else he has to do."

"Especially when he's obviously running for vice-president," said Brothers. "And what's more, I get the impression that he's running with the President's encouragement."

"Of course, maybe he is writing a book. But then why lie? And he did lie about that report from Carlson. He told me he had no written report from Carlson, but I'm sure I saw it on his desk yesterday afternoon, and then last night Carlson admitted to me that he'd made a written report."

"And why should this Roger Carlson go around the country under an assumed name?" Brothers spoke as though questioning himself.

"Not only did he use an assumed name," said Smith, "but he told people he was from Omaha. Of course, MacVeagh explained that readily enough. He said if Carlson went under his real identity, people would clam up and refuse to talk to him."

"Does that make sense to you?"

"Not exactly. Who'd know Roger Carlson? And, of course, when I asked MacVeagh if it wasn't unusual for a fellow to write a book about a man whose running mate he might be, he just laughed and said it was pretty unlikely the lightning would ever strike him. But if it did, he said, such a book would be unique. I agreed there, but then asked him the name of his publisher. He looked startled and said he didn't have one yet, that he was just getting started."

"Has MacVeagh ever written a book?" asked Brothers.

"No. We checked that out. Not even a magazine piece."

Brothers had the appearance of a man being pestered by sand flies. His face bunched in irritation. There had to be an easy answer, but it eluded him.

"Maybe he's doing a book and maybe he's not," he said, "but I wonder if there isn't some political angle. It's a cinch he's investigating the President's early life, but why? Well, suppose he's afraid Hollenbach may not take him for vice-president. And suppose he manages to come up with some unsavory odds and ends about the President that Hollenbach would rather not have revealed. All right, then MacVeagh's in a position to put the squeeze on Hollenbach."

Smith shook his head, pursing his lips in dissent. "Aw, Mac-Veagh's not that kind of guy. I can't see him mucking around like that. You're talking blackmail. This guy's a pretty straight shooter."

"Still," said Brothers, "Hollenbach is a very proud man who'd hate to see his image tarnished, even by some old incident. And MacVeagh probably understands that about the President as well as we do."

"Forget it, chief," said Smith emphatically. "Jim MacVeagh's not the type. There's no malice in the guy and he's no conniver. And what's more, I don't buy that explanation of Griscom's either. MacVeagh's too stable a man to get upset and go into an emotional funk just because he happens to sleep now and then with some dame he isn't married to."

"Well, then, what's the answer?" Brothers eyed Smith accusingly, as though he'd let the Service down by becoming the courier of bad news.

"I don't know yet. But I'm as sure as I'm sitting here that we've nothing to worry about. Whatever MacVeagh's reason, he's no oddball. He's not about to harm the President. And after all, chief, that's our only concern, isn't it?"

"Not quite. I've got to be ready in case Hollenbach finds out about this. Somebody could always call him from La Belle." Brothers sniffed. His eyes were watering. "I keep coming back to one thing. It keeps bugging me."

"What's that, chief?"

"Those knives you saw in MacVeagh's den."

"You mean that old surgical collection?"

"Yes. Now, that's a mighty weird hobby, Luther, for a United States senator."

"Oh, it isn't a hobby of MacVeagh's. He says his father collected surgical instruments and the senator just keeps the tray around as a souvenir of the old man."

"I don't like it." Brothers sighed. "I don't know what this is all about, but I don't like the smell of it."

"It is strange," admitted Smith.

"We've only got one obligation in this mess," said Brothers, "and that's to protect the President. I don't know what's going on yet, but when a fellow who keeps little knives around the house begins asking suspicious questions about the President, I want to know why."

Brothers stood up and shook his head. A man only a year away from a full pension had enough troubles without this sour brew being thrown in his face.

"Luther," he said, "I don't like to do it, but I want Senator MacVeagh kept under constant suveillance. And I want the interviewing continued. But be careful, for God's sake. Maybe there isn't anything wrong with MacVeagh, but if there is, you know something?"

"What?"

"He wouldn't be the first crazy congressman in this cruddy town."

Chief Arnold Brothers shrugged sadly. Then his nose began to itch and he whipped his sodden handkerchief aloft just in time to meet another violent sneeze.

10.

Routine Field

The MacVeagh-for-Vice-President drive gathered headway like a sailboat which swings off a close tack and begins running before the wind. Every day brought a new gust of support, just as planned by President Mark Hollenbach, the master planner.

The Wisconsin Democratic state chairman announced that he would back Senator MacVeagh for vice-president. A salute to a great man from a great sister state of the Midwest, he said. A day later, the lone Democratic senator from Wisconsin and all Democrats in the state's Congressional delegation added their support. Another MacVeagh write-in office opened in Green Bay, supplementing the original one in Milwaukee. Cards circulated throughout the state, instructing Democrats how to write in MacVeagh's name on the ballot of the otherwise meaningless presidential primary.

National Chairman Joe Donovan at first refused to talk to newsmen, but pressure mounted and he was forced to hold a press conference. He denied that he or anyone else at the national committee was lending covert support to MacVeagh. When newsmen countered with a statement from the Appleton city chairman, who said he'd been called by Donovan, soliciting support for MacVeagh, Donovan said the Appleton chairman completely misunderstood him. All he'd done, said Donovan, was to assure the Wisconsin people that any move for any candidate would not be frowned upon by the White House. While the President reserved to himself the right of final selection, he nevertheless welcomed evidence of support for any candidate around the country.

As for Hollenbach's own press conference, the vice-presidency monopolized the entire half hour in this second week since the announcement that Patrick O'Malley would not run for re-election because of the Kennedy sports arena scandal. Hollenbach sparred deftly, declining to single out MacVeagh for special praise and refusing to identify the seven persons reputedly on his list of possibilities. Obviously savoring the gathering suspense, Hollenbach stated his position as "of March, April and May."

"I have, as I said, narrowed my own preferences to seven persons," he said, "but as a Democrat I will always take counsel with my party. Therefore, I intend to listen carefully in the weeks ahead. If the Democrats of this country have a choice for vice-president and make it evident, I won't ignore the advice, but I do reserve the right to overrule it if circumstances so dictate. At this juncture, I am endorsing no one and opposing no one."

Press interpretation: A boost for MacVeagh.

A constant target for reporters himself, MacVeagh never varied his stance in scores of interviews. He appreciated the support of the many friends he appeared to have in Wisconsin, but he was not an active candidate for the nomination. The choice was the President's alone. The producer of NBC's "Meet the Press" program begged him to appear on the popular political panel inquisition, but MacVeagh steadfastly refused. It would place him in the role of a candidate, he said, and a candidate he was not.

An article about his declination appeared in the Washington *Post*, and President Hollenbach phoned MacVeagh as soon as he read the story, calling Jim away from the breakfast table.

"You did exactly right, Jim," said Hollenbach. His heartiness at eight in the morning was dismaying. "You don't need the exposure of a national TV show. Things are off to a booming start as it is. I'm very pleased the way things are going."

"Thanks, Mr. President," Jim answered, "but I must say I don't like this dissembling. I don't like to twist the truth."

"But you're not tampering with the truth," Hollenbach chided. "Have you been nominated for vice-president?"

"No, sir. I haven't."

"Neither have you been selected finally by me. I told you that as of now you're my preference and that we need to build you up. And that's exactly what we're doing, Jim."

The President was toying with him. Lord, how he enjoys this cat-and-mouse game, thought MacVeagh. "I realize that, Mr. President. But it's difficult to pretend that I'm not receiving White House support."

"This part is just the mechanics, Jim. You let me worry about it. What I want you to do is to begin giving some serious consideration to the grand concept." The President's voice took on a lilt and an eagerness. "We're going to need another good long talk about that soon. Some new ideas are percolating that I want to try out on you."

"Yes, sir," said Jim. "I'm anxious to hear them."

The phone call cracked the layer of normality which had formed like a crust over Jim's profound misgivings. For several days he'd felt remarkably like his old self. The excitement of the political maneuvering, the parry and thrust at sessions with the press, the phone calls from wondering politicians around the country, the ballooning requests for speeches—some with quite fancy fees—all combined to make him forget his suspicions. The ugly thought which led him to Griscom's sleek offices in the World Center Building had been smothered by the bustle of activity, the clamoring reporters, the telephones which jangled far into the night. The flurry and bounce of a campaign year clattered about him, and Jim felt almost normal again. He was too busy to reflect.

But the President's phone call, with its pointed reference to "the grand concept," plunged him into a quick, brooding depression. If Hollenbach's state was a temporary one, as Griscom had suggested, why this prolongation of the super-union fantasy? Life was not the same, after all. There was this other world, sinister, baffling, unreal, the shadowy world of Aspen lodge, and its banks of clicking computers recording every telephone call, its lurid spectacle of a consolidation of nations, and its petty, frightening rages against O'Malley, Davidge and Spence, three good men who meant no harm.

Jim left his McLean house absent-mindedly, forgetting the usual kiss for Martha and neglecting to pull down the garage door, a daily habit as ingrained as brushing his teeth.

Driving his convertible over the George Washington Parkway, he turned the windows down. The sharp morning breeze, bearing the scent of budding springtime, whipped through the car and plucked at the fabric top. His doubts about Mark Hollenbach refused to drift away. They lay heavy on his mind again, shutting out the fragrance of this new day of late March. He felt obstructed and thwarted, as though penned by a slowly rising fence. Paul Griscom had been no help at all. Instead, the lawyer thought that MacVeagh himself needed psychiatric aid. And that curious visit from Luther Smith. Why would a Secret Service agent question a United States senator, unless . . . Could it be that Smith actually suspected that he, MacVeagh, had harmful designs on the President? No, that was preposterous. Nobody could get such a wacky idea. Still, why the visit then? And why was he the only one who wondered about Mark Hollenbach? He'd asked around the Hill, cautiously, probing with questions tucked innocently into the flow of conversation. But not a single person had indicated that he'd noted anything strange about the President's behavior. Were those nights at Camp David only a dream, after all? Jim laughed derisively at himself. As an investigator, he'd make a good dump truck operator. About all that he'd accomplished so far was to make at least two people, Griscom and Smith, suspicious of Senator MacVeagh.

Glancing in the rear view mirror before making the loop to cross Memorial Bridge, MacVeagh's eyes held a moment on a gray sedan behind him. It resembled a hundred other cars, but something about it seemed vaguely familiar. He glanced again while curving around the Lincoln Memorial and again when he turned into Constitution Avenue. The gray sedan was still behind, driven by an apparently youngish man in a snap-brim felt hat. Of course. Now he realized. He had seen that same automobile behind him a number of mornings recently, but until now the fact had failed to register. He could not see the driver's full face, but the outline of the head and features triggered his memory. Was he being followed? MacVeagh turned left, just beyond the old Navy Building, and drove along 17th Street toward Pennsylvania Avenue. He eyed the rear-view mirror. The gray sedan also turned left into 17th. When MacVeagh turned right on Pennsylvania, so did the gray sedan with the snap-brimmed driver. Both cars passed the White House, bright in the morning sun. Why, damn it, he *was* being followed!

Suddenly a mental shape materialized as though the last pieces of a jigsaw puzzle had transformed meaningless bits into a logical whole. He thought he'd seen the same man near him a number of times recently, a tall, young man in snap-brim hat, his face blank and unconcerned. The man had been near him at a drugstore counter in McLean, again on Connecticut Avenue near

DuPont Circle, where he'd stopped to buy flowers for Martha, and once again when he took Chinky to the movies. Now he was sure. Also, at a Senate hearing, he'd seen another face that seemed familiar, a youthful face. Hadn't he seen those features on a campaign trip somewhere? Oregon, California? It began to fit together now, all of it. He, Senator James F. MacVeagh of Iowa, was being tracked. He was under surveillance by persons who knew their business.

Now he kept shifting his eyes constantly to the rear-view mirror. The gray sedan clung there, never more than one or two cars behind him. When he turned into the Senate Office Building's underground garage, he could see the sedan continue on down the street, slackening its speed.

The certainty that he was being watched, probably by federal agents, deepened his mood of dejection. He knew he should be either outraged or laughing out loud. The idea of a vice-presidential candidate being trailed by federal sleuths was either sinister beyond belief or it was utterly ridiculous. But Jim couldn't shake the black mood. He felt forlorn and vacant, as though slowly spiraling downward in an unknown void. Even a morning of more than ordinary activity failed to dispel his despondency. He dictated letters to prominent constituents, talked about the ever-inflating vice-presidential balloon with Flip Carlson, took a dozen phone calls, and received three sets of callers, including a group of 4-H youngsters from Iowa who filled his office with wholesome, rosy-cheeked exuberance. There was even a farcical episode that diverted Jim's mind for a few minutes. Mrs. Jessica Byerson, a dumpy, saccharine woman who had lobbied for years to get Congress to proclaim the white chrysanthemum as the national flower, waddled past the staffers in the outer office and flowed, unannounced, into Jim's sanctuary. He cringed at the sight of her, for Mrs. Byerson, the "mum's mum," was famous on Capitol Hill for her sudden ambushes of legislators. He shoved her out into the corridor through his private door by grasping both her elbows and trundling her ahead of him like a loaded cart. She wheezed a protest as Jim locked the door behind her. But even this interlude of heave-ho-manship failed to dispel his dark mood. The thought quickly returned and would not be erased: he was being shadowed by specialists at the trade of surveillance.

When the bell rang for the Senate session, he walked warily to the subway car, occasionally glancing over his shoulder. At his desk on the Senate floor, he found it difficult to concentrate on the debate, even though it involved a phase of defense policy on which he had specialized. Instead, he looked about the galleries, inspecting the faces, wondering which one, if any, was there to watch him. MacVeagh realized that he'd never been followed before—or tailed, as they termed it in the paperback mysteries. It unnerved him. Who, for instance, would believe him if he stated such surveillance as a fact? He saw plump, aging Fred Odlum sitting in the second row. Odlum, a shrewd, sardonic septuagenarian, whose eyes still darted covetously toward a swaying rump, was the senior senator from Louisiana, chairman of the Appropriations Committee, probably the most powerful man in the Senate. Suppose he were to ease over to Fred and whisper that he, MacVeagh, was being followed? Old Fred would fix him with those pale-gray hawk's eyes and tell him he ought to lay off the bottle until at least sundown.

MacVeagh sat for perhaps an hour, his thoughts moving fitfully from Camp David to Pat O'Malley to young men in snap-brim hats, his ear catching only fragments of debate. Then a page appeared respectfully at his elbow. The boy whispered his name and handed him a slip of paper: "Please call Briarwood 9-8877 at once. Urgent."

Rita's number. Rita, who had threatened to summon the police and the Associated Press simultaneously if he ever telephoned her again, now wanted him to call. He walked from the chamber, avoiding the telephones in the Democratic cloakroom. Instead, he dialed from a pay booth in the corridor.

"I have to see you immediately," she said. It was the voice of a stranger, crisp, commanding.

"The Senate's in session, Rita," he said. "We'll be here until late."

"This won't wait. You'd better come right now."

"What are you doing home this time of day?"

"I'm not feeling well," she said. Her tone was flat, did not beseech sympathy. "Something very distasteful has happened that involves both of us. I can't discuss it over the phone."

A thought hit MacVeagh like a clap of thunder. Oh, my God, she's pregnant. His hands became quickly clammy and he felt water in his legs.

"I'm supposed to be following this debate," he said, "but I'll get there as soon as I can."

"All right." She hung up without saying good-by.

It was after three o'clock when MacVeagh mounted the four brick steps on O Street after parking his car in a new place near Georgetown University. Leaving the Senate Office Building, he'd glimpsed the gray sedan again, but he had headed toward the Baltimore expressway, then doubled back and lost the sedan after several swift turns in the residential section of northeast Washington, far from Georgetown. The three blocks' walk from his parking space to Rita's apartment had seemed like ten miles, but he saw no snap-brim hat behind him.

Rita was wearing a prim black dress with a lace collar snug about her neck. She had on her thong sandals, but Jim noted her toenails had no crimson tint. The usual wide slash of matching lipstick was missing too. She motioned him to a straight-backed wooden chair in the small living room. In all his times in this apartment, Jim never before had sat in the parlor. The room had a formal, unused air, and he could see dust on the China knick-knacks on a wall shelf. Rita seated herself on a small sofa facing him. She did not smile.

"This is as disagreeable for me as it is for you," she said. "I'll get to the point right away."

"Rita." Compassion tugged at him, fighting to surmount his worry. "I'll do anything. You know that. The first thing we have to do is to get you examined by the best specialist we can find."

"Specialist?" Her black brows arched. "I'm not that sick. I don't need a doctor."

"Of course you do. How long has it been? . . . When did you first notice?"

"Notice what?" she asked coldly. "Would you mind speaking some semblance of English?"

"All right. How long has it been since you learned you were pregnant?"

"Pregnant!" She stared at him. Then she threw back her head and laughed, a loud, convulsive laugh that shook her mass of wavy black hair and filled the room like an explosion. She ended on a thin, high-pitched note which trailed into a dry giggle.

"That's rich," she said. "So you came scurrying over here, thinking I was—how do we say it stylishly? Enceinte? Did it scare you, MacVeagh?"

The use of his last name cut. He nodded.

"Good," she said. "At least something concerning me has managed to get under your skin. No, Mr. Senator, I'm not with child—yours or anybody else's. That problem I could handle. The one we're faced with I can't."

Jim hoped he hid his enormous relief. Nothing that he could imagine would be quite as bad, right at this time, as a pregnant Rita Krasicki. Absolutely nothing. It was hard to keep from smiling, but inwardly the tension broke and fled.

"This, my friend, is worse than fatherless babies," she said.

"Last night and again this morning I was visited by federal agents. The one last night was from the FBI. This morning, while I nursed this repulsive case of flu, my caller was a Secret Service agent. They both wanted to know approximately the same things."

"What, for God's sake?" asked MacVeagh, but he sensed the answer already. The gray sedan. The young men in the snap-brim hats.

"They wanted to know about you and me. The FBI man, very polite and circuitous, said this was just a routine field investigation. He beat around the bush for a while, then asked me point-blank whether you had ever visited me here. I hesitated for a minute, but then I realized it was useless to lie to the FBI. They have ways of checking—and I have my job to think about. So I said yes. He wanted to know how many times. I said maybe a dozen. Then he asked me, after apologizing for asking, whether we were intimate. I told him it was none of his damn business. That, I presume, is one thing still beyond the powers of the invincible FBI to find out."

"What did he say to that?"

"Nothing. He didn't even smile. He asked a few more questions about us, how long we'd known each other, that kind of thing, and then he left. Now, MacVeagh, I want to ask you a question. I haven't mentioned my—uh—friendship with you to a soul. Have you?"

"Never," said Jim promptly. Then he thought of Paul Griscom and his nonchalant disclosure of seeing a man on O Street who resembled a senator.

"Then how could the FBI have learned about us?" she asked, holding his eyes with hers.

"Paul Griscom lives across the street from you," he said. "I heard the other day that he thinks he's seen me entering and leaving your apartment."

"Isn't that just ducky?" She wrinkled her nose in distaste. "And so the FBI has been talking to Griscom about us, huh? Why? Just why, I'd like to ask."

"I haven't the foggiest," said Jim. The feeling returned, the feeling of being hemmed in by a slowly rising fence. They were silent a moment while she continued to stare at him. "I've only got one possible answer," he said. "It could be that Hollenbach has ordered a routine field check on all the men under consideration for vice-president."

"That would be highly unusual," she said. "No president has ever done a thing like that."

"Mark's a very unusual man," he said, "as we both know. If it's true, he's got one hell of a nerve, investigating a member of the United States Senate."

And, he added to himself, a man whom Hollenbach personally picked out of the crowd. His ire rose. He hadn't asked for this vice-presidential business. It was all Hollenbach's idea. And yet, apparently, the President distrusted him so much he put a tail on him as though he were a common crook. MacVeagh forgot Rita in his mounting anger.

"That doesn't add up," she said sharply. "The FBI, maybe yes. But how do you explain the call from the Secret Service? They don't have anything to do with security investigations."

"What did the Secret Service man want?"

"No," she said. "You tell me first. Why am I being questioned by the Secret Service?"

"I don't know, baby." The word slipped out by force of habit.

"Don't you dare 'baby' me. I want an answer."

"Honestly, Rita," he pleaded, "I don't know. How am I going to make a guess unless you tell me what happened?"

She glared at him. "He wanted to know the same things as the FBI man. How long had we known each other? Was it an affair?

Did you stay here overnight? The whole thing was absolutely disgusting and degrading. I felt undressed. And it was especially humiliating because I know the agent."

"Oh."

"Yes. His name is Luther Smith. I've known him awhile and I've always liked him. But now he must think I'm a cheap whore."

"Rita, please."

"Oh, it's all nice and proper for you, safe family man. Nothing ever touches the great, secret lover. But I feel filthy and common. Everybody in town will be talking about me."

"That's just not true, Rita. You know perfectly well that neither of those agents will ever say a word to anybody."

"They make reports, don't they?" she flared. "And how about your gabby friend, Paul Griscom? After talking to the FBI, he'll probably tell all his friends at Burning Tree—in the locker room. Need a girl in a hurry? Call Briarwood 9-8877 and ask for Rita." Her voice had an edge of fury, and her black eyes flashed. "Damn you, MacVeagh. I wish to God I'd never seen you."

Suddenly she began to cry, uncontrollably. Her broad shoulders heaved and she bunched into a corner of the sofa, rubbing at her tears with the back of a hand. Jim went to her side and touched her gently on the shoulder, but she wrenched away.

"Don't touch me," she cried.

When the sobbing ended, she at last accepted his proffer of a handkerchief, and she dried her eyes.

"And so," she said, "after the brief intermission for laughs, how do you explain the call from the Secret Service?"

"I don't." Jim felt his voice sounded far away. He wanted to tell her, but he couldn't, not without opening up the whole fantastic story of the nights of Camp David and his doubts about the President. She would never believe him, and even if she did, he could tell no one until he was sure. And when, if ever, would that be?

So, it was true. He was under surveillance and investigation by the Secret Service. Luther Smith, or perhaps Chief Brothers, had cause to question Jim MacVeagh's own mental processes. They knew of his recent late visits to Camp David, of his investigation in La Belle, and they must have concluded that MacVeagh bore watching lest he have designs on the safety of the President. Was that it? Was that their devious reasoning? The mood of depression lowered over him again like a black hood. He felt alone, divorced from this real world in which Rita sobbed for her shredding reputation.

He spoke softly to her. "I don't know what this is all about, Rita. All I can say is that I'll do my best to find out. And when I do I'll let you know."

She stood up to face him. Her olive face, bare of lipstick and rouge, seemed worn. Her shoulders slumped. Jim pitied her, but he noted there was no pang of the old desire. Lust had eroded like a shining piece of metal too long exposed to the rains. She seemed another Rita, defenseless, shorn of the stubborn Krasicki confidence.

"Forgive me, Jim," she said. "Our affair has always been more my doing than yours. I keep forgetting that it was I who called the last time. You didn't really want to come."

"No regrets. Remember? Rita, don't worry about this thing. There has to be some simple explanation, and as soon as I know I'll call you."

She brushed the cleft of his chin with a quick kiss. "Thanks . . . Jims."

MacVeagh walked down the four steps again, casting one hostile glance at the Griscom house across the street. Then he sank into his bewildering maze of thoughts, and he did not remember to look up and down O Street. He did not see a young man in snap-brim hat standing at the corner. Nor did he see the family station wagon in which Martha and Chinky were riding.

It passed as he started to walk toward Georgetown University.

"Hey, Mom," said Chinky inside the car. "There's Pops!"

Martha looked over her shoulder as she drove.

"No, Jane," she said quickly. "You're mistaken."

Chinky twisted around in the front seat and looked back into the drawing twilight.

"It is so too," she insisted. "No hat, and that mat of black hair, and the white alligator coat. And he walks just like Pops. Come on, Mom, stop and pick him up."

"You're mistaken, Jane," said Martha firmly. "Your father is at the Senate. They're still in session."

She pressed the accelerator and drove on. Chinky continued to stare back through the rear window, watching a man in a white coat who strode rapidly along the sidewalk.

11.

Patrick O'Malley

Heedless of other pedestrians, Jim MacVeagh walked toward
Georgetown University. The sinking sun still held a spring
warmth, but an evening breeze played along O Street, ruffling
Jim's thatch of black hair and plucking at his clothes. Automatically Jim buttoned his white all-weather topcoat. His
thoughts were on Rita and this new baffling development of the
FBI. A single investigation of a United States senator by a federal agency was extraordinary enough, but to become the magnet
for two sets of government sleuths was unheard of. Most certainly, he thought, the FBI questioning had been prompted by
Mark Hollenbach. Never before had Jim known of a president
ordering an investigation of his proposed vice-presidential candidate.

MacVeagh walked with his head down, his eyes on the uneven
brick sidewalks of Georgetown. Mark had a colossal gall, he
thought, sending FBI men around to question Jim's friends. The
very idea was insulting. And now of course, the FBI knew about
Rita, and soon, he surmised, a formal government report, as
colorless as a traffic summons, would be on the President's desk.
He could imagine the language: "Subject has visited the apart-

ment of a Mrs. Rita Krasicki, a widow employed at the Democratic National Committee, numerous times over a two-year period. Mrs. Krasicki refused to discuss the nature of their relations. Subject's visits customarily at night. A neighbor, R. Paul Griscom, an attorney, reports that subject often looks up and down the street before leaving Mrs. Krasicki's domicile. When interviewed, Mrs. Krasicki became angry. . . ." An emotion, thought MacVeagh, which could not approach the flashing rage of President Hollenbach when he read the document.

And so, Jim's brief fling at the vice-presidency would come to a tawdry and abrupt end. Rita? Jim felt a welling of sympathy for her, but he noted that his feeling was passionless. If their affair hadn't been over anyway, it had died forever in the little front parlor. Love might survive a hundred torments, but lust waned rapidly under duress. . . . But Mark's impressment of the FBI was of a piece with the gaudy grand concept of Camp David and the spluttering explosions over his supposed persecutors.

Jim's thoughts, a blue tangle of knots, were cut by a voice from a radio. A sweatered young man, probably a Georgetown University student, was standing at a corner curb, holding a tiny portable radio near his ear. Jim thought fleetingly that the youth must have eardrums of lead, for the volume was turned high. An announcer's voice was blaring:

We interrupt this program to bring you a special news bulletin. The White House has just announced that President Hollenbach will meet with Premier Zuchek of Russia on April 20 in Stockholm. An authoritative source says the summit conference will deal with the possibility of a united nuclear front against the threat of Red China which last month detonated its fifth "dragon bomb," a hydrogen weapon thought to be of a magnitude of 75 million tons of TNT. Repeating, President Hollenbach will meet with Premier Zuchek on April 20 in Stockholm, Sweden. Stay tuned to WRC for more details on the six o'clock news program.

Jim stood still for a moment, and once more he felt a twinge of apprehension, an increasingly common experience recently. Was time running out? In only about three weeks Hollenbach was to confront the stoic and practical Russian premier—in Sweden. Jim wondered if Hollenbach had stipulated the site and, if so, whether this was another cunning offshoot of the grand concept for a union with Scandinavia. Perhaps of a kind with Hollenbach's choice of a vice-president whose wife happened to be of Swedish stock?

Suddenly the thought struck MacVeagh: President Hollenbach must not be allowed to go into this conference with Zuchek. My God, Mark might be capable of anything. Who knew what fantastic secret agreement might emerge from such a meeting? Zuchek, a patient, steel-nerved negotiator, utterly devoted to Russia's self-interest, vs. Hollenbach, whose once brilliant mind now was obsessed with fancied tormentors and played like a child's with the toy blocks of destiny. The meeting had to be prevented, somehow, some way. And who else would attempt to stop it besides MacVeagh? Who else, indeed, even suspected what MacVeagh knew? He had to act at once. He knew it now. His own small concerns no longer mattered. Now it was a case of the country. The realization brought a faint smile to his face. Jim MacVeagh, playboy turned patriot. Country before self. All right, he thought, it may be corny, but it's true. Do something. Now.

Still in the trance of thought, MacVeagh looked uncertainly about him. A block away he saw a corner telephone booth. He walked quickly to it. He had to tell Martha he would be delayed. He dialed, and waited, but there was no answer at the McLean home.

Jim retrieved the dime, then consulted a small memo book which he always carried. In it he found the unlisted home telephone number of Vice-President O'Malley. He dropped in the coin and dialed. Mrs. Grace O'Malley, her voice as bright as a warbler's, expressed surprise. Not many important people wanted to talk to Pat these days, she said. But she called her husband to the telephone. O'Malley said he was just having his first belt of bourbon for the day. Urgent? Nothing was urgent any more, he said wistfully, but sure, come on over and have one before dinner.

Settled in his car, Jim remembered the gray sedan. He kept his eyes on the rear-view mirror as he drove. There was no gray sedan, but he soon became aware of a black one. He turned twice to test, and each time the black car turned up behind him. Jim drove to the garage on L Street behind the Statler Hilton Hotel, shoved a dollar in the attendant's hand, and then ran out the back, through the long, covered passageway to K Street. He took the first taxi at the cab stand and promised the driver a tip for extra speed on the way to Capitol Hill. O'Malley lived in a renovated two-story stone house, a block behind the Congressional Hotel, within easy walking distance of his office on the Senate side of the Capitol. Jim was relieved to find, when alighting, that no moving black sedan was in sight.

Grace O'Malley, a little woman with merry gray eyes and a quick laugh, hooked an arm through Jim's as she welcomed him. "He's in the library," she said, "probably thinking murderous things about sports arenas and contractors."

The library door was open. Vice-President Patrick O'Malley heaved himself out of a well-worn easy chair. His left hand was fastened about a glass; bourbon and water, Jim guessed. His right hand, large and fleshy, came out to shake MacVeagh's. Pat O'Malley had a long, jowly face which drooped comfortably like that of a basset hound. His paunch was solid and conspicuous, and he moved slowly. To meet Pat O'Malley for the first time was to relax immediately, as though one were entering a familiar saloon where the talk would be frank and never too refined.

O'Malley pumped MacVeagh's hand several times.

"You're a surprise, Jim," he said. "I thought the young Scot would be out in Wisconsin, making sure he got the mick's job."

"I'll admit I've got the bug now, Pat," said MacVeagh, "but only after you said you wouldn't run again. Pat, I've never told you I'm sorry, but I am, sincerely. You got an unlucky break."

O'Malley waved his big hand. "None of that, young fellow. That's all over and done with. These days, I'm wondering how an old pol goes about earning an honest living—for a change. Drink?"

Jim nodded. "Scotch-on-the-rocks."

O'Malley shook his head, the jowls swinging slightly. "They raise these Iowa boys on bourbon and branch water, and then they come east and get seduced by Scotch."

The Vice-President poured a drink from a row of bottles on a lower bookshelf, handed the glass to Jim, then lumbered back to his easy chair. It was dusk outside now, and O'Malley turned on a floor lamp beside his reading chair. Crowded bookshelves lined two walls of the room and the other paneled walls were thick with autographed pictures of politicians of both parties.

O'Malley, noting MacVeagh's eyes on the pictures, held his glass toward the rows of blurred faces. "Not many live ones left up there," he said. "I've been around a long time." The Vice-President grunted, leaned forward heavily toward a cigar box resting on an end table and took out a cigar sheathed in silverish foil. He unwrapped it slowly, bit off the end, spat the fragment into a large green ashtray, and fussed with the lighting. At last he blew out a doughnut of smoke and eased back in his chair. *The image is all against Pat*, thought MacVeagh. *With that fat cigar and those sagging jowls, he looks like a ward boss who'd play it low and crafty, but he isn't that way at all.*

"I'd offer you one, Jim," said O'Malley, "but I know you don't have the habit. Well, young fellow, what's so urgent?"

"Pat, there's no use puttering around the edges," said Jim. "Something frightening is happening here in Washington, and if what I suspect is true, this country's in deep trouble."

"And what do you suspect?"

"I suspect . . ." Jim paused, then lunged ahead. "I suspect on the basis of personal observation—and some collateral evidence —that President Hollenbach is suffering a severe mental ailment."

Jim intended to go on, but he stopped involuntarily, checked by the sound of his own words. He had thought and brooded over this thing for days, had sketched it without names for Griscom, but this was the first time he'd said it aloud. The words seemed to come from afar as though rocks had been thrown into a canyon and one had to wait for the series of crashes below. Then the imagined echo faded and there was silence in the room. O'Malley puffed noiselessly at his cigar. His eyes centered on MacVeagh, seeking to extract the intent behind the words.

"I've been in politics almost forty years," he said at last, his voice steady, "and that's the most serious charge I've ever heard."

"I know it, Pat. I've lived with this for two weeks now, and it's about to undo me. I've come to you only because you're the only one to go to. It's a long story and I think you ought to hear all of it."

O'Malley said nothing for a moment. Then he rose from his chair, went to the door and called his wife.

"Grace," he said when she answered from the foot of the stairs, "let's put dinner off for an hour or so, if we can. Senator MacVeagh and I need a little time to chat."

"Don't worry, dear," called his wife. "It's only stew. It'll keep."

O'Malley closed the door and returned to his chair, trailed by a funnel of smoke like an ancient steam locomotive. "All right," he said. "Let's have it."

This time, unlike his session with Griscom, MacVeagh told everything with names, omitting only the identity of Rita Krasicki. He began with the initial scene at Camp David, its intentional gloom and its wild, illogical outburst against O'Malley. He told of the similar eruption against Craig Spence, and again, from another source, of the causeless explosion over Davidge, the banker. Jim went into detail to describe his second session at Camp David when the grand concept was unveiled. He told of Hollenbach's glittering eyes, his tumbling speech, and his maniacal vow to use force, if necessary, against the nations of Europe. Then he recounted the events since his second eerie meeting at Aspen lodge: Flip Carlson's trip, the quizzing by Luther Smith, the shadowing by federal agents, and even the questioning of Rita. Although he did not name her, he hinted at the intimacy of their affair and told of his talk with her that afternoon. The recital consumed more than half an hour.

O'Malley did not interrupt, but he kept his eyes fixed on MacVeagh, shifting them only occasionally to inspect the coils of smoke from his cigar. The room became hazed. Again there was silence while O'Malley squashed out the butt.

When O'Malley spoke, his voice was keyed unnaturally low. "Jim, I wonder if you realize the impression you convey by that story?"

"What do you mean?"

"I mean that anyone listening to you might arrive at the conclusion that you're the paranoid, not Hollenbach."

Jim felt the pit of his stomach go hollow. First Griscom, then Luther Smith and now Pat O'Malley.

"Good God, Pat!" he exclaimed, and he realized at once that his voice squeaked with strain. He tried to resume a conversational tone. "Honestly, Pat, you don't think I'm nuts, do you?"

"Look at the facts," said O'Malley, ignoring the question. "Here you are at age thirty-eight, a first-term senator, really a kid at this business, and you're running a write-in campaign for my job. Delusions of grandeur? And these investigations by the Secret Service and the FBI, the stories about being followed by fast sedans driven by inscrutable young men. Persecution complex? And, let's face it, young fellow. You're obviously in a highly agitated state."

Jim found it an effort to throttle his emotions, to keep his voice on an even pitch. "Pat, since you won't answer my question, let me ask you another one. What sort of mood was Mark Hollenbach in that Tuesday night when he called you to the White House and demanded your resignation?"

O'Malley looked startled. "Well, he . . . he was goddam mad. Frankly, he blew his stack."

MacVeagh took a chance. "Flipped his lid is the common phrase for it, isn't it? And isn't it true that he accused you of trying to sabotage him by the way you handled your defense on the Jilinsky charges? That you plotted the whole thing just to defeat Hollenbach in November—the same screwy charges he made to me about you? Well, am I right?"

O'Malley bit his lower lip and fingered his jowls as he thought. "Well, yes, you're right. He really let me have it. If it had just been Jilinsky and the arena case, I'd have understood. But I thought his charge that I'd intentionally plotted his downfall was absurd. It didn't make any sense."

"Of course it didn't," said MacVeagh quickly. "It made no sense at all—and from a mind that prides itself on logic. Pat, that kind of accusation could only come from a warped mind.

"Take another thing. How about Hollenbach's weird idea for a national wiretapping law? That was no joke at the Gridiron dinner. The President told me at Camp David that he was utterly serious about it. Just imagine hundreds of FBI agents combing through all the private phone conversations in this country? And that from a long-time champion of civil liberties. It's not only idiotic, it's insane. For Christ's sake, Pat, admit it."

It seemed to MacVeagh that O'Malley was about to nod agreement, but checked himself. Instead, the Vice-President huddled deep into his chair, his full face brooding and his eyes staring at MacVeagh again.

"Jim," he said, "let me ask you a blunt question. Why are you so anxious to prove that the President of the United States is insane?"

MacVeagh had the sensation that he was butting his head into mist. O'Malley's doubts were thick in the room, and nothing he had said seemed to have dispersed them. He wanted to lash out in anger, and again it was an effort to control himself.

"Pat," he said, very slowly, "believe me, I'd rather find my own daughter with a deranged mind than to have this forced on me. And why, in God's name, would I want to right now? You probably don't know it, but Mark called me into his office and said he wanted me to be his running mate. I didn't start this vice-presidential business. He did. It was all his idea. He proposed it and planned it. The write-in in Wisconsin is all his doing. I'm not exaggerating a bit. So, obviously, if I keep quiet now, I'll be Vice-President next January 20. You know that, Pat. The Republicans don't have a chance against Hollenbach. So why would I want to spoil all that?"

"That's what I'm wondering, Jim," said O'Malley quietly, "but I'm not getting an answer."

"Now look, Pat. Don't make me go into all that jazz about the system, the Constitution, and the country. Sure, we all honor them, and we'd do anything to preserve them. But it's more simple than that. I'm beginning to think of myself as a pro at this business even if you don't think so. And, as a tradesman, I don't want some crazy man running my business at the top."

O'Malley grinned, suddenly, for the first time since he'd poured the Scotch. "You're talking my language," he said. He reached out for MacVeagh's glass. "You need a refill, and so do I."

When he fetched the drinks and seated himself again, O'Malley hoisted his glass and smiled. "I like you, Jim. I always have. No, of course I don't think you've lost your buttons. But that doesn't mean I come to the same conclusion you do. I'll grant you that Hollenbach has a mean temper, but, Christ, man, I've seen a dozen worse in my time."

"I'm sorry I can't describe those nights at Aspen the way they were," said Jim. "His eyes, the way he looked, the gloom, and that torrent of words. If you'd heard and seen what I did, Pat, you wouldn't be doubting."

"Maybe, and maybe not," said O'Malley. "Another thing bothers me. Even if you're right, perhaps it's a temporary state, as Griscom indicated. What makes you think that something has to be done right now?"

"The meeting with Zuchek in Sweden, of course. I don't think a man suffering a mental ailment—of whatever nature or duration—should be representing the United States in any two-man conference with a guy as tough as Zuchek."

"Zuchek? Sweden?" asked O'Malley. "What are you talking about?"

"You mean you don't know about the summit conference—for April 20—that the White House has just announced?"

O'Malley shook his head. "Nobody tells me anything in advance any more." His small smile was bitter. "They don't even trust me around an arena these days."

"The White House made the announcement about five o'clock," said MacVeagh. "That's why I called you and said it was urgent. It is. We've got to stop Hollenbach from going to Sweden."

"Assuming, that is, that your analysis of Hollenbach is correct." O'Malley unwrapped another cigar and went through the tedious ritual of lighting it. "Let's backtrack a minute. As I get it, there's only one person besides yourself who has observed Mark in one of these tantrums that you claim are evidence of a persecution complex."

MacVeagh shook his head. "No. Two. You saw one instance yourself. You just admitted that."

"I don't count that," said O'Malley. "That was just a case of a man who got so angry he said things he didn't really mean."

"But it's all part of the pattern," insisted MacVeagh.

"Not if you don't concede the existence of a pattern."

"Good Lord, Pat. How much corroboration do you need?"

"Well, for one thing," said O'Malley, studying a fat smoke wreath, "I think if I were making a similar accusation I'd be willing to reveal the name of the woman you say heard this eruption over Davidge."

"I can't, Pat." MacVeagh's tone was pleading. "I've told you we were very close. Isn't that enough? Why do I have to drag her into this—to say nothing of my wife?"

"Ah, man and woman. And they talk about deceit in politics . . ." O'Malley's voice trailed off.

It occurred to Jim that O'Malley must be comparing his own situation to that of MacVeagh. He had been broken from the vice-presidency for a violation of ethical standards involving finances, and now here was a young senator, with only a fraction of O'Malley's experience, being selected for the same office despite an offense that both Hollenbach and O'Malley would consider more repugnant than O'Malley's own lapse. Jim could sense that this big, friendly man before him felt the injustice and yet, curiously, he knew that O'Malley would never say a word about Jim's marital transgressions. O'Malley had his code. "Man and woman" relations were never to be mentioned.

"Jim," said O'Malley, "I can't buy your conclusions, even though I know you're telling me the truth as you see it. But, assuming for a moment that you're correct, why come to me? What can I do about it?"

"That's obvious, Pat. You're the man who has the inability agreement with the President. As I understand it, and I've read an awful lot on the situation recently, you're the only one who can act. You're the one man who can invoke the disability clause."

"Clause?" asked O'Malley. "You mean the disability thing in the amendment we put through a few years ago?"

Jim nodded.

"That provides," said O'Malley, "that the President can declare himself in writing, stating he's unable to continue in office. Or, lacking that, the Vice-President can take over with the written consent of a majority of the Cabinet."

O'Malley took a sip of his drink and studied MacVeagh over the rim of his glass.

"Obviously you don't think President Hollenbach would put anything in writing indicating he's of unsound mind?"

"No, of course not," replied Jim. "But you can take over the presidency with written backing from a majority of the Cabinet."

O'Malley set his drink aside. His lips shifted his cigar to a corner of his mouth in a curious movement that left the cigar tilted belligerently upward. He stared at MacVeagh and shook his head as though in rebuke.

"I guess you haven't thought this thing through, young fellow," he said. "The provision we passed in the sixties after the hearings of the Birch Bayh committee was all right as far as it went, but nobody ever supposed it could be used to handle anything as complex as a mental ailment. A heart attack, a stroke, some obvious and apparent physical accident, sure, then anybody can see the President is disabled. But this mental stuff is something else. It's all too hypothetical, too sticky. It's like trying to find a dime in a pot of glue." O'Malley shrugged. "I wouldn't want any part of it," he added, "even if I were convinced you were right."

MacVeagh persisted despite his feeling of dismay. "But Pat, paranoia—and that's what I guess it is with the President—could be even worse than a physical handicap. Imagine a paranoiac bargaining with Zuchek or suddenly facing a major decision on use of the bomb."

"I grant all that," said O'Malley, "but look at the practicalities. How would I ever convince a majority of the Cabinet on the evidence you have? There wouldn't be one chance in ten. In addition, the President of course would hear about it, and then there'd be sheer hell to pay. It would tear the administration apart."

O'Malley blew a fat, gray smoke ring which floated lazily upward and slowly disintegrated. Jim, watching it, felt his own hopes of action dissolving, yet he felt an inner compulsion to press on.

"You're talking about the Constitution and the amendment," said MacVeagh, "but how about your own special agreement with Hollenbach? Under that, you're required to act if you have evidence the President can't carry on his duties."

"Required!" O'Malley snorted and looked at MacVeagh in disbelief. "You can't be serious, Jim. Have you read the agreement?"

"Of course," said MacVeagh, somewhat testily.

O'Malley hoisted himself out of his chair and walked to the bookcase. He drew down a tan, ridge-backed volume.

"This is my annotated volume of the Constitution," he said. "Mark has the original of our agreement, but I keep my copy in the front of this book. Here, read it."

MacVeagh took the paper. It was a single-spaced typewritten sheet, dated three days after the Hollenbach inauguration, signed in ink by both men and impressed with the presidential seal.

Agreement between Mark Hollenbach, President of the United States, and Patrick J. O'Malley, Vice-President of the United States.

The undersigned state it to be their joint intention that under no circumstances shall the continuity of government be permitted to be broken by reason of inability of the President to discharge his duties. Even a hiatus of a few days might do irreparable damage to the nation. Following the precedent established by Dwight D. Eisenhower and Richard M. Nixon in the 1950's, and adhered to since by their successors, the undersigned agree:

1. That upon clear evidence that Mark Hollenbach is no longer able to discharge the duties of the office of President, Patrick J. O'Malley shall act promptly to set in motion the procedures provided by constitutional amendment and by law.

2. That, upon such clear evidence, Mr. O'Malley shall in no case delay longer than 24 hours in carrying out his obligations under Point One (1) above.

The undersigned have studied all prior agreements between Presidents and Vice-Presidents and have taken special note of a letter written by former President Eisenhower to Senator Birch Bayh of Indiana on March 2, 1964. Mr. Eisenhower concluded that letter on the problem of presidential inability by stating:

"There is, of course, no completely foolproof method covering every contingency and every possibility that could arise in the circumstance now under discussion. We must trust that men of good will and common sense, operating within constitutional guidelines governing these matters, will make such decisions that their actions will gain and hold the approval of the mainstream of American thinking."

The undersigned realize, with General Eisenhower, that not every contingency can be foreseen. We have decided, therefore, to keep this agreement, as embodied in Points One (1) and Two (2) above, as simple and as broad as possible, thus affording the utmost elasticity to cope with unforeseeable events of the future, while at the same time stressing the need for dispatch in ensuring continuity of government.

The undersigned rely on mutual good faith and trust to carry out this agreement in the spirit of the Constitution and the laws of the United States of America, and they urge the citizens of the United States to accept this agreement in similar faith and trust.

Mark Hollenbach
Patrick J. O'Malley

When MacVeagh finished reading, he held the paper toward O'Malley, indicating the first numbered paragraph with a finger.

"There," he said, " 'Upon clear evidence,' you 'shall act promptly.' It doesn't say 'may.' It says 'shall.' You've got no alternative. You're required to act."

O'Malley shook his head and smiled gently. "Jim, you ought to have better sense than that. You're skipping over the most important words—'upon clear evidence.' Clear evidence? What clear evidence do I have that Mark is unable to discharge his duties?"

They were standing by the bookcase, and MacVeagh grasped O'Malley's elbow, pulling the larger man toward him.

"What the hell do you want, Pat?" His voice rasped with frustration. "Jesus, do you need a medical report, signed by fifteen psychiatrists? Or a vote of Congress? Or an affidavit from the dean of Johns Hopkins medical school, or something else that would take us umpteen months to get hold of? I tell you the President of the United States isn't in his right mind."

O'Malley pulled his arm away, slid the paper inside the book again, and replaced it on the shelf. Then he put his arm around MacVeagh and guided him to his chair. O'Malley didn't speak again until he'd lowered himself into his own easy chair and taken another swallow of bourbon. Then his voice was low and friendly.

"Look, Jim, I know the pressure you've been under, and I can imagine the anguish you've suffered before you could bring yourself to come talk to me. Believe me, I do. An outsider might not, but anybody in our business knows there'd be a lot of sleepless nights before a United States senator would make that kind of a charge that you have—even in private.

"But, young fellow, you just don't understand the circumstances under which that agreement with Hollenbach was made. In the first place, I didn't have a thing to do with writing it. Hollenbach just called me in one afternoon, three days after the inauguration, and asked me to read it. He said the Attorney General had written a long, legal document, but it was too cumbersome and complicated, so he'd just written one of his own. He asked me if I wanted to make any change. I said no, it looked all right to me. So we signed three copies and sent the last one to the Attorney General.

"Now, in the second place, I'll never forget what he said afterward. He said, 'Pat, this thing is just for the record and it doesn't mean a thing.' He said he was sound of mind and body, that the only thing he'd ever had was a slight heart murmur some years before, but that it was all gone now. And then he added, with a laugh, that he didn't want me ever trying to invoke the agreement on mental grounds. He said he was no Woodrow Wilson and never would be."

MacVeagh had calmed as he listened. He rubbed the bridge of his nose pensively.

"In my book, Pat," MacVeagh said, "Mark Hollenbach is a lot worse off now than Wilson ever was. At least, Wilson's trouble had a physical source. He'd had a stroke, and there was always the expectation that he'd recover. But with Mark it's a psychic thing, a case of a disordered mind that may never be set right again."

"We're talking at cross-purposes, Jim," said O'Malley. He was puffing on his cigar again, his head tilted back against the chair. "You see, you're convinced that Mark's mind is deranged, and I'm not at all sure of it. And so we come down to a basic dilemma of presidential disability that has vexed constitutional lawyers ever since the document was drafted almost two hundred years ago. Let me go into a little history for you."

O'Malley talked, slowly and patiently as though instructing a college seminar. The Vice-President sketched the history of dispute and inaction over the "inability" subsection of the Constitution. He recalled how Vice-President Chester Arthur had declined to assume the presidential duties even though President Garfield lay wounded and almost inert for eighty days before his death from an assassin's bullet, and how Vice-President Tom Marshall let Mrs. Wilson and the White House physician, Cary Grayson, virtually run the country during almost two years of President Wilson's incapacity. No man, said O'Malley, could ever act lightly in attempting to remove the President of the United States. The office, if not always the man, commanded a respect and an awe that almost amounted to reverence. And so it should always be, said O'Malley. As the Vice-President talked, his jowls wobbling and his fleshy hands waving points of emphasis, Jim realized how little he really knew of this Irish politician who resembled a cartoonist's version of a Tammany boss. O'Malley obviously had steeped himself in the history of a vice-president's relationship to his superior. What's more, he brought to the subject a sense of fitness and proportion that no amount of scholarly research could develop. Pat O'Malley, decided Mac-Veagh, was a wise man. The Vice-President talked uninterrupted for half an hour.

"I've always thought," he concluded, "that the best solution— there is no perfect solution—is the one we've got right now, the one enacted under the Johnson administration. It may be cumbersome, but it's workable."

"It doesn't seem to be working now," observed Jim wryly.

"The machinery's there," retorted O'Malley. "You just don't have the evidence—or the confidence—to use it. You want me to take the initiative, and I won't do it. I wouldn't make a move any more than did Chester Arthur or old Tom Marshall."

"Would you," asked MacVeagh, "if you were convinced his mind was abnormal?"

O'Malley flipped a lengthening ash into the green ashtray, frowning and studying the act as though it were a complex mechanical operation. He shook his head. "No, Jim, I wouldn't —not without solid backing from the leaders of the party. In the special circumstances existing right now, a move like that would rip the country to pieces. Have you forgotten Art Jilinsky and the Kennedy memorial sports arena?"

"No, of course not."

"Well, then, who do you think would believe me now?" O'Malley's tone was caustic. "They'd say I was an ugly old crook, bent on revenge for being dumped as vice-president. And what about Hollenbach? Assume he's the paranoid you think he is. Why, he'd be patronizing and righteous, and he'd dismiss me as a meddling fool. Let's face it, Jim. The country would either drown me in ridicule or I'd be written off as a power-mad scoundrel who was trying to get even."

It was full night outside now, and Jim could feel his resolution being smothered in the folds of darkness. It was as though the last window light had winked off in a blind alley. He made a final effort.

"Look, Pat," he said. "You say you wouldn't invoke the agreement unless you had the solid backing of the leadership. I know you have reservations about everything I've said, but couldn't it be true that your doubts are compounded by your own particular position at this time? Suppose, then, you let me tell my story to a small group of leaders whom you'd name. The Cabinet, we both realize, is too unwieldy and too prone, frankly, to leak anything that's said. But a small group could meet privately, with a stipulation that everything said was off the record.

Then, if the group didn't believe me, that would end it. But if it felt action was necessary, then you'd have real support to invoke the agreement and go to the Cabinet formally. Or maybe some further investigation could be figured out. What about it?"

O'Malley showed interest. "That's possible," he said.

MacVeagh brightened. "Okay, suppose you invited the three most influential men on the Hill, say Speaker Nicholson, Fred Odlum and—the House Republican leader, to make it bipartisan?"

O'Malley bridled. "No Republicans," he said. "I'm not going to have any Republican listen to the kind of pure conjecture that's involved here."

"But, Pat," protested MacVeagh, "this is a matter for the nation, not the party. Suppose you had to act? Suppose it came down to that? You'd want the support of both parties."

"I'm not going to trust any Republican with that kind of ammunition in a campaign year," said O'Malley flatly. "I may have been thrown off the ticket, but I'm no turncoat. No, that's out."

MacVeagh beat a judicious retreat, but he refused to surrender now that O'Malley appeared to be in the mood.

"All right, then," he said, "how about Grady Cavanaugh? He's got the stature, on the Supreme Court, and he's one Democrat everybody trusts."

"Grady would be fine," agreed O'Malley. "And, besides, he's got a great mind for sifting evidence. Frankly, I'd place a lot of reliance on what he thinks of your story."

And so it was settled. They talked about the arrangements, and both agreed that if Cavanaugh assented, it would be best to hold the meeting at his country home. Cavanaugh was a widower who owned 200 acres with a farmhouse on a high hill overlooking St. Leonard's Creek, about 60 miles from Washington. The Supreme Court justice spent his weekends there. The place was isolated and secluded, set off from the main highway by thick woods. This was a Monday night, and they agreed on Thursday night for the meeting, if it was convenient for the others.

O'Malley accompanied MacVeagh down the stairs and through the narrow hall to the front door. Grace O'Malley leaned out of a doorway.

"Do you two connivers realize it's nine o'clock?" she asked. "You've been talking—or drinking—for more than three hours. And Pat told me he was through with politics."

"But we're not through with him, Grace," said Jim.

"I can see—I mean I can smell—that you aren't. Say hello to Martha for me, Jim."

At the front door O'Malley shook Jim's hand in a friendly grip.

"Jim," he whispered, "I can tell you right now that your story won't be believed Thursday night unless you can produce the woman who can tell us about Hollenbach and Davidge."

"Pat, please," Jim pleaded.

"I mean it."

Jim frowned. "We'll see," he said.

12.

Martha

The mood of dejection which enveloped him like a cocoon almost constantly these days was upon Jim again as he rode away in a taxi. The only consolation, a thin one, was the realization that apparently he had not been followed to O'Malley's house. There was no evidence of pursuit as the taxi rolled down Constitution Avenue to the garage on L Street, near 16th, where he'd left his convertible.

But even that minor victory dissolved when he reclaimed his car and drove toward McLean. The rear-view mirror disclosed a black sedan maintaining the pace about a hundred yards behind. Jim watched the trailing vehicle for a bit, but then dismissed it. Now that he was on his way home, he really didn't care how many diaries of surveillance recorded the fact. Jim's thoughts centered bleakly on O'Malley. The Vice-President, Jim surmised, probably had an instinctive feeling that Jim was right, but O'Malley's mind obviously refused to accept the fact. Only unanimous agreement by the leaders Thursday night would propel O'Malley to action. Jim knew that somehow he must convince these four men of the nation's danger. But wasn't Pat right? Would they ever believe him unless they heard the Davidge story from Rita herself? And how could he persuade her to talk, especially when she had no inkling of his conviction about Hollenbach's mental state?

Thinking of Rita made him realize that Martha had no idea where he was. It had been four hours since he'd called from the Georgetown phone booth and gotten no answer. MacVeagh pulled into a gas station at the foot of Key Bridge and called home. Martha listened in silence to his explanation.

"Where are you calling from?" she asked.

"A pay station on M Street near Key Bridge."

"Oh, yes. Georgetown." She sounded dispirited.

When Jim turned into his driveway in McLean, the open garage was dark, but his headlights framed a figure standing inside. It was Martha, leaning against the workbench which Jim hadn't used in weeks. She held the collar of a cloth coat about her throat against the chill of the night, and she blinked in the glare. When Jim turned off the ignition, she leaned inside the convertible.

"Jim," she said, "take off that white coat and put it in the trunk of the car."

"Why?"

"Don't ask questions," she said, her tone peremptory. "Just do it."

He leaned across the front seat to kiss her, but she pulled back. Jim questioned, blankly, but Martha merely jerked her head toward the rear of the car. Jim took off the topcoat, unlocked the trunk compartment and stowed the coat beside the spare tire.

"What the devil . . . ?" But Martha was walking across the lawn to the front door, a hand clutching her coat collar.

In the vestibule, Chinky greeted him with a hug and a kiss on the cheek. The pony tail stretched her hair tight from her forehead, and her wide, brown eyes shone with pleasure. Chinky rubbed a hand over his sleeve.

"It's cold out, Pops. Where's your topcoat?"

Martha, standing beside them, spoke quickly. "He lost it," she said. "He left it in a restaurant this noon, and somebody took it.

Your dad's getting absent-minded in his middle age."

Jim stared at his wife. She returned the look without smiling, her face impassive. Martha turned to the closet and removed her coat, then stood fluffing her brown, close-bobbed hair before the closet door mirror.

"Oh, so it wasn't you after all this afternoon?" asked Chinky.

Jim stared again, this time at his daughter.

"What are you talking about, Chinky?" he asked. "Who wasn't me? Where?"

Chinky planted her legs wide apart, her favorite stance. She tilted her head as she surveyed him.

"Mom and I saw a man coming out of a house on O Street this afternoon," she said. "He had messy black hair, just like you, and no hat, just like you, and he wore a white alligator coat too. I was sure it was you, Pops. I even wanted to stop and pick the man up."

Jim shot a glance at Martha, but she was intent on the mirror. Her lips were pressed tightly together.

"No, it wasn't me," Jim improvised. "I've been in conference with Vice-President O'Malley, up on the Hill, ever since the Senate quit."

"Pops," said Chinky, "you'd better watch out. You've got a double. The guy better behave himself."

Jim could not bring himself to look at Martha. It was all plain to him now, and he could feel color creeping into his cheeks. So Martha knew. How did she find out? Suddenly, he felt a thrust of pride for his wife. She knew, but she was shielding Chinky from the knowledge. He turned to thank her, mutely, but Martha was already walking toward the kitchen, her high heels clicking a brisk tattoo on the floor.

"I'll fix the leftovers for you," she said.

Jim ate alone in the kitchen. The cold meat loaf seemed tasteless and he pushed it away, half eaten. Instead, he drank two glasses of milk and foraged in the freezer top of the refrigerator until he found a pint of chocolate ice cream. Martha stayed out of the kitchen. From Chinky's room came the usual discordant sounds. She was on a telephone extension, prattling to some unknown teen-age confidante. Jim felt like a stranger in his own house. He dawdled over the ice cream, trying to put off the moment when he had to face Martha alone. Later, in the upstairs den, he tried to read, but his eyes kept roving over the same column of type in a news magazine, and he realized he was absorbing nothing.

When he finally went to bed, Martha was lying far to her side. When he settled himself, almost a foot separated them. The middle of the bed stretched as vacant and cold as new snow. Martha's breathing was regular, but forced, and Jim knew that she was feigning sleep. He wanted to reach out and fold her to him, as he did every night, but he could not make his arm move. They lay there unspeaking, both rigid, their breathing clamoring over the unseen wall between them. Finally, she turned slightly and spoke. Her tone was flat.

"Jim," she said, "I know something has been troubling you lately. I've sensed it ever since we got home from Iowa. Do you want to tell me?"

"I do, Marty." He answered eagerly. "It's a frightening thing and it's worrying the hell out of me. I want to tell you, but I can't."

There was a long silence. The air hung heavy between them.

"Jim," she said in almost a whisper, "I know her name."

He said nothing. He waited, tensed, and he was conscious of his heart beating against the lower sheet.

"I've known for four or five weeks," she continued. "I heard about it quite a while before Jane and I went to Des Moines."

"Martha." He felt limp and lost, and he was reminded of the time he'd undergone a spinal tap, testing for polio. When the needle struck, his body went totally slack, a bottomless feeling, as though every source of energy had been drained at once by a huge suction pump. The sensation lasted only a few seconds, but it seemed timeless. And so it was now.

At last Jim touched Martha's back awkwardly. He searched over the sheen of her nightgown for her hand and when he found it, he squeezed hard.

"Marty," he said softly, "all I can say is that I love you deeply. I made a terrible mistake, a thoughtless one, but it all ended— some time ago."

And as he said it, three weeks seemed not just "some time ago" but an eternity in the past. At this moment he wished with all his being that he had never met Rita Krasicki.

"But, if it's all over," asked Martha, her face still averted and the pillow swallowing her words, "why were you at—at her place —this afternoon?"

"I can't tell you, Martha. It's all mixed up with this other thing, this thing about national security, I guess you'd call it. Someday I can tell you, but not now. You'll just have to trust me, Martha."

His response was instinctive, but no sooner had he made it than Jim began analyzing his reasons for refusing to tell Martha everything. It would be natural to tell her, his own wife, the entire haunting story about President Hollenbach, from beginning to end. But to her, he knew, it would sound fantastic, incredible. A crazy president? She would immediately assume he'd concocted the whole weird tale to distract her from his affair with Rita. And if he did tell everything, how could he explain where —and when—he learned Rita's story of the President's savage indictment of Davidge. No, his instinctive reply had been the correct one. He just couldn't tell Martha—not now.

Martha said nothing. Jim lay taut as a steel band under tension. His skin felt hot and dry. He got out of bed and went to the bathroom for a drink of water, then fumbled in the medicine cabinet for a sleeping pill. He took one, gulping down a full glass of water afterward. Back in bed, he found the frigid gap still between them.

"Jim," she said, "I'd give anything on earth if I could trust you again."

And he realized that the gay, twittering woman, abrim with a hundred ventures, was no longer with him. This Martha was withdrawn, lonely, remote. He put his hand on the smooth curve of her hip, but she thrust it away and turned on her stomach. She began to sob, quietly, into the pillow. Then the crying became louder, and her body twitched with the convulsive sounds in her throat. Jim sensed that the tears were flowing from her eyes and that her pillow was becoming wet. He put both arms around her and drew her into the hollow of his body. She did not resist. She merely lay inert, like a lifeless bundle. Slowly the crying faded into scattered sobs and her muscles began to relax. At last she wriggled slightly, moving closer to him. Then her breathing became rhythmic, and she fell asleep in the nest of her husband, as she had done night after night for more than fourteen years.

But Jim still lay awake while distorted images moved through his mind. He could see Martha, small and frail, her cloth coat clasped about her throat. He could see Rita sitting stiffly in her Georgetown parlor, and he could see Pat O'Malley's drooping jowls through a haze of cigar smoke. Behind it all there came and went the vision of a huge window and a blanket of snow stretching away from Aspen lodge toward a pale horizon. It was almost an hour before the sleeping pill took effect.

Jim felt prickly and unrested the next morning. His head throbbed with each passage of the electric shaver over his jawbone. And then, as he finished shaving, the thought came to him.

Of course. It was the only honorable way. He had to do it.

Why hadn't he realized it before? It was so simple. Unless he took the step, his situation was impossibly compromising and stultifying. The decision made, he felt somewhat better, and he hurried his dressing, anxious to get the scene over with.

Chinky had left for school, and Martha was alone at the breakfast table in the little alcove with its gingham curtains. Martha's face was drawn, but her snub nose crinkled when she saw him, and she smiled shyly. Steam curled from the cup of coffee by his place. Martha slid the *Post* across the table toward him. The morning routine was unchanged, as though there had been no night of sobbing.

"The President is going to meet Zuchek," she said.

"I know," said Jim. "That's why I had to talk to O'Malley last night . . ." He checked himself, then met her eyes across the table.

"Marty," he said, "I'm not going to run for vice-president, Mark Hollenbach or no Mark Hollenbach. I'm going to tell him this morning."

Her pale lashes fell and she avoided looking at him. He frowned, puzzled for a moment, but then he knew. Of course, she thought he couldn't run for vice-president because of fear that the affair with Rita would be exposed.

Martha raised her head and smiled, a weary smile, but a fond one. Quickly she moved around the table, buried her head against his neck and kissed him. Her arms held him, and he could feel moisture from her eyes.

"Thank you, Jim," she whispered. "I love you so. And I've been foolish too. Too much dashing around. Too many zombie clubs. Some of them have got to go."

"Take it easy, Marty," he said. "I like you when you're excited and busy. It's your way."

She shook her head, rubbing his nose with hers. "But not too busy. From now on, my big project is you."

He grinned. "Well, maybe the Committee for More Effective Urban Renewal could get along without you."

"And the embassy tour and the Smith alumni fund drive too," she said.

"Okay."

She kissed his cheek. "Please, Jim," she whispered softly, "please don't ever leave me again."

"Never, Marty." And this time he felt he meant it, as he had never meant anything before in his life.

And then, while the ringlets of her hair still brushed his cheeks, he realized, with a shock, that she was expressing gratitude. She believed that he'd decided to abandon the vice-presidency so that no scandal would embarrass his wife. She must think he feared a campaign revelation of the Rita affair and that he was determined to spare his wife the injury to her pride. Lord, what a slithery mess this was getting to be. First, Martha thought he lied about the affair being over, and now she was embracing him as an instant hero.

Actually, he thought, concern for Martha had little to do with his decision. Nor concern for Rita, nor for himself, for that matter. What really impelled him was the threat to the country and his own responsibility to function as a free agent. Who would ever understand that? Would anybody? The feeling returned, the feeling he experienced fitfully earlier—that of a noose being tightened slowly but irresistibly about his neck. He could feel Martha's arms still about him, and he wondered if he could any longer trust his own impulses.

A feeling not unlike panic closed about him, but he made an effort to ward it off. One step at a time, Jim, he told himself. He kissed Martha and pushed her gently away.

"Honey," he said, "I might as well get it over with. I'm going up to the den and call the White House."

Rose Ellen's drawl seemed filmed by sleep. The President's

personal secretary was not enthusiastic about her employer's early-morning work habits.

"This is Jim MacVeagh," Jim said. "Could you let me talk to him, Rose Ellen? I can't say it's urgent, but it is very important."

"We're telepathic, Senatah," she said. "The President just asked me to get you out of bed."

"Oh?"

The President's voice came on, fresh but cold. "All right, Senator." He snapped the words out.

Jim plunged ahead. "Mr. President, I've decided that I cannot run for vice-president. I say this most regretfully, sir, with sincere appreciation for your confidence in me, but I just can't do it. I've given this a lot of thought, Mr. President—"

"Never mind." Hollenbach's voice cut in, sharp as a knife. "Just a minute . . ." Hollenbach turned from the phone. "Would you mind leaving the room, Rose Ellen," MacVeagh heard him say. "I want to talk to Senator MacVeagh in private, please."

There was a pause. Then Hollenbach turned back to the mouthpiece. "She called it telepathy. It certainly was. I was just about to call you to tell you the same thing, MacVeagh."

Jim was taken aback by the harsh use of his last name. "Oh, you were?" he said.

"Yes, I was," said Hollenbach, biting off the words. "It took a little investigative work, Senator, to come up with the name Rita Krasicki, but fortunately I took the precaution of ordering an FBI security check on you." The President was speaking swiftly now. "I admire your taste, MacVeagh, but I abhor your duplicity in failing to tell me the other day in this office that you had this—this thing—in your record."

Hollenbach's indignation triggered something in MacVeagh, and the image flashed before him of Tina Faraday, the actress, standing beside a fountain and drunkenly describing the day

Mark Hollenbach, as a college boy, fled from her house in Columbus.

"You double-crossed me, MacVeagh," continued Hollenbach, his speech seeming to stab over the phone lines. "It was a complete lack of square shooting on your part, and there's nothing I detest more. The Republicans would have been sure to find out about anything as filthy and dirty as that, and so we would have faced it right in the middle of the campaign. And I, in my innocence, thought you were many cuts above O'Malley."

The President halted, as though for breath, and MacVeagh said: "I did consider telling you, Mr. President, but frankly the affair was over, and besides, well, I was too excited that afternoon to think straight, I guess."

"That's a pallid excuse," replied Hollenbach. His voice rose in key. "And it doesn't pass muster with me. Frankly, I don't believe you. But what I do suspect is that you're in league with O'Malley and the rest of that cabal. You've joined the plot to discredit me and disgrace the administration—for what exact purposes, I don't know yet."

The accusation, delivered on a piercing, rising inflection, tore something loose in MacVeagh. All the frustration of days boiled up suddenly in him and the words began to fly from his mouth uncontrollably.

"That's a baseless charge, Mr. President," he said, "but I'll tell you something that is a fact. You are guilty of snooping and now you want a national wiretap law that will let your administration snoop on a grand scale. No wonder you want such an ugly law. You called in the FBI to ferret around in a man's private life. Is that what you call playing square with a man you asked to run with you? I didn't ask to run. It was all your idea. And tell me, what vice-presidential candidate in all history had to suffer the indignity of being shadowed and investigated by the footpads of the President of the United States?" MacVeagh, in his rush of anger, was about to add the Secret Service, but he caught himself with the thought that undoubtedly Hollenbach did not know of that agency's surveillance.

"And if there had been no security check?" Hollenbach laughed harshly. "You wouldn't have said a word about the voluptuous Mrs. Krasicki, would you? You'd have passed yourself off as a respectable family man. And then, the Republicans would have found out and we'd all have been destroyed—you, your lovely wife, your daughter, the administration, the party."

"And Mark Hollenbach?" asked MacVeagh. He couldn't resist it.

"Yes!" The President almost screamed it. "Yes, and Mark Hollenbach too. You were out to get me, weren't you, MacVeagh? But you didn't bring it off. You're lazy and ineffectual, and you can't even succeed in the department of dirty tricks."

MacVeagh's anger ebbed now before the President's swelling outburst. Jim felt as fragile as tinfoil from lack of sleep, and an ineffable sadness came over him.

"Again, Mr. President," he said in a low voice, "we understand each other, but in a way I regret with all my heart, believe me, sir."

"At least," said Hollenbach in a more normal tone, "you were man enough to make a clean breast of the thing, even if you were late as usual, Senator. I feel sorry for you. I wish it could have ended as it started."

"I do too, Mr. President."

There was another pause. Then Hollenbach spoke quite formally. "I'd appreciate it if you would mail that silver fountain pen back to me."

"Of course, sir. Good-by."

"Good-by, Senator."

Bruised, feeling as though his muscles had been pummeled in a street brawl, Jim walked slowly from the room and down the stairs.

Martha was standing in the living room, nervously straightening the new draperies. She turned to him.

"I told him," said Jim. "He understands. I'm off the ticket." He sniffed in disgust. "Not that I was ever on."

Wordlessly Martha crossed the room and put her arms around him. She fastened his lips with a longing kiss, one that seemed to be filled with all the blind and nameless hurts that human beings inflict on one another. He held her tight for long moments and when he released her, she smiled.

"Jim," she said, "I think you'll make a fine senator from Iowa —for a long time."

"Even with a wife who's neutral about urban renewal?"

"Neutral?" She smiled her old bantering, teasing smile. "Honey, I'm anti."

They kissed again, briefly this time, and Jim knew that the home in McLean was a warm place again, no matter how cold and forbidding might be the White House and the maniacal world of the man who inhabited it.

13.

Out and Down

By noon that day Jim MacVeagh sensed that the FBI surveillance of him had been withdrawn and the bureau's security investigation ended. There were two small signs in the morning: no young men in snap-brim hats at the McLean shopping center where he stopped to leave a suit at the dry cleaner's, and no casually sauntering man in the corridor along his Senate office. Then, when he returned to his office just before noon, Flip Carlson brought confirmation.

Carlson sat on the edge of Jim's desk as he briefed the senator on a variety of trifling legislative and constituent matters.

"Say, Jim," said Carlson, "something funny is going on around this place."

"It's your talent for attracting oddballs," retorted MacVeagh with a grin.

But Carlson wasn't in his usual playful mood. "Seriously, Jim, I've got a hunch this thing involves you in a way you're not telling."

"Why? What's up?"

"Last night," said Carlson, "I get a call from a guy named Phillips who says he's an FBI agent. He wants to come around to the apartment to interview me, but I say I have a date and I'll see him this morning at the office. Right? The guy says he'd prefer to meet me some place else, that it's a matter of some delicacy involving the office. So I agree to meet him at the Carroll Arms for lunch today. Then, about a half hour ago, he calls and says the interview won't be necessary after all, that the personnel check he'd been working on had been closed out."

"Nothing unusual about that," said MacVeagh. "The bureau must call off a dozen checks a day, for one reason or another. Why do you jump to the conclusion that I'm involved?"

"Oh, sometimes you get a feeling. Right? So why wouldn't this agent see me in the office? I bet I've talked to a dozen of them since I came to work for you, and none of 'em minded sitting around the office."

"Still, it doesn't sound peculiar to me." Jim feigned a yawn.

"Not alone, no," said Carlson, "but how about that Secret Service agent who came around asking me questions about my trip to La Belle and the West Coast? That was damned funny, if you ask me. And now this. Listen, Jim, are you in some kind of trouble?"

"Of course not, Flip." MacVeagh laughed, swung his feet up on the desk, and leaned back in his swivel chair. "Everything's going okay. As for the Secret Service, they just got interested because somebody in La Belle thought you were extra-thorough in your questioning. Routine stuff."

Carlson, frowning, studied MacVeagh's face. "So how's that biography of Hollenbach coming?"

"Pretty good," lied MacVeagh. "It's keeping me up nights, but I guess I'm about half finished."

"Damned if I see where you get the time." Carlson got off the desk and folded his shirt-sleeved arms. "I dunno, I got a feeling something offbeat is going on. Anyway, if you need help, Jim, don't forget I'm your man."

"Thanks, Flip. Everything's all right, but I'll remember the offer."

Yes, thought Jim when Carlson had left, the FBI undoubtedly had been called off by Hollenbach this morning, probably right after Jim's phone call to the White House. The fact should have brought him a measure of relief, but despondency clung to him like a rain-soaked shirt. He could imagine Mark Hollenbach as he read the FBI dossier, probably late last night in his upstairs study. The President, with his starched view of sex, probably tightened his lips as he read the fragrant implications of the government report. The thought repelled Jim. What right had Mark Hollenbach, whatever his position in the nation, to intrude on the private lives of men and women as though he were a common Peeping Tom? And remembering Tina Faraday's guess as to Hollenbach's own bedroom behavior—"he gets as much loving as a Tibetan monk"—Jim surmised that Hollenbach got a vicarious thrill from the report. Jim felt useless and soiled, and he found himself beginning to detest this relentlessly encircling power of the White House.

And now the nice big fat file on MacVeagh and Rita Krasicki probably rested in a cabinet of the Federal Bureau of Investigation. Since the bureau seldom threw anything away, the folder would lie there unseen for years, perhaps never to be inspected again. But there it was, nevertheless, a sapless chronicle of suspected passion and adultery. The very existence of such a dossier on a U.S. senator carried an implied threat—to vote right on FBI appropriations and all legislation desired by the bureau. With data like that about himself in the FBI raw files—and the word "raw" carried a caustic connotation in this case—what legislator would take the chance of raising questions about how the bureau spent the taxpayers' money? Oh, well, he thought, on balance he had to admit the FBI was a fine institution. Not under J. Edgar Hoover, or since, had there been any indication of such tacit blackmail. The bureau drew a steel curtain between its files and its legislative operations. But still they had MacVeagh catalogued now, and for decades, perhaps, his trysts with Rita would lie in some air-conditioned government recess, microfilmed for posterity. Thank you, Mark Hollenbach.

MacVeagh sighed, lifted his feet off the desk, and buzzed for Carlson.

"Flip," said MacVeagh when his aide entered, "my mind's wandering today. I forgot to tell you that I want you to call the press galleries and tell them I'm having a press conference this afternoon. Let's make it two o'clock so it'll hit the late evening papers and still get a good ride in the A.M.'s."

"You decided to campaign in Wisconsin?" Carlson's eyes lighted.

"No. I am going to announce that I am not a candidate for vice-president."

"You're what?" Carlson stared at him, stupefied.

"I'm not going to run, period."

Carlson stood staring down at him.

"Jim, are you out of your mind?"

No, thought MacVeagh. You've got the right idea, Flip, but the wrong man.

"Never been more sane," he said with an attempt at cheeriness. "I've thought it out, Flip. I can be a senator from Iowa for a long time, but I'm too young, too inexperienced for the other job." Seeing the look of incredulity deepen on Carlson's face, Jim winked at his aide. "Besides, I've got an inside tip that Hollenbach will never pick me, so I'm quitting before he can turn me down in public."

"God Almighty, Jim," protested Carlson, "the dope is all the other way. The White House is fanning this thing for you. Joe Donovan's working for you. Unless I heard it otherwise from Hollenbach himself, I'd swear the President is backing you one hundred per cent."

"Was, maybe," corrected MacVeagh, "but no longer. Believe me, Flip, I've got the straight word. Whoever Mark picks, it won't be me."

Carlson flopped into a chair, his beefy form seemingly as deflated as a spent balloon. Carlson, Jim knew, had envisioned soaring onward and upward with MacVeagh, perhaps to the very pinnacle of power—the White House.

"Aw," said Carlson, "why don't we make a fight of it? Even if you're right on your dope, you could put on a campaign that would carry you to the top of every poll in the country."

"And the descent would be all the more precipitous," said Jim. "I don't aim to make a fool of myself. Some other year maybe, Flip. Now go call the press galleries. Tell them it's a good political story. We might as well get maximum mileage out of it."

"Okay," said Carlson. But the bounce was gone, and he left with a slump to his shoulders.

By a quarter of two the throng of reporters and photographers in the corridor outside MacVeagh's office had grown to such size that the conference had to be shifted to the Senate Office Building's large caucus room, scene of countless hearings and investigations over the years. A sprinkling of Senate employees and a score of the usual roaming, eager-eyed tourists had joined some two hundred newsmen when MacVeagh walked to the center of the long committee table and faced the crowd. He held up his hands to quiet the gesticulating cameramen who were bombarding him with querulous orders.

"Ladies and gentlemen," he said, "I am here to announce that I will not be a candidate for vice-president and that I will not permit my name to be presented in nomination at the Detroit convention.

"Accordingly, I am requesting that all activity in my behalf, in Wisconsin and elsewhere, should cease. I appreciate the support I've received in Wisconsin, but I request that no Democratic voters in that state write in my name for vice-president, as such votes would be wasted.

"As you all know, President Hollenbach has made no effort to discourage evidence of support for vice-presidential candidates. Since he, in a sense, welcomed such evidence, I thought it only fair to inform him first of my decision. So I called the President early this morning and told him. He indicated that he respected my wishes. Well, that about ends the short-lived Mac-Veagh-for-vice-president business, ladies and gentlemen. Any questions?"

They came flying at him like projectiles. A dozen voices shouted at once: "Why?"

"Frankly," he said, "I just decided that I don't have the seasoning. I'm only a first-term senator and I have a lot to learn. While I feel certain I could handle the office of vice-president, we must never forget that this office is only a heartbeat from the presidency. It would be a disservice to the country to pretend that I have the capacity and the experience to deal with the grave issues facing the President of the United States." He grinned. "Now, five, ten years from now, it may be another story. Right now, no."

"Come off it, Senator!" shouted one newsman. "What's the real reason?"

Jim smiled easily as the crowd laughed.

"Seriously," he said, "I think every voter in this country should pay just as much attention to the caliber of man running for vice-president as that of the presidential candidate. The vice-president, as we all know too well, could become president in a fraction of a second. And again, seriously, I think our party has a number of men who are far more qualified to run this nation than I am."

Who? they chorused. Well, there were at least seven, he said, adopting Hollenbach's figure. Were Karper and Nicholson among them? Of course. Both were exceptionally capable men.

"Jim," asked a reporter, "did the President try to argue you into remaining a candidate?"

"No, he didn't." MacVeagh smiled. "I assume he does not dissent from my view that I need more seasoning."

"Senator MacVeagh, are you willing to take a Sherman?"

"Indeed I am," replied Jim. "In the words of General William T. Sherman—now don't hold me to them exactly—if nominated I will not accept, if elected I will not serve. Now, having said that, it sounds a bit presumptuous, since the selection of a vice-president is entirely in President Hollenbach's hands. Still, it does mirror my feeling and my intentions."

"Good Lord," remarked one newsman, "I've been around here thirty years, and this is the first time I ever heard any politician take a Sherman."

"Mind you," warned MacVeagh, "I don't promise to emulate Sherman forever. Come talk to me a few years from now."

The press conference broke up in good-natured ribbing. MacVeagh was well liked on any day, but on this afternoon the newsmen regarded him with special fondness. He had provided the only thing a newspaperman ever really wants from a politician—hard news.

Craig Spence walked back with Jim to MacVeagh's office. The columnist matched Jim's long stride with his own gangling gait.

"You beat me, Jim," he said. "You looked like you had the world by the tail. I just don't understand it, especially, who knows, the way Hollenbach drives himself, you might have ended up as president in a couple of years."

"Craig, I'd like to level with you, but I just can't. Someday, when this thing is all ancient history, maybe I can tell you. It's quite a story."

"Then there is another reason?" asked Spence.

"Don't press me, Craig. Let's just leave it that I was completely honest in what I did say. I am too young and I've a lot to learn—some of which has to be learned pretty quickly."

"But you didn't tell the boys everything?"

"Does anybody ever tell everything?" asked MacVeagh. "Does he ever know enough to tell everything?"

Spence shook his head. "You're being enigmatic, Jim, and it's not like you."

"Craig, you'll just have to trust me for a while—maybe a long while."

There's that word again, thought Jim as he parted from Spence. Trust. He'd asked Rita to trust him, and Martha, and Pat O'Malley—and now Craig Spence. But trust resembled credit at the bank. The notes had to be redeemed someday, not on time perhaps but within a reasonable period. Otherwise, the credit withered like the smile on the banker's face. The brief feeling of excitement provoked by the skirmish of wits at the press conference melted away, and Jim's mood of dejection returned.

Headlines of the late-afternoon editions played the story. The front page of the tabloid Washington *Daily News* used huge type: "Like Cal, Jim Does Not Choose To Run." It was the top story in the red-bordered final of the Washington *Evening Star:* "MacVeagh Takes Sherman. Keeps Senate Seat." A friend in New York called Carlson to read him the *World-Telegram's* headline: "MacVeagh's Out. Who's In?"

In the Senate press gallery Craig Spence frowned at a typewriter, scratched his freckled, bald head, then began a two-finger drumming on the keys. It was his daily offering for the syndicate which that night would wire his words to 150 newspapers from Jersey City to Honolulu:

The real reason Senator James F. MacVeagh of Iowa suddenly withdrew his name from consideration for the Democratic vice-presidential nomination may not be revealed for years.

Some future professor of history undoubtedly will print the reason in a dry, dull little book which nobody will read, because nobody will care any longer. And therein lies the frustration of political writing. The motivations that produce the big stories only rarely are revealed at the time, and sometimes never. "There is no history," President John F. Kennedy once told his confidant, Kenneth O'Donnell. Kennedy, with his acute political perception, recognized that what we call history is a patchwork of guessing, thirdhand reports and formal state documents, most of which penetrate the kernel of truth only occasionally.

This is by way of warning the reader to take all speculation on MacVeagh's astounding renunciation with reservation, for all of us who write political commentary will only be guessing at the truth.

James MacVeagh is known for his refreshing candor, and deservedly so, but in this instance even his best friends find it difficult to accept MacVeagh's own stated reasons—youth, inexperience, lack of capacity to handle the presidency in event tragedy should move him into President Hollenbach's office. He is young, but he is not inexperienced. As for his capacity, the potential is enormous, even though as yet the junior senator from Iowa has been tested but rarely on major issues of the day.

Jim MacVeagh is one of the most forthright, intellectually honest, and unusual young politicians to reach Washington in many years, and he will not fade from the limelight. Instead, a certain mystery will cling to his unexpected announcement. . . .

Spence lit a cigarette, crossed his long legs, and sat staring at what he had written. He sat for a long time, his stomach knotting as his deadline approached, and when he finally resumed writing, he realized that his words merely proved that he was right in warning the reader against all speculation, including his own. For Spence, despite his close friendship with MacVeagh, had not the smallest clue as to why Jim had slammed the door on his own future.

MacVeagh's own mind was fastened on a future only two days away, the Thursday night meeting at Cavanaugh's home, which O'Malley informed him cryptically by phone had now been arranged. Sitting blankly at his office desk, isolated from his staff by orders that he not be disturbed, Jim tried to erect the case for the plaintiff, Jim MacVeagh, Citizen, vs. Mark Hollenbach, President. The more he thought the more he visualized ponderous, bulky Speaker Nicholson and adroit, incisive Fred Odlum. For these men would his story have the texture of floss? Cavanaugh was another matter. With his judicious temperament and his zest for truth, the Supreme Court justice at least would weigh all the evidence. O'Malley, Jim knew, was halfway convinced already, but O'Malley would do nothing unless the others insisted that he act. Somehow, Jim felt, he must persuade Nicholson and the cynical Odlum, but unless they could hear Rita with their own ears, scrutinize her features as she talked, they would never believe him. There was no way out. She must come to St. Leonard's Creek Thursday night.

He reached her on the phone only after a long delay. Calls were stacked up for Donovan's office, the national committee's switchboard girl explained, in the wake of Senator MacVeagh's surprise announcement. Rita accepted his call without comment.

"Rita," he said, "I need your help badly. Something has come up that involves—well—national security. There's a private meeting Thursday night of some important men, and I want you to come along with me and repeat that story you told me about President Hollenbach and that Chicago banker, Davidge. I know this is asking a lot but, Rita, it's vital to the country."

"Has this got something to do with those agents who called on me?" Her voice was wary.

"Yes, in a way."

"You mean you want me to tell that Davidge story to the FBI?"

"No, no," said Jim. "These aren't FBI men. It's an allied matter, but it's something much bigger than any security check, Rita—"

"I don't repeat conversations with the President," she cut in, her tone hostile. "And I don't like what's going on. Have you any explanation for that other agent's visit yet?"

"No, I haven't, not yet. But, Rita, this is something else, much more important. Believe me."

"Believe you?" Her laugh was brittle. "You're acting mighty strange lately. This press conference of yours tops everything. You'd hardly begun to run when, suddenly, you quit."

MacVeagh hurried into the opening. "You know why I did that, Rita. After that FBI security check, how could I possibly risk the chance that your name would be dragged into the open? I don't blame you for being upset, but at least give me credit for trying to protect you."

She softened. "I do, Jim. Of course, there's you and your wife too."

"I don't deny that, Rita."

"Now that you've quit the race, things aren't much different than they used to be, are they?" It was her old voice, low, throaty.

"Meaning?"

"Meaning that if something is already in FBI files anyway, there isn't much more to lose, is there?"

"Oh." He could hear Martha's racking sobs, and he wanted to reiterate that the affair with Rita was over forever, but he didn't. He needed Rita Thursday night, desperately. "No," he said, "I suppose there isn't."

"I'm sorry I lost my temper yesterday, Jims."

"That's okay, baby," he said hurriedly, "but that's got nothing to do with this other thing. You've just got to come Thursday night."

"What's the purpose?" she asked.

"I can't tell you. You've just got to trust me now. Later, sometime, I can tell you."

"Trust you. Haven't I heard that before? That's becoming quite a word in your vocabulary."

"I know it." The desperation was with him again and his tone reflected it. "This is urgent, Rita. It concerns the safety of the country. It really does. You've just got to come to that meeting. Please—for my sake."

She was silent a moment, and he could hear her breathing. "Damn you, Jim," she said. "You're in my blood and you know it. Sometimes I wish I'd never met you."

"But you will come?"

"Yes, Jims, I will—for your sake," she said quietly.

"Thanks, baby. You're a sweetheart."

"Forget it," she said, briskly competent again. But she mouthed a kiss into the phone as she hung up.

When he replaced the receiver, MacVeagh found that his palms were sweating. It had been close. He had played on her emotions, letting her think that their love could be renewed, and he felt like a heel for the forgery. But at this juncture he would do anything. She had to be at Cavanaugh's. Without Rita there would be little chance of convincing Nicholson and Odlum. Now there was a possibility.

There was a rap on the door, and Carlson put his head into the room.

"I know you're not supposed to be disturbed," he said, "but I've got a favor to ask you. An awful problem is bugging me, and it won't wait."

"That's okay," said MacVeagh. "Come on in, Flip. What can I do for you?"

"This sounds ridiculous on a day like this," said Carlson, "but that fat little dame who wants to make the chrysanthemum the national flower is driving me batty. She's staging a sit-in in the reception room, and she claims she won't leave until you agree to see her."

MacVeagh grimaced and waved an arm as though to ward off a blow. "Oh, Jesus, no, Flip. Not that. Not today. She's nutty as a fruitcake. If she gets in here we won't get her out for two hours."

Mrs. Jessica Tate Byerson, with the enormous white chrysanthemum at her challenging bosom—symbolizing, according to Mrs. Byerson, purity, generosity, love which would transform American foreign policy into a thing of beauty forever—padded the marble corridors of House and Senate day after day.

She knew every legislator by sight, and none could elude her when once observed. Seeing her enter the rotunda, men had been known to blanch and scuttle down a flight of side steps into the bowels of the Capitol. She haunted the Congressional offices, made life miserable for secretaries, and gave impromptu lectures to tourists, many of whom signed her long, crackling petitions to canonize the chrysanthemum. Never had a flower had such a belligerently saccharine advocate. Terrorized by her tactics, which centered on target like a dentist's drill, several hundred congressmen had agreed to vote the mum into national saint-hood. Mrs. Byerson, the "mum's mum," was the most persistent threat to the untrammeled freedom of the American legislator since the birth of the first veterans' organization.

"Please, Jim," pleaded Carlson, "if you agree to see her for ten minutes—ten minutes only—I'll guarantee to get her out, if I have to smother her with her damned handbag. Otherwise she'll sit in that outer office all week. She's a menace to navigation. Everybody who comes in the door goes into a state of siege."

"Ten minutes?" asked Jim. "You promise . . . on pain of getting fired if she stays one second longer?"

"I do."

MacVeagh grinned. "All right, send her in. But, man, you'll really owe me one after this."

"Anything, boss, anything. Right?"

Jessica Tate Byerson sailed into the inner office like a bloated spinnaker. Her fat face, flushed with the exertion of the long campaign, was damp and she tapped at her brow with a lace handkerchief. She beamed at MacVeagh, plumped her handbag on his desk, and handed him three pamphlets simultaneously. When she sank into a chair, her feet barely touched the floor, but her pulpy thighs swelled over the sides of the chair. She wore a purple suit, the pockets stuffed with newspaper clippings, and her layered straw hat sat on her stringy blonde hair like a stack of wheatcakes. A white chrysanthemum was pinned to her ferocious bosom.

"You've been trying to avoid me, Senator," she admonished him. Her voice had a tinkling, bell-like cadence, strangely delicate from such a muffin of a figure. "I can't understand what you've got against mums."

"I have absolutely nothing against the chrysanthemum." Jim

decided he would not be bullied. "But neither do I think we need a national flower."

"Ah, Senator," she trilled, "how woefully shortsighted! Do you realize that practically every garden club in Iowa has joined the crusade to make the white mum America's flower?"

"Indeed, I do, Mrs. Byerson. The letters come in here by the bale, and while I think that's a tribute to your skill as a lobbyist, I also think the whole business is downright silly."

"Silly?" Mrs. Byerson's damp face lost its smile and her brow wrinkled as though she were recoiling from a stab of pain. "Oh, Senator, how could you be so cruel—and so ignorant of the true facts."

"Facts are facts, Mrs. Byerson," said Jim tartly. If he could offend her quickly, she might leave within the ten minutes. "There are no such things as true facts, for then we'd have to have false facts, wouldn't we?"

"You're trying to trap me with words," she said indignantly, "and I do so terribly with words. I deal in sentiment, Senator, in what the heart speaks. And, if you would but listen, the heart of America is speaking today, imploring you to give this great country a national flower that it can wear proudly—"

"I went all through that with the rose and the sunflower. The corn tassel too, for that matter," said Jim, "and I maintain it's all utter nonsense. Mrs. Byerson, you may not realize it, but we are elected to legislate on the demanding problems facing the country, the balance of payments, ending unemployment, keeping the peace, you name it. We're not here to worry about idiotic trifles."

"Ah!" She brightened. "That's just it. Once we adopt the white mum—purity, generosity, love—every aspect of foreign policy would take on new meaning. Our deeds would shine like our words, and our friends across the seas would find a new sincerity in all that we proposed."

Mrs. Byerson tinkled along, rippling like the upper keys of a piano. She heaved and squirmed in her seat as she delivered her "A" lecture—for the intelligent but unenlightened—and she dabbed now and then at her temples with her limp lace handkerchief. Jim looked at his wrist watch. Four minutes to go. His mind veered to Mark Hollenbach, to the Thursday night meeting, and to his own perplexing dilemma. The lady lobbyist's voice seemed as remote as faraway chapel bells. She must have noted the absence in his face, for she suddenly turned up her volume.

". . . and if my crusade is so ridiculous, how do you explain the fact that the White House has endorsed my legislation?"

"What's that?" Jim realized he had been questioned.

"I said, how do you explain the fact that the White House has endorsed my idea?"

"Oh, come now, Mrs. Byerson," said Jim, "let's not play games with each other. The White House has turned thumbs down on the chrysanthemum bill at least twice to my knowledge."

"Ah." Mrs. Byerson breathed deeply, mysteriously. "The White House did take that position, but no longer. The next report from the White House will be favorable, you watch."

"I won't hold my breath, dear lady."

"You won't have to. I have President Hollenbach's personal promise on behalf of the mum."

Jim frowned skeptically. "President Hollenbach told you he would support your national flower legislation?"

"Not exactly." The little bells of her voice clanged conspiratorially. "He told me something much more interesting. If I tell you, can I swear you to secrecy?"

"Absolutely." Puzzled, Jim was alert now.

"Well, you mustn't whisper a word of this, because the President warned me not to tell a soul, but he's working on a project for a big union of some kind—with other countries, you know—and he promises me the white mum will get priority consideration as the symbolic flower of this union. He's going to have a special tree too, the aspen."

Her face glowed with triumph. Her straw hat perched raffishly on her head, and she began a happy tapping with her feet, stretching slightly to reach the floor. Jim MacVeagh leaned across the desk, studying her.

"When did you see the President?" he asked.

"Last Wednesday afternoon." She winked at him. "Two weeks ago I told his press secretary that I was going to sit in the lobby until I got to see the President. He tried to pull me out, physically, but I resisted him. The next morning they wouldn't let me in the front gate, so I just went to Senator Hempstead's office and told the senator that I was going to sit in *his* office until he got me an appointment with the President. It took twelve days, but in the end I got in to see the President."

"What time did you see him Wednesday?"

"At four-thirty-five," she said, beaming. "And I didn't stay just five minutes. He kept me there 15 minutes, he was so interested."

Jim crossed to her chair, took her chubby hands and pulled Mrs. Byerson to her feet.

"I'll make you a promise," he said. "If you can get a unanimous report from the Judiciary Committee and your bill gets to the floor, I'll vote for it."

"How lovely and thoughtful, Senator MacVeagh." Her smile was angelic, blissfully distant, as though these victories were fashioned, after all, in heaven. She took her vast handbag from MacVeagh's desk, rummaged a bit, and withdrew a pencil and notebook.

"I'm marking you down, Senator," she tinkled. "Just two more names, and I'll have a majority of the whole Congress."

"Great." Jim was edging her toward the door. "Never under-estimate the power of a woman."

"When her cause is just," she said. She blew him a wet kiss, and then she was out the door, her handbag swinging on her wrist like a pendulum and news clippings dripping from the pockets of her purple suit.

Jim buzzed at once for Carlson. "Flip," he said, "Our chrys-anthemum tigress claims she got in to see Hollenbach on that nutty bill. Says she saw him at 4:35 last Wednesday. Call Howard down at the White House and see if she's telling the truth. I want to know right away."

Carlson was back on the intercom within minutes. "Yep," he said. "The old dame wasn't lying. Howard says she was in with the President from 4:35 to 4:50. Howie was ready to shoo her out after five minutes, but Hollenbach let Mrs. B. have fifteen."

After clicking off the intercom key, MacVeagh sat quiet, gaz-ing across the room at the color photograph of a tractor plow churning through the rich, black soil of Iowa. He rubbed the bridge of his nose, and slowly a feeling of exhilaration mounted within him. Confirmation! Now there were three other people who had glimpsed some recess of this strange, tangled mind of Mark Hollenbach. Rita had heard him explode over Davidge. O'Malley heard himself being accused of deliberate sabotage of Hollenbach's re-election chances. And now tubby Mrs. Byerson, obsessed with her own floral crusade, had stumbled into a hint of the grand concept. A mum for the union of Aspen! Jim knew that this new indication of Hollenbach's derangement should sadden him, should evoke again the fear that gripped him after he left Camp David that second Saturday night. Instead he felt curiously elated. His conjectures were right. There was no doubt about it now, thanks to a dumpy little woman whose hat resem-bled a pile of pancakes and whose talent for boring people was unrivaled in Washington. He began to leaf through his correspondence, making rapid decisions on a myriad small problems and whistling thinly to himself. He rattled off a dozen letters into the dictating machine before quitting for the day.

He was his old self at the dinner table that night. He joshed Chinky about her ever-phoning girl friends, kept both Chinky and Martha laughing with wry comments on the afternoon press conference, and asked Martha for a second helping of the beef Stroganoff, clear proof that he was in good spirits, for he privately detested the dish.

After dinner he and Chinky listened to the entire album of Porky Jones on the drums. They turned up the sound on the stereo set, and the living room became a pandemonium of drums and raucous yells. Chinky screamed ecstatically, while Jim beat the floor with a fly swatter. Martha appeared at the kitchen door, holding her ears and imploring them to dampen the uproar. They ignored her, Jim turning his back and leaping up to do a wild jig that shook the walls. Chinky began to weave in a spell of euphoria, somewhat like a kitten after a saucer of rum. When the album at last concluded on a heady, savage beat, father and daughter collapsed on the carpet in a spasm of laughter.

"Pops, you're a swingin' cat," said Chinky, and then she giggled helplessly.

Later, after Chinky had gone to bed, protesting as ever, Jim and Martha sat in his upstairs den. Jim closed the door and tried to temper his ebullient mood for the serious business at hand.

"Marty," he said, "this is going to hurt, but it's got to be said. On Thursday night I have to escort Mrs.—well, the woman in Georgetown—"

"You mean Mrs. Krasicki?"

"All right, Mrs. Krasicki." He couldn't look at his wife, and the name dragged on his lips. "I've got to take her to a meeting. I can't tell you what it's about, but it has to do with the security of

the country. The . . . the thing . . . with her is all over and buried.
This is something else. I've just got to do it, but I wanted you to
know."

"You want me to trust you, Jim?" she asked softly.

"You've got to, Marty."

"I do, Jim, I do." Her face clouded and her little nose wrinkled in annoyance. "But I can't understand why you can't tell me
what it's all about. You've never held anything back before.
Have I ever once let out one of your secrets since we got into
politics?"

"No, you haven't." They held each other's eyes, each searching for understanding.

"Well, then, why can't you tell me?"

Why not, indeed? thought Jim. It was different now. Now
there were no longer any doubts. Jessica Tate Byerson, that
fey little bundle with the enchanted flower, had erased the last of
the misgivings. That alone gave him strength to make the fantastic seem credible to Martha. And with the vice-presidency cast
aside, for Martha's sake, she believed, she would be in a mood to
credit his lurid discovery. But, above all, his Thursday night
mission with Rita had to be explained, somehow. Suddenly Jim
could withhold the story of President Hollenbach no longer.

"Martha, this is the most frightening thing that's happened in
this country in a long while," he said. "I'm going to try to tell you
everything I know."

And he almost did. He told the story in great detail, but when
he came to Rita's conversation with Hollenbach about Davidge,
he saw Martha wince at the mention of Rita's name and he could
not bring himself to tell the exact truth. He said that she had told
him of the incident back in January, and that it had made no
impression on him until after his session with the President at
Camp David. Then, he said, he'd had to consult Rita to hear the
story again. Also, when he told of the Secret Service and FBI

investigations, Jim did not mention the fact that agents called on Rita as well.

Throughout the recital, Martha busied herself removing pale-red lacquer from her fingernails. Her snub nose twitched with the sharp fumes of the polish remover, and she raised her head only occasionally to look at her husband. Then she applied a new coat and held up her fingers to let the lacquer dry. When Jim finished, Martha spread her fingers, fanwise, and inspected them thoughtfully. How to explain women, thought Jim. The country faced the worst crisis he'd known, and she sat admiring her nails. Then she rose slowly and came to the arm of his easy chair. She clasped his head to her bosom and caressed his hair.

"Dearest Jim," she whispered, "forgive me for making you tell me. But I'm glad, darling. I understand. You need help so badly."

"I've just got to make Nicholson and Odlum believe me," he said, his voice muffled by her breasts.

She tilted his head upward and kissed the cleft of his chin.

"Of course, dear," she said. "Of course you do."

Then he saw a questioning, pitying look in her eyes, and he wondered why the miseries of President Hollenbach should touch the woman of her so deeply, why her affection should flow because she'd learned the mind of the President was unsound. The mystery of woman, he thought, was boundless.

In bed, she covered his face with small kisses and then she held him tightly as though he might leave.

"Jim," she said suddenly, "I'm going to drive you to work tomorrow and prove to you that nobody—Secret Service or anybody else—is following you."

He hoisted himself on an elbow and stared down at her face in the dark. "Marty, for God's sake," he began, but she pulled him down beside her and stroked the nape of his neck.

The transient ebullience of the afternoon and evening was all gone now, and loneliness struck deep in his being. He did not have the will to argue with her. If Martha thought his mind was disturbed, there was nothing he could do about it tonight. He kissed her tenderly, trying to make the senses reassure where words could not, and soon, silently and somewhat sadly, they were making love.

14.

St. Leonard's Creek

All his years Jim MacVeagh would remember these two days, Wednesday and Thursday, as the longest of his life. He felt he was alone, a prisoner in a jail of glass, high on a hill, watching helplessly as the valley crumbled beneath him. Mark Hollenbach made his feverish plans to meet Zuchek in Stockholm, and only Senator MacVeagh, from his lonely vantage point, knew that it was a psychotic president who would fly to Sweden. If James MacVeagh yelled, none would hear him. If he warned, they would turn away, for the senator himself was suspected of aberrations—by Griscom, the lawyer, by Arnold Brothers, the Secret Service chief, and now by his own wife.

The hovering FBI agents were gone, but it was no consolation, for the surveillance by the Secret Service seemed to have tightened. Jim felt the presence of the Service everywhere. At a committee session he recognized a face in the rear row. It was an agent from the West Coast whom he'd seen briefly during the Hollenbach campaign. On Wednesday morning, when he stopped at a gas station in McLean, MacVeagh saw Luther Smith sitting in a car across the street. The agent was averting his head when Jim looked, but Jim caught a glimpse of the swarthy face. At his office Jim looked up Smith's address in the phone book. Smith lived in Silver Spring in Maryland, a 40-minute drive in traffic from McLean.

Vexed and harried, MacVeagh called Arnold Brothers at Secret Service headquarters. He accused the chief of assigning agents to shadow him and demanded to know by what right or authority in law the Secret Service placed a net of surveillance about a United States senator. Brothers expressed shock at the charge, but Jim thought his voice too bland to be convincing. It was almost as though Brothers had anticipated such a call. Senator MacVeagh, said Brothers, certainly must be imagining things, for no detail had been assigned to trail him. The Service had merely checked on a call two weeks ago from La Belle, Florida, had found that Roger Carlson had made some inquiries there on MacVeagh's instructions, and that was the end of that. Purely routine. Why would the Service go further? No, no. The Service had agents all over town. MacVeagh must have seen men on other missions. If the senator had been given cause for worry, the Service was sorry. Brothers was insistent, sympathetic and reassuring, but MacVeagh hung up feeling again the noose being drawn about him. If he had been a smoking man, he would have consumed a pack.

At home Martha was solicitous, almost cloying in her maternal attention. She did not again hint that his mind was fraying, but she questioned him frequently about his experiences with Hollenbach, and he found her pursing her lips in disbelief when he described the nights of Camp David. In the retelling Jim found the ghostly, frightening quality had worn off. He could no longer be sure, in memory, that Mark acted and talked like a madman. The scenes were blurring, and doubts again began to nag him. Only the recent episode with fat Mrs. Byerson, innocently revealing that she too had heard of Hollenbach's grand concept for a super-union, remained vivid. Simpering, pathetic Mrs. Byerson, he thought, what a waxy reed to lean on.

Wednesday afternoon the Washington *Evening Star* printed a story by Cousins and King, the nation's leading political gossip columnists. The story said that the real reason Senator James F. MacVeagh bowed out of the vice-presidential contest was because there was a mark on his private life which he feared would be revealed had he continued. The writers did not hint at the nature of the blemish, but they stated their accusation as though it were a fact well documented. They seemed to relish the use of words as provocative as possible, as though daring MacVeagh to sue them for libel.

The story uncapped a geyser of rumors and gossip. MacVeagh's office switchboard was flooded with calls. The Democratic state chairman ·phoned from Iowa, pleading with MacVeagh to issue a denial. Deny what? retorted MacVeagh. He hadn't been charged with anything. Then sue for libel, he was urged. Senseless, replied MacVeagh. Libel litigation only opened a man's whole life for ruthless lawyers to poke and prod about in. The state chairman wasn't satisfied. MacVeagh had to run again two years from now. People remembered things like this. Then Craig Spence came to see MacVeagh, enraged for his friend and anxious to write a column excoriating Cousins and King for trafficking in baseless innuendo. MacVeagh urged him to write nothing on the matter, argued that further words would only prolong a brief tempest into a wind that would howl about him for months. Spence bristled and left the office in ill humor. Nothing, Jim thought, sours charity so quickly as an unwilling recipient. But while MacVeagh managed to weather his friends and political associates, the scene with Chinky hurt.

Chinky greeted him that evening with a brushing kiss, then planted her feet wide apart in a bellicose stance, pointed to the *Star* which was open to the Cousins and King column.

"That's the rottenest thing I've ever seen in a newspaper," she said. "Pops, aren't there laws or something to prevent lies like that?"

"That's just politics, honey. It doesn't mean a thing. You've got to get used to it."

"I'm going to write a letter to the *Star,*" she said. She blinked rapidly as she often did when angry. "I'm going to dare them to say just what they mean, or shut up."

MacVeagh patted her cheek. "None of that, Chinky. That will just make a mountain out of a molehill. Let it lie."

"A molehill?" she shrieked. "Why, every filthy little sneak at school will be gossiping about it. I'll hate to show my face."

"Now, Chinky," he consoled her, "who's the story about, you or me? If I can take it, you can. It's a low blow, but that's the way politics is."

She stepped quickly to him and hugged him. "Aw, gee, Pops, you're the straightest guy on earth." She rubbed her cheek against his coat sleeve, and Martha, who had been standing in a corner of the room, stepped quickly through the swinging door to the kitchen.

The two days seemed to stretch interminably, with MacVeagh abrasively on the defensive, with his friends, with newspapermen, with his family, and with his own shuddering doubts. When Thursday evening finally came, Jim faced it with a sense of inadequacy and almost futility. Why, of all the thousands of public officials, had he appointed himself the guardian of the nation? But something thrust him onward, like a small unseen hand at the back.

By prearrangement he met Rita on the street beside the Supreme Court Building. She came by taxi, and he waited in a rented car which he had obtained at the Hertz garage on L Street after making sure that his own cab was not being followed. Rita wore a fog coat with flaring collar, and she jiggled a pair of smoked glasses at him as she got in the car.

"As long as we've got all this mystery," she said, her voice low, "I thought I'd go as Mata Hari."

She squared the glasses on her nose and lit a cigarette. Her lips were crimson against her delicate olive skin, a shake of black hair fell over one eye, and a faint aroma of perfume began to fill the car. Jim shifted uneasily in his seat.

They drove in silence over the South Capitol Street bridge, out the Suitland Parkway, past Andrews Air Force Base.

"Remember this road, Jims?" she asked. "The time we borrowed your friend's sailboat? What a heavenly weekend."

"Yeah," he said, but he pushed from his mind the picture of the gently rocking boat and its deck checkered with moonlight.

"Jims, why did you give up on the vice-presidency?"

"I'm not the caliber," he bantered. "Remember? I'm sweet and kind and usually on the side of the angels, but I don't use half the brains God gave me. Besides, I'm lazy."

She touched his chin. "Don't forget the cleft when listing your assets. Seriously, why did you quit?"

"As I told you Tuesday," he said, "once the FBI knew about us, it was bound to get out, and Hollenbach was sure to hear, since he apparently ordered the security check in the first place. And when he read the report, he'd have thrown me off the ticket head first. Our President doesn't tolerate—how shall we put it? —indiscretions of the flesh. So I just beat him to the punch."

"You mean the President is going to read about us?" She turned to him, her face tight and reddening.

"Of course, Rita. You must have figured that out."

"No, I didn't." Her voice had lost its warmth. "Why, that's detestable—the President reading that kind of thing. He'll think I'm some kind of cheap pushover."

"Baby!" He reached over and squeezed her hand, but she snatched it away. She sat staring out the car window, her dark glasses oddly reflecting the lights from the dashboard. It was several minutes before she spoke again.

"Damn it, Jim. What's this all about? Where are you taking me?"

"To a house on St. Leonard's Creek," he said. "It's a little way this side of Solomon's."

"That's too spooky for me." She lit another cigarette, but mashed it out in the dashboard tray after a few puffs. "Jim, turn this car around. I want to go home."

"You promised, Rita," he pleaded. "We'll be there in half an hour. I'll tell you everything as soon as I can. But, believe me, it's all tied in to national security."

"Security!" she blazed. "I've had enough of that word for a lifetime."

But she protested no more, and they drove on, speeding through southern Maryland under a night sky that was shrouded with cloud. At the hamlet of Lusby, Jim turned right on a gravel road, then turned right again at a swinging, wooden sign which read "Grady Cavanaugh."

"Is that the Supreme Court justice?" asked Rita. Jim nodded. "You could at least have told me that," she said reproachfully.

The road wound through thick woods, and the car's headlights played on the new buds of the maples, oaks and dogwoods. Then they traversed an open field, newly plowed, and mounted toward a great, white frame house which crowned a hill overlooking the dark waters of St. Leonard's Creek. Several cars were parked in the pebbled roadway behind the barn.

A long low wing ran from the side of the house, and by prearrangement with Cavanaugh, MacVeagh escorted Rita to a guest room nearest the back entrance. The room was simply decorated in early American style, with cherry furniture and an oval, hooked rug on the floor. A floor lamp burned beside a slip-covered easy chair, and magazines were spread over an end table.

"Make yourself comfortable," said Jim. "I'll come for you in half an hour or so."

She sniffed as she took off her fog coat. "Prisoner Krasicki, No. 87114. Take your time, Senator. I wouldn't walk back along that lonely road for a million dollars."

Jim made his way to the living room of the main house. A log fire was crackling in the wide stone fireplace, and the shadowed sweep of pasture through the front windows reminded Jim of Camp David. The walls were paneled in antiqued oak and rough beams supported the cathedral ceiling.

Five men were ranged in a semicircle about the fire. A sixth vacant chair awaited MacVeagh. The men rose as he entered, and Jim took in their faces at a glance. There was Associate Justice Grady Cavanaugh, a cheerful, even-tempered man with a habit of arching his black eyebrows, as he did now, when greeting a friend. Speaker of the House William Nicholson, fourth generation of one of America's proudest political families, stood stolid, austere and heavy. Old Senator Frederick Odlum of Louisiana, chairman of the Appropriations Committee, short and squat, followed MacVeagh with roving, cynical eyes. Vice-President Patrick O'Malley rolled a cigar above his drooping jowls. Jim was surprised to see the fifth man, a Negro, Senator Sterling Gullion of Illinois. He had large, moist brown eyes and skin the color of tanbark. As always, he was dressed immaculately. MacVeagh shook hands with each man, registering his reactions as he did so. With Cavanaugh, O'Malley and Gullion he felt at ease, but Nicholson was too forbidding of mien and stance, and Jim feared the first question from Odlum's waspish tongue.

All six men seated themselves, awkwardly and formally, as O'Malley spoke.

"Jim," he said, "I invited Sterling after checking with the others. Five old heads are better than four." O'Malley unclamped his cigar and smiled. "Besides, I didn't want any historian to claim that this meeting was segregated."

Gullion laughed. "Well, I'll sit in the same room with Fred Odlum, but I won't swim in his pool."

Odlum grunted. "You're welcome, Sterling," he said. "If you'll risk pneumonia and swim in that pool tonight, I'll call AP wirephoto and let them get a picture of it."

"If the case comes up to the court," said Cavanaugh with a wink at Gullion, "we'll rule for you, Sterling. The Odlum pool is not a public facility, and you don't have to swim in it if you don't want to."

All joined in the laughter, and the slightly forced joking continued for several minutes. Then O'Malley raised a hand and asked for quiet. His face was serious and the big jowls seemed to sag with a new burden.

"As you all know," he said, "Jim MacVeagh came to me three nights ago with a very alarming story. I thought all of you should hear it. We've all agreed in advance not to mention this meeting or anything connected with it outside this group. Is that still understood?"

They all nodded.

"I've got a completely open mind about Jim's story." O'Malley turned to MacVeagh. "Well, Jim, that's enough introduction. You've got the floor."

"I apologize for fetching you all out here," said MacVeagh, "but I've become convinced this country is facing a crisis. All I can do, as I did with Pat, is tell you exactly what I've seen and heard."

And once again Jim launched into the story. He told why he'd gone to O'Malley—because of the announcement of Hollenbach's April 20 meeting with Zuchek and Jim's own conviction that it must be canceled. Then he began with the first night at

Aspen lodge, trying to relate precisely what occurred. He sought to reflect Hollenbach's moods of rage and exaltation and to communicate to them the feeling of the President's erratically racing speech in the dead of night after the floor lamp had been turned off. But as he retold one incident after another, Jim realized that he was failing to convey the frightening reality of the paranoia he saw in the President. Instead, to his own ears, Jim's story sounded a bit disorderly and vague, as though the events had lost their graphic outline and some of their meaning. But he continued, a bit doggedly, relating Hollenbach's latest charge Tuesday morning that MacVeagh had joined a conspiracy to destroy the President. He concluded with the odd episode of Mrs. Byerson and her surprising revelation that she too had heard the President mention a super-union of nations.

When he finished, Jim saw Fred Odlum's little eyes fixing him from the wrinkled, pinched face. Jim felt the pressure of disbelief in the eyes, and he hoped he could survive the questioning without flinching. But Cavanaugh spoke first in an even, conversational tone.

"I think we get the picture as you see it, Jim," he said, "but perhaps you should sum up for us what you think. What's your conclusion?"

"I think," said MacVeagh slowly, "as I told Pat the other night, that the President of the United States is either demented, lost in some severe case of paranoia, or else he's suffering some temporary mental lapse. I pray to God it's the latter. But, either way, I don't think he should be allowed to go to Stockholm."

Odlum's first question came in the gritty voice he used for evasive committee witnesses. "Senator, you seem to put a lot of emphasis on this business of turning out the lights at Aspen lodge. What's so sinister about that? Didn't Lyndon Johnson make a big thing about clicking off lights?"

"That was a symbol of economy, Fred," replied MacVeagh,

"more for laughs than anything else. With President Hollenbach, there's something eerily spiritual about it."

"Spiritual? Not very scientific terminology," snapped Odlum.

"I'm just trying to give you the whole picture." Jim knew it sounded limp.

"Do you think the idea of a union with Canada has to be the notion of a diseased mind?" asked Gullion.

"No, of course not," replied Jim. "But it's of a pattern with everything else."

"Ah'm glad to hear you say that," drawled Gullion, "because there's a group of important businessmen in Chicago who favor a union with Canada, and I'd hate to think they were all crazy."

"Of course," said Cavanaugh, "let's not start off with the assumption that this is an impossibility. Don't forget Woodrow Wilson. Obviously he wasn't in possession of his full faculties for months while the Versailles Treaty was up, and Mrs. Wilson was running the country more or less. And I remember that Eisenhower himself said that in his case, he couldn't speak properly after his small stroke, which mercifully cleared up in a few days.

"But still, Jim, with that background for an appreciation of your concern, couldn't Hollenbach's suspicion that Pat here was deliberately trying to sabotage him, couldn't that have been the normal exaggeration of a man who was hopping mad?"

"Sure," said Jim, "but don't forget what he said about Davidge, and to me—and his dark hints that there was some kind of conspiracy operating against him. Also, Mark prides himself on mental precision, and those kinds of charges are plain wacky."

"Still," insisted Cavanaugh, "what he said to O'Malley would not in itself indicate a mental ailment."

"No," said Jim defensively, "not in itself it wouldn't."

Cavanaugh frowned. "On the other hand, the most damaging

thing you've said, to my mind, is that the President actually is considering a national wiretapping law. That seems incredible to me. It flies directly in the face of everything he's advocated in the area of personal freedom."

"Exactly," said Jim hurriedly. "That's just the point. His mind has to be radically disturbed to come up with a thing like that. And don't forget, he told me he could have used a wiretap on Pat here if he'd had the law."

"I just can't believe that you're accurately quoting the President," said Nicholson archly.

"I can't either," said Gullion. "For one thing, the President is too smart politically. That kind of plan could defeat him in November."

"He was serious," said MacVeagh doggedly. "He convinced me that he was. That's all I can tell you but, believe me, I'm not exaggerating."

"Now that business about Scandinavia," said Odlum. His tone was acid, unbelieving. "Certainly a man who is married to a lovely woman of Swedish descent would not contend that praising the characteristics of the Swedes is the act of a tortured mind?"

"No, of course not." Jim had to struggle to control his temper. Odlum was trying to bait him. "But union with Scandinavia is something else again. Hollenbach pictures that as some kind of utopia, and you and I know it would raise hell with our real power allies, Germany, France, England, even Japan. What the hell, Fred, you know that's nutty."

"Well," said Odlum dryly, "just try telling that to Mrs. MacVeagh's Swedish kinfolks and see who they think is crazy." The squat little Louisiana senator fingered the wrinkles in his cheek. "You know, maybe Hollenbach hasn't got such a bad idea. A union with Scandinavia would redress the racial imbalance in this country. We whites need some help. Gullion and his people are about to make this a black republic."

"Now, Fred," said Gullion, shaking a warning finger, "where's your sense of gratitude? You got 66 per cent of the Negro vote in Louisiana last time."

Cavanaugh laughed. "That proves the point Fred is making—when the Negroes gang up to keep a low-brow like himself in office."

"A couple of low-brows on the Supreme Court," retorted Odlum, "and you fellows might hand down a sensible decision for a change."

Everyone laughed except MacVeagh. Jim had a sinking feeling that the heavy-handed humor was intended as a wake for his mission. They weren't taking him seriously.

"Let's get back on the track," said O'Malley, and MacVeagh flashed him a grateful look.

"All right," said Speaker Nicholson. "The trouble with Mac-Veagh's story is that there's no corroboration from the people who know the President best." He spoke ponderously, as though ruling on a point of order in the House. "What about his wife, Evelyn, that son of his at Yale, the White House physician, the people on the staff who are close to him? What do they think?"

"It would be impossible, Mr. Speaker," protested MacVeagh, "to pursue a line of questioning like that without a go-ahead signal from the leadership. That's what I'm arguing for here—some arrangement for further investigation of my . . . well . . . my convictions."

"Of course," said Cavanaugh, "under the present setup, only the vice-president could pursue this thing. The law itself is clear, and besides, Pat has his own written agreement with the President under which he's required to act speedily. Gentlemen, I do agree that Jim's story merits further inquiry. After all, we're not back in Wilson's day. With all these nukes, push buttons and go-codes, we just can't afford any presidential 'hiatus from normality,' if I can phrase it that way."

"But so far we've only got one man's word to go on," said Nicholson.

"That's not quite correct," said MacVeagh. "Pat heard himself charged with intentional sabotage, and then there's Jessica Byerson. She'd be easy enough to question."

"Looniest old crone in Washington," said Odlum. "I should listen to that crackpot again!"

"What about this mysterious person who talked to the President about Davidge?" asked Nicholson.

O'Malley nodded to MacVeagh. "I think Jim has arranged for that," he said. "Let's take five while Jim fetches his witness."

Rita was sitting in the guest room, a mound of lipstick-marked cigarette stubs in the ashtray beside her. She came willingly enough, after primping her hair and smoothing her charcoal linen dress. Surveying her, Jim had a twinge of anxiety. She looked too sensuous, too inviting, for this cold business with the leaders. But there was no retreating now, and he squeezed her hand as they walked to the big living room.

The group was as startled as was Rita when she entered the room. The men all rose and there was a brief introduction by O'Malley before she took the chair the Vice-President held for her. Except for Cavanaugh, Rita knew every man in the room.

"Mrs. Krasicki," said O'Malley, "I gather that you're the person who had a conversation with President Hollenbach relative to a banker named Davidge. Would you mind repeating that story just as you remember it."

"I'm not in the habit of repeating confidential political conversations," she replied. Her tone was her crisp, bookkeeper's one. "May I ask the purpose of this? Is it some kind of investigation of Mr. Davidge?"

"We're not at liberty to say," said O'Malley, "since it's a matter of national security. Of course, you're under no compulsion to talk. This is completely informal and we have no power of subpoena."

Rita's black eyes, flicking from face to face, were hostile. Oh, God, thought Jim, she's going to refuse after all. He caught her glance and pleaded mutely with her. Finally, he said aloud: "Please, Rita. You promised."

"May I smoke?" she asked O'Malley.

"Certainly," said O'Malley, brandishing his own cigar.

The seconds dragged silently as she produced a cigarette and leaned forward for a light from Fred Odlum. Her small movements and her first inhalation stirred old memories of desire in MacVeagh, and he looked quickly away, lest the others sense his feeling.

"All right," she said, and she told the story of her telephone conversation with President Hollenbach. But her tone was flat, arid, and she conveyed none of the fire of the President's voice and mood as she had with Jim.

"Isn't it true, Rita," Jim asked when she finished, "that you told me that story because I had said the President had talked strangely to me, and you said everybody's a little strange at times, and then I asked you to explain?"

"Yes, that's right."

"And what was your conclusion, the way you told me?" he prodded.

"I think I said that . . ." She frowned. "That it showed the President had a human side, after all, and that even Mark Hollenbach, who preaches perfection isn't always perfect. Something like that."

Senator Odlum bored in at once. "And where did this conversation with Senator MacVeagh take place?"

Rita dropped her eyes. "At my apartment in Georgetown."

"When?" asked Odlum. He was treating her sharply, as he would a balky committee witness.

"Let's see." She did not lift her eyes to Odlum's. "A Sunday, about three weeks ago, in the evening."

Odlum leaned forward, his pinched face intent. "And why did

Senator MacVeagh come to your apartment, Mrs. Krasicki?"

Justice Cavanaugh, as though sensing the situation, interrupted. "Is that necessary, Fred? What difference does it make why Jim was there?"

Odlum's little eyes darted from Rita to Jim. "It has a direct bearing," he said. He was in his full, relentless role of committee chairman now. "We all read that Cousins and King story yesterday. Suppose, for the moment, that for some reason unknown to us our colleague, the distinguished junior senator from Iowa, is not telling the truth. Then, of course, if there is a . . . well, uh . . . an understanding between MacVeagh and Mrs. Krasicki, then I'd say it tends to color the testimony of both."

"This isn't sworn testimony, Fred," flared MacVeagh. "My God, I'm just trying to do what I think is right, not trying to put something over."

"All right," said Odlum, his voice harsh and challenging, "but we were brought out here in the middle of the night, out in the woods, and I, for one, want to get to the bottom of all this."

Rita looked beseechingly at Jim. He could see the hurt in her eyes, and he experienced a sinking sensation within him.

"Don't worry, gentlemen," said Rita suddenly. "I don't know what this is all about, but if it matters, Jim and I were once close friends."

She said it defiantly, her shoulders drawn back and her eyes fastened on Odlum. With her black eyes and her tensed muscles, she reminded Jim of a cornered animal, a wild and beautiful animal. He felt a surge of pity for her. God, suppose he was wrong, he thought, all wrong? How many persons were being sacrificed for one man's suspicions?

"You mean you were intimate friends?" asked Odlum. He stressed the word "intimate" in a drawl that taunted.

"Fred," said Cavanaugh, "I think that's quite enough."

"It is enough," said Rita, interrupting. She glared at Odlum.

"Draw your own conclusions, Senator. I notice that you seem to enjoy drawing the spiciest ones."

"My dear young lady," said Odlum, "I didn't ask you to come here. I didn't even volunteer to come here myself."

Rita lit another cigarette hurriedly, her hand trembling. She looked numbly at MacVeagh, and he felt as though he'd like to seize her hand and whisk both of them away.

"Rita," said Speaker Nicholson gently, "I hate to do this, but there is one question that occurs to me. Are you quite sure you got all of Davidge's speeches? Isn't it possible his secretary didn't send them all to you, and that perhaps Davidge did make some vitriolic speech about President Hollenbach or the administration?"

Rita nodded with a puzzled frown. "That's possible. I only read those speeches that were sent to me."

"But had Davidge made such a speech, Mr. Speaker," observed Cavanaugh, "considering his stature and influence, I'm sure it would have made all the papers."

"I guess that's all, Rita," said O'Malley. "Thanks for coming and being so cooperative."

MacVeagh walked Rita in silence back to the guest room. Only then did he see that her eyes were moist and a tear streaked the powder on one cheek. He put an arm around her shoulders to comfort her, but she shook it off.

"What in God's name are you trying to do to me, Jim?" she asked, her voice breaking. "First the FBI and now this. I'm beginning to think you're an ugly excuse for a man."

She turned her back to him, and after a moment he left the room. Yes, he thought, what was he doing to her? Mingled sensations of shame, pity and charred desire churned within him, and he felt undone as he re-entered the living room.

There was a brief, stiff discussion of whether MacVeagh should be permitted to tell Rita the purpose of the meeting.

Justice Cavanaugh settled the matter. MacVeagh's suspicions, he said, whether true or false, were so inflammable, that absolutely no one else should know. MacVeagh nodded an assent.

"By the way," asked Odlum, "have you communicated these fears of yours to anyone else?"

"Only to Paul Griscom," said MacVeagh, "and as I told you, I didn't identify the President. I pretended it was someone else. And I'll be honest with you, Fred, I think Griscom believes I was describing a mental condition of my own. He wanted to help me." Jim paused. "Oh, yes, I told my wife too, but she wouldn't tell a soul."

"And what does Mrs. MacVeagh think of your story?" asked Odlum.

"I don't think she believes me," he said, "because of . . . well . . . because of other things. I think she thinks I'm having hallucinations of my own."

They all stared at him, and Jim knew they surmised that his wife suspected his relationship with Rita. And now Jim understood how Rita felt, for he too had the feeling that he'd been stripped naked.

"Well," said Cavanaugh after a moment, "what should we do?"

Nicholson got up from his chair, his movements cumbersome, officious.

"I'll tell you what I'm going to do," he said. "I'm going to leave. I've had enough."

There was astonishment on every face. Nicholson held the back of his chair and spoke as though addressing a sizable audience.

"I don't know what is prompting Senator MacVeagh," said Nicholson, "whether it's an overly suspicious mind or something more devious. I note that he has withdrawn from the vice-presidential contest, a curious move to my mind. Then I find this

business of Mrs. Krasicki and the Cousins and King story a
trifle too much to digest right now. I'm not sure just what's going
on, but I don't like it, gentlemen.

"I refuse to sit here any longer and listen to more maligning of
a great president. I think these aspersions on his mental condition are fantastic, and I think this meeting damn near amounts to
sedition. Frankly, I feel disloyal and unclean for having taken
part in it."

With that, Speaker Nicholson turned and walked from the
room in his slow, lumbering gait. Jim, in a flash, thought of the
high irony of Nicholson's defending Hollenbach when the President at Camp David had dismissed Nicholson as "too heavy":
"He smothers me with that elephantine way of his."

The five remaining men sat stunned. Senator Gullion tried a
light remark. "Well, there goes the House. We're left with no
shelter." But nobody smiled.

"I think," said Cavanaugh at last, "that I favor some more
inquiries. Just how that should be done I'm not sure, but perhaps
we should all keep our ears open, make what discreet soundings
we can, and then meet back here again in a week. What do you
say?"

"No," said Odlum. "I favor dropping the whole thing right
here. I'm not as upset about all this as Nick is, and I appreciate
Jim's effort to do his duty as he sees it. If he comes up with anything more, I'll be glad to listen, but as of now I just don't
think there's enough substance to his story."

"But the whole pattern, Fred," said Cavanaugh. "There does
seem to be a pattern of instability, at least. I'm worried enough
. . . or uncertain enough . . . to proceed further."

"Look," said Odlum. He had dropped his inquisitional manner. "Nobody is normal, and even if we could find a completely
normal president, would we want him that way? Can any man be
an outstanding leader who doesn't have some flights of imagina-

tion, some ideas that set him apart? I doubt it. At any rate, this thing is too vaporous for me. I just can't get my fingers on anything solid."

"I agree," said Gullion, "and it's probably the first time in my life I ever agreed with Fred on anything."

"You build a swimming pool, Sterling," said Odlum with a derisive chuckle, "and someday I might come and integrate it for you."

"It's a bargain." Gullion's coppery features split in a wide grin.

MacVeagh experienced an empty feeling. The country faced one of its greatest perils and these men, cynically disbelieving, were treating it all as a joke.

"My hands are tied," said O'Malley. "Because of my own compromising situation on the arena, we all know I can't act without the support of you men. Personally, I do have doubts about the President's mental processes, but doubts aren't enough in a case of this kind. I propose that Jim and I stay out of this, and that the other three of you take a vote. Should we continue the inquiry or drop it right here?"

"I vote to continue," said Cavanaugh.

"I say drop it," said Odlum.

"Ditto," said Gullion.

Vice-President O'Malley slapped the arm of his chair as though with a gavel. "Meeting's adjourned," he said.

Each man shook MacVeagh's hand in friendly fashion, and Odlum even gave his arm a squeeze as he whispered, "I'm sorry I put the heat on you and Rita, but I had to know whether you were playing straight with us." But the parting was misery for Jim. He felt that he'd lost not only the battle but the war. And now, MacVeagh was sure, several other people, Nicholson especially, either thought his own mental structure was faltering or that he was some kind of vengeful political feudist. Cavanaugh held MacVeagh back as the others filed out the door.

"Jim," he said, "if I were in your spot, there's one line I think I'd follow up. Suppose your theory is correct? If it is, the President may have had symptoms before. After all, that's why you looked up the material on his boyhood. Why not have some friend at the Pentagon look up Hollenbach's service record for you? He fought in the Korean War. Army, wasn't it? There might be something there, maybe not. But at any rate, if his mind was normal under pressure of combat, at least you'd feel a little easier."

MacVeagh thanked him and agreed to follow the suggestion. But he wondered if he really would. He felt disjointed, vapid, drained. God, he hoped he could sleep for a change tonight.

The ride home with Rita began in sullen silence. The sky showed only patches of gray beyond the fringes of a muddy overcast that seemed to weigh on them like lead. They could hear gravel snapping under the tires as the rented sedan picked its way over the winding road to the highway. The village of Lusby was dark and only an occasional farmhouse light flickered as Jim pressed back to Washington at seventy miles an hour.

"Jim," said Rita, "I was never made to feel so shabby in my life."

"I'm sorry, Rita," he apologized. "That's all I can say. I'd have given ten thousand dollars to spare you that scene."

"That nasty Fred Odlum," she snapped. "I might have expected that from a man who's pinched half the fannies on Capitol Hill."

"Rita. It's over. Forget it." He was bone weary and he did not want to talk about anything.

"Aren't you going to tell me why I was put through that crawly third degree . . . like some streetwalker the cops picked up?"

"I can't," he said. "We were all sworn to secrecy. And if I could ask one thing more of you, please don't mention anything about that meeting to anyone, Rita."

"Don't worry," she said bitterly. "How could I ever reveal such a dismal, degrading scene to anyone?"

She turned to the window and once more Jim heard her sob. It was a brief, dry cry. Then she wiped her eyes under the dark glasses and smoked in silence as the night fled by.

They were passing the entrance to Andrews Air Force Base when she suddenly said: "Jim, you are in some kind of cabal to destroy President Hollenbach, aren't you?"

"No," he said. "I'm trying to help him, not hurt him. But I can't talk about it, Rita. Not now."

She lit another cigarette after crumpling an old pack and reaching in her purse for a new one. "That's it, isn't it?" She was angry and accusing now. "He threw you off the ticket only three weeks after inviting you on it, so now you're out to get even with him. You're in some plot to discredit the President. I've a good mind to tell Joe Donovan tomorrow."

"Don't, for God's sake, Rita," he implored. "That would raise all kinds of hell to no purpose. I'm not in any plot of any kind."

She said nothing.

"Please, Rita," he urged. "Trust me."

She turned, and her dark glasses faced him bleakly like lumps of coal. "Trust you, MacVeagh? After tonight? Never again."

And Jim realized there was no arguing with her. He felt sad, for her, for himself, for his country, and he wondered whether his fight was worth it. Perhaps he should drop the whole thing. Or, again, perhaps he was having hallucinations and had dreamed it all. He drove in silence through the deadened streets of Washington and when he reached the house on O Street, it was almost 2 A.M. Rita left the car without a good-by, banged the door, and rushed up the four brick steps to her front door.

15.

Green Turtle

Jim arrived at the Senate Office Building Friday a few minutes before eight o'clock. The elevator boy yawned over a law textbook open on his knees. Otherwise the old structure was empty. Jim's footsteps echoed in the wide marble corridor as though he were a platoon of wearily marching men.

The first of Senator MacVeagh's staff would not begin work until 8:30, and Jim was alone in his big room with its glass-windowed bookshelves, its autographed pictures, its photograph of spring plowing in Iowa, and its desk with the neat stacks of correspondence awaiting his attention.

He felt wretched. The whites of his blue eyes were streaked with red, his head throbbed, and his skin felt as though it were flaking away, a sensation usually produced by lack of sleep. He had slept only fitfully, and no body position or mental counting game had carried him far from consciousness. Then, just after dawn, he had awakened from a light dozing spell to find his leg and arm muscles twitching.

He had dreamed and the instant memory of it was vivid. He dreamed that President Mark Hollenbach, in a choking fury, had accused Jim of plotting his downfall. Jim, unable to contain his temper longer, lashed out savagely at Hollenbach with his fist, struck the President full on the cheekbone and felt, horribly, his hand go entirely through the President's skull, emerging on the other side. When he pulled out his arm, as he would from a pail of water, Hollenbach fell dead at his feet. Then had come Arnold Brothers, shaking his head and clucking as though Jim had been a naughty child. Brothers snapped handcuffs on Jim and led him away to a barren cell in a damp prison where iron doors clanged ceaselessly. There Jim sat on a stool, desperately castigating himself for slaying a man without cause and wondering why he had not thought before he acted in violence.

Now, in his Senate office, Jim could still feel the terror of the dream, even if he could no longer remember all the scenes. Was the dream some subtle warning from his subconscious? Was he guilty of trying to harm the President of the United States? Were his conclusions as to Mark's sanity but flimsy conjectures that had no substance in fact? Were Nicholson, Odlum and Gullion right in believing that Senator MacVeagh was imagining what was never there? Perhaps Martha, Griscom and Chief Brothers were correct, and his shocked mind was drifting from the mooring which had always held it so snugly.

The man who once shied from self-analysis was now again deep in the process, and he wondered if some unknown, twisted part of him was luring him on a surrealist venture without earthly goals. Again he could feel the noose tightening about him, and he physically shook his shoulders to be free of it. No, he told himself firmly, nothing had changed. The man whose mind was shredding was not Jim MacVeagh, but Mark Hollenbach. Two stable men, Cavanaugh and O'Malley, gave credence to his story. Settle down, Jim, he cautioned himself. One step at a time. Don't panic. All right, that's better.

When Jim later buzzed for Roger Carlson, the aide swung in with his cocky stride and was about to assume his customary slouching perch on the corner of Jim's desk. Then he saw Mac-Veagh's face and he stopped.

"Jeez," he said, "have you been doing the town all night? You look like something the rats left over."

Jim smiled wanly. "I stayed up too late, Flip, working on that Hollenbach book."

"You musta had a belt of Scotch with every paragraph," said Carlson.

"Nope, just the ravages of work. Flip, I want you to pull some strings over at the Pentagon and get me Hollenbach's service record. I need it for the biography. Maybe, if it's not too long, I could even use text on the thing."

Carlson folded his shirt-sleeved arms and shook his head.

"Come off it, boss. You're not writing any book about Mark Hollenbach. Something else is up. Right? Come on, tell me. What the hell is going on?"

Jim was startled. "What do you mean?"

"Just what I said. You're bluffing."

"I am not. I'm working on a lot of material about Hollenbach. What makes you doubt it?"

Carlson pulled a chair to the center of the room and sat facing his senator. "Look, Jim, I've come to the conclusion that a lot of screwy things are happening all at once. The way that FBI agent hinted around, I'm sure he was going to question me about you, not somebody else in the office. Then he calls it off, suddenly, just when you apparently called Hollenbach and bowed out of the vice-presidential thing. And how about that visit from the Secret Service agent after my La Belle trip? Some of the stuff he asked me was pretty far out, as though he had some zany idea that you and I were out to harm the President, for God's sake. He got pretty detailed for the routine check he claimed it was. For instance, he asked me if I'd made a written report to you, and I said I had."

"Oh." Jim couldn't hide his surprise. God, he thought, he'd forgotten to cover that one.

"What's the matter?" asked Carlson.

"Well, you see, that agent, Luther Smith, called on me too, and I told him you hadn't made a written report, only a verbal one."

"But why did you say that?"

"Because," said Jim, "it was right in front of him. He was looking right at it and I was afraid he'd realize what it was and ask for it. Naturally, I didn't want him to have it. Anyway, I guess now Smith probably has reported to Chief Brothers that I'm a liar, and they'll think I'm the one who's—" Jim checked himself. He averted his head and simulated a cough.

"Who's what?" asked Carlson.

"Nothing, I mean . . ."

"Say, boss," persisted Carlson, "let's level. Have you some kind of hunch that the President isn't all there in the head?"

"No, no, Flip. What gives you that idea?"

"Well, as I say, a lot of stuff around here is beginning to add up. Take that report of mine. Mark Hollenbach was a pretty offbeat kid and college boy, wasn't he? There were no kids like that on my block, or around the fraternity house either. Then these two investigations, and suddenly you get bounced off the ticket—or were going to be, according to you—only a few days after I got the clear idea that Hollenbach had picked you."

"I resigned," said MacVeagh. "I took myself off."

"Yeah, I know. But all this studying of Hollenbach you're doing, like you're trying to psychoanalyze him. And now you want his service record."

"Flip," said MacVeagh, with a show at firmness, "you're imagining things. Your penchant for flashy speculation has got the best of you. I'm writing a biography of the President. It's as simple as that."

"I don't believe you. And if that's cause for firing me, go ahead."

"Now, don't get on the muscle." Jim sought to placate him. "Just go ahead and get me that service record. The best way, probably, is through that Army legislative liaison officer, Colonel Josephs. He owes us plenty for all my votes for the Army. If he gives you any static, just remind him how much we've done for him in the past."

"All right." Carlson got up to go, but his eyes held Mac-Veagh's in a lingering and doubting gaze. "When you get ready to tell me, boss, I'll be ready to listen. I might be able to help, you know."

And when Carlson closed the door behind him, Jim realized that one more friend had been added to the growing list of those who no longer believed what Senator MacVeagh told them. He felt helpless and isolated, and he realized that if he didn't get some sleep soon he would become physically ill.

By noontime, luckily, a great weariness settled over him. Jim welcomed the feeling of exhaustion, and he could visualize the sheets on his bed as a cool haven. He informed his staff he was going home and he quit for the day just as the noon bell rang for the Senate session.

Martha met him at the door in McLean.

"I'm whipped, Marty," he said. "All done in, and I'm going to bed. No calls, please, huh?"

"Is it this thing about the President that's got you down?" she asked.

"Uh-huh." He did not have the energy to say more.

She grasped him by both arms and smiled, her eyes roving fondly over his weary face.

"Jim," she said, "I've got it all figured out."

"You have?" He felt drugged and lifeless.

"Yes, I have. We're going away for a few days. Just the two of us, to that quiet little inn on Green Turtle Cay in the Bahamas. You know we love it there."

Yes, thought Jim. They had spent their fifth and tenth wedding anniversaries there. He could see the shifting pastels of the water, shimmering in the sun like a vast green mosaic, and he could feel the luxury of the lazy salted air. But he shook his head.

"I can't, Marty. Not now."

"Why not?" She squeezed his arms and implored with her eyes. "April is lovely in the outer islands. You can rest. We'll watch the sunset and walk on the beach. You can fish, if you want. Please, Jim, please. You need it so, darling."

Well, he thought, why not? She believed that his mind was drifting, and perhaps it was. What could he do in Washington anyway right now? Nobody would listen to him. He was not convincing anybody, merely sowing a wider field of doubt whatever he did and wherever he went. But down there, in the soaking warmth and the silky nights, maybe he could think things out. Just maybe. Why, sure, Marty was right.

"Okay, honey. You fix everything while I take a nap. Get us on a night jet to West Palm Beach and then we can fly over tomorrow morning."

She hugged him, planted a moist kiss on his ear, then tugged him toward the stairs.

"While you're asleep, the good fairy will wave her wand, and then we'll be off," she said.

They flew south that night from Dulles International Airport after Martha had farmed out Chinky to friends and after Jim had called Flip Carlson, giving him the Bahamas address and leaving instructions that he was not to be disturbed for anything short of a declaration of war.

Green Turtle Cay, off the eastern flank of Great Abaco, lay like an emerald in the sun as the battered powerboat took Jim and Martha across three miles of sheltered water from the airstrip on the larger island. The white Bahamian boatman, his withered face the color of tobacco stain, rattled off the cay's gossip since their last visit. Jim loosened his tie and turned his face to the warm wind as the boat cut into the harbor, crossed White Sound, and moored at the pier below the inn.

The MacVeaghs were greeted as old friends by the proprietors of Bluff House, a lemon-yellow frame inn which sat atop a high hill amid a profusion of golden chalice vines, bougainvillea, coral hibiscus and yellow crotan shrubs. Jim changed into trunks and Martha into a swim suit, and they half ran down the coral rock path to the beach 100 yards below. Jim played porpoise in the water, nudging at Martha and pulling her under by grabbing at her heels. Then they lay on the powdery sand, feeling the sun pour into their bodies and listening to the breeze whipping at the madeira and ficus trees. Jim fell asleep and had to be wakened by Martha because his back was turning pink in the afternoon sun. They swam again in the salt-water pool beside the inn, and then there were cocktails with the proprietors and the four other guests, followed by a candlelit dinner, featuring coq au vin and a full red wine that left a rich taste on the tongue.

The two other couples were both young, one a honeymooning pair who held hands furtively under the table and occasionally exchanged reverent glances when they thought they were unobserved. The second pair apparently was not married, for they had registered under the improbable name of Mr. and Mrs. "Godspeed," which happened to be the name of a rakish racing sailboat at nearby Elbow Cay which they had just visited. Also Mr. Godspeed frequently responded to his name with a baffled and hesitant look. The non-Godspeeds were skin divers and spent most of their time brooding and bickering over a mountain of gear, including hoses, tanks, spears, masks and motors, which littered a good part of the pier. They were both bony, parched and leathery, and they carped so much over the care of their diving accessories that Martha speculated that the non-God-speeds would soon be parted by a nondivorce.

Martha was adding new spice to her theories about the skin divers that night while Jim buttoned his pajamas and prepared to slip into bed. He was drowsy and content, and he hadn't thought about Washington since he toiled up the hill to Bluff House that afternoon. He knew he would fall asleep in five minutes. Martha wore a pair of sheer black lace pajamas, belted at her waist. She took Jim's hand.

"You're not going to bed yet," she said. "You're coming with me."

"And where are you going, lady adventurer, at ten o'clock at night on this island? The only thing still up is the moon."

"Sometimes you talk too much, Jim," she said. "Just shut up, put on your shoes, and come with me."

He did as bidden, and they walked out of their room hand in hand. Martha carried two towels in her free hand. The dome of the sky arched clear and fresh above them and millions of stars were strewn about like jewels on black felt. A crescent moon perched above the thicket of gumbo limbo and poisonwood trees as though pinned there as an ornament for a lawn party. Holding Jim's hand, Martha picked her way down the path which led to the beach. When Jim stumbled once and cursed the coral out-cropping, she shushed him. The pale night light shimmered thinly on sand and water. The ocean, placid now, nibbled at the shore with soft, suckling sounds.

Martha undid her lace pajamas and let first the top and then the bottom drop to the sand. She stood before him nude and, placing one hand on her hip, she pirouetted slowly. Her nipples were taut and the breasts cast small shadows on her flesh in the moonlight.

"Now, Jim," she said, "you'll have to admit this is more chic than Rita Krasicki's basic foundation."

He stood watching her, fascinated, as she turned with a saucy toss of her head. As a husband, he felt a stab of guilt and remorse at the mention of Rita's name, and he wondered what vagaries of emotion had swept him into unfaithfulness. But the man quickly took over from the husband, and he found himself challenged carnally by her comparison. Yes, he agreed that Martha, as she stood there under the moon and the stars, was an alluring sculpture in flesh. Her belly was trim and smooth, her white thighs gleamed in the fragile light, and her face wore a mocking smile.

"Undress!" she commanded. The buoyancy of her tone startled him. What the devil . . .

But she was beside him, fumbling feverishly at the buttons on his pajama top. He slid off the trousers himself, and she yanked at his hand, pulling him across the beach into the water.

The cool night waves, rolling gently toward the shore, had the caress of velvet on his bare skin. Jim reached for Martha's waist through the water, but she took several swift strokes, swimming away from him and kicking a bubbly froth in his face. The chase lasted several minutes. Each time he touched one of her limbs, she squirmed away and slid, dolphinlike, out of reach. At last he grasped her firmly about the shoulders and drew her to him. The sensuous merger of water and flesh, never before experienced, aroused a desire almost suffocating in its power. They stood in waist-deep water, lavishing each other with wet kisses and holding so tightly their arms ached. Then, as they laughed shyly at their surge of passion, Jim guided her to the shore. There, on the beach, they were one, and for long minutes they alternately fought for consummation and to thwart it, whispering feverishly like children and expending themselves wildly. Lust fired them as a fever, and Martha felt an immense, welling hunger for her man. At last, in the mysterious seizure of fulfillment, she uttered a sharp cry, and then they were both still.

They lay mute and exhausted, clasped in an embrace in which

sweat and sand mingled with the sting of drying salt water. And then, as quickly as the sudden breeze which whistled through the madeira trees, Jim felt an enormity of guilt for his long affair with Rita. In a swift tumble of thoughts, he castigated himself for sliding heedlessly into a liaison that carried his body and his mind to another woman and which robbed Martha of him for precious months. It was as though, in a fit of madness, he had looted his own home. Remorse ate at him like acid, then slowly ebbed away, engulfed in a wave of deep tenderness. He stroked Martha's throat and he said softly: "Marty, please forgive me for what I've done. I love you."

To his surprise, she smiled, patted his face and got up quickly from the sand. She found the towels and threw him one.

"Quit your mooning and rub hard," she said, "or you'll wind up with pneumonia."

They dressed in their pajamas again and sat hunched on the sand, looking across the sound to the little village of New Plymouth. Several lights still twinkled, and the cluster of single-story houses was framed faintly by the moonlight.

Jim wondered at the transformation in Martha. Gone was the skittering, frothy, cluttered woman who slid from project to project like a bug on ice. Instead she seemed composed, poised, appearing as content as he felt.

"Jim," she said as though she had a window to his thoughts, "it was as much my fault as yours. No man should have to put up with a wife who races around chairing committees. He needs a woman in his home, and if he doesn't have one, he'll go out and find one."

"Aw, Marty—" he protested, but she cut him short.

"I know I'm right," she said. "But I know something else now. You're my man, Jim MacVeagh, and I'm going to keep you any way I can."

They both stood up, and she brought her face close to his. Her close-bobbed hair was matted to her head in wet strands, and her face, bare of cosmetics, broke into a teasing grin.

"Wouldn't you like to keep me as your mistress, Senator? I think I'm good enough, don't you?"

He clutched her and smothered her again with kisses. "God, you're wonderful, Marty. Anything, anything. What would you like?"

She tilted her head and looked skyward. "Oh, just a few little things—in mink. Or sable maybe. Nothing ostentatious, you understand."

"I love you," he said.

"It's not enough," she replied. "You've got to worship me."

They laughed and then, hand in hand again, they walked up the winding path to the little inn, couched in its fragrant bed of flowering shrubs. Jim hadn't felt so serene and happy in months.

In the days that followed they became a rollicking, teasing pair, reveling in each other and in the glitter of Green Turtle Cay. Neither calflike nor somber like the honeymooners, they nevertheless seemed as fresh as a newly married couple to whom everything shone with a recently washed face. They fished. They sailed. They swam. They wandered through the hamlet of New Plymouth, which had been settled by refugee Tories from the United States during the Revolutionary War. They inspected the crumbling tombstones in the old graveyard, and they idled by the wharves to watch the inter-island schooners unload. They joked, they kidded each other unmercifully and once again they stole down to the beach near midnight. They found it difficult to keep their hands from each other, and Jim wondered at the waves of virility which swept over him time and again, unbeckoned. Once, after lovemaking, Martha broke into a fit of laughter.

"We've got to stop this," she said, "or I'll be a nervous wreck when we get back home. Do you know how many times we've made love here?"

"I never mix statistics with romance," he said.

"Nine." She giggled. "Nine times. If I ever told that to the Senate wives, they'd make you start a harem."

He leaned over her with a look of mock rage. "Do you mean to tell me that while I've been lost in love you've been counting?"

"I dote on higher mathematics."

"And the lower lusts too," he said. "Marty, it's plain concupiscence."

"Concu-what?"

"Never mind. You know too damn much already. I've a good mind to tell your mother on you."

"Oh, Jim darling, I adore you."

And so it went through the blissful hours, and it was not until Monday afternoon, as they lay baking in the sun on the little beach, that Jim let his mind return to President Hollenbach, Aspen lodge, the tangled mysteries of the grand concept, and the President's haunted charge that he was beset by a conspiracy of persecutors. What exactly, thought MacVeagh, should he do, now that he had this new perspective of distance and personal contentment? Somehow now it seemed that Fred Odlum had been right. The proper course, the one he should have followed all along, was to do nothing. The best action was no action. There was no question that President Hollenbach was not "normal," but precisely what did that mean anyway? Mark probably was suffering from some small, temporary disturbance, but didn't everybody at one time or another? Take himself and Rita. No, he refused to think about her, and he found it easy to dismiss her from his thoughts.

The sun beat down on Jim's tanning body, and he fingered the warm, loose sand. Sure, of course, under the tensions of Washington, he had exaggerated. Here, in the lazy, lulling breeze, Hollenbach's once hurtling speech seemed to slow and his jerky motions at Aspen lodge seemed to fade into familiar reactions.

The President was imaginative, alive, certainly strange at times, but he wasn't mad. Of course not. And even if he was somewhat abnormal, the infirmity would show itself to others soon. It couldn't be hidden forever. And why should Jim MacVeagh be the lonely crusader? By what God-given right did he appoint himself the savior of the country and the umpire of the sanity of men's minds? Yes, doing nothing—at least for some time—was really the wisest course. At the meeting with Zuchek in Stockholm there would be a score of State Department advisers to keep Mark in check. Jim had worried unduly about that. Odlum and Gullion, the white man and the black man, weren't so dumb. They were right. And Jim's face, upthrust to the sun, relaxed with the effortless decision he was making.

Martha, watching him idly, saw the change.

"What are you thinking, honey?" she asked.

"I was deciding," he said. "I've decided to do no more on this Hollenbach business. If he's off his rocker, and he's probably not, somebody else will discover it soon enough. It's not my job to psychoanalyze."

She traced a finger around his lips. "Of course, darling. I knew you'd understand finally."

He grinned. "The man has at last become as wise as his woman, huh?"

"And, Jim, you weren't being followed," she said quietly. "You know that now, don't you?"

He sat bolt upright and sand showered from him. "No, damn it . . ." he began, but then he checked himself. Why argue with her now and stir up her latent fears? Of course he had been followed. For all he knew, a Secret Service agent was staying in the hotel in New Plymouth right now. The surveillance of Jim MacVeagh had been an observed fact, regardless of the accuracy of his surmises about Hollenbach. Still, there was no sense in upsetting Martha.

"I was too being followed," he said with a grin. "You were following me—to force me into sexual bondage."

"You make a handsome slave," she said.

"Never give me liberty—or death," he said. And they kissed again.

Another night and day slipped by, luxuriously carefree, and they decided to stay the remainder of the week. But on Tuesday night Jim got a call from Washington. The inn had no telephones, but the owner maintained a ship-to-shore phone on his power barge, and Jim walked down the hill to answer the summons of the Miami marine operator. The connection was bad. Rattles and squeaks decorated a wavering beat of sound which alternately boomed and faded. Jim had to strain to hear. It was Flip Carlson.

"A couple of interesting things have happened, boss," said Carlson. "I knew you'd want to be filled in."

"All right. Shoot."

"First," said Carlson, "Colonel Josephs reported back to me today that Mr. H's service record is missing from the microfilms of the Army service records in St. Louis."

"Missing?"

"Yeah. A guy named Andrate from the Pentagon came out a couple of days ago and took the microfilm. Josephs wasn't supposed to tell me that, but he did."

"Who's Andrate?" asked MacVeagh.

"Your memory's failing in that tropic sun, boss. Butch Andrate is the confidential assistant to Mr. Defense, Sid Karper."

"Karper? You sure?"

"Right," said Carlson. "And here's the other interesting thing. You didn't tell me, but the head of the legislative reference service at the Library of Congress called you today, then talked to me. He says he still can't get you the full packet on the subject of presidential disability because somebody else has it."

"Did he say who?"

"Yes." Carlson uttered a name, but the connection faded.

"Who? Who?" asked Jim. "I couldn't catch it."

"Karper. Sidney Karper."

Jim was seized by a quickly mounting excitement. Lethargy dropped away like a spent shell.

"Flip," he said, "we'll fly back tomorrow. I'll arrive on that late-afternoon plane from West Palm. Meet me at Dulles, will you?"

"Sure, boss." There was a pause. "You still won't tell me what this is all about?"

"Later, Flip." Jim found that his nerves were quivering. "I can't tell you right now. Pick us up at Dulles."

"Okay," said Carlson, "and if you're so interested in Karper right now, it's good you're coming back, because he's slated to testify before your subcommittee on defense costs the day after tomorrow."

Jim walked rapidly up the hill to Bluff House but, fast as he went, his steps could not keep pace with his thoughts. Sidney Karper, probing into President Hollenbach's service record and reading material on presidential disability? Could that mean . . . ? Martha, waiting for him at the top of the hill, could tell by the absorbed look on her husband's face that the second honeymoon was over.

16.

Cactus II

At 10 A.M. Thursday Senator MacVeagh and two other senators, one Democrat and one Republican, seated themselves in black leather chairs at the head of the long, oblong table with green felt topping, traditional place of business for the Armed Services Committee of the U.S. Senate.

A large wall mirror over the old-fashioned marble fireplace reflected the gathering group of officials. Senator MacVeagh, chairman of a subcommittee conducting a continuing study of defense costs, nodded a greeting to the Secretary of Defense, Sidney Karper, who eased his huge body into a chair several places down the table from the three senators. The bronze tint of Karper's skin might blend with the metal nameplates on the committee table, but the seating protocol served as a tacit reminder to the Cabinet officer that in the halls of the Senate he was an alien on sovereign territory. Karper was neatly attired in a subdued pin-stripe suit, in contrast to the assistant at his side, whose clothes were rumpled and who had a pair of eyeglasses casually straddling the top of his head.

A committee aide walked past the cluster of service flags on a side wall and hung a small sign, EXECUTIVE SESSION, on an outer knob of the main door. Then he closed and locked it.

Jim MacVeagh, who had been studying Karper intently since

the Secretary entered the room, rapped his gavel smartly.

"No introductions are necessary here," said MacVeagh. "We're all old friends—or perhaps veteran acquaintances is a more appropriate term."

"Well, no," said Karper. "My special assistant here, Carmine Andrate, is new to this particular group. However, he's fully cleared for all security material, so there's no problem there."

MacVeagh nodded. "I think it's of a piece with Secretary Karper's grasp of the defense establishment that he comes here on complicated matters with only one assistant. At some hearings here, the colonels outnumber the bulbs in the chandeliers."

"Thanks," said Karper. His broad smile was genuine.

"All right," said MacVeagh, "this morning we're going to review the financing of the Pentagon's classified projects." He inspected a paper in his hand. "I see we have twenty-three of them this morning, so you might as well begin, Mr. Secretary, and take them up in order."

"Number 1," said Karper, clearing his throat and studying the top page of a sheaf of papers, is Project AWARE. The annual funding for this is $87 million and there's no change this year. As you gentlemen know, this involves the delicate recording stations we maintain in cooperation with the Atomic Energy Commission to detect nuclear explosions in Communist countries, or anywhere else for that matter. Our system, while expensive, is worth the money. Last year we detected the fourth big hydrogen blast by Red China in the vicinity of Luho not far from the Tibetan border. Then this February the system identified the fifth so-called dragon bomb detonation, measuring it at 75 megatons, or about 5,000 times the power of the Hiroshima bomb back in '45. The President was immediately notified and, as you know, the Hollenbach-Zuchek conference in Stockholm later this month is one of the diplomatic outgrowths of our findings—that plus the auxiliary intelligence that Red China now has the missile delivery capability. Our detection system is expensive, but we think it pays off. For your information, we know we measured the Chicom blast within an error margin of one megaton."

The senators raised no questions, and Karper ran through explanations of six other projects, including a new diving "igloo" for the Navy and support of the secret countersabotage school run in cooperation with the Central Intelligence Agency.

"This brings us to No. 8," said Karper. "This is Project CACTUS, financed with $250,000 from my own contingency fund. Unfortunately, this project, on which I'd placed so many hopes, came to nothing. It wasn't money down the drain, for at least we now know what we cannot do in this highly sensitive area. Still, I'm frankly discouraged at the lack of results."

"I don't think the committee has ever heard of CACTUS," said MacVeagh. "Could you go into that a bit, Mr. Secretary?"

Butch Andrate leaned over to whisper to his superior. Karper nodded. "Oh, yes," he said, "you haven't heard of this project because it was born and it died since our last report on classified programs to you gentlemen last spring. Essentially this was an effort to improve our command and control of nuclear weapons. You senators know many of the problems of C and C. They are vast."

After Karper described the establishment and functioning of the committee headed by General Trumbull, the Republican senator asked: "Just what phase of C and C were you trying to perfect, Mr. Secretary?"

Karper hesitated a moment, biting his lip. "Let's say the human element. The National Command Authorities—or the Big Three, if you will—must consult swiftly within a few minutes should a nuclear response or attack be indicated. While the President has final authority, it's assumed he wouldn't go against the combined opinion of myself and the Chairman of the Joint

Chiefs. Frankly, I've never been satisfied with the safeguards in this system."

"Why not?" asked MacVeagh.

"Well," said Karper, "suppose one of the three is ailing and finds it difficult to think clearly at just that moment. My concern is how do we protect ourselves, the country—the world, for that matter—against the possibility that a mind is not functioning properly."

MacVeagh, who had been slouching in his chair, came suddenly upright. He stared at Karper and, tilting his head, turned an ear toward the Pentagon chief.

"Did you say a mind that's not functioning properly, Mr. Secretary?" he asked.

"Yes." Karper's face registered no emotion.

"You mean," asked MacVeagh's fellow Democratic senator, "what happens if one of the men goes berserk?"

Karper nodded. "Well, that would be an extreme case you wouldn't look for in any of these three men, but one could suffer a sudden stroke or incapacity of some nature. At that point C and C becomes highly vulnerable. Last fall I became concerned and wondered whether there wasn't some way to insulate the system from 'human aberrations,' the phrase I used in setting up CACTUS. But after five months, as the committee reported to me three weeks ago, they could come up with no feasible recommendations. In short, the committee felt we'll just have to rely on the stability of the three men."

"Why last fall, Mr. Secretary?" asked MacVeagh. "Did anything special happen that caused you to act at that time?"

Karper shot a quick, appraising glance at MacVeagh from under his dark brows. MacVeagh thought he appeared startled. "Frankly," said Karper after a moment's hesitation, "I had reason to examine myself. I'm in good physical shape, I think, and I believe I'm normal. I work and I play hard. But if you recall, gentlemen, the same thing was thought of Forrestal in 1949. Yet it turned out he was suffering a severe mental breakdown that caused him to take his own life."

"You mean you had cause to question your own mental health?" asked the Republican senator skeptically.

MacVeagh thought Karper's quick laugh was forced.

"Not the way I am today," replied Karper, "or was last fall either, Senator. No. But what of the future? None of us can guarantee his mind's stability a year from now. So I groped for an answer, perhaps naïvely. But, at any rate, we're right where we started. Apparently there's no workable system of insurance."

MacVeagh looked closely at Karper, who sat as impassive as an Indian chief. If Karper had questioned his own stability, thought Jim, what had happened to cause him to do so? Was it really himself he was concerned about? Jim had never before seen Karper, usually blunt to the point of embarrassment, so discreet, so guarded, almost like a soldier picking his way through a mine field. Jim stared at Karper, but the Defense Secretary dropped his eyes and toyed with the sheaf of papers before him.

"This is a fascinating subject," observed the Republican senator. "It's too bad I'm under the total security rule here, because this year's election is one where my party could use an unbalanced Secretary of Defense as a target. However, I'm not sure that even that would save us this year."

They all laughed and MacVeagh added: "How about me? A lot of people are accusing me of being lightheaded for declining to run for vice-president."

The Republican snorted. "You're a good chairman, Jim, but you're not important enough to help us, crazy or not. But Sidney Karper, now there's a real game fish."

Karper chuckled, but again Jim had the impression the mirth

was synthetic. "My brain tends toward the Democratic party, Senator," said Karper, "if that's any indication of a lack of balance."

MacVeagh rapped his gavel. "We could stay on Project . . . what was that name again, Mr. Secretary?"

"CACTUS."

"Yes," said Jim. "We could stay on Project CACTUS all day, but we've got a lot more ground to cover in the sensitive areas, and I suggest we move along."

"I won't disagree, Mr. Chairman," said the Democratic senator, "but I think we ought to devote a whole day to this sometime soon."

"We'll consider that another time," said MacVeagh.

Karper, appearing relieved, took up the next classified item on his list. There were no further questions, and he managed to complete an explanation of all 23 programs just before the bell rang for the noon session of the Senate.

"Right under the wire," said MacVeagh. "We'll adjourn for the day and meet here again at 10 A.M. next Thursday, when we'll try to finish up on the classified programs."

As the group filed out, MacVeagh drew Karper aside. They stood next to a huge globe beneath the hanging banner of the Marine Corps.

"Have you got time to stop by my office for a moment?" asked MacVeagh.

Karper looked toward Andrate, who stood a few paces away. "What's my schedule, Butch?"

"You've got a 12:30 appointment with the Boeing people at your office," said Andrate.

"This is very urgent," whispered MacVeagh.

Karper looked at MacVeagh in surprise, then spoke to Andrate. "In that case, Butch, you keep the group happy for a while. I'll come over as soon as I can."

MacVeagh escorted Karper to his own suite in the old Senate Office Building, entering by his private door. He locked it behind him and then crossed the room to lock the door fronting on the outer secretarial offices. He motioned Karper to a chair and then called on the intercom to tell the receptionist he could take no calls from whatever source until further notice. Karper watched these proceedings with a baffled look.

"Mr. Secretary," said Jim, "I'd like to pursue something here in private. Could you tell me exactly what happened last fall that caused you to initiate Project CACTUS?"

Karper sat, blank, with folded arms. Once again the big head, imposing beak, and coppery tint of the skin gave Jim the impression that he was facing an Indian chief. Karper did not reply.

"Before you answer," said Jim, "let me tell you something. Two things have struck me rather forcefully. If there had been just one, I'd say it was coincidence, but two makes it startling to me."

Leaning forward on his desk and eying Karper closely, Jim told the Secretary of his call for the full presidential disability file and of his later request for the Korean service record of President Hollenbach.

"In both cases," said Jim, "I find that you have the material."

Still Karper said nothing. The two men sat staring at each other in silence. Jim had a strange, intuitive feeling that Karper was duplicating his own thoughts. He experienced an odd sense of shared awareness, as though they were two persons each recognizing in the other an old acquaintance after many years.

At last Karper spoke quietly, his eyes still fixed on MacVeagh's. "Let me ask you a question, Senator. Why did you want to see the President's service record?"

Jim felt his heart beating faster. "My excuse," he replied, "was that I'm doing a biography of him and I needed all available data."

"You say 'excuse,' " Karper was wary.

"Yes," said Jim. "I'm not writing such a book."

A crinkling of the flesh about Karper's eyes was the only movement in his face. "And what about your call for the file on the presidential disability question?"

Jim still held Karper's eyes with his own. "I had no excuse," he said, "but I have cause to believe that the subject of presidential disability is of vital concern right at this moment."

There was a heaviness of suspense in the room, yet Karper's face showed only a flicker of emotion.

"It's time," said Jim, "to be completely candid, Mr. Secretary. I had cause to doubt the mental stability of a high government official. Did you too—last fall?"

"I did."

"Was it . . . was it the President?"

"It was," said Karper.

There was momentary shock in the air, as though a shell had burst. Then Jim felt a sensation of vast relief, and he thought he detected a similar reaction on Karper's face.

"Have you told anyone else?" asked Jim.

Karper shook his head. "I couldn't."

"Perhaps," said Jim slowly, "in view of the circumstances, I ought to tell you first what I know."

And while Karper sat immobile, but with an expression of dawning understanding, MacVeagh told the whole story once more. Karper slumped in his chair, his great head resting on pressed fingertips, but not once did he take his eyes from MacVeagh. When Jim finished, Karper smiled sadly.

"Senator," he said, "or I'd prefer to call you Jim, if you don't mind—and please call me Sid—I couldn't help thinking during your recital what a curiously involved and compartmentalized government we have here in Washington. You and I know how this town works, but what ordinary citizen could believe that two officials could suspect what you and I have without ever meeting to share their views?"

"I've thought the same thing, Sid," said MacVeagh. "But, actually, how could we know? You don't shout this kind of thing from the housetops."

"No, you don't," replied Karper. "You know, it may sound heartless under the circumstances, but your story lifts a great burden from me. I've been struggling with this thing alone, losing sleep, going back and forth over a scene with the President, until, like you, I'd begun to doubt myself. What an upside down world, to think that corroboration of a President's mental troubles could actually make me feel good. But it does. Jesus, I'm not seeing phantoms, after all."

"Make that two of a kind," said Jim. "Sid, I felt as if I was dropping into a deep well of mist, losing all contact with reality. The nights have been frightening, some of them pure torture. But now let's hear your side of it."

Karper rose from his chair, his big body towering in the room. He clasped his hands behind his back and paced about. Then he resumed his seat, put a quill toothpick in his mouth, and blew through it as though it was a boatswain's pipe.

"Let me see if I can tell it precisely as it occurred," said Karper. "Last October the President summoned me—late at night—to the White House. I was in bed asleep when the white phone rang. He said it was urgent and that I should come right over. Of course I thought an invasion had started somewhere. We met in that oval sitting room right off his bedroom on the second floor in the family quarters. As he did with you, he turned off the only light. But this night there was no moon whatsoever, and we were in almost total darkness, except for the street lamps beyond the iron fence on the south lawn and the red lights at the top of the Washington Monument.

"It was the most bizarre scene in all my years in Washington. The President had no small talk at all. He immediately began striding up and down the room, in small, jerky steps, and his speech was running along so fast it was hard to follow him. It took some time to get the drift.

"He was raging against Carter Urey. He said that Urey was running the CIA like a separate empire, that he was insubordinate, paid no attention to the President's directives, and that he was trying to grind out a foreign policy of his own. When a break came, I asked why, if he felt that way, he didn't fire Urey. He said he couldn't for political reasons. Urey had too many friends on the Hill, the President said. He said Urey seduced congressmen by his lavish off-the-record dinners and his practice of filtering out secret information to flatter the congressmen. He contended Urey was power mad and that he was out to supplant him, Hollenbach, as head of the government."

"My God," interrupted Jim, "Urey has positively no political ambitions. He hates Washington. He's told me privately that he longs to chuck the whole thing and go back to Kansas City."

"Exactly. It was a fantastic charge," said Karper. He was leaning forward now, his elbows resting on his knees. "Urey is the soundest, least power-conscious man in Washington for my money. I know. I deal with him all the time. He's one fellow who's dedicated and selfless.

"Anyway, there was no containing the President. I disagreed with him and tried to defend Urey, but he'd have none of it. He raged on, in that spooky gloom, not a light in the place. Finally I asked what he wanted me to do. He said he wanted the Secretary of Defense to take over direction of the Central Intelligence Agency and said he'd hand me a directive giving me authority over Urey. I said that made no sense, that I wasn't equipped for the job, and that Congress would never approve it. He said—and he was furious—that he didn't care what Congress thought, that he'd issue a secret directive. Nobody had to know, not even Urey, except the President and myself.

" 'Great Jesus, Mr. President,' I said, 'you're talking like a madman.' With that, he stopped dead still beside a little writing desk. Although it was dark, I could hear him breathing hard and I could make out his hand closing about an object on the desk.

" 'Karper,' he said in a voice like a steel ghost, 'you're another one. You want to destroy me too, don't you?' I said nothing. He raised the thing—I saw it was an inkwell—and he pulled back his arm as if he were going to throw it at me. I took a couple of steps and wrapped my arms around him—I'm pretty strong, you know—very firm, but as gently as I could. 'Now, Mr. President,' I said quietly, 'put that thing down.' He was rigid for a moment, but all at once he went limp. I released him and he put down the inkwell. Then he kind of sank into a chair and said nothing for a while. Needless to say, there was ink all over the rug.

"When he spoke, he was very calm and actually he didn't say much. He just said that perhaps we both ought to sleep on the problem, and we could come up with an answer in the morning. He took me to the elevator and told a Secret Service man in the hall that he was very tired and was going to bed, and to please ask his valet, Bob, not to wake him early the next morning. I said good night and went home. Naturally, I was damn glad to get out of there, but also, naturally enough, I didn't sleep much that night.

"Next morning, about nine, just as I was leaving for the Pentagon, he called. He was cheery and very full of command and authority, like his regular self. He told me to forget what he'd said the night before, that he was upset and had said the wrong things. Don't mention it again, he said, as he'd find a way to work with Urey. He apologized for overstating the case. Urey was basically all right and he'd just have to learn to cooperate, or something to that effect. He was as bright and chipper as a squirrel.

"But the scene plagued me. Command and control of nuclear weapons has always bothered me and I got to thinking: What if we'd had a nuke decision—the big one—before us that night? Then I thought of Woodrow Wilson and Forrestal, and so—well —in three or four days, I'd written the directive for CACTUS. I checked it with the President, although of course I didn't mention the mental thing to him. I just called it a study to improve the command decision mechanism. Sure, he said. Fine. Go ahead.

"That was all until I sent him over by courier the two-month interim report of the committee. Of course, that showed that they were dealing with the mental problem. He called me right away, wanted to know why the CACTUS people were getting into that area—and what if they came up with an idea that the Big Three should be examined by psychiatrists? Oh, I said, nothing like that. But he demanded the study be canceled. He was mad again. Finally I argued him into letting it continue and I said of course nothing would be set in motion without his complete approval. He agreed very reluctantly.

"Then about three weeks ago I told him on the phone that CACTUS was a flop, that the committee could suggest nothing. And you know what he said? He said, 'Sid, I don't trust those five fellows, I've got information they've joined the conspiracy against me, and I want you to keep a close eye on them.' I was so thunderstruck I couldn't say anything but a 'yes, sir.'

"Well, that's when I decided I'd better do something. What, I didn't know, but I got to wondering about his early life, so I called for his Korean War record. The service is a natural place for stress and strain to show up. And, of course, I requested that disability file from the Library of Congress. I wanted to make sure of the law and of the agreement between Hollenbach and O'Malley."

"What did the service record show?" asked MacVeagh.

"Nothing," said Karper, "but there was something damned funny about it. The Army only recently got around to microfilming records of men in that particular division, the one in which Hollenbach served. The microfilming shows the numbered pages in each file, but in Hollenbach's case it jumped from page five to seven. What was missing was the medical record. Obviously somebody had it scissored out of the record.

"Of course it would be a mess to try to piece his medical history together now. Some of the medics in that division may have died, and even those you could find probably wouldn't remember anything. And obviously such a search would stir up a devil of a lot of talk. Another thing. You probably know that Hollenbach got the Silver Star for gallantry in action in Korea. The citation in his record shows that he got it for holding firm, with his platoon, in the face of a heavy Chicom attack. Frankly, Jim, that kind of cooled me off. Even with his medical record missing, it's doubtful it would reveal anything bearing on our present situation—not for a Silver Star man. So, I just haven't done a thing about it."

Jim dug at his desk blotter with a letter opener. "Sid, you've been more perceptive about this whole thing than I've been. For instance, at the Gridiron dinner, you sensed immediately that something was wrong when Hollenbach made his suggestion for a national wire-tapping law. Remember? I laughed, but you said it was a 'chilling suggestion.' "

Karper smiled. "Of course, I had some background to fit that into. At the time, you didn't. Now, in some ways, I find his serious idea of such a law the most conclusive evidence we've got as to the state of his mind. Even Hitler didn't dream up anything so methodically diabolical in the way of invading personal privacy."

"You're right," said Jim. "I wonder why he hasn't mentioned his wiretap plan to other people?"

"Maybe he has," said Karper, "and we just don't know about it."

"The same thing goes for this whole story," said Jim. "It's a big government. Maybe a dozen people have gotten separate pieces of the President's mental trouble, but lacking any pattern to fit them into, the incidents don't mean anything to them.

"Look, Sid, you've just got to tell your story to the same group that met at Cavanaugh's. They'll believe you. They sure didn't believe me. Actually, my feeling was that a majority of the men there thought there was something wrong with *my* mind."

"I can understand that," said Karper. "Nobody wants to believe the President of the United States is deranged."

Jim rubbed the bridge of his nose reflectively. "So, why isn't the simplest and most direct plan to convene that group again and let you talk? You carry an awful lot of weight around this town, Sid."

"I'm not sure that's feasible," said Karper. "In the first place, there's the security problem. CACTUS carries the highest classification and I know Odlum, Gullion and Cavanaugh aren't cleared that high. And I'd have to describe CACTUS, with the problem of the command decision on nukes, to have the impact. After all, Mark's blowup over Urey was almost six months ago. Far more telling, to my mind, was his contention that the CACTUS committee had joined a conspiracy to destroy him—and he said that only three weeks ago. But I couldn't go into that without breaking security on CACTUS."

"Of course," said Jim, "if you talked to O'Malley, I'm sure we could get him to convene the Cabinet and then invoke the legal provision on succeeding a disabled president."

Karper shook his head. "We can't do anything that formal without an airtight case. That Cabinet leaks like a sieve. We might as well phone all the newspapers." Karper thought for a moment. "No, I guess we have to go back to that original small group first. But I also think we've got to have more solid evidence before we approach them. You really can't blame them for being incredulous. You and I know that a person has to experience Hollenbach's rage—see it personally—to understand what we both feel. We need more corroboration."

They sat silent, thinking. Karper chewed absently on his toothpick while Jim fingered the bridge of his nose again. It occurred to Jim that this same thought—the need for more corroboration—had harried him for days.

"But where are we going to get it?" he asked after a few moments. "We can't just go around polling people on whether the President is all there."

"I know," said Karper. He fell silent again, and Jim experienced a sinking sensation. The dilemma was unchanged, and two men seemed no more capable of solving it than one. This time the silence lasted for several minutes.

"The doctor," said Karper at last. "I'm not sure it promises much, but I think our first move is to have a session with General Leppert."

MacVeagh considered the name. Brigadier General Maury Leppert, formerly a practicing physician in Denver, had been brought to the White House by President Hollenbach and given an Army commission. He was a gaunt, melancholy man who seldom appeared in public and who steadfastly refused to discuss any aspect of the President's health with newspapermen, confining himself to an annual report filled with bleak statistics on blood pressure, cholesterol count, urine analysis, and pulse rate.

"Certainly," said Karper, "if the President is crazed, his own physician should have some inkling of it. I thought of consulting him before, but alone I had no standing, no excuse really. With two of us, and our positions, perhaps we could base our questions on some unclassified aspect of C and C procedures. We'd have to be adroit, but it's worth a try."

"All right, let's do it. When?"

"The sooner the better. How about 4:30 this afternoon if he'll agree to see us then?"

"You make the date," said Jim, "then call me. I'll be there."

Karper rose and Jim automatically followed suit. They shook hands, wordlessly, in the center of the room and then moved toward the private door to the corridor.

"This is a sad business," said Karper, "but actually I'm approaching it pretty cold-bloodedly now. All the days and nights of frustration and doubts are gone. It boils down to just one thing. We've just got to get Mark Hollenbach out of that White House before something terrible happens."

Jim merely nodded. His own feelings were an elusive combination of pity for the President, dread over the inevitable clash of wills to come, and a fierce pride—pride that his own judgment had been vindicated by this strong, resolute man.

"Jim," said Karper, "what exactly do you think Mark's trouble is?"

"Just from poking around the fringes of abnormal psychology since this thing started," replied Jim, "I'd say he's a paranoid."

"That's my curbstone diagnosis too," said Karper. "Let's see what we can pry out of the doctor."

They shook hands again, and then Karper was out the door and walking rapidly down the corridor.

17.

Saybrook

That Thursday afternoon, several hours after Defense Secretary Karper drove back to the Pentagon, Mark Hollenbach, Jr., the 21-year-old son of the President, slumped on his spine in a splotched leather chair in a top floor suite of Saybrook College, Yale University. He wore khaki pants, sweat socks, loafers, and a reversed crew-neck sweater through which his varsity Y showed in discreet outline.

Yale men, in a judicious accommodation of pride and modesty, never wore the Y outside. Such self-advertising was considered too blatant, too Ohio State. In a word, a Yale word, it was not "shoe." On the other hand, a man did not want it forgotten that he had played three years at right end on winning teams, especially when the happenstance of being a President's son created untold psychological hazards on the field. Had the coach favored him or purposely refused to give him the breaks another man would get? Had the Cornell linebacker, who snapped one of Mark's ribs on a hard tackle, hoped to put a famous name out of the game? Had he been favored when his pass pattern was called, out of sequence, for the last, unneeded touchdown against Harvard? Mark felt he would never know. But whatever the truth, his sweater could not be permitted to speak his secret pride in lasting three years of college football. So he turned the sweater inside out and pretended he was disenchanted with such transient status symbols as university athletic letters.

In manner and ritual Mark Jr. was of a brand with his roommate, "Little Doc" Peyster of Saragosa, Texas. He differed but little from the other young men of Saybrook College—the chief difference being the Secret Service agent who lived next door, accompanied Mark to classes, and hovered in the background as Mark moved about the campus.

Record albums, books, playing cards, and a Fence Club tie rested in disorderly companionship on the fireplace mantel. In the wastebasket stood a metal marker, "Visitor Parking, Connecticut College," which Little Doc had uprooted one night in a fit of joy after achieving conquest of one of Connecticut College's more nunlike juniors exactly seventeen months after he had set his erotic sights on her. In another corner of the room was a pile of dirty laundry, and in still another a stack of old copies of the *New York Times*. Through the open door and the casement bay window came the mingled sounds of higher education: the slamming of doors, a gust of laughter, feet thudding on steps as young men raced downstairs. In the York Street courtyard below could be heard the slap of a bat, for it was the first warm afternoon of the year in New Haven, and the boys of Saybrook were playing whiffle ball.

Mark Jr. resembled his father. He had a similar long, sensitive face and his brown hair was crew-cut. But he was taller, six feet two, and his muscles were tough and wiry. Mark admired his father, and on top of the record player, only partially obscured by two tennis racquets, was a framed photograph of President Hollenbach taking the oath of office on the Capitol steps. The son, who enjoyed rambling political discussions with his father, got along fairly well with the older man, chiefly because Mark Jr. refused to heed every echo of his father's stern call to excellence. In the boy's opinion, excellence was akin to everything else—all right in moderation. And, anyway, even if a man privately dedicated himself to excellence, too much prattling about it spoiled the effect. Passionate devotion to a cause was not "shoe."

This afternoon Mark Jr. was deep in the old leather chair which still showed a dusty footprint on the arm, where Little Doc had stood last night to declaim on the virtues of wine, wanderlust and women. With his loafered feet propped on the seat of another chair, Mark was reading a letter on pale-green White House stationery. After finishing it he frowned, crumpled the letter into a ball, and hurled it at the wastebasket. He missed. He sat glaring at the letter a moment, then retrieved it, smoothed out the wrinkles, and put it in his hip pocket. He went to the casement window and looked down at the ballplayers in the courtyard. Then, lying on the cushioned ledge, he took out the letter and read it through slowly for the third time. At last he shoved the letter in his pocket again, went to the telephone and placed a person-to-person call, collect, to Mrs. Evelyn Hollenbach in the White House.

When his mother answered, they exchanged the small talk, with its affectionate fumbling for understanding, that characterizes the communications between close relatives of different generations and sexes. Evelyn Hollenbach loved her son, but could not quite comprehend what he was up to or why. Mark loved his mother, but had little insight into her matronly world and even less curiosity about it.

"Say, Mom," he asked at last, "how is Dad feeling?"

"Fine," she said cheerfully. "You know your father. He's on all cylinders as usual, working too hard. But who can stop him? He thrives on it. Why do you ask, Mark?"

"I got a funny letter from him," he said. "It kinda worries me. It doesn't sound like him at all."

"What do you mean, dear?"

"Oh," said Mark, "he's bawling me out for my semester

grades. Jeez, I thought they were pretty good, an 85 average, which puts me in the top quarter of the class. But he seems to think that's lousy. God knows what he'll think about my comps in history."

"You know our Mr. President," she comforted. "He wants everybody to be first. I say, well, then, who'd be left to be second, but he can't see that. Everyone connected with him has to be first. But I agree with you, dear, I think they're fine grades."

"It's not so much the idea of it, but the way he said it," said Mark. "He sounded kind of sour and mad as though I'd disgraced the family or something. Bitter almost. And a little snide from a guy's father."

"Can't you read it to me?" she asked.

"No," he parried. "I'd rather not. There's a lot of man-to-man stuff you wouldn't understand."

"Oh." She sounded relieved that the letter would go unread.

"Honestly, Mom, it's pretty dreary stuff. You wouldn't like it."

"All right," she said, "but please don't worry about your father. He's in fine shape. Why don't you have a good, long talk with him about your grades when you come home for spring vacation next week? He probably doesn't realize you're in the top quarter."

"Okay, Mom."

"And how are the girls, dear?" she asked.

"Plentiful," he said, "but chaste. My roommate has all the luck."

She clucked a reprimand. "I've got a nice date for you here next week. You'll adore her."

He was immediately suspicious. "Not another cherry blossom princess? I got a dog last time."

"This one's a beauty," she said. "Gracious and intelligent too."

He groaned, and they said a laughing good-by.

But the telephone call did not appease Mark's anxieties. He fingered his father's letter again and stood for a moment brooding over the language.

Then, through the windows, he heard the cries of the whiffle-ball players, and he ran from the room, yelled a warning to his Secret Service guard, pounded down the steps like an upended trunk, and joined the game. He was deep in play, sweating freely, an hour later when a letter carrier appeared in the courtyard and was directed to young Hollenbach. The mailman brought a special delivery letter. Mark glanced at the envelope, noted the postmark, Saragosa, Texas, and surmised it was news from Slim Carmichael about his summer job. He jammed the letter in his hip pocket and continued the game.

A half hour later, dirty and tired, Mark mounted the steps again, joking as he went with his Secret Service guard. He took a hot shower and cannonaded the tiled walls with off-key songs. He dried himself, wrapped a towel about his hips, and turned on the record player.

Then he remembered the letter. He took it from the hip pocket of his khaki pants and sank into the easy chair again to read. A sheet of pale-green White House stationery accompanied the letter, and Mark fingered it idly while reading Slim Carmichael's cramped, penciled handwriting:

Saragosa, Tex.
Tuesday, April 6

Dear Mark:

This is an awful hard letter for me to write, as you'll realize as soon as you've read the enclosed letter from your father, which I got some days ago. I wasn't going to tell anyone about it, and Betsy wanted me to save it until you got out here. But your father's letter keeps worrying me. Sometimes I get mad, and then sometimes I feel a little scared.

I got a nice letter from the President in January, about a suggestion of mine that the federal government should figure out a way to conserve the water in these parts, but this last letter from him has got me upset. Mark, either your father never wrote this letter I'm enclosing or he completely misunderstands my position.

I'm not trying to get a thing from the government. You know me well enough for that. I've worked hard all my life, made it on my own, and never took a nickel of public money, price supports, crop loans, disaster relief or anything else. Cotton has been good to me out here, and I figure success or failure is entirely up to me.

All I was trying to do was to suggest a way that we could conserve this great river of water underneath the land. I'm willing to cut back voluntarily, but a lot of fellows aren't. I just want to conserve our resources, as I'm sure you understand from our talks about it. But now your father treats me like a criminal or some kind of riffraff.

I figured you'd be going to Washington soon for spring vacation. If you get a chance, would you straighten your father out on this? As I said, maybe he didn't write the letter at all. If not, please let me know, as I've always thought him a great president up until now.

Your job is waiting for you this summer. Pedro and the boys say to be sure to bring your guitar with you. Me, I'll settle for those football arms and legs, because mine are slowing down.

Sincerely from Betsy too,
Your friend,
Slim.

Mark read his father's letter to Carmichael slowly, pausing and frowning over such phrases as "Frankly, my dear Carmichael, you are completely out of bounds . . . a problem that is one of your own making . . . every citizen should do his utmost to find his own way over the personal obstacles which face us all." The boy pulled out the letter written to him by his father, and compared the handwriting. There was no mistaking the high, careful looping of letters, the meticulous, prim style. Not a single word was illegible. Excellence in all things, even handwriting. Mark had seen that familiar hand style hundreds of times. There was no doubt that the letter to Slim had been written by his father.

Then Mark reread his own letter from his father. This time, after reading the letter Slim had forwarded, the phrases on the White House stationery seemed angrier, even ugly:

". . . a dismal showing in the senior year for a Hollenbach . . . you've managed to disgrace not only yourself, but the office of the presidency . . . are you planning to enter law school on your father's name rather than your own merits?"

One sentence now seemed fairly to leap from the page:

"I had hoped that my own son would spare me vexations at this particular time when there is an obvious conspiracy afoot to sully and demean me, even to destroy me."

Mark stared for a long time at this sentence, wondering, conjecturing. The cries of his friends in the courtyard seemed remote, and the room was cloaked in an orange haze from the fading sun. Although the afternoon was still warm, he felt a chill as from an unseen shadow, and involuntarily he rubbed his arms. He reread all three letters twice, and he thought some more.

Then suddenly he got up and went to the telephone in the wall niche. He dialed the long-distance operator.

"I want a Mr. R. Paul Griscom in Washington, D.C.," he said. "He can be reached at his law office in the World Center Building, or at his home on O Street Northwest."

18.

East Entrance

Joe Donovan always felt slightly ill at ease in the presence of Speaker William Nicholson. Old Nick wasn't Donovan's swinging type of politician. Donovan shared President Hollenbach's view that the Speaker was too ponderous, inclined to be pompous and stuffy. Nick was about as subtle as an ax handle, Donovan thought. The Democratic chairman preferred the pols with the light touch and he often pined for the old days with Jack Kennedy's Irish Mafia.

But he had to concede, as he faced Nicholson in the Speaker's ancient, musty office off the House floor, that Nicholson's demeanor fitted the occasion this afternoon. Donovan's mission was a curiously serious one and he was more perplexed than he cared to be.

"Well, what's your problem, Joe?" Nicholson appeared to be already brooding over expected bad news.

"Just checking, Nick," said Donovan. He threw one leg over the arm of his chair. "It's a screwy story and maybe there's nothing to it, but I've got to find out."

Nicholson squinted at him, rubbed his grizzled chin, but said nothing.

"My secretary, Rita Krasicki, has been acting funny for about a week," said Donovan. "I knew there was something wrong, but who knows about a woman? This morning she comes in and talks. She's got quite a story. She says that a week ago tonight, she was invited to a private meeting of a bunch of Democratic leaders at Grady Cavanaugh's place down on St. Leonard's Creek. She was taken before this group by Jim MacVeagh, according to her, and put on the grill. They asked her a lot of surprising questions about a conversation she had with the President.

"No use going into a lot of details, but Rita said MacVeagh was agitated and upset and refused to tell her what the meeting was all about. As I say, the questions put to her were queer ones. Anyway, she got to thinking about it and came to the conclusion that some kind of secret cabal was operating to damage Hollenbach politically, maybe even to try to deny him renomination at Detroit."

Nicholson broke in. "And she gave you a list of names of the men who were there—and I was one of them?"

"That's right." Donovan was grateful for the Speaker's candor. "So, that's why I'm here. Let's level, Nick. What's up?"

Nicholson tilted back in his swivel chair until the springs squeaked in protest. He looked moodily at Donovan for a moment.

"We were under a pledge of secrecy," he said, "and I'm no man to break my word. Still, you came to me and you're the party's chairman and you've got a right to know. The fact is, Joe, that O'Malley and MacVeagh called that meeting to consider a sensational charge by MacVeagh—that President Hollenbach is mentally unbalanced and that incidentally he, MacVeagh, is being followed by the Secret Service."

"What?" Donovan gulped and stared at Nicholson in amazement.

"That's right. Jim claims that the President is suffering some kind of mental breakdown."

It took Donovan a moment to get his voice. "He's got to be kidding," he said in awed tones.

"No, he's not. He's serious. He presented us with a lot of so-called evidence."

"What do you mean 'so-called'?"

"I mean I didn't believe it," said Nicholson. "As a matter of fact, Joe, I walked out on the meeting before it ended. I thought that MacVeagh was either out to get the President for some unknown reason of his own or that Jim's own mind was sick. I must say I incline to the latter view, the more I ponder it."

"What about the Secret Service following him?" asked Donovan.

"I don't believe it. I think he's having hallucinations."

"Have you checked any of this out?" asked Donovan.

"No," said Nicholson. "I don't believe in moving too fast on something like this, and frankly I didn't know just what to do. I thought of telling the President, but then decided there was no sense in alarming him unnecessarily."

"As long as you've told this much, would you mind filling me in on the meeting at Grady Cavanaugh's?"

"Not at all." And Nicholson proceeded to relate the sequence of events at St. Leonard's Creek, including MacVeagh's story of calling on Paul Griscom and MacVeagh's belief that Griscom thought it was MacVeagh who was having mental problems. Nicholson also told of Rita Krasicki's tacit admission that she'd had an affair with MacVeagh.

"God love us," said Donovan. "Jimmy and Rita! The things a boss doesn't know about the help. I wondered why it took her so long to tell me about that meeting at Cavanaugh's and why she was so shook up this morning."

"Apparently the affair had been going on some time," said

Nicholson with obvious distaste. "I assume that's what that Cousins and King story was hinting at. My own theory is that Jim MacVeagh is a badly confused young man and that, as a result, he's developed a psychotic desire to damage the President in some way."

"You don't think he's actually dangerous, do you, Nick?"

The speaker shrugged. "He may be. I know little about such things, but I admit I'm concerned."

"I've been wondering about Jimmy ever since he quit that vice-presidential race," said Donovan. "That seemed nutty to me. Especially since—with all due deference to you, Nick—I happen to know he had a good chance to be picked."

"Oh." This intelligence obviously did not please the Speaker.

"Look, Nick," said Donovan. "If Jimmy's off his rocker, we ought to know more about it and try to help him. How about getting Griscom over here to see what he knows about Jim? And Chief Brothers too. Let's see if the Service ever did put a tail on MacVeagh. It seems a pretty far-out story to me."

Nicholson pondered a moment. "I think you're right," he said. "Let's get them both up here."

An "invitation" from the Speaker of the House amounted to a command in Washington, second only to a summons from the President, and Paul Griscom and Arnold Brothers arrived at the Speaker's office within fifteen minutes. Griscom left no word at his office as to his whereabouts, so efforts of a New Haven long-distance operator to reach the man whom Mark Hollenbach, Jr., called "Uncle Paul" proved fruitless.

When the two newcomers were settled in the Speaker's office, Nicholson wasted no time on banter before driving to the core of the problem.

"Gentlemen," he said, "I'm worried about the mental condition of our good friend, Jim MacVeagh." He sketched, briefly but somewhat pontifically, the St. Leonard's Creek meeting for

Griscom and Brothers. "To my mind," he concluded, "Mac-Veagh's charges against the President are preposterous. I think the young man needs psychiatric help, the sooner the better, and I'll grant I was laggard in not doing something about it last week. But Joe's call on me just now has crystallized my thinking. What do you think, Paul?"

The lawyer's deep eye pouches could be seen through his rimless spectacles. He brooded a moment like a somnolent lizard, then took off his eyeglasses and carefully polished them on the lower part of his shirt.

"Frankly, Nick," he said, "I had no idea until now that Mac-Veagh was trying to tell me he thought the President's mind was shot. That just never entered my head. I assumed he was talking about himself, while pretending he'd come on behalf of some other senator. Later, of course, that Secret Service call on me did seem odd. However, I failed to put two and two together, a common failing in this town, but an error a man in private practice shouldn't be making. So, Jim is actually accusing the President of mental incapacity?"

"Indeed, he is," replied Nicholson. His tone was heavy, indignant. "It's patently absurd."

"A very, very strange charge to come from MacVeagh," said Griscom. His manner and voice were dispassionate. "I don't quite understand the whole thing."

"Look, Paul," said Donovan, "you see the President more than any of the rest of us, being a friend of the family. Have you noted anything oddball about his behavior?"

Griscom shook his head emphatically. "Not a thing. He's brimming with enthusiasm. I was over there yesterday on a matter, and I've never seen a president more in command of the situation. Of course, he bubbles and boils more than the rest of us, but he's always been that way."

"That goes double for me," said Donovan. "He's so hearty on

the phone he makes my ears ring. He's the same old Mark, full of fire and twenty new ideas an hour."

Donovan looked at Chief Brothers, whose usually bland, impassive face was knotted in astonishment over the course of the conversation. "How about you, chief?" asked Donovan. "Have you or any of your men on the detail seen anything abnormal about the President's actions recently?"

"Not a thing," said Brothers, "but I wish I could say the same for Senator MacVeagh. He's worrying the hell out of me."

"What are the facts about MacVeagh's claim that you have him under surveillance?" asked Nicholson.

A pained expression came over Brothers' face. Here he was, so close to retirement, and now this increasingly involved and messy business about the junior senator from Iowa came to harass him in his final months on the job.

"We hate to tail a public official," he said, and he looked at them as though beseeching understanding. "But in this case we had no choice. First, we get a tip that Senator MacVeagh's assistant is asking curious questions about the President's early life. Then MacVeagh lies to my man Luther Smith. And then we find a set of surgical knives in his study at home—"

"Knives!" said Griscom.

"Yes, sir, knives." Brothers described Luther Smith's discovery in the MacVeagh home on a Sunday afternoon almost three weeks earlier.

"And then," continued Brothers, "there was MacVeagh's unexplained chucking of the race for vice-president, and his curious contention that he was writing a biography of the President, although there's not the slightest clue that he's doing anything of the kind. So I couldn't take a chance. After all, it's our job to protect the President."

He said it defensively, and he did not add that the shadowing of MacVeagh had been undertaken as much by fear that President Hollenbach might hear of MacVeagh's inquiries and demand an explanation from the Service as by Brothers' own suspicions about MacVeagh's motives and intentions. From long experience in the bureaucratic jungle, Brothers had found it wiser to say too little than too much.

"My own feeling," said Speaker Nicholson, "is that we ought to get psychiatric attention for Jim MacVeagh. I don't know what's eating him, but he's obviously out to harm the President in some fashion, perhaps only politically, but who can be sure? I suspect this woman thing has got him more upset than we realize."

"The affair went on quite a while," said Griscom. "I know. I live on O Street across from Mrs. Krasicki. But that's really beside the point now. I agree with you, Mr. Speaker. We ought to take steps to get Jim into a hospital where he can get some mental clinic help."

"That's pretty sticky business," offered Donovan, "trying to commit a United States senator."

Nicholson nodded heavily and there was quiet in the room for a moment. Nothing was more zealously guarded in Washington than the multifold privileges and immunities of senators and congressmen. Some were protected by law, but most, such as the unwritten permission to ignore parking restrictions, were shielded by tradition. It definitely was not the custom to invoke the police powers against members of Congress.

"Yes," agreed Griscom, "it is. But it is possible."

"How?" Donovan was skeptical.

"It can be worked through the Secret Service in this case, I believe," said Griscom. "I seem to remember some old cases our law firm got involved in. Am I right, chief?"

"Well," said Brothers, "in the District we don't have much problem on the original detention, provided the man is picked up in some public place. No warrant is needed then, although we do need a warrant to go into a man's home and fetch him. But anywhere outside, if we have cause to believe the President is threatened by anyone, we can pick up the suspect and take him to D.C. General Hospital. He's placed under the care of staff psychiatrists. Then, within forty-eight hours, we have to file an application for detention and examination, and the suspect is examined by the chairman of the Commission on Mental Health and two psychiatrists. If they conclude the person is of unsound mind, they must report the fact to the district court within twenty-five days. That's about the procedure."

"But members of Congress are different, aren't they?" asked Donovan. "I thought there was something in the Constitution, giving them immunity from arrest."

Griscom shook his head. "They're privileged from arrest while in session, or going to and from Congress, except in cases of treason, felony or breach of the peace, I think the language is. That narrows their immunity pretty severely. Of course, the question here is whether detaining a senator for mental examination would constitute an arrest in the constitutional meaning. I would think not. What do you think, chief?"

"We've never had to face the issue with a member of Congress in these circumstances," said Brothers, "but I don't think there's much doubt that we have the legal right to take Senator Mac-Veagh in for an examination. Still . . ."

He paused and his face clouded. "I'd hate to do it on my own authority alone. If we pick up Jim MacVeagh, we open a can of worms, believe me. Law or no law."

"You're not kidding," said Donovan. His pale eyelashes were almost closed, a sure sign that his political sensibilities had been alerted. "You pick up Jimmy MacVeagh, and you couldn't keep it quiet overnight. It would be a page one sensation within twenty-four hours."

There was a moment of silence, punctuated by the squeak of Speaker Nicholson's old swivel chair.

"We'd have to face the publicity," said Nicholson, "but I think MacVeagh should be put in a hospital right now. I'm afraid of the man. If you'd seen his face and his behavior at Cavanaugh's, you'd know what I mean. He's potentially dangerous, in my book."

"Maybe Jimmy would consent to a voluntary commitment for a few days," suggested Donovan, "long enough to have a thorough examination."

"I doubt it," said Nicholson. "It's obvious he's got an obsession on this thing about the President."

"Still," said Griscom, "Joe's idea is worth a try. I'd be willing to talk to MacVeagh and try to persuade him. Then, if that didn't work, we could decide what route to take. What do you say?"

"Okay by me," said Donovan. Nicholson nodded assent as well.

"All right," said Griscom, "I'll call him right now."

The lawyer picked up the telephone on the Speaker's desk. He was connected with MacVeagh's office, asked for the senator, then listened for a moment before hanging up.

"MacVeagh just left for the White House," he said.

The four men exchanged surprised glances.

"That's funny," said Donovan.

"Funny is not the word." Nicholson heaved himself out of his swivel chair. "I think you'd better take over, chief. I don't know what MacVeagh is up to at the White House, but I don't think he should be allowed in there right now."

"You want him detained?" Brothers scanned three faces, seeking unanimity. Donovan looked doubtful, but Griscom nodded.

"Absolutely," said Nicholson. "If you get any static later, I'll take responsibility for it."

Brothers took the phone at once and asked for the White House number.

"Luther Smith on the detail," he told the White House operator.

288 | NIGHT OF CAMP DAVID

Agent Luther Smith left the west lobby of the White House on a trot, ran past the front portico of the mansion and fetched up, panting, at the police cubicle at the east entrance. It was 4:22 P.M. Two minutes later, Senator James MacVeagh descended from a cab at the gate and paid off the taxi driver.

Smith walked casually toward MacVeagh, grasped his right arm firmly, and propelled him across East Executive Avenue toward the basement entrance to the old Treasury Building.

"I'm sorry, Senator," said Smith in a low voice, "but we've got orders to detain you."

MacVeagh tried to wrench his arm free. "What the hell for?" he exploded.

"I don't know," said Smith, "but you've got to come with me."

MacVeagh, a larger and stronger man than the swarthy Secret Service agent, again sought to free his arm, but Smith now had one hand on Jim's right biceps and another clamped on his wrist. By the time Jim had decided how to break the grip, he was already being pushed into the shadows of the Treasury garage. A second agent grabbed Jim's left arm and MacVeagh was thrust bodily, although not roughly, into the back seat of a sedan.

"D.C. General," Smith commanded the driver.

"Am I supposed to be sick?" asked Jim.

Smith looked away, embarrassed. "I don't know, Senator. We've got orders to take you to the psychiatric clinic."

The Pentagon limousine of Defense Secretary Sidney Karper pulled up at the east entrance of the White House just as the car carrying Jim MacVeagh left the Treasury basement garage at the other end of the short block.

Karper looked at his wrist watch as he backed out of the limousine. He was two minutes late for the appointment which he and Senator MacVeagh had with Brigadier General Maury

Leppert, physician to the President. Karper nodded to the White House policeman standing in front of his white guard cubicle.

"Has Senator MacVeagh arrived yet?" Karper asked.

"Senator MacVeagh?" The guard looked puzzled. "Why, yes, Mr. Secretary. He got out of a cab here a couple of minutes ago, but he was led away over to the Treasury Building by one of the Secret Service agents."

19.

Paul Griscom's

Sidney Karper, inwardly seething, strode across East Executive Avenue to the Treasury Building, entered the Secret Service suite of offices and demanded that the girl receptionist take him at once to Chief Brothers.

The girl, accustomed to dealing with cranks and crackpots, patted at her stringy black hair and sought to appease him with a forced smile. But a middle-aged administrative assistant at the desk behind her recognized the Secretary of Defense. He bolted forward as though shot from a catapult. Fussing over Karper's rank and calling him "Mr. Secretary" three times in one obsequious sentence, he explained that Chief Brothers had just left a conference on Capitol Hill and was expected back momentarily.

"I'll wait in his office," said Karper, scowling.

"Yes, sir. Of course, Mr. Secretary."

When Brothers returned a few minutes later he found Karper pacing about his office, his hands clasped behind him and his lips compressed in a thin line. Karper wheeled on him.

"Just what in the hell has the Service done with Senator Mac-Veagh?" he demanded.

Brothers, taken aback at the ferocity of Karper's inquiry, took a moment to settle himself behind his desk. Then he tried a placating smile.

"That's an administrative matter," said Brothers. He could think of no better word.

"Administrative!" Karper roared it. "What does that mean— in English?"

"I'm not at liberty to reveal the circumstances." A tremor in Brothers' voice betrayed his anxiety behind the officious tone. How did the Secretary of Defense figure in all this?

"I'm a Cabinet officer," said Karper coldly. "James MacVeagh is a United States senator. I have an official right to know what you've done with Senator MacVeagh. I know he was escorted to this building by one of your agents."

Brothers hesitated. In these last months the swirling crosscurrents of Washington politics had buffeted him more than at any time in memory. He felt an urge to sneeze and he eyed Karper bleakly, accusingly. Didn't the Secretary of Defense have enough to worry about with his missiles and nuclear fleets?

"Senator MacVeagh has been detained for investigation," said Brothers with a sigh. "We were forced to do it as a precautionary measure."

"By whose authority?" demanded Karper. "I didn't know this was a police state."

"Now, Mr. Secretary," said Brothers, essaying a soothing tone, but not quite bringing it off, "while I agree it's highly unusual to detain a United States senator, we had reason to believe that Senator MacVeagh had designs on the President. In such circumstances, the Service can take no chances."

"Tommyrot!" boomed Karper. "Jim MacVeagh wouldn't harm a bird. I demand to see him at once. Where is he?"

"I'm sorry. I can't reveal that."

"I am a member of the Cabinet and I have a right to know."

"And I'm an agent of the President of the United States, and I'm only doing my duty," said Brothers. He sighed again, wearily, and inwardly cursed MacVeagh for fetching him this packet of woe. "Why don't you appeal to the President? Perhaps he can help you."

Karper shot a glance of frustration at Brothers and hastily changed course.

"You say 'we' have reason to believe Senator MacVeagh has designs on the President," said Karper. "Who is 'we'?"

Chief Brothers eyed Karper balefully. Why, he thought, should he, a beleaguered civil servant, take the heat alone for the apprehension of a senator?

"The 'we,' " said Brothers, "includes the Speaker of the House, Mr. Nicholson, the chairman of the Democratic committee, Mr. Donovan, and a prominent Democratic attorney, Mr. Paul Griscom. We've just had a meeting in the Speaker's office. They made the decision. I merely concurred in it and ordered MacVeagh picked up as he entered the White House."

"Thanks," said Karper, and he marched from the office without further word.

Karper's temper cooled somewhat as he strode along the old Treasury corridors. He considered calling Speaker Nicholson or Chairman Donovan, but dismissed the idea. He knew neither man well enough. Instead, he decided to call on Paul Griscom, the lawyer every Washington official knew and with whom Karper had been paired occasionally for golf at the Burning Tree Club. He found his limousine and chauffeur awaiting him at the rear driveway of the Treasury and he gave orders to be driven to Griscom's home on O Street.

A maid answered Karper's summons, two rings of the doorbell plus one loud clap of the shiny brass door knocker. A narrow hallway, with marble flooring, ran back into the recesses of the Georgetown house. Two sliding oak doors, similar to those used in nineteenth-century parlors, opened to the left on a spacious living room. At the foot of the hallway, Paul Griscom was talking on the telephone.

"All right then," Karper heard Griscom say. "We'll discuss it in detail when you come down next week for spring vacation. Okay? Now don't worry, Mark. Sure. Good-by."

Griscom turned to Karper and smiled. If he was surprised to see the Cabinet officer, he did not show it. Griscom's colonial O Street residence had received scores of prominent government officials over the years.

"Good evening, Sid," he said. He gestured toward the telephone. "That was Mark Jr. up in New Haven. The boy's worried over some letter or other from the President that he thinks overdoes the parental bit. Grades, I gather."

Griscom advanced and shook Karper's hand. The lawyer's trousers bagged at the knees and his face looked as lived in as the old house about him. "Nice to see you, Sid." He eyed Karper inquiringly. "Anything the matter?"

Karper nodded. "Did you say young Hollenbach is worried about a harsh letter from his father?"

"Harsh?" echoed Griscom. "No, I don't believe I described it that way. But, well, I suppose it is harsh, as young Mark read it to me. Actually, it concerns two letters his father wrote recently. Both are a bit strange, I'd say." He shrugged. "But it's just one of those family things. The boy needs somebody's shoulder to cry on. What can I do for you, Sid?"

Karper ignored the diversion. "What do you mean, 'strange'?"

"Now, just a minute, Sid," said Griscom. He adjusted his rimless spectacles on his nose and peered at Karper. "This is a personal matter, and I'm not really at liberty—"

"If young Mark got an ugly letter from his father," cut in Karper, "it's my business as well as yours. As a matter of fact, it's public business. If I were you, I'd get that boy on a plane down here right away. Tonight."

Griscom removed his spectacles and stood staring in bewilderment at Karper. "What the devil are you talking about?"

Karper hesitated as he watched Griscom's reaction. Ordinarily, he would lead into the subject gingerly. But there was no time left for caution. He might as well lay it on the line.

"I'm talking about insanity," said Karper. He thrust his big head forward and fixed his eyes on Griscom's. "Paul, President Hollenbach is in very, very bad trouble. You've made a terrible, although understandable, blunder. It isn't Senator MacVeagh whose mind has deserted him. It's the President."

The two men stood facing each other in the hallway. Above the veined pouches, Griscom's eyes scanned Karper's face as though seeing it for the first time.

"I think you'd better explain that statement," said Griscom slowly. His look was one of skepticism, but his tone seemed to reserve judgment. "Let's go into the living room."

Griscom motioned Karper to a brocaded sofa while he seated himself in a painted wooden armchair. The room was furnished in a stilted French seventeenth-century style that seemed as out of character with Griscom's unpressed suits and his Wyoming twang as was his opulent law office. Karper leaned forward, his long arms resting on his knees.

"Paul," asked Karper, "do you think I'm crazy?"

"No, of course not."

"You're right," said Karper. "I'm not. And neither, my friend, is Jim MacVeagh. We're two of a kind. We both have become convinced that the President's mind is not all there. We're convinced he's suffering some kind of paranoia. We arrived at this conclusion independently, based on independent evidence, and only today was either of us aware of what the other had found out. We were on our way to consult General Leppert by appointment when the Secret Service apprehended Jim."

The lawyer played for time, removing his spectacles, yanking out a shirttail and polishing the lenses with it. "That's a pretty strong dose, Sid," he said. "I could use a drink. How about you?"

Karper nodded. "A martini on the rocks."

When the drinks had been served by Griscom from a portable corner bar, Karper told the whole story, including his exchange with MacVeagh that noon. Only with Project CACTUS did he grow cautious. He referred to it only as a classified Pentagon study.

"And so," he concluded, "I think the situation is growing worse. There's absolutely no evidence that Mark's mind is straightening itself out. On the contrary, the aberration I noted about six months ago appears to have become fixed. He thinks he's the victim of conspirators who are plotting to destroy him, and he has obvious delusions of grandeur."

Griscom remained silent a moment as he toyed with his glass. "Those letters of young Mark did seem strange," he said in a half-voice, as though musing to himself. "What worried young Mark was a sentence in his father's letter that spoke of a conspiracy that was afoot to harm him in some way, or at least ruin his reputation. The other letter was an extraordinary one too. Apparently the President wrote an accusing letter to a fellow named Carmichael out in West Texas, the cotton farmer young Mark worked with last summer."

Karper nodded assent. "It all fits in," he said. "Paul, I don't think this thing can be allowed to slide any longer. Hollenbach's meeting with Zuchek is only twelve days off. We just can't permit a deranged president to go to that meeting. Several defense matters—I can't discuss their nature—are hanging fire. When I think of what a paranoid president might tell the Russians, the kind of deal he might make, God, it gives me the shivers."

"I just can't bring myself to believe it," said Griscom, shaking his head. "I see him two, three times a week, and I can't remember a single thing he's done or said that appears the least bit abnormal. There's his hyperactivity, of course, but he's been that way ever since I've known him."

"But," protested Karper, "the paranoid's ability to fool people is uncanny. With some people, he can always appear completely normal, and in fact, he is. With others, his logic can be brilliant —if you accept his fantastic premises."

"I realize that." Griscom frowned. "I recall that when Jim MacVeagh called on me and described the symptoms of a man he refused to name, I thought many of the ideas made sense, if you were willing to accept the premises. I've experienced the same thing in a number of legal cases involving paranoids. Still, Mark Hollenbach. It seems incredible."

"But look at that absurd conspiracy delusion he has," said Karper. "It reappears over and over again, with O'Malley, with Davidge, with MacVeagh, with me. He even mentioned it to his own son. That's the symptom of a diseased mind, Paul, and you know it."

Once again Karper went over the series of incidents, from the hoisted inkwell in the White House to the promise to Mrs. Byerson to make her chrysanthemum the flower of the new superunion. Griscom listened without interrupting, his lanky body slouched in a chair and his eyes fastened on the drink which he held cupped in his hands.

At last the lawyer held up a hand. "That's enough, Sid. You've convinced me. I'll just go tell my wife to cancel me out of dinner, and see if I can't get us a couple of sandwiches. I suppose we ought to get the leaders over here, the same ones who were at Cavanaugh's. What do you think?"

Karper nodded. "Yes, we ought to get that same group, plus Joe Donovan and Arnold Brothers, since they're in on it now. Also, you ought to get young Mark to fly down here and bring those letters."

Griscom smiled a bit sheepishly. "And get Jim MacVeagh out of custody?"

Karper grinned. "Yes, I almost forgot Jim. Where is he, by the way?"

"At D.C. General, for psychiatric examination."

Griscom went to the hallway telephone and quickly got Mark Hollenbach, Jr., at Yale. "Mark," he said, "you'd better fly down here on the first plane. Yes, tonight. Something has come up that makes it imperative. Come straight to my place and bring those letters with you. No word to your folks, please. I'll explain when you get here."

After a few more words with Mark he hung up, then called all those involved, Vice-President O'Malley, Senators Odlum and Gullion, Speaker Nicholson, Justice Cavanaugh, Chief Brothers, and Joe Donovan. All were at home except Odlum, who answered a page at Dulles International Airport, where he'd just arrived from a New Orleans speaking date. He too promised to come at once. While Griscom telephoned, Sidney Karper paced the living room. His big hands swung at his sides and a frown held his great forehead.

Some of the group arrived within a few minutes, but it was almost an hour later when Odlum, the last to reach the house, came in, puffing his apologies. Griscom closed the sliding oak doors and invited all hands to serve themselves from the portable bar.

"I think we've made a grave mistake," Griscom said simply when the amenities were finished. "It's President Hollenbach whose mind we should be worrying about, not Jim MacVeagh. There isn't a man in this room who would question the integrity of Sid Karper. I think we should all hear his story."

Karper told it again, graphically depicting the President's maniacal rage against Carter Urey, the CIA director, and his threatening gesture with the inkwell. He told of the missing medical data from Hollenbach's service record, of Hollenbach's charge that a Pentagon committee had joined a conspiracy against him, of the letters received by Mark Hollenbach, Jr., and of his own shuddering concern over the nuclear firing decision and the coming conference with Premier Zuchek.

Griscom took over when Karper finished. "You all know my part in this business. For several weeks I was under the misapprehension that my friend Jim MacVeagh was ill. Now, speaking as a close family friend of the Hollenbachs and as a lawyer accustomed to weighing evidence, I think there's no longer much doubt in this matter. Apparently the President's mind is off balance. If so, we're faced with a grave national crisis. It's fairly obvious, I think, that we must consider invoking the formal procedure on removal of a president."

"What do you suggest we do?" asked Justice Cavanaugh.

"Two things," said Griscom. "First, we ought to review Pat's agreement with the President and decide precisely how and when he should take the matter to the Cabinet—with our backing. Second, Chief Brothers must get Jim MacVeagh out of the hospital and bring him here right away." The lawyer turned to O'Malley. "Where's the text of that agreement, Pat?"

O'Malley had been brooding, trance-like, while Karper and Griscom talked. His big jowls sagged and he seemed sunken within himself.

"What do you mean, take the matter to the Cabinet, Paul?" he asked.

"He means prepare to take over the office of president," said Karper bluntly. He stared at O'Malley, challenging him.

"My God," said O'Malley. He recoiled as if struck across the mouth. "Do you know what you're saying? I'm a ruined man politically. The country would never accept any move that would put me in the White House. It's unthinkable."

"You're the Vice-President," said Karper. "You're the only man who can act. It's as simple as that."

O'Malley slumped in his chair. The look of incredulity on his face resembled that of the convicted man who cannot accept the sentence the judge has just passed upon him.

Griscom, watching the Vice-President, spoke hurriedly. "We

can go into all that later. The thing to do now is to get the text of the agreement over here, so we can study it. Can you get it, Pat?"

O'Malley nodded, as though in a stupor. "It's at my house on the Hill. I'll go get it." And he walked slowly from the room, his head bent, his sagging face sad and lined.

Griscom turned to Arnold Brothers. "Now, chief," he said, "you'd better go over to D.C. General and fetch Jim MacVeagh back here."

Brothers squirmed slightly in his chair. His ordinarily bland face looked perplexed, and he dabbed at his nose with a handkerchief, as though fearing a return of the spring cold which had dampened him for several weeks.

"I'm not sure of my duty here," he said.

"Just what does that mean?" asked Griscom.

"I'm the agent of the President," said Brothers in a pleading tone. "We detained the Senator because we had reason to fear he might harm the President."

"But you did that on our recommendation," countered Griscom. "Now, certainly, any reasonable man would say MacVeagh was picked up without justifiable cause."

"How about those knives at MacVeagh's home?" asked Brothers doggedly.

"Coincidence," said Griscom.

Brothers said nothing and Karper leveled a finger at him. "Good God, man, don't you realize what's involved here? The President's mind is unbalanced. Jim MacVeagh is as sane as you are. Do you want us to resort to a writ of habeas corpus—with Justice Cavanaugh here signing the writ? Do you want to make a federal case out of this, and have the Service the laughingstock of the country?"

Brothers kneaded his hands and frowned. A pension less than a year away . . .

"Does everyone here agree with the Secretary?" asked Brothers plaintively. He was playing for time.

There were several nods from men about the room, and then Speaker Nicholson said quite formally: "If any question arises, Arnold, you have us as your authority for acting. This looks like a long night, but whatever happens, I think Senator MacVeagh should be here for it."

Brothers, his face reflecting his discomfort, rose and walked toward the hallway. "In that case," he said, "I'd better do the job myself."

The Secret Service chief was back in half an hour, entering the house with MacVeagh just ahead of the returning Pat O'Malley. Brothers delivered MacVeagh to the group like a man washing his hands after carrying a messy package. Karper quickly explained the suddenly altered circumstances to Jim.

"We're sorry, Jimmy," said Joe Donovan. "You're not really nuts. You just act that way."

"Thanks, pal," said Jim, but his laugh was less than cheerful. He had been boiling for more than three hours since Luther Smith and another Secret Service agent had registered him at the hospital's mental ward and then escorted him to a private room. First had come a nurse, solicitous and patronizing, to bring him a white gown. When he refused to don it, she merely smiled angelically and took his temperature and pulse rate. Then came a young, serious, white-coated hospital staff doctor with a clipboard and two pages of questions which he put to MacVeagh apologetically but firmly. Jim was advised to get a good night's sleep, call for a sedative if he needed one, and be prepared for his first session with a staff psychiatrist at nine o'clock the next morning. Then came dinner on a tray, the food tasting as though it had been stolen the day before from a cafeteria. More solicitude from the nurse and a grudging agreement to bring him the late edition of the Washington *Star*. He considered demanding a lawyer, thought better of it, wondered what Secretary Karper did when he arrived at the White House gate, decided against calling Martha, damned Chief Brothers, and glowered at the locked door and at the wire mesh at his bedroom window. In all, by the time Arnold Brothers arrived to end his detention, Jim was seething with frustration and anger. Brothers' guarded apologies on the ride to O Street did nothing to appease him.

But his ire ebbed in Griscom's living room as he was swept into the discussion. MacVeagh had arrived late at many Washington conferences, but never at one where the mood was as unrelievedly somber as this one. There was no jesting after Joe Donovan's remark and few wasted words.

Griscom asked Chief Brothers to step into an adjoining room, explaining that a question of Democratic party policy had to be determined and that Brothers, as a civil servant, would feel more comfortable out of hearing. Brothers, mirroring relief for the first time that night, agreed. Then Griscom asked O'Malley for the text of the presidential disability agreement and read it aloud.

"The whole emphasis of this agreement," he said, "is on speed. O'Malley is required to act 'promptly' upon 'clear evidence' and in no case is he to delay more than twenty-four hours in setting the legal procedure in motion. Now I would suggest that this entire group should draft and sign a statement, urging O'Malley to assume the presidency because of President Hollenbach's disabled condition. Then O'Malley should summon the Cabinet, get written statements from a majority stating that he should take over, and then request TV time to explain it to the nation. After that, we get him sworn in."

"That's an awful lot of drastic action all at once, Paul," observed Speaker Nicholson. He was obviously loath to entertain such a sweep of movement.

O'Malley, who had been unwrapping a cigar, now lighted it and puffed reflectively. He had recovered his composure, but his great drooping jowls seemed to accentuate the fatigue etched in his face.

"Before there's much discussion of this thing," said O'Malley, "let me say my piece. I thought about this riding to and from my house. No man here is under any illusions that I'm the kind of man who could fill Mark Hollenbach's shoes—the old Mark Hollenbach, that is. I can handle the job all right, but we all know public confidence in me would be down below the zero mark. What's more, it would be disastrous for the party if people thought I would become a candidate for president this summer.

"Therefore, I want to make it crystal clear right now that if I'm forced to take over at the White House, under no conditions would I become a candidate for an elected term as president. That would be plainly and irrevocably stated to the country over television. Anything else, with my background in the arena case, would murder us. I just think you all should know that in advance."

"Thanks, Pat," said Karper. "Enough said. We all understand."

MacVeagh spoke for the first time. "Not that anybody cares much, but the same thing goes for me on vice-president. After my part in this—well, this investigation of the President—I could never be a candidate for vice-president. It would be presumptuous to include the presidency in that, but of course, it's included too."

Fred Odlum's small pale-gray eyes darted from man to man. He had said nothing so far, an unusual restraint on his part. Now he spoke, his voice as barbed as a trolling hook.

"These great renunciations are very magnanimous on your part, gentlemen," he said, nodding to O'Malley and MacVeagh, "but I'm a lot more interested in what we're going to tell the country. I'm not anxious to enter a campaign in which we've just told the people that they've been governed by an insane man. The voters might get the idea it's some contagious Democratic disease."

"I agree," said Karper, somewhat to Odlum's surprise. "Fred is right. But it's not domestic politics that bothers me. Such an admission could be terrifically damaging abroad, especially with this conference with Zuchek coming up." He whistled through his quill toothpick, then shook his head. "I'm not sure, but perhaps the way out would be through General Leppert. Perhaps we could persuade him to certify that the President is suffering from a physical ailment. And maybe, who knows, there is some tissue damage to the brain."

"Now just a minute," said Sterling Gullion. "How do we know that General Leppert will concede that the President is ailing, either mentally or physically? How do we know that he won't claim, after hearing everything, that Hollenbach is sane?"

They all looked at the Negro senator in surprise. His large, moist eyes returned their gaze, and he smiled softly.

"Good God, man," exploded Karper. "How could anyone doubt evidence like this? Do you?"

"No," said Gullion, "but I'm a layman, not a physician. Leppert might demand all kinds of medical proof, psychiatric examinations and that sort of thing, before he'd lay his own reputation as a doctor on the line."

"I think that's a strong possibility, Sterling," said Speaker Nicholson. He spoke in measured, rhythmic tones as though rendering a parliamentary decision in the House of Representatives. "You all know I didn't believe this at first. Now I've come to the reluctant conclusion that perhaps something is wrong with the President's mind. But who knows how bad it is? Maybe it's only temporary. Maybe, unbeknownst to us, it has already cleared up. Who can be sure just what a professional man would certify?"

"Gentlemen," said Karper, "this condition of the President's has been under way for at least six months. There is just no blinking the facts." His voice grew harsh, almost brutal in intensity. "I live with this nuclear decision day and night, and I just could not face my children or yours if I didn't do everything in my power to get Mark Hollenbach away from the go-code. It is sheer folly to have that man anywhere near the command and control machinery. It might lead to wholesale murder."

Karper's stand provoked an argument that lasted more than an hour. Odlum, Nicholson and Gullion maintained that the chance of a decision requiring firing of the massive atomic arsenal was exceedingly remote. Karper, backed by Cavanaugh, O'Malley, Griscom and MacVeagh, contended that the threat always hung over the nation, especially now that the Red Chinese had detonated five hydrogen bombs of frightening power and had exhibited the missiles needed to carry the warheads. Gullion inquired how the go-code of the National Command Authorities actually functioned. Karper begged off on security grounds, explaining that it was the most tightly held secret in government and that he would be subject to imprisonment if he revealed it. But, he added, it was common knowledge that the basic atomic law stipulated that only the President could authorize use of nuclear weapons.

"Men," pleaded Karper, "we just can't temporize with this situation. There is no compromise. Mark Hollenbach's hand must be removed from the button. And if this group refuses to act behind the scenes, then I'll just have to take the case to the country—with all that that involves."

"You couldn't," said Odlum. "Think what it would do to the party."

"I'd chance that," said Karper grimly. "This is bigger than party."

"That's easily said by a man who doesn't have to face the

voters," said Odlum. His pinched face appeared wizened under the lights of the chandelier and his hawklike eyes seemed to accuse Karper.

"I live with the bomb decision," said Karper. "You don't."

"Let's get this straight, Sid," said Odlum sharply. "As I get it, you're willing to wreck the Democratic Party over this issue."

Color swept over Karper's bronzed face. "I mean precisely that," he blazed. He shot a warning finger at Odlum. "And I think it's a damned outrage that Louisiana sends the kind of senator to Washington who has the gall even to mention party advantage in the same breath with a madman's finger on the trigger."

Odlum's pinched face hardened until the grooves stood out like cracks in a rock. "I think you'd better retract that statement, Mr. Secretary," he said. His tone was frigid.

"Retract, hell," roared Karper. "Your kind of approach to life and death on this planet disgusts me deep down in my belly."

"I might point out to the morally indignant Secretary of Defense," said Odlum with exaggerated gravity, "that if President Hollenbach is removed, Mr. Sidney Karper would become one of the leading candidates for the Democratic nomination." His tone taunted now. "And I'd like to know whether that cheap political thought has ever crossed the Secretary's mind?"

"Are you accusing me of trying to get rid of Mark Hollenbach because of personal political ambition?" bellowed Karper.

Odlum glared at him without flinching. "Please lower your voice, Mr. Secretary," he said, "or people may begin to wonder just whose mind it is that's disturbed."

Karper sprang to his feet. "Damn you, Odlum. I've had about enough."

Griscom rose quickly and thrust his body in front of Karper. Odlum had risen too, and Griscom placed a hand on each man's chest.

"That's enough, gentlemen," said Griscom. "That's quite enough. I think a double apology is in order here."

The little senator and the huge Cabinet officer stood glaring at each other. The room was so still that the heavy breathing of Speaker Nicholson could be heard. Karper clenched his fists at his sides and Odlum's mouth looked as though he had just bit into a lemon. Joe Donovan broke the silence. He got up from a sofa and put his arm around Odlum's shoulder.

"Come on, Fred," he said. "He's got seventy-five pounds and at least four inches of reach on you. Pick on somebody your own size."

Odlum smiled faintly. "I will accept an apology from the Secretary," he said. His tone was as starched as a boiled shirt front.

"I apologize," said Karper archly. "I lost my temper."

"So did I. Please be kind enough to overlook it."

Joe Donovan grinned and held an arm of each man aloft.

"Now shake on it," said Donovan.

They did so. Jim MacVeagh, knowing Odlum's acid temperament, had a fleeting fear that the Louisiana senator would remind Karper that another man, under similar circumstances, once lost his temper with his hand on a White House inkwell. The opening, thought Jim, was too obvious for Odlum to ignore. But Odlum merely smiled, nodded his head at Karper, and went back to his chair.

"God, it's hot in here, Paul," said Grady Cavanaugh. "Can't you open a window?"

"I'll turn on the air conditioning," said Griscom. "I'd rather not take a chance on open windows."

The hum of the cooling machinery seemed to calm the atmosphere. Tension ebbed and the discussion resumed in a normal key. Nicholson urged that the group recess and continue the talk in the morning. MacVeagh insisted that no one knew the extent of the President's mental disturbance, and that they should continue through the night, if necessary, until some plan of action was evolved. Gullion suggested that the Chairman of the Joint Chiefs of Staff be brought into the meeting because of his stature with the country and his intimate knowledge of the nuclear decision mechanism. Cavanaugh countered that the issue of presidential removal was a purely civilian one in which a military officer should have no part. And so the talk went on for an hour, with no definitive course of action emerging.

It was past midnight when Griscom answered the ring of the doorbell after carefully closing the oak doors behind him. Mark Hollenbach, Jr., stood on the stoop.

"What's cooking, Uncle Paul?" The boy's voice jested, but worry lines in his face showed his concern.

"I'll tell you upstairs," said Griscom. "There's a meeting on down here."

He led young Hollenbach to an upstairs bedroom.

"Did you bring the letters?" asked Griscom.

Mark nodded and held out two envelopes. Griscom read the three letters, ran his eyes again over several passages, then handed the sheets back to the boy.

"Mark," said Griscom, "this is going to be hard to take. A number of us have come to the conclusion that your father is suffering some kind of mental ailment, just how severe we don't know. A group of party leaders is meeting downstairs now, trying to decide just what to do."

"I guess I knew there was something like that." Young Mark went to a back window and stood gazing into the night. "Does Mother know?"

"I don't think so," said Griscom. "Things have happened so fast today we haven't had a chance to talk to her."

Griscom briefly reviewed the gathering evidence while young Mark slouched on a bed and listened.

"I guess I'm not really surprised," said Mark when Griscom had finished. "Dad's a complex guy with all that tension and the drive for excellence. I used to wonder sometimes why he didn't crack." The boy chewed moodily on his lower lip. His handsome features, with the delicate bone structure, showed his strain. "It's a sad break, Uncle Paul. I was just getting to the age where I could appreciate the old man, talk to him on his level, I guess you'd say . . . and now this."

Griscom put a hand on Mark's shoulder. "I know," he said.

"I suppose it means he'll have to give up the presidency," said Mark.

"Yes. I don't see any other way out. But, of course, Mark, we have to face the fact that he may refuse to relinquish the office. In that case—and this will be rough, kid—we'll have to use those letters of yours. I sincerely hope not."

"I understand," said Mark. "You go on back to the meeting. I'll try to get some shut-eye. And listen, Uncle Paul, don't worry about me. I'll do whatever you say has to be done."

Griscom came back to the living room to find that a consensus had been reached. As Grady Cavanaugh explained it, all agreed that whatever else was done, the only logical next step was to summon General Leppert and quiz him in detail on the President's mental and physical condition. The chore of calling the doctor fell to the man who knew him best, Fred Odlum, who observed sourly, after glancing at his watch, that he hadn't heard of a physician in thirty years who would make a house call at 12:45 in the morning.

"He's coming," said Odlum when he returned from the hallway telephone. He glanced at Karper. "I told him it was a matter of life and death," he added sarcastically.

Chief Brothers was brought back into the room to hear the White House physician, and, fifteen minutes later, Brigadier General Maury Leppert arrived. He was a withdrawn, haggard man with a thin, corn-colored mustache and eyelids that blinked rapidly when he was addressed. Odlum introduced him to the men he did not know, then Cavanaugh took a stance in the center of the room.

"General Leppert," he said, "we've invited you over here on a matter of the utmost gravity and, we think, possibly of great urgency. To put it bluntly, all of us in this room have cause to question the normality of the President's mental processes. We would like to ask you, doctor, do you have any cause to doubt the President's sanity?"

Leppert blinked swiftly as he stared at Cavanaugh, then searched the faces of others in the room. He was obviously stunned. "That's the most astounding question I've ever been asked in my entire career," he said.

"I don't doubt it," said Cavanaugh. "But what is your answer?"

"No, of course not," said Leppert. Although he nervously fingered his thin mustache, it appeared certain to Jim MacVeagh that the doctor was not lying. "I have absolutely no reason to question the President's sanity," added Leppert.

"Is there anything wrong with the President, either mental or physical?" asked Cavanaugh.

"He has an occasional heart murmur," said Leppert, "to use the layman's terminology. I consider it a matter of some concern, but no cause for alarm."

"Outside of this occasional heart murmur," pressed Cavanaugh, "there is nothing else?"

"No infirmity, no," replied Leppert. He hesitated. "Of course, as his physician, I don't care for his pattern of strenuous activity. He goes all hours, and he doesn't get enough sleep. As a matter of fact, I know he was still up—probably telephoning—when I left the mansion."

"Couldn't such habits lead to a mental breakdown?" asked Cavanaugh.

"They could," said Leppert slowly, "they could, but in President Hollenbach's case, I've seen no indication of mental fatigue. He's been doing it for years. I'll wager he doesn't average six hours sleep a night."

"Some men thrive on that kind of regime," offered Speaker Nicholson.

Leppert nodded. "The chemistry of each human body varies. Mark Hollenbach is one of those fortunate men who require less rest than most people."

Cavanaugh pressed again. "But he has no definite medical problem of any kind other than the heart murmur?"

"Nothing," said Leppert. "He seldom even has a cold."

Jim MacVeagh began to feel uneasy again. He looked across the room at Sidney Karper. The Defense Secretary's face was clouded, and Jim thought he detected a look of hostile suspicion as Karper studied the physician.

Cavanaugh spoke quietly. "General, would you believe evidence gathered by the men in this room as to the President's mental condition?"

Leppert blinked and rubbed the tip of his forefinger over his pencil-like mustache. "I think you're all men of integrity," he answered cautiously. "I certainly would believe that you would honestly report what you observed, but that doesn't mean I'd come to the same conclusions."

Cavanaugh nodded. "I realize that, doctor. And now I want you to hear the whole story. If I misspeak in the slightest degree, I want my friends in this room to correct me."

It took Cavanaugh a half hour to go through all the evidence. As the Supreme Court justice talked, Jim MacVeagh could see again the ghostly, flickering firelight of Aspen lodge, could feel the chills of apprehension as Hollenbach raged against O'Malley and Craig Spence, and could hear the wild, frayed texture of the President's voice when he alluded darkly to a conspiracy that had been formed to crush him.

"Now, General," asked Cavanaugh when he concluded, "in the light of all that, would you say the President's mental processes are normal?"

"Mr. Justice," replied Leppert, "what is normal? You define the word, and I'll answer the question."

"Oh, come now, doctor," objected Griscom, "let's not quibble over semantics. The word 'normal' has a generally accepted meaning."

"To a layman perhaps," said Leppert, his eyelids closing and opening like mechanical shutters, "but not to a medical man. Normal has no precise meaning in physiological terms."

"Look, doctor," said Griscom. The lawyer rose and walked over to the marble fireplace. "I don't think Grady made quite enough of the President's proposal—seriously made—for a national wiretapping law under which the FBI could listen to any private phone conversation, and, as a matter of fact, computers could store up millions of phone calls for future reference. To my mind, this obviously is linked with his desire to spy upon and 'get even' with the conspiracy he thinks is after him. Now, as a man who prizes the doctor-patient relationship, doesn't such an idea disturb you?"

"Yes, of course." Leppert blinked rapidly as he spoke. "I think such a law would be foolish and dangerous, but that doesn't mean that the man who advocates it is insane."

"What about the President's letters to young Mark and Mr. Carmichael?" asked Griscom. He studied the doctor over the tops of his rimless spectacles. "I have just read them upstairs and some of the phrases are still pretty fresh in my mind. One in particular. The President wrote his son that there was 'an obvious conspiracy afoot to sully and demean me.' Then—and I don't remember his exact words—he enjoined his son not to add to his problems at a time when he had to deal with this alleged conspiracy. Now, as a close friend of the Hollenbach family, I ask you, don't you think those letters emanated from a troubled mind?"

This time the physician thought for some seconds, pressing his lips together and knuckling his mustache. "Troubled? Yes. But deranged? I would hesitate to draw such a conclusion."

"Let me put the whole case more explicitly, doctor," said Grady Cavanaugh. "Assuming that everything you've heard reflects the facts accurately, would you say that the President is suffering from some form of paranoia?"

"I am not a psychiatrist," said Leppert promptly. "Unless the President were adequately examined by the best psychiatric specialists in the country, I would withhold a medical judgment."

"Doctor!" It was almost a command from Sidney Karper. The Secretary of Defense's big frame leaned forward tensely and he sought and held General Leppert's eyes.

"Yes, sir," replied Leppert.

"Forget for a moment your professional status." Karper's tone was icy. "As an American citizen, are you satisfied that President Hollenbach is sufficiently normal of mind to make the final decision to launch a hydrogen warhead that might kill ten million people in a matter of minutes?"

"No!" The voice came from the hallway. It was loud, clear, weighted with authority.

The thick, oak panel doors were flung wide and there, stiffly erect in the doorway, stood the President of the United States.

20.

Command and Control

President Mark Hollenbach stood perfectly still for a moment. His shoulders were squared like those of a military officer, his crew cut seemed to bristle aggressively, and his eyes mirrored the confidence of command. Then, with a slight movement of his shoulders, he visibly relaxed and walked easily into the room with a gait that was almost a saunter.

There was a chiding smile on his lips and his face was composed, curiously free of strain. He wore a tweedy sports coat and he thrust his hands casually into the side pockets as though he were out for an evening stroll.

All eyes were riveted on the President. The only sound in the room was the ticking of a gilt-framed clock on the marble mantel. The clock's hands showed the hour—2:35.

The President bowed slightly toward Karper.

"Pardon me for eavesdropping, Sid," he said.

He turned to Cavanaugh. "And you too, Mr. Justice. I've been standing outside there in the hallway a minute or so . . ."

In the background could be seen a figure standing against a wall in the hallway. "Wait outside for me, will you, Luther," said the President over his shoulder. "These men are all my friends. Besides, I see Chief Brothers here, so security is in good hands."

The President stood in the center of the room, ringed by the circle of men who watched him in shocked fascination as though he were a sudden visitor from another planet. His aplomb, subtly bolstered by the authority of office, recalled the old Mark Hollenbach that millions of Americans had seen on television and on the campaign platform. Jim MacVeagh, stunned as he was by Hollenbach's unexpected appearance, could sense the indefinable magnetism of the man, the aura of leadership. When the President spoke, his tone was quiet, firm.

"Does Mark Hollenbach," he asked, "have the mental stability to enable him to make the decision that might consume all of civilization?"

He paused and scanned the faces, still dazed with shock, which ringed him.

"No," he said, "he does not. I repeat. No, he does not."

He was silent again, merely standing there with a wispy, faintly reproving smile about his lips, and his hands tucked idly into his coat pockets as though he were back on the college campus with a group of his favorite students.

"No, he doesn't," he continued in a conversational tone. "This is especially true, gentlemen, when you realize that under certain conditions he must make that decision within two or three minutes. Does Sidney Karper have such soundness of mind—or should we call it omniscience? Does Mr. Justice Cavanaugh?"

The President's eyes went from one man to the other, the chiding smile still playing about his mouth. "Does anyone in this room? Each must speak for himself, gentlemen. In a matter of this gravity, I wouldn't presume to speak for another."

The leaders sat as though in a trance, listening to Hollenbach's rhetorical questions drift about, unanswered, in the high-ceilinged room. During his pauses only the soft whir of the air-conditioning machinery could be heard. Jim MacVeagh could feel the old yielding to the presidential presence come creeping back into the room like a physical thing, as pervasive and as captivating as an evening mist.

"And how did I happen to drop in on this little gathering?" asked the President. He grinned. "Well, I was up late—telephoning as usual. I had just learned about this harassment of Senator MacVeagh and I called Chief Brothers at once to ask him to desist. It seemed a foolish thing to me. Chief Brothers, it turned out, was at Paul Griscom's. Then I called Jim to apologize for any embarrassment to him, and I found, somewhat circuitously, that he was thought to be here too. And, since I was working on this knotty business of the foreign aid appropriations, I called Fred Odlum at home. He too, it turned out, was at Paul Griscom's. And finally, seeking a sedative from the good doctor, I found that, lo and behold, General Leppert also was at the famous house on O Street. Well, says, I, there must be a party of my old friends at Paul's, so I'll just drop by."

The President continued in his chatty manner, as though he were idly gossiping on a hot summer afternoon. "Gentlemen, from what I've heard tonight and from a few little hints picked up here and there, I take it my mind is under question."

Karper flashed a glance at MacVeagh from under his heavy brows, but the other faces remained immobile, centered on the President as though transfixed.

"Everyone here, I take it," said Hollenbach, "has either heard me blow my top on some subject or other, or has heard about it. You've matched notes, haven't you? The President, you've decided, suffers from delusions of persecution and perhaps of grandeur as well. Oh, by the way, may I sit?"

Griscom hurried to a corner and brought the President one of the painted, antiqued wooden chairs. Hollenbach pulled it back toward the doorway, so that he became part of the circle. He settled himself comfortably and stretched out his legs. Resting his hands on his thighs, he began flexing the fingers forcibly.

"Oh, yes," he said lightly, "and my isometrics, I suppose, has been discussed, as well as my perfectionist pleas for excellence. He's taut as a drumhead, you've probably been saying, no wonder he explodes. And he turns off the lights in the small night hours, an odd eccentricity. And he stays up half the night, working and telephoning. Yes, I suppose you've gone over all my quaint little habits."

No one else had spoken yet, and the leaders were heeding Hollenbach's every word with the hushed fascination of desert tribesmen listening to a prophet down from the hills. The President's tone became more serious.

"Delusions of grandeur?" he asked. "Yes, I suppose I am guilty of grand dreams. The union with Canada, for instance. I'm sure Jim has told you about that. Well, if a merger with Canada is the product of a tainted mind, so be it. Frankly, gentlemen, I think such a union should have taken place a century ago. We and Canada have every reason to combine for our mutual strength and profit, and only rabid nationalism, customs, and outworn modes of thinking prevent it."

Here is the Hollenbach of old, thought Jim, Hollenbach in his most persuasive mood, brilliant, convincing, alternately challenging and pleading. MacVeagh could feel the vibrations of sympathy in the room as though all were anxious to help the President. Senator Gullion spoke first in his soft drawl.

"As you know, Mr. President," said Gullion, "we've got an active group of businessmen in Chicago that agrees with you. They're plugging Canadian union with us."

Hollenbach nodded and smiled. "I know, Sterling. Of course, they're for it. Most Americans and Canadians will be in another decade. It makes sense, that's why."

He paused again and his eyes searched the ceiling for a moment. "Ah, but my union with Scandinavia, that indeed must be the offspring of a demented mind, so divorced from reality and common sense. Eh, Jim? I suppose you've told them about my grand concept?"

MacVeagh nodded dumbly, and he felt suddenly, irrationally, as though he had betrayed a cause. The pull of the presidency, he thought, is so powerful that even a president on trial before his peers can dominate them all. Jim felt disloyal, as a man who had broken his word and compromised a friend.

"But isn't Scandinavia a starter, gentlemen?" pleaded Hollenbach. His eyes glowed now. "I firmly believe that a parliament of the free world is the best guarantee for lasting peace, and we have to start somewhere. Britain, France, Germany are all too proud to make common government with us, but if we could begin somewhere—and the Scandinavians are as sound a people as any to start with—wouldn't the others join us later? I think it makes sense."

But that's not at all the way he outlined his scheme at Aspen lodge, thought Jim. Hollenbach derided Europe then, and spoke of using force—even hinting at military force if necessary—to drive the European nations into union. And what about Hollenbach's messianic desire to lead such a union, to become the prime minister of super-government? Jim again could see Hollenbach striding in the gloom of Aspen, obsessed with his quixotic passion. How different was that seized zealot from this relaxed and apparently fully rational man sitting here in Georgetown. Jim saw once again the crazed soldier gesticulating in the medic's shack in Viet Nam, and he felt intuitively that the image was closer to the real Hollenbach than this logical, self-possessed man sitting near him now. Jim was enveloped by a weird sensation that Hollenbach was going to talk himself out of his cul-de-sac. By God, he was. Jim sat mesmerized, waiting like the snake before the charmer for the next sound of the pipe.

"And I suppose you've discussed my alleged persecution complex," said the President calmly. "Yes, Sidney, you did hear me raise the roof about Carter Urey and his one-man control of the CIA, his failure to report adequately to me, and his attempts to make foreign policy on his own. But, on the other hand, you've never known how many times that man disobeyed my instructions. Of course, I've got a temper. I admit it. I occasionally say things I shouldn't, but I regret them and I apologize."

Throughout the President's comments, except for his brief glance at MacVeagh, Karper had remained rigid, his large, bronze face coldly impassive. Now he leaned forward, sharply questioning.

"But that's not quite the way it went, Mr. President," he said. "You threatened me with an inkwell, remember?"

"Sid, Sid, I'm always doing my isometrics. You know that." He spoke gently, as though reproving a child. "I do it in times of relaxation and sometimes in moments of stress. I was merely putting pressure on that bottle. It helps me get myself under control. Don't you ever get mad, Sid?"

Karper nodded silently, and threw a helpless glance at Mac-Veagh, as though to say that the President was making everything sound too normal, too commonplace. It wasn't that way at all, his glance seemed to say. No, it wasn't, thought MacVeagh. But he knew the President had scored, unknowingly, a blow for himself, for Karper's eruption against Odlum was still fresh in the minds of all who listened.

Speaker Nicholson moved ponderously in his chair and addressed Hollenbach.

"Mr. President," he said, "I wish you wouldn't go any further into this, sir. I let myself be persuaded of your—uh—instability —against my own better judgment. I don't agree with your proposal for a merger of major free nations, not at all. But that's beside the point. I'm in this room against my every instinct. We all have times of mental turbulence in this city, and you're as human as the rest of us. But now I think it's time for a little tolerance and understanding—and time for us all to go home."

Hollenbach smiled his appreciation, but shook his head. "No, Nick, I know there are other charges, and we might as well clear the air of them here, tonight."

"But," protested Nicholson, "we're into an area where the Constitution never intended us to be, an area where we're judging one man's mind against another. We're just not wise enough to play God."

"In this city, we always have to try," replied Hollenbach. "Let's take these other things. MacVeagh, for instance, has heard me accuse the Vice-President—" he nodded pleasantly toward O'Malley "—accuse the Vice-President of trying to sabotage me. That, I grant, was overstating the whole case. Pat, you did let your country and your party down, but I erred when I accused you of trying to hurt me intentionally. I realize that and I regret it."

The President slid into his most effective and persuasive tone, the tone that had carried hundreds of points during his political career. "Gentlemen, this office does change the man. The President is in command so constantly. He is Number One. He is never denied. He is king for his term. So, it is only natural that a president begins to think of himself as the country. Anything that harms America, he takes as a personal affront. Every beneficial development, he takes as a personal tribute. You all help to foster that attitude, by your kowtowing to the President, and by your refusal to state your case consistently and stubbornly when you know the President thinks ill of it. Every one of you helps build the power complex of the White House, gentlemen, every one of you."

He definitely is talking himself out of it, thought MacVeagh. My God, what a superb performance. And perhaps . . . who could say? Perhaps, logical as he is tonight, perhaps he is sane, maybe saner than any of the others in the room. Perhaps Hollenbach's mental trouble, whatever it was, was only temporary after all. Jim began to feel guilty for starting it all, and he wondered how Karper felt now. Why had Karper been so persistent?

"There was my outburst over Davidge, the Chicago banker," continued the President. "I'm guessing you've all heard of that too." He smiled kindly at MacVeagh, and Jim thought the President was trying to indicate to him privately that he knew how the Davidge story might have got out.

"There again," said Hollenbach, "my temper got the better of me. But did any of you know that Davidge and I had a conference in which I specifically told him that the whole interest rate policy was under review? And yet he insisted on making a speech criticizing the very things I told him I planned to remedy. That, you'll grant, smacks of double-dealing. But, I readily confess, I was too hard on him. I was too hard on Davidge, and on you, Pat, and on Carter Urey. But in each case I recognized it after the temper passed and I tried to make amends."

Jim felt a twinge of embarrassment to hear the President thus baring his emotions before his subordinates. Since he himself shied from self-analysis, Jim felt acutely uncomfortable to hear another, especially a president, do so. But then his thoughts ran to the substance of what the President was saying. Had he really tried to make amends, as he said? The President had never apologized to O'Malley before tonight. And he had accused MacVeagh too of trying to ruin him, of joining a conspiracy. What about this absurd cabal theory of Hollenbach's? He had given no explanation of that. No, Hollenbach was making it all sound too normal, too neat, as though the incidents were no more significant than spats with a wife. Had it really been that way? Jim exchanged baffled glances with Karper. The Defense Secretary moved restlessly in his chair during a brief lull in the talk.

"I repeat my suggestion, gentlemen," said Nicholson, breaking the silence. "We should disband and go home to bed. We've no business sitting here like a court of psychiatrists. Frankly, this whole thing is damn repugnant to me. I apologize to you, Mr. President, for ever attending this kind of session."

The Speaker turned to MacVeagh with a courtly bow. "And I apologize to you too, Jim, for ever questioning your mental processes. I think we've all learned a lesson in humility and mutual tolerance here tonight."

"Ditto, Mr. Speaker," put in Joe Donovan. "Let's let the Republicans hire the headshrinkers. They give me the itch."

Karper, whose eyes seldom left the President, raised a hand as though to still Nicholson and Donovan.

"Not so fast," he said coldly. "I'd still like to pursue several lines here."

"Mr. Secretary," objected Nicholson, "I think we've had about enough of that kind—"

"No, Nick," interrupted the President. "Let Sid continue. We want to thrash this thing out."

"Mr. President," said Karper, "with your permission, sir, I'd like to question you about five specific points you haven't mentioned. First, is it true that you are seriously considering a law that would give the FBI authority to tap any telephone conversation in the country at any time?"

For the first time a flash of hostility crossed Hollenbach's eyes. He shifted uneasily in his chair and glanced toward the high windows fronting on O Street.

"Of course, when they . . ." The President's voice, suddenly high-pitched, had a querulous ring.

"When they . . . ?" repeated Karper.

"When they are trying to . . ." Hollenbach spoke harshly, but his voice quickly trailed away for the second time. He looked down at his lap, his shoulders slumped and color seemed to fade from his face. There was a momentary hush in the room.

"You were saying, Mr. President?" Karper's tone was low, gentle.

Hollenbach looked up again and Jim MacVeagh had the impression, watching him, that the President had wrenched his mind back in focus by sheer force of will. Hollenbach smiled at Karper. "Yes, Sid," said the President, "I did indicate to Jim that my joking proposal at the Gridiron dinner had a serious basis. I think such a law could be of tremendous benefit in curbing crime in this country."

"And did you indicate you would have used it to eavesdrop on Pat O'Malley's conversations?" asked Karper bluntly.

"I may have." Hollenbach hesitated. "But if so, I was wrong. Of course I would not have the law used in such a manner. I suppose I was overwrought about the Vice-President at the time."

"But, Mr. President," pursued Karper, "wouldn't such a law constitute the greatest single threat to individual freedom since the alien and sedition acts?"

"Absolutely not. My idea is that the law would be most scrupulously drawn to protect personal liberties."

Karper sighed, then pressed on. "I'd like to ask you about four other matters. First, about your temper outburst over the columnist Craig Spence. Second, why was an FBI investigation ordered of Jim MacVeagh? Third, what about your belief that some kind of conspiracy exists with the goal of destroying you? Finally, I'd like to know why your medical record is missing from your Korean service file?"

Hollenbach obviously was surprised at the last question. "I didn't know any medical data was missing," he said. He faltered a moment. "I can't explain that. It may have been deleted by some overzealous friend. But I don't mind telling you frankly that I once had a psychiatric examination after breaking under fire. I turned and ran. But the phase—it was pure cowardice and

I admit it—the phase passed and I returned to my company three days later. The next time the Chinese Communists charged our position, I held."

There was a hush, then Nicholson turned on Karper. "You're damn right he held—and he got the Silver Star for it. What the hell kind of business is that, Mr. Secretary?" he blazed. "That's a despicable act, sneaking around and digging into the service file of a President of the United States—a soldier decorated for gallantry in action."

Karper faced Nicholson. "I had reason to believe," he said roughly, "that we were dealing with a constitutional crisis. I still do."

"I think it's an outrage," Nicholson sputtered.

Hollenbach waved a calming hand. "No, Nick, the Secretary was within his rights. And I'm not through yet. Without answering Sidney's other questions specifically, let me just say that I've had cause to consider my behavior in recent weeks. I've done a little investigating of myself, delving into my own thought processes—a personal review, as it were. It's a pursuit I recommend to all hands."

The room was again so quiet that only the ticking of the mantel clock and the hum of the air-conditioning system could be heard.

"I did some studying and some reading," said Hollenbach, "and I came to the conclusion that I haven't always acted normally—if that is the word. However, I don't blame General Leppert for not recognizing my lapses, for every time I've consulted him I've felt fine. Whatever the name for my condition, I'm sure it was only temporary."

Could that be true? wondered MacVeagh. With the exception of a brief moment, Hollenbach was so "normal," so plausible tonight, just as he had been at Camp David when he talked about his crusade for excellence falling on O'Malley's deaf ears.

Damned convincing. But, good God, how about those letters his own son brought down here?

Jim looked at Paul Griscom, and Griscom tilted his head upward as though he too were thinking of the letters. Griscom, the President's closest friend in the room, obviously was not persuaded. Griscom returned his gaze to the President, cocking his head quizzically and studying Hollenbach as though he were a witness who had yet to tell the full story. Karper was sunk in his chair, his eyes fastened on Hollenbach. Not a muscle in the Secretary's bronze face was moving.

"But gentlemen," continued Hollenbach, "something else has happened to me recently. I have heart murmurs, as you probably know—since Dr. Leppert is here and this appears to be one of those confess-everything sessions. But recently the murmurs have grown worse. I can feel a sharp pain at times. And so, to bring this somewhat unsavory business to a finish, I must tell you that I'm concerned about my heart."

General Leppert appeared surprised, but the other faces were void of expression as the men waited, tensely, for the President's next words.

"As a result," continued Hollenbach, "I've decided to postpone the conference with Zuchek. At nine A.M. tomorrow, or rather today, I propose to hold a news conference in my office and let the people know." He paused once more. "I'm going to let the people know, for the best of all concerned, that I've decided to take a long vacation."

The room was soundless. Outside could be heard the whine of tires as a lone car sped along O Street in the early morning hours. The headlights flashed briefly at the windows like the sweep of a searchlight.

Nicholson, Gullion and Odlum looked startled, yet relieved, as though welcoming any compromise that would avoid a judgment on what Hollenbach called "this unsavory business." Chief

Brothers, opaque and neutral as always, showed no emotion. Cavanaugh, Karper, Griscom and MacVeagh exchanged anxious glances. O'Malley chewed on his cigar and frowned, lost in his own thoughts of what a presidential vacation would mean to him. Griscom again motioned his head toward the upstairs bedroom where Mark Jr. was sleeping, but Karper, seeing the gesture, shook his head.

"I think, Mr. President," said Nicholson laboriously, "that this is a wise and patriotic decision. We'll keep the show on the road while you're gone and try not to bother you too much. But of one thing I'm convinced, Mr. President. You're as sane as I am."

MacVeagh, knowing Hollenbach's opinion of Nicholson, found this to be the first faintly humorous observation of the night. Jim could tell by the amused look on Hollenbach's face that he too appreciated the irony.

Hollenbach smiled at the Speaker. "And how sane is that, Nick? But let's not confuse the issues here. It's my heart that bothers me. Of course, gentlemen, I would assume that with my announcement tomorrow there would be no necessity of ever revealing our other discussions here tonight, would there?"

"Never, Mr. President," said Fred Odlum.

Griscom looked at the White House physician. "And you, General Leppert, do you agree that the President is taking the proper step here?"

"Any man with a heart tremor should take it easy," replied Leppert. "To continue at breakneck pace under pressure is tempting the fates. I've consistently urged the President to take a vacation."

The men began to rise and stand awkwardly, as though they were actors fatigued by a drama long rehearsed. Nicholson stepped to the President, grasped his hand, and shook it heartily.

"Good luck, Mr. President," he said, "it's a wise decision."

"Wiser than you know, Nick," replied Hollenbach.

Each man stepped forward in turn to shake the President's hand. As he did so, Jim MacVeagh felt guilty and confused. Did this postponement really solve anything? After their handclasp, Hollenbach handed MacVeagh a silver fountain pen.

"Here, Jim," said the President in a low voice, "please take this back again. I want you to have it in memory of the days that might have been. If it hadn't been for them . . ."

The President's eyes glazed. Jim waited a moment, then asked: "Them?"

"You know who they are, Jim," said Hollenbach in a whisper. "But it doesn't matter any more. Just remember, we could have been a great team."

Jim's eyes moistened, and he was too numbed to say anything significant.

"Thank you, sir," was all he could say.

Hollenbach straightened suddenly, slapped his hands together and flashed a cheerful smile.

"Well," he said genially to the group at large, "let's not look like a bunch of pallbearers. This is a great country. It can survive any of us. I've got to go now. Good Lord, it's almost five! Come along, Pat. You ride back to the house with me. With you in charge while I'm gone, there are a few things you ought to be briefed on—right now."

And President Hollenbach, his right hand guiding Vice-President O'Malley at the elbow, walked out of the room.

The group clustered in the outer doorway as the President and the Vice-President, accompanied by three Secret Service agents, climbed into the long White House limousine. The first thrusting of day was streaking the sky and the morning air was cool and sharp to the skin. Mark Hollenbach waved to his friends and rode away into the quiet dawn.

21.

Heart of Aspen

It was 8:15 A.M. when Sidney Karper's SECDEF limousine rolled into the driveway of the MacVeagh home in McLean. Jim was descending the stairway, rubbing his cheeks and blinking torpidly in the manner of a man who has had only two hours' sleep and is not yet ready to accept the world. Chinky, gathering her schoolbooks, called to him.

"Hey, Pops, look at that taxpayers' sports car out there."

She swung out the front door with her neatly banded pony tail, her fresh linen dress, and her armful of textbooks. Sidney Karper backed somewhat gingerly out of the car and nodded to her.

"Good morning, young lady."

"Good morning, sir. There's an awful lot of early and late comings and goings around here. Are we in a crisis?"

The sun already stood bright in the east, and Karper was aware of beads of moisture on his forehead. It would be a hot April day in suburban Virginia and in the capital city across the Potomac.

Karper smiled wearily. "No more than usual," he said.

"That's good," said Chinky. "I'll tell my civics class."

She walked out toward the highway school-bus stop, crooking her books in her arm and humming a favorite tune from her Porky Jones album.

Jim shook hands with Karper at the door and led him to the television room, where Martha was laying out orange juice, scrambled eggs, and coffee on a card table before the television set.

"I'll leave you two conspirators alone for a while," she said, "but when the President comes on, I'm going to watch too."

The two men talked as they ate. Jim merely pecked at the eggs. His head was cloudy and his mouth felt dry. Fatigue seemed to bolster Karper's appetite, for he consumed the eggs in great mouthfuls and washed them down with copious draughts of coffee.

"I worried on the way home," said Jim, "but now, this morning, I think maybe it's the best solution. Perhaps, who knows, with some expert treatment, he'll be as good as new when he returns."

Karper shook his head dubiously. "I'm not happy about the arrangement. How could I ever trust him again in the Command and Control setup? After what I've seen, even affidavits from a flock of psychiatrists wouldn't mean much."

"But," said Jim, "you've got to admit he was his old self last night. He was brilliant. Even the dramatic timing, leaving that vacation bit to the last. He was as good as a professional actor."

Karper took a quill toothpick from his vest pocket, poked at several back teeth, then held it in his lips and whistled through it.

"Yes," he said, "but he colored everything his way. You know that as well as I do. We both know it wasn't that way at all. I know, for example, that he was going to throw that inkwell at me until I grabbed him." Karper sniffed. "And he tried to pass it off as an isometric exercise."

"Of course, he never did answer your questions," said Jim, "about his explosion over Craig Spence, which was utterly silly, and ordering that FBI investigation of me. Most important, he didn't even mention his charge that a conspiracy of some kind was out to get him."

"He didn't mention it," said Karper, "but he really confessed to us without knowing. Remember when he got mad and started to talk about 'they'? He meant the conspiracy, I'm sure, but he caught himself in time."

"He talked about it again to me later," said Jim. "He referred vaguely to the days that might have been except for 'them.' The 'them,' I guess, were the plotters he imagines, although for some reason at the last minute he excluded me."

"The conspiracy thing is the key," said Karper. He shook his great head sadly. "Millions of ordinary people like to imagine there's a conspiracy behind everything, from the Kennedy assassination to the fluoridation of water. But when a man of Mark's caliber and education imagines there's a cabal operating to persecute and to destroy him personally, well, there's only one word for it—paranoia."

"Still," said Jim, "the strange part is that he seems to recognize it himself. Didn't he indicate pretty plainly to us that he thought he had suffered a temporary mental disturbance?"

Karper nodded in assent.

"Well," said Jim, "Maybe he's right. Maybe it was only temporary. They call it a paranoid state, I think."

"Temporary?" asked Karper. "When he was still hinting at some mysterious 'they' last night? Anyway, when he comes back from his vacation, we have to face the same thing all over again. Just imagine. We'd be studying his every move, wondering whether it was the act of a sane man or not."

Karper struck the table with the palm of his hand. "Jim, you just can't run a government like that."

"No, I suppose not," said Jim. "Still, this vacation of Mark's gives us all a breathing spell. We can figure out a course of action while keeping in close touch with General Leppert. After last night, you can bet the doctor will be on the alert for any signs of mental trouble. Then, later, if it ever comes to another showdown, we've always got those letters of Mark Jr. as a final card to play."

Karper shook his head. "You mean Mark Jr. has them. And suppose he decides later that his father is mentally sound, even if the President actually isn't? And suppose he refuses to let us use the letters? Then where are we?"

"I think Paul probably could persuade the boy," said Jim, but he said it without conviction.

Karper sipped at his coffee, then pushed the dishes aside and leaned his elbows on the card table.

"Jim," he said, "this whole affair has convinced me of one thing. The mental business is almost impossible to handle at the apex of government. We thought the disability problem was solved when the succession amendment was passed and ratified in the Johnson administration. But it isn't, is it? If Mark comes back and claims he's normal, but we have evidence he isn't, then the fight would rip the government apart—with God knows what dangerous results abroad."

"But there ought to be some mechanism," said Jim, "especially now when mental ailments can be diagnosed and catalogued almost as well as a lot of physical illnesses."

Karper shook his head moodily. "I don't think so. We went all through that with the CACTUS committee. And I keep remembering something General Trumbull told Butch Andrate—that nobody in this country can tell a president of the United States that his mind is sick."

Jim was about to protest, but the doorbell rang and Martha called: "Jim, it's Craig Spence to see you."

The columnist came loping into the TV room before Jim could intercept him. Spence was startled to see Karper there.

"Oh, I'm sorry," he said. "I didn't realize I was barging into a private breakfast conference. Could I see you alone for a minute, Jim? There's something I need to check."

Jim glanced at his wrist watch and shook his head. It'll have to wait. The President is going on the air in two minutes."

"The President?" Spence scratched his bald head and looked at MacVeagh with a puzzled frown. "What's that all about? I've been out of touch with my office. . . . I hadn't heard that the White House had announced any speech."

"I think he got the time just an hour or so ago," said Mac-Veagh. He called to his wife, then drew the window draperies and turned on the TV set to Channel 4.

In the darkened room, a handsome male visage slowly took form on the screen. The man was speaking.

"The regular Friday morning Monica and Muriel show," the announcer was saying, "is being pre-empted today to bring you an important message from the President of the United States. The White House asked for this time only a short while ago and very few newsmen have been alerted as yet. We do not know the nature of the President's talk, so we simply take you now to the fish room of the White House in Washington."

The camera focused on the blue and gold seal of the President and then moved upward to show Mark Hollenbach standing behind a podium which reached barely to his waist. The long, thin face, delicately boned, wore no smile, but it appeared fresh, even youthful under the sturdy crew cut with its mixture of sandy and gray hair. Behind the President on his right stood his wife, Evelyn, and Jim was immediately struck by her sad, haggard look. It was the face of a woman who might have been crying recently. To the left in the rear stood Mark Hollenbach, Jr., handsome, forcibly restrained, obviously saddened. Then the camera panned over not more than a dozen newspapermen who were sitting in chairs with open notebooks ready.

"Good morning, fellow citizens," said Hollenbach. His tone was pleasantly conversational. "While it is unusual to come to you so early in the day, I thought it best to speak to you at this hour, so that you could know the facts at once and not be harassed with gossip and rumor throughout the day. I wish to read a brief announcement."

President Hollenbach took a sheet of paper from the podium, held it before him, and began reading:

"My fellow Americans, for some time I have been bothered by palpitations of the heart. My physician, General Maury Leppert, has advised me repeatedly either to slow down or to take a vacation of some length, but I declined to do either. In these crucial times, I felt the nation could not afford a president who either had to work part-time at the job or who had to leave Washington for extended periods. I had hoped, naïvely, that the heart irregularity would improve. In recent days, however, I have become aware of an increased heart tremor."

He stopped and sipped at a glass of water.

"Accordingly," he resumed, "after consulting with General Leppert and others, I have decided to resign this office."

In the McLean home, MacVeagh and Karper exchanged amazed glances.

"Did he say 'resign'?" asked Jim.

Karper nodded, a bewildered look on his face. Martha gasped and clapped her hand to her mouth. Craig Spence stared at the television screen as though he had seen an apparition.

"I am," continued Hollenbach, "resigning the presidency under the law and the Constitution and under the terms of the disability agreement signed by Vice-President Patrick O'Malley and myself shortly after the inauguration."

To the rear of the screen, the camera caught Mrs. Hollenbach quickly dabbing at her eyes with a handkerchief. Young Mark's lips were pressed tightly together.

"My family," said the President, "has been informed of my decision and both my wife and my son approve of it. Democratic leaders, who met through most of the night, have gone over the situation thoroughly.

"While Vice-President O'Malley was understandably reluctant to undertake the burdens of this office, he is a man who knows his duty and his responsibility, and he has agreed to take the oath of office at twelve noon today in the Cabinet room. I am hopeful the Chief Justice of the United States will be able to administer the oath. I understand that after taking the oath, President O'Malley will have an important announcement as to his own future plans in this election year, plans to which Democratic leaders gave their assent last night. I urge my countrymen to give the new President every ounce of encouragement and support for such time as he holds the presidency.

"The first clause of our disability agreement requires Vice-President O'Malley to act promptly to initiate succession procedures upon clear evidence that I am no longer able to discharge the duties of this office. While the clear evidence may be lacking in this case, there is no indication that my condition will improve in the future, and it would only contribute to confusion and chaos in the nation's affairs should there remain any uncertainty as to whether I could again take up the reins of authority. Therefore, in the interest of a smooth and orderly transfer of government, I am tendering my permanent resignation. The official papers, under the law and the Constitution as we understand them, are now being prepared by the Attorney General and will be signed shortly."

The President paused. His eyes appeared to mist slightly and he coughed, then cleared his throat before resuming.

"I cannot leave this great office of responsibility and trust, which I sought to conduct in the best interests of all the people, without thanking you, my fellow countrymen, for your support and your faith in me. You showed it first in the voting booths, and then by letter, telegram, phone calls, and word of mouth as the months passed. You have heeded my summons to excellence and you have proved that every citizen can share the American dream in all its beauty if he but puts forth the effort. I have an abiding faith in the destiny of this immense and wonderful country.

"I hate to leave you, but I must. Thank you, God bless you—and God be with us all."

The camera showed the President slowly lowering his paper, then caught the pack of reporters bursting for the door of the fish room. Mark Jr., with obvious tears in his eyes, stepped forward and shook his father's hand. Evelyn Hollenbach slipped her arm protectively through that of the President and, as the picture faded, she was turning him gently away from the podium.

Jim MacVeagh switched off the set, and as the picture contracted to a vanishing dot of light he exchanged a look of wonderment and relief with Sidney Karper.

"I can't believe it," said Martha.

"I can't either," said Karper. He got to his feet. "I have to get to the office right away. I'll call you later, Jim."

"Did either of you have any inkling this was coming?" asked Spence.

Karper shook his big head. "Not a word. He spoke with some of us early this morning, but it was my understanding he merely intended to take a vacation."

MacVeagh nodded agreement. "A long vacation is the way he put it."

"Long is right," said Spence.

Karper walked from the room and out of the house, his bearing erect and resolute, and Jim wondered if he was watching the exit of the next Democratic candidate for president. As Martha accompanied Karper to the driveway, Spence spoke in a low voice to MacVeagh.

"Jim," he said, "I really came here this morning on the damnedest story. I got a tip that you were apprehended by the Secret Service and taken to D.C. General yesterday."

MacVeagh laughed. "God, how things get exaggerated! Craig, I was due at the White House to meet Secretary Karper for a joint appointment, the nature of which doesn't really matter now. Suddenly I felt faint on the sidewalk by the east entrance. Agent Luther Smith was there and he was kind enough to drive me to the hospital."

"But," protested Spence, "my source over there claims you were taken to the psychiatric section."

"Well, there are times when I think I ought to go there on purpose." Jim grinned. "But yesterday it was just a mistake. Smith got mixed up on where he was taking me."

Spence eyed him closely. "Are you okay now?"

"Oh, sure," said MacVeagh. "I felt much better in a few hours, and I'm completely back to normal this morning. After all, Craig, I've been under a lot of conflicting pressures lately, what with running and not running for vice-president. But I'm glad it's all over, and I can go back to being the junior senator from Iowa again."

Spence, apparently convinced, hurried off for the White House and a newspaperman's long day of digging into the background of President Hollenbach's startling resignation.

When the door closed, Jim and Martha found each other's arms and clung together in a tight embrace. Jim thought wryly that Washington was the only city in the nation where events of state could trigger romantic impulses in the inhabitants. He held Martha close, he felt a surge of affection, and he did not once think of Rita.

Martha brushed his chin with a kiss, then pushed him away.

"Now that it's all over, Jim," she asked, her eyes searching his face, "what do you think? The President looked so calm, poised, and so sure of himself just now. Do you still believe he was suffering from a mental breakdown?"

"I don't know for sure," he said, "and I hope to God I never have cause to find out."

"But what about his heart?" she asked.

Jim grinned down at her and, in the recess of his coat pocket his fingers toyed with a silver fountain pen.

"Mark Hollenbach's heart?" he asked. "I was never quite sure about it until right up to the end this morning. Now I believe he has the finest heart in America."

penguin.co.uk/vintage